HELL
Spring

ADVANCE PRAISE FOR *HELL SPRING*

"....the mix of sorrow and shame powering these stories lends substance to the scenes of horror. The shocking moments deliver serious jolts."

—Booklife Review by *Publishers Weekly*

"...packed with tension and credible characters that propel readers forward."

—BlueInk Review

"It is disorienting, grotesque, absurdly funny and oddly hot..."

—Drew Rowsome, *My Gay Toronto*

"The small town and the store are compelling, claustrophobic backdrops to this drama, and the book's tension mounts at an exponential rate."

—*Foreword* Clarion Reviews

"Thorne does a fantastic job of creating a wide cross-section of society..."

—Steve Stred, Splatterpunk-nominated author of *Sacrament* and *Mastodon*

HELL
Spring

ISAAC THORNE

Lost Hollow Books
Franklin, Tennessee

Copyright © 2022 by Isaac Thorne

All rights reserved. No part of this book may be used or reproduced in any form or by any electronic or mechanical means, including information storage and retrieval systems, without permission in writing from the publisher, except by reviewers, who may quote brief passages in a review.

ISBN 978-1-938271-53-3 (Hardback Edition)
ISBN 978-1-938271-54-0 (Paperback Edition)
ISBN 978-1-938271-55-7 (eBook Edition)

Library of Congress Control Number: 2022902651

This is a work of fiction. The characters, events, locations, and dialogue are either products of the author's imagination or are used fictitiously. Any resemblance to actual events or persons, living or dead, is entirely coincidental and not intended by the author.

Cover design by Paula Rozelle Hanback
www.paulahanback.com

Published in the United States of America
First printing September 2022

Published by Lost Hollow Books
PO Box 1193
Franklin, TN 37065

www.isaacthorne.com
www.losthollowbooks.com

For the shamed:
the recovering, the recovered, and the broken.

Information about the tropes and other contents of this story
can be found at the author's website:

www.isaacthorne.com/hell-spring

The books that the world calls immoral are books that show the world its own shame.
—Oscar Wilde

Tell the truth and shame the devil.
—Francois Rabelais

Here, here!
It is the beating of his hideous heart!
—Edgar Allan Poe

TIME
Unknown

CHAPTER ONE

She ran. The thing was after her again. She could sense it. From the day of her birth—or her creation, or her evolution, or whatever process had belched her into existence—the gigantic phallus in the center of the fiery arena had wanted her for its own. But she was more intelligent than the others who cavorted around its base, the dogs begging for scraps. Any scrap. Mostly she lurked along the circle's edge near the line where the charred forest of tree corpses began. This spot lay outside the reach of the ever-flowing fountain of acidic pre-cum streaming down the sides of the enormous crimson glans.

The giant was growing ancient, nearing the end of its millennia arc of life. Or so it claimed whenever she dared venture within range of the thoughts it injected into her mind. It was dying and sliding into insanity as the end of time approached. She could glean that much from the sporadic, dissociative, and maniacal transmissions it spat at her intermittently. It sent them less frequently these days. That lent some credibility to her theory. The longer she waited, the more likely it seemed the thing would wither and die before it could erupt its thick, impregnating goo onto her back. If it ever struck her, the goo would split her wide, divide her into new shadows like herself.

She didn't know whether the rest of the dogs could communicate with the thing in the same way. She couldn't share with them nor they with her. They were simpletons, drone-like and stupid, seeking nothing for all she knew. They ran on survival instinct alone. She may have once been like them, but she could not remember a time when she was not sentient.

How many times had she been destroyed by the gunk, only to be reborn as another two or three entities, none of whom retained her memories? How many eons of lifetimes had she, born again out of herself, spent trying to avoid the inevitability of becoming glazed in the living mountain's ejaculate? How many times had she relearned her fate by watching shadow dogs torn in half as the creature's splatter rained down on them after an eruption?

The deflated remains of one of her sisters lay on the cracked stone landscape yards away. She'd watched from the safety of the tree line when it happened. A spherical glob of white and yellow had fallen on her while she fed. It intersected between her shoulder blades and decapitated her. Moments later, the head of the corpse sprouted brand new baby legs. It raised on them, lifted its muzzle skyward, and shot a brand new set of forepaws out of its neck along with a new tail, torso, and shoulders. An identical creature crawled from the neck hole of the remaining half, leaving behind a flattened shell. The corpse would eventually melt and fade and burn away in the heat of the eternal fire raging beneath the stone and dirt floor. Both freshly born demon dogs bounded off toward the center of the arena as if they'd been alive forever.

The only time she dared venture toward the monster was when she needed to feed. The souls of the damned were the only food source for her and every dog in the arena. They were ensconced in the thick, bubbling soup of white-hot lava just below the blackened crust on which she and the rest of the shadow dogs danced and ran and tried to avoid birthing more of themselves. Sometimes she sensed the guilt of those condemned to burn in the forever fire as it boiled up from the depths of the hellish concoction below and broke through the surface: their anger, their shame for the sins of their previous lives. The scent of it enticed her and those like her to partake. To suckle. To risk narrowing the radius between themselves and the impregnator so they could eat. Her belly filled up, she would retreat again to the perimeter of the arena, near the charred forest. Always she pined for the safety of its darkness and the obscurity beyond its border.

Few of those before her fled to the forest, whether by intention or instinct, she did not know. All were slain. She'd watched them, seeking trial and guidance for her eventual breakthrough. They ran from the eruptions, the serpentine white goo close on their heels. Those capable of outrunning the stuff were eventually cornered by it at the forest's edge. There they had a choice. They could allow themselves to be destroyed and reborn. Or, if they crossed the border, they could be consumed by whatever invisible force lay just beyond it. Those who chose the latter were immediately shredded, mulched into charcoal dust by hidden blades that protected the lands outside the arena. These were the same lands from which the damned wandered before being cast into the lava. How did *they* survive it?

So escape eluded her. She'd never dared to try, clinging instead to the hope that the impregnator would either die or run out of seed before it could nail her again. Its time was short. But she was hungry.

Enticed by the scents of guilt and shame wafting from the lava, she crept nearer to the glans, carefully avoiding the acid pre-cum as its rivulets trickled along the landscape and opened new cracks in the land beneath her feet. She must know when it came for her. The timing was everything. Eruptions, like its telepathic communications, happened with less frequency these days. They were always preceded by a repulsive and noisy swelling when they did happen.

The gigantic head flattened on top as it engorged with the juice it would eventually spill over the arena and all within it. Its sides flared outward, the flesh there sometimes splitting as it did, revealing cracks and folds out from which hairy eight-legged mites scurried and plummeted to their deaths in the fiery lake beneath them. If she saw its skin begin to stretch in that way she would, like so many times before, bolt to safety.

Beside her, a ragged new fissure opened in the crust. Spice and honey scents emanated from within. They overpowered the ammonia odor of ejaculate all around. She gazed into the flaking cavern. In its depths, she could see the swirling colors of anguished souls writhing in torment. Together they formed a terrible landscape of beauty: a kaleidoscope of terrified expressions, a cacophony of screams, and a carnival of tantalizing aromas. She collapsed on her phantom haunches and stabbed at the soup with her muzzle, lapping greedily at the mixture of flavors and textures that arose from the putrid red steam below.

The metallic taste of shame from avarice tingled her tongue first, its texture a combination of silvery smooth coin and rust. It tried to lodge itself in her throat as it went down. She forced it through with an extra gulp. The guilt of an adulterer followed that appetizer, a prickly and salty flavor that left a slimy, wormlike trail along her uvula when she swallowed. Oh, but next came the best flavor: the shame of the murderer. The steam from one who took the life of another was always unique. It was hot, with a bite that caused her flesh to quiver and break out in a phantom sweat. Often it was laced with a sweetness, a heat she couldn't quite identify but supposed might be rationalization or justification.

Dessert came next. Just a taste, she warned herself. The steam of the addict intoxicated her above everything else she had sampled so far. If she ingested too much of the addict's shame, her senses dulled, her judgment and agility became impaired. If the glans erupted while she was in such a state, she would miss her chance.

She cautioned a look toward the tip of the giant as she lapped at the sugary delight. Had it pulsed? Had it flattened some? Were those wrinkles and folds of flesh that flowed from the rim of the meatus down the glans beginning to look wider than they did a moment ago? Just one more sip at the fountain, and she would back off, return to her safe space along the edge. Just one more tiny drink and—

A mite emerged near the rim of the giant's hole. It tumbled delicately down the length of the beast, tossed hither and yon along the descent by the cracking of the surface on which it rode. It disappeared in a black puff of smoke where the corona of the quivering mountain had begun to widen against the parched crust of the surrounding land.

An eruption was imminent—time to move.

Her legs betrayed her at first. She'd lost track of the amount of steam she had ingested while monitoring the mountain. She tried to stand, turn, and run but instead slid flat to her belly. The sharp edge of the crevasse from which she'd been drinking sliced at her snout when she struck. She yelped in surprise, then scrambled back to all fours, struggling mightily to control the demon dog muscles that thrummed beneath the gray fabric of her skin. She shrugged off what remained of the intoxicant and fled, glancing back to gauge how much time she lost by indulging herself.

That was when the thing erupted.

A geyser of milky yellowish goo suspended inside a sticky transparent gel spewed high into the orange sky above the arena. It separated in mid-air and rained down globs upon all within. Some smaller, lower-weight drops struck the edges of the forest and were immediately shredded in a brilliant, glittery display. The heavier ones remained inside the diameter of the arena and landed with a splattery *smack*. Those drops boiled immediately. Thin, bubbling membranes rose and burst within them as they sizzled on the hot ground. Others struck her fellow demon dogs directly.

Some of her sisters split into two or three parts upon impact. The bellies of some unfortunates who were not bombarded instantly became engorged with spawn. Their middles expanded rapidly with new life, ballooning each dog to such spherical distortions that their legs, tails, and heads all but disappeared. They burst into a waterfall of shadowy skin and muscle. Their mewling young plummeted from their ruptured wombs and began to feed instinctively on the shame of the damned.

Many of the remaining blobs tumbled into the ravines of exposed lava, never to be seen again. The rest became elongated as they glided toward the cooler areas of the arena. There they transformed into eyeless, sickly white snake creatures. They launched themselves like springs from a coiled start and then serpentined across the land to pursue the demon dogs who fled in every direction. When captured, a shadow dog first became encased in the stuff and absorbed it. After that, they suffered the same fate as the impregnated, exploding into a new batch of more minor but rapidly evolving shadows.

Yet she remained untouched for now.

A new blob, steaming and stinking, thudded to the ground nearby. It had formed a coil before she found her legs again and took flight. As always, she aimed for the edge of the arena. If the snake managed to chase her that far, she might dodge its strike at the last second, forcing it to launch itself into the forest so that it was shredded at the border. The charcoal trees looked impossibly far away, though, her approach alarmingly slow. Something unseen was holding her back. The harder she ran, the slower she thought she was moving.

A second glance back at her pursuer did nothing to reassure her. The snake gained on her. Every sideways thrust of its body propelled it closer, perceptibly shortening the distance between them. This time, the glans wanted her badly, enough to have targeted her with the strongest and fastest of its faceless sidewinders. Somehow the thing held onto enough of its waning sanity to telepathically direct some of the brainless creatures it ejected from its hole. Or maybe it had gone insane enough to become capable of that feat.

She faced the forest, searching for and ultimately finding the strength for a fresh burst of speed. Hope crept into her heart. The edge of the forest neared. Within, she could see one upright tree that remained unburnt by the heat and fire of the arena. She blanked all else from her mind save that tree. It was her goal. A last-second dodge to the left or the right may well save her and propel the snake to its doom if she could get close enough to it without crossing the boundary. No more glances backward. No time was left to chance it.

Faster.

Her legs tingled with exhaustion. Her demon muscles cried out for respite. She would not allow it. The edge of the forest closed in, near enough that the arena had vanished from her periphery. Too close? Could she change course and send the snake over the boundary without launching herself through it as well? Even if she wasn't, she thought that she would rather be shredded and winked out of existence than suffer the impregnation, explosion, and recycling of life. If each demon pup took with it some of the consciousness of its mother, how many of her were racing around the arena? Dozens? Hundreds? She couldn't know, and it didn't matter. Not now.

She arrived at the border. Only a second remained to make her turn. She thought she could feel the invisible blades churning wind against her face from the edge of the arena. She thought she could feel her shadowy flesh prickling against their tips. She tried to halt her forward momentum, to pivot before the first blade of scorched grass touched the pads of her feet. Left. She veered left. Too late.

Her attempt to turn and run alongside the border ended in a one-hundred-and-eighty-degree spin so that she faced the snake that had chased her to the end. She plunged tail-first into the forest at the edge of the arena and tumbled into the single healthy tree that remained standing at the border. The snake was closer than she had dared imagine. Its round, featureless head bobbed at the tips of her toes.

This was the end, then. She was going to die, to vanish forever into whatever darkness, whatever nothing lay beyond the shredding of her demon form. She might simply cease to be. But so would the thing chasing her. That was what mattered most—that and the glans could no longer force her to reproduce endlessly.

She had won.

Finally, she had won.

She closed her eyes, steeling herself, anticipating the forest doing to her what she had seen it do to countless others. She hoped it would not hurt.

From behind her came a thunderous electric crackling sound. A bright blue bolt of light surrounded her. Her eyes were shut tight, but she could see the flash even through the fabric of her eyelids. Surprise and confusion overcame her as she continued falling backward instead of being shredded into bits of nothingness.

Down. Into billowy clouds of warmth and light. She sensed no cuts or nicks or slices in her flesh. She felt no stings or burns or heat of agony.

She thrust her eyes wide in time to see the snake bounce off some new invisible barrier between them. It looked like it had been trapped in an oval surrounded by tree bark through which she alone had been allowed to pass. Before her eyes, the thing was shredded into a billion tiny globs of mucus that vaporized along with the rest of the scene through the portal as she plummeted.

She landed on her back, eyes open. Above her, an angry gray and black sky dripped clear liquid onto her face. It stung, but it did not cut her in half or kill her. Something was different. The world had changed. Her body had changed as well.

Suddenly she was covered in a thick, black hairy material she did not recognize. She opened her jaw, testing it, and startled herself when a low, guttural groan escaped her muzzle. She snapped it shut again when a drop of the clear stuff landed on her tongue. Whatever it was, it wasn't ejaculated from the giant. She had only a second to taste it, to register its lack of consistency before it sizzled and evaporated on her tongue. The spot where it had landed was sore, as if whatever it was had singed her taste buds.

She righted herself and examined the tree beside her. It could be the same tree, the healthy one she had aimed for while fleeing the snake. It was charred, however. It smoldered and was aflame in some places. All around it were other trees, but they were not the ones she knew from the edge of the arena. They were whole trees, healthy, with green things growing from the ends of their branches. These were trees she had never seen before. They were strange and wonderful.

Above her, the sky rumbled angrily. It did not dump any more of whatever the clear substance was on her. Not yet. She was grateful for that.

Rain, a voice in her head chimed. It was also outside her head. Not the thoughts of the giant this time. She was picking up telepathic transmissions from something else. *It looks like it's going to rain.* Her head hurt. More sound, a deluge of static interspersed with coherent thought, threatened to shut out all her own. Then, just like that, it subsided.

Instantly, she knew all kinds of things about this new place. The green clumps on the ends of tree branches were called *leaves*. Right now, they were small, having just emerged this month following a particularly nasty winter freeze. The hardness under the skin of her new head was called a *skull*. The black hairy material all over her body was called *fur*. The form she had assumed was usually labeled a *dog*, although she could be a *coyote* or a *wolf*. The liquid that had poured on her from the sky was indeed called *rain*, and *they* were calling for a lot of it to fall today. That would be dangerous if the *creek* overflows its *banks*.

She heard a new sound on her left and outside her head: *whistling*. It was a means of making *music*, a form of entertainment peculiar to those who walk alone. The melody spewed from a creature who walked through the woods nearby. He strolled down a narrow dirt path that he had worn through these woods over all these years of collecting *groceries* for the *missus*.

Elijah. The creature was called Elijah. Eli for short. He was on his way to buy flour for Mrs. Blalock, the farmer's wife for whom he worked. He resented the errand because it was going to rain, but he also reckoned with guilt about feeling resentful. There was something else, though, a more primal urge that pulsed inside him with each throb of his heart. She could feel it, but she could also smell it wafting off him. Lust. She had feasted on it in the arena before. Its scent rode the air of this new world like sulfur on the hot winds of her old one.

Eli was a male, and he lusted for a female. Her name was Marilyn, but he did not know her. Not personally. Sometimes he imagined her naked. Often, really. When he could, he sought naked pictures of her on paper. It was something he called a *calendar*, a tool he and others like him used to track time. Except that this calendar with the naked woman atop was a personal calendar, hidden from most eyes. It lay closed in a drawer and was looked upon occasionally when his friend Jerry Beard allowed it. The pages of the calendar, the markings of time, had never been turned.

Eli liked this timeless calendar. It made his skin tingle. It painted his imagination with lurid, colorful daydreams that pleased him greatly. They also shamed him. If Mrs. Blalock ever found out he had been looking at pictures of a naked woman, she would give him *the knowing look*. In Eli's estimation, there was nothing worse than *the knowing look* from Mrs. Blalock.

She learned all these things because Eli knew them. The flood of information overwhelmed her, sapping her strength.

Her stomach panged.

MARCH 21
1955

CHAPTER TWO

Jesus, he thought. *That was close.* The blinding bolt of lightning struck so near Eli Wynn that he had almost said the swear out loud. He was not sure that he had not, so it was a good thing that some Blalock horses had bolted before he left the farmhouse to go on Mrs. Blalock's flour errand. Otherwise, she would have sent Smarty Marty to accompany him. Marty would've relished an opportunity to tell on Eli for taking the name of the Lord in vain.

Beard's General lay just beyond the small forest of trees that soldiered Hollow Creek Road at the perimeter of the Blalock farm. From there it was a hop, skip, and a jump across the road and over the creek. Eli happened to be the farmhand of least renown on Mr. Blalock's roster. So when Mrs. Blalock suddenly found herself out of flour (or short on any kitchen ingredient that the farm couldn't make for itself), she inevitably sent Eli to retrieve the goods.

Marty, the little snitch of a Blalock who was just as often sent along on errands to make sure Eli received the correct change, indeed would have told on him. He would have tattled even though the late Jacob Wynn's son Eli was eighteen years old, going on nineteen. He might not look it, but years were years, even if they weren't wrinkles. Mr. Blalock liked to say that whenever Mrs. Blalock caught him casting sidelong glances at the younger and more attractive ladies in the parking lot after church. Cherub cheeks or not, Eli figured he should be allowed to swear by God if he wanted to swear. Sometimes he swore aloud in protest when he was sure no one was around, least of all Smarty Marty.

Eli had never been so near a lightning strike before. An entire minute after his vision cleared, he could still feel a sunburn-like tingling against the sensitive skin of his clean-shaven mug. The post-flash darkness was accompanied by a stiff, warm breeze that at first caressed his face, then threatened to set it ablaze. The ground undulated beneath him. He'd heard the rumble of the violence in the earth beneath his feet. The ordinary sounds of the woods around him—chirping birds, buzzing insects, and the *splat* of an occasional heavy raindrop on the blanket of leaf corpses that covered the ground—had been replaced for a moment by a monotonous, high-pitched whine. That sound began to fade at the same time his vision began to clear. His nostrils filled with the electric blue smell of burning ozone and then, close behind it, the aroma of scorched wood.

Jesus, he thought again. His lips split in a wide, shit-eating grin at the novelty of the thought in his head. *Jesus, Jesus, Jesus*. Then it faded.

On repetition, the twinge of shame that stabbed him over taking the Lord's name in vain crept to the forefront of his mind. The back of his neck, which had not been in the path of the lightning flash, felt as hot as his face and prickled. Its sting crept over his skull and down his forehead, blistering the smattering of freckles over the bridge of his nose like a red morning sun draining away the shadows of the night.

The fine hairs that faded down the nape of his neck from the thick bowl cut of yellow hay on top of his head stood at attention.

Eli had experienced shame and humiliation before. Many times, thanks to Smarty Marty's steady watchful eye. If he so much as scratched his balls while growing up a farmhand with Mrs. Blalock's son, he'd find himself sent to bed without supper. It wasn't the act of ball-scratching itself that fueled his embarrassment so much as Mrs. Blalock *knowing* he'd scratched them. He could practically hear her gears grinding over it as she glared down her nose at him from what in those moments looked like a good twenty feet of height.

However, this embarrassment wasn't precisely the same as the ones before it. The heat on the back of his neck and top of his head radiated off him in a way that seemed very much like he'd spent too long in the sun without his hat or his work shirt. Moisture erupted from the pores on top of his head in tiny bubbles that popped when he ran his hand over them. A red-tinged vapor arose from them. It was held aloft on the wind, snaking toward a scorched tree that stood smoking in the distance.

That must have been the tree that was struck. It was *really* close. Maybe he had gotten more of a shock from it than he'd initially thought. Weakness overcame him, settling a heaviness about his shoulders. His lanky knees buckled. He collapsed to the earth, squatting atop them, head bowed in the direction of the steam flow.

"It's the Lord," he muttered. "He's damned me for taking his name in vain."

He hadn't uttered the Savior's name. Not out loud. But he shouldn't have thought it, either.

From a copse of trees that mostly hid the scorched one from his view in his submission, Eli thought he could hear the wet, ragged breaths of a hungry animal. A bear, maybe? Or a wild dog? He'd once heard Pastor Mark describe the voice of Jesus as the sound of many waters. That didn't seem right. If it wasn't Jesus, then it perchance could be the Devil. Maybe Jesus had sent the Devil, and the Devil had come to claim him for his blasphemy.

"I'm sorry," Eli whispered hoarsely. "Please. Give me a chance to be sorry. Give me a chance to make it right."

And he would. On Sunday, when Mrs. Blalock invariably dragged him to Hollow Creek Nazarene Church for the weekly preaching and singing, he'd repent. Pastor Mark allowed the folks in his flock to repent of their sins without saying them out loud. All he had to do was kneel at the altar while the preacher prayed over him. The congregation was supposed to close their eyes during that part. Sometimes Eli peeked, though, just to see who might've been sinning and who else was spying on the penitent.

Once, his curiosity got the better of him for six Sundays straight. On all of them, the one person who showed up at the altar for forgiveness was Peter Mayberry, the church piano player. That set Eli's imagination to conjure all the fanciful ways the doughy man with thin chestnut hair could sin. Did he touch himself? Or was it something less salacious? Was he a glutton? It couldn't be wife-beating because Peter Mayberry was a confirmed bachelor. Murder? Defiling the deceased?

Those last two possibilities set off an explosion of grotesque and bloody imagery inside Eli's head. There stood meek Peter Mayberry, slicing the ears off wayfaring victims and shoving knitting needles up their nostrils to poke at their brains in a dank basement somewhere. There he stood, pouring their organs and intestines into a meat grinder, patting the result into perfectly shaped discs to fry up for his dinner or to freeze for a rainy day.

Eli's stomach had protested the vision in the sanctuary at its loudest volume. He'd had to swallow the large lump in his throat. Both sounds had reverberated throughout the room, causing more than one head to swivel his way. That got Mrs. Blalock's attention. She'd swatted him on the thighs with her hymnal and elbowed him in the ribs hard enough to make him gasp. On the seventh Sunday, Eli pushed Peter Mayberry's potential iniquities from his mind and kept his peepers shuttered.

Except for that one incident, Mrs. Blalock almost always kept her head primly bowed toward her lap while Eli peeked. Even if she did open her eyes, all she likely saw was her folded hands and the shapes of her knees under her Sunday dress. If he sat in a different row from her, which he did on days when Smarty Marty had been particularly pesky, she'd never know he'd sinned at all, much less the nature of that sin.

So it would be a Sunday morning repentance six days from now for the first day of spring crime against The Almighty. If he forgot to do it on Sunday, he was sure to be absolved in three weeks when Pastor Mark and the elders passed around the Easter communion. He did forget things sometimes. From this point on, there would be no more taking of the Lord's name in vain, even if a bolt of lightning struck him directly.

As if confirming the notion, Eli felt the burden lifted from the back of his neck. A remarkable shift in the wind dried the sweat of his panicked repentance just as he both intuited and heard a patter of fresh raindrops dotting the canopy of forest around him. How long had he knelt here?

The incoming weather cooled the prickly top of his head and dampened his work shirt. With it, strength returned to his legs and arms. He tested them by planting his hands palm down on the earth and pushing against it to regain his feet. He wiped the remaining sweat and raindrops from his face with one grimy hand and restarted his path through the woods. To Beard's General on Hollow Creek Road. To get a bag of flour for Mrs. Blalock.

Another loud clap of thunder startled him, but this time he managed to keep his thoughts free of any potentially sinful reactions. The rain patters picked up seconds later, transitioning from a fine mist to a pelting of pregnant droplets that changed the color of the dirt from a dusty peanut shade to a rich and ominous fudge. Something rustled in the copse. Whatever beast was hidden there may have decided to have him for lunch after all.

Eli broke into a jog and then a run. Rationally, he knew better than to turn tail on a beast and flee, but his rational mind was not in control of his heart and leg muscles.

Less than a fifth of a mile down the path, he arrived at the shoulder of Hollow Creek Road. Across it, Hollow Creek babbled fast but low through its five-foot deep and more than twice as wide bed. Eli leaped from the line of trees that bordered the Blalock farm and dashed across the road. He did not bother to look for oncoming traffic, not at this time of day. Once across, he scrambled down the embankment that led to the creek bed.

He could have simply run to the bridge that connected Hollow Creek Road to Beard's parking lot, but he'd never liked the looks of that dilapidated thing. How many cars crossed its rickety planks every day? How many more would succeed before it collapsed under their weight? No, if he were going to end up in the creek, he would do so under his power.

Eli deftly navigated the four exposed chunks of granite riprap that had, over time, become dislodged from the roadside bank and plunged into the creek bed. Sediment serving as mortar and mild erosion during high water days had forged them into a nearly perfect set of stepping stones, each about one Eli-stride apart from the next. He'd crossed them so often that he hardly bothered to look when he leaped anymore. His muscles had memorized the correct number of steps to the jumping-off point as well as the perfect amount of power and thrust to shore his footing as he crossed. The routine familiarity of the act caused the lightning and the copse of trees to dim in his memory. He welcomed the amnesia. The farther the distance between him and the stricken tree, the less it seemed like he had nearly lost his salvation.

He glanced at the sky. He had dallied too long in the woods. The clouds were all but sure to release before he could return to the farmhouse with Mrs. Blalock's fresh bag of flour in tow. It was after the school bell on a Monday, to top it off. That meant Kathy Beard's only son Jerry would be working the cash register. He posed a greater danger of distraction.

Eli liked Jerry. He was an older boy but slow on the uptake, just like Eli. He'd been held back a year because of it when he was in grammar school. Jerry was always friendly to Eli, unlike most young men their age. Eli himself had been taken out of school just before the eighth grade during the summer that he'd been kicked in the head by the Blalocks's mule Jenny. They said they pulled him out of school because they needed his help for planting and harvests. They never pulled their own boy out, however. Smarty Marty was just about to end his ninth grade year. Sometimes Eli wondered if the Blalocks thought the mule kick had knocked out his smarts the way it had knocked out his lights. Truthfully, he couldn't say he had learned very much new since then. The school wasn't really for boys like Eli, anyway. The main thing he learned from looking at books was how looking at books confused and bored him.

Jerry was a hoot. He was a big fan of knock-knock jokes and had bent Eli's ear with several of them over the years. He also had a secret stash of pictures of naked ladies near the cash register that his mother Kathy did not know about. If she happened to be in the back while Jerry was working the register (and while snitchy Marty Blalock's eyeballs stayed glued to the shiny jars of candy on the opposite counter), Jerry would allow Eli a peek at some of that treasure.

Somehow, his friend had recently acquired a new calendar emphasizing a photo of the most beautiful woman Eli had ever seen. She was naked, of course, and reclined against what looked like red velvet. Her hips and legs were positioned just so, protecting her modesty in a teasing way. She lay with her knees bent, her right foot resting atop her left one, her toes curled. Her left arm was straightened into a prop. Her right one was stretched into the air and bent at the elbow so that her right hand was hidden behind a gloriously curly mane of strawberry blonde hair.

The pose was intended to highlight her completely nude breasts. Even so, it was her face that rendered Eli dumbstruck. Partially hidden behind her right arm, the half of the woman's face that Eli could see melted his heart. It straightened his pants in a way he had not experienced when he'd pored over previous pinups. Her left eye was half-lidded and decorated with blue eye shadow, contrasting beautifully with her rosy cheeks. Her parted cherry lips revealed a perfectly straight row of gleaming white teeth.

Jerry claimed that the woman in the picture atop the calendar was a young Marilyn Monroe. He said she'd been paid fifty bucks to pose for it before she became a movie star. He said that she had admitted to it a few years ago. She'd done it because she needed the money at the time. Eli was skeptical. The woman didn't look like the pictures he'd seen of Marilyn Monroe in the copies of the *Hollow River Echo* newspaper that Mr. Blalock always brought back with him from Saturday stock markets. He also couldn't imagine the woman in the picture on that calendar, wearing that comfortable, knowing smile, *needing* anything at all. Ever.

The memory of the first time Jerry had shown him the calendar triggered a longing in Eli as he scaled the wall of the creek bed and jaunted across Beard's parking lot. A part of him wanted Jerry to be there, wanted his friend to give him another peek at the loot. Especially if there was no chance of Marty catching him.

But the part of him that feared Mrs. Blalock's reaction if he returned to the farmhouse with a bag of flour soaked through by a heavy downpour overrode it. If she discovered her flour was ruined because Eli took time from his errand to harden his prick over a picture of a naked lady, he might again endure that awful glare of her *knowing* he had indulged his lust, as if she had seen his hard-on herself.

Please let Mrs. Beard be behind the counter today, Eli prayed. He bounded up the three steps that led to the wooden porch and dashed through the door, nearly knocking over one of Kathy Beard's potted ferns that sat just outside as he did.

Another clap of thunder rolled across the sky as Eli vanished into the store. A black furry snout appeared from the edge of the woods out of which he had emerged. Above it, flaming red eyes stared at the threatening heavens. A deluge was coming, if she had correctly read the boy's mind. Creatures great and small should seek shelter.

Her stomach protested the idea, and she understood why. The accidental transition from her hell world to this one had used her up. She'd tried to feed on the boy whose flash of guilt for having sworn in vain the name of the god he worshipped had a pleasing tart flavor. But it had been too fleeting, a mere morsel barely tasted when what she needed was to feast.

If the stories she'd siphoned from the boy's head were true, the prey in this world, like the souls of the damned in hers, could be ripe with the shame and guilt she needed to sustain her. In the short time since she'd first encountered him, Eli Wynn himself had experienced shame and remorse for at least three different acts, past and present. He felt shame for what he called "peeking" (the penitent Peter Mayberry fellow he'd recalled sounded like a promising source of nourishment). Next was his guilt over the oath. Finally, there was the shame of his lust for the creature in the photograph, the female that he thought Was Not Marilyn Monroe.

Above her, the sky let go. A soft pattering of rain began to fall. Instinct combined with the sting of the stuff when it struck her eyes and the end of her nose pressed her to flee, to hide until the storm subsided. But her hunger was too powerful. That, and the fact that her thick pelt seemed to be protecting the bulk of her skin from the wet stuff. Regardless of her discomfort, it was not time to hide.

This was the time to hunt.

CHAPTER THREE

P astor Mark MacDonald sat at his kitchen table, forehead cradled in one hand. With the other, he wiped salty tears off the aquamarine laminate as they ran from the end of his nose and splattered in front of him. An inch to the left, and they would've blotted the ink on the check he'd just written to the Hollow County Utility Company, the last item in the stack of bills he needed to drop in the mail to prevent himself from being considered delinquent. After that payment, the balance sheet math worked out to precisely six dollars cash remaining in his pocket and almost nothing in the bank. It was just enough money to buy one week's worth of groceries from Beard's with some left over, but not enough to gas up his Plymouth.

The rusted P15 sat at a quarter of a tank when Mark returned home from church the day before. It was good that he didn't have anywhere he had to go except for Beard's. Not until Sunday anyway, when the congregation expected him to deliver the second of his four Gospels sermons that would end, as it reliably did every year, with Easter's glorious Good News.

They were demanding bastards, his flock. Not to mention cheap and lazy. Oh, they would make a joyful noise all morning long if the sun was shining and the bars had closed early the night before. As soon as they were asked to volunteer or tithe, they were up and gone like a fart in the wind. The Fed's recession had ended nearly a year ago. The Depression? More than a decade previous. You wouldn't know it by the contents of the collection plate, in any case. If Mark dared preach to them about giving their ten percent, he inevitably received the after-service earful about how Bessie didn't bring her price at the stockyard or that corn prices were on the decline thanks to the Federal Reserve trying to fix post-war inflation. Not Eisenhower's fault, of course.

For going on ten years, he'd guided the faithful in Lost Hollow through their triumphs and tragedies. He'd celebrated the return of our boys in '47, only a year after he'd first mounted the pulpit. He'd mourned every loss of life or farm since. For all that time, he'd begged the congregation for one volunteer—just one—who would find it in his heart to help maintain the church by taking on the role of the treasurer or dropping in during the week to give the pews a polish before Sunday service.

It made no difference. The elders, who were pretty much elders in title only, primarily wanted to hear themselves lecture their Sunday School peers. Meanwhile, their wives whispered behind their hands about the latest marriage on the rocks because the good-for-nothing came home drunk again late last night. To Mark, it was as if everyone in Lost Hollow had escaped The Depression with cash in hand and nothing to worry about but gossip and scandal. Everyone except him.

"Ten years," he said to his kitchen. His voice rang foreign against the walls. "Ten years without a volunteer and a raise. Hell of a thing."

Despite the Fed's efforts, and contrary to Mark's piteous ego, inflation had indeed taken a toll on Lost Hollow residents since the war ended. He knew that because he relied almost exclusively on the congregation's contributions for his income. Thus, Mark MacDonald had been hit harder than most, but only because he had been honest.

The Hollow Creek Nazarene Church's board had offered him thirty percent of the weekly tithes for his salary. The rest was to be deposited directly into the church's bank account where it would be used for emergency maintenance on the church itself or charity when times got tough for any single parcel of Lost Hollow's vast swaths of farmland. Well, for any of those farmers who happened to attend Hollow Creek Nazarene, anyway. Most Lost Hollow residents considered themselves Baptists, not Nazarenes. Since the nearest Baptist church was on the outskirts of Hollow River, a good fifteen miles from Lost Hollow, Mark figured there probably weren't very many local Baptists who attended service regularly.

He sat up straight against the back of the kitchen chair and tore the utility payment from his checkbook. A glint of light on the brass collection plate on the opposite side of the table caught his eye. His thirty percent of that take had paid his bills and were about to buy his groceries for the week, but that was all. He was a preacher, treasurer, and janitor for his small community church, three jobs his ungrateful flock squeezed out of him for the price of one. So who would miss it if he decided to go around the board and grant himself a small pay raise?

The church hadn't donated money to any local farms even at the height of The Fed's recession. The only person maintaining the church building was Mark himself. An extra ten percent in his pocket would go a long way toward ensuring that ends continued to meet. He might finally afford a few things he'd wanted lately, too. Perhaps he could buy some books to read beyond his battered old copy of the Good one. Or maybe he could buy a radio or, Heaven help him, a television set so he could finally see an episode or two of that *I Love Lucy* show everyone was always talking about.

However, there were stories about the star of that show being a dirty commie. That's how the television folks got the Devil into you. They secretly insert their politics in their funny shows so it all seemed *normal* somehow. The thought sent a shiver down his spine. The Devil box may be a form of mind control. That explained how a congregation could be so stingy with their tithes during a supposed economic boom.

Mark slid the stack of freshly paid bills aside, then hooked the lip of the collection plate with his index finger and dragged it toward him. He'd counted and banded the bills just that morning and had already set aside his thirty percent, the aforementioned six dollars, for his groceries. Bumping his take up to forty percent meant that he could pluck an additional two dollars out of this week's collection and add it to his pocket. That would put at least seven gallons of gas in the P15. Seven gallons should be more than he needed if he didn't make any trips to Hollow River for a while.

Yesterday's tithes had been particularly low: twenty dollars out of a congregation made up of about fifteen families. He figured the community was saving up for Easter tithing, which was always the highest tithing day of the year. It meant he could expect to pick up an extra two-fifty or even three dollars on a perfect Sunday. He would never be a rich man, but he could be comfortable at least.

A tingle of taboo ran up his arm when he lifted two creased and limp singles from the banded bundle of donated farm income. A bittersweet grin curled his lips as the sensation crawled down his back and into his balls, causing his scrotum to prickle and scale upwards inside his boxers. It pressed itself against the wall of his groin. Was *this* actual sin? If so, it was no wonder the sheep often strayed from the flock. If peeling a couple of extra dollars from the collection caused this type of sensation, what must it feel like to drink a glass of beer on a Saturday night? Or fuck a whore under a broken streetlamp in an alley by the bar? Pastor Mark MacDonald felt good for the first time since he'd left the church sanctuary following Sunday service.

He pushed back from the table and folded his arms across his chest, smiling broadly. Even if he only netted an extra two dollars per week with his new pay increase, it could add up to a significant lifestyle increase by the end of a year. Two dollars a week is an additional hundred and four per year. Not quite enough to buy a television, but it would get him about halfway there.

Of course, that's assuming he *only* added two dollars per week to his pocket. If Eisenhower's economy continued to improve and progress made its way from Hollow River into the surrounding countryside like Lost Hollow, the offerings in the Sunday collection plate could only grow.

Increased offerings that added to Mark's happiness could also improve his sermons. He could finally find some inspiration somewhere, could move his congregation to do more. Lord knows he would love to get the perpetually atoning Peter Mayberry off his knees and into some volunteer work for the church itself. If he busied himself with holy things, he wouldn't have to worry so much about whatever ungodliness was dropping him at the altar of repentance every Sunday morning after the sermon.

Of course, Mark's guilt could catch up with him, in which case he would end up like Peter. Imagine being a man so paralyzed by fear of discovery of whatever was pricking his conscience as well as the threat of being cast into the fiery depths of Hell by his judge and maker. Best not to think about that.

Mark stood and swept the kitchen table's contents into his arms. He carried the collection plate with the remainder of Sunday's offerings in it to the bathroom. There, he pulled open the medicine cabinet, removed an empty Phillies box from its depths, and stashed the bills inside. He'd retrieve them on Wednesday when he made his once-per-week trip to First National Home and Farm over in Hollow River to make the church deposit. Lost Hollow, bless its heart, had no branch of the bank for itself. That's why most folks around here simply carried cash and stocked up on a good supply of mason jars. Occasionally, there was talk about opening a branch in Lost Hollow's town square, but so far, no progress on it. Thanks to Mark's new raise, he could afford some patience. He could comfortably buy the gas to make the drive to Hollow River.

The offerings stowed, Mark shut the medicine cabinet. He winced as he turned away from it, his knee twinging in protest at the sudden strain. Getting old. He was forty-two, and it showed. The flame of wavy, reddish-orange hair atop his head had thinned ever so slightly around his temples. The luster and ambition that used to sparkle just beyond the layer of green in his eyes had dulled as his eyelids grew heavier with age, their corners cracked with crow's feet. On Sunday, he had tried grinning at himself as he readied for church, hoping it would make him look younger. It only succeeded in revealing the extra layers of jowl that had congealed under his skin during his decade in Lost Hollow. Alongside his bulbous cherry nose, they made him look hangdog and tired. Money had been too much on his mind for too long. His weary countenance was proof of that.

Mark ambled to the kitchen where he dropped the empty collections plate back on the table. It would sit there until next Sunday morning when he took it to church for another round of begging and disappointment. He donned his father's plaid tweed sport coat, a ratty thing from the early 1940s handed down to him after his dad passed on. Then he grabbed at his front and back pockets to verify that he was, indeed, carrying his keys and wallet and started for the front door. Groceries and gas were the order of the day from here on out.

He was just about to close the door behind him when he heard the patter of raindrops on the dead leaves around the singular maple tree that adorned the center spot in his meager front yard. A rolling clap of thunder and visible, heavy droplets darkened the Tennessee chert that topped his driveway.

Mark stretched an arm through the half-ajar door and retrieved his beige porkpie from the hatrack just inside, another relic of his father's. Today was the first day of spring in Middle Tennessee, after all. That meant that a man who planned to run errands for an hour or two in the afternoon might need his hat.

Ten minutes later, Mark swung the P15 into the parking lot at Beard's Grocery, bringing it to a leisurely stop at the farthest of the two gas pumps that sat out front. He pressed the horn twice—two short beeps to summon service—and watched the door for a response. Eli Wynn, the farmhand that Jimmy and Georgia Blalock sometimes dragged to church with them, was darting inside. Seconds later, the door banged open again. Jerry Beard emerged wearing a pair of navy-blue coveralls with a long, white shop rag flapping like a dog's tail from the back pocket.

"Fill 'er up, would you?" Mark asked when the boy approached.

"Yessir," Jerry replied. "Want me to wash the windshield and check the oil for you?"

Mark glanced at the sky. "Nah. I don't think a windshield washing will do much good today, do you? Just park it and bring the keys inside if you don't mind. I've got to get cracking on my grocery list."

"Yessir," Jerry repeated. He set to work on the pump.

Mark exited the P15 and strode up the porch steps just as a fresh clap of thunder rumbled overhead. A burst of raindrops rang loudly on the metal roof that covered the porch.

Just in time, he thought. *Hope it passes soon.*

CHAPTER FOUR

Donna Gilliam split the main bedroom door down the middle when her body crashed shoulder-first into it. The left side of her face followed hard after. She collapsed to her knees and sat on her haunches, eyes closed. She cradled her elbows, trying desperately not to cry. Ted's blows only landed harder if she showed any sign of tears.

A trickle of blood oozed down her right temple. She must've cut herself on the clothes hook as she slid down the door. Or she reopened the scab that had barely crusted there from the last time he'd thrown her against it. Had that been yesterday or the day before? The hours and days of the week all blurred together lately.

Donna's infant son Theo wailed incessantly from his crib in the nursery across the hall. It was a shrill, maddening sound that never seemed to let up. Not when he had been freshly changed. Not when he had just been fed. Not when he went down for his nap.

That wasn't what had set Ted off this time. They had both way overslept and he was late for work. The bloodshot in his angry brown eyes cracked the whites like fiery bolts of lightning. Premature grains of salt had filtered into his oily black hair over the past year. That slick look combined with the pointy, slightly upturned nose he'd inherited from his mother made him resemble a rabid, raging anthropomorphic skunk in a white T-shirt and beige coveralls. A puff of thick striped chest hair that curled from the neck of his tee exacerbated the effect. Theo's role as alarm clock this morning was just the straw that might break his mother's back. His grandmother, Ted's mother, said the babe was colicky because Donna wasn't nursing him naturally.

"That formula shit them modern doctors are gonna give you is the Devil's milk," she'd cried as Donna's due date neared. "Your wife should give your baby the tit, else you're gonna have a sicky or a half-wit. You mind me, now."

Donna couldn't give Theo the tit even if she'd wanted to. She'd tried in the hospital. The milk flowed a little at first, but only a trickle. The nurses told her that formula was the only thing that would keep Theo from starving to death before he was old enough to wean.

Ted was having none of it. On the morning that he had lingered before work, towering over the nursery rocker and screaming at her to produce while Theo wriggled and shrieked in her arms, she had dried up completely. She hadn't been able to squeeze a drop since.

In the four weeks since Theo's birth, Ted had decided the child's every cry was because Donna had somehow been neglectful. Evening feeding violence was followed by morning feeding violence as her husband, annoyed by the newborn, directed his anger at Donna with escalating ferocity. What had started as a simple tug at the length of her hair had become a twice-daily wall-to-wall bedroom wrestling match: slaps, punches, kicks, body slams and all.

Donna had come to fear for the baby in the last two days. The unsolicited sculpting had taken a toll on her. What had once been narrow, pretty features that gave her an illusion of height had shriveled. It made her look emaciated now. The curly copper hair she once painstakingly groomed and coiffed hung loose and limp at the sides of her head. Her previously glistening blue eyes had dulled and sunken behind puffy purplish bags of skin. The perky cheekbones she had once blushed for her high school dances were stained a chronic blotchy red. Had she fairer skin and a more rounded face, she thought the accents might've made her look a little like her late mother's china doll collection. After they'd aged and cracked, of course.

"I already told you," Ted puffed as he knelt by his crumpled wife and leaned into her left ear. His scruffy beard tickled the red palm stain that adorned that cheek. "Shut that kid up. All it ever does is cry. And all you ever do is lie around and let it. I'm *sick of it*, Donna. If you don't shut him up, I will."

He snarled the fingers and thumb of his right hand into her hair, near the part and used the leverage to wrench her backward. Then he shoved her with the palm of the same hand into the door. A cracking sound echoed inside her head as her left temple smashed into the solid wood.

Startled by the sickening thud of his mother's head, Theo wound himself up for another round of inconsolable shrieking.

"Shut. That. Kid. Up!"

Ted rose, yanking Donna to her feet by a fresh fistful of her hair gripped in one cracked and calloused hand. He grabbed the bedroom doorknob and pulled on it, throwing the door wide. It slammed against the bedroom wall. The concussion shook the single photo of the unhappy couple on their wedding day from the adjacent wall, causing it to plummet to the hardwood floor. The glazing shattered when it hit. A shard skidded from the frame and came to rest an inch from the construction boots Ted would eventually don for work that morning.

Donna saw the light from the ceiling glint off the fang-shaped spike just as Ted pulled her through the door frame. He dragged her upright by the hair into the nursery. There, he shoved her into the rocking chair beside squalling Theo's crib and released her. She saw a thin clump of her copper locks drift to the floor from between the first and second fingers of his right hand. Donna buried her face in both of her hands, preventing him from seeing the tears that had escaped her will and crept from the corners of her eyes.

"You're gonna feed him," Ted bellowed at her. "You're gonna feed him now!"

He stretched an arm into the crib and snatched the newborn from it single-handed. He knotted his fingers around the throat of Theo's onesie, balling it up in his fist in the same way he might grab the neck of a cloth sack or the way a mother cat carries her kitten by the scruff. Theo's tiny head lolled backward. A crescent sliver of tongue protruded from between his lips as Ted hoisted the newborn into the air. Donna dropped her hands from her face just in time to see him thrust the child at her. Spit bubbles emerged from Theo's mouth, popping just as they broke the surface.

"Oh my God, you're going to kill him!" she screamed, unable to fight back her tears any longer. In that instant, she knew what she said was not hyperbole. Killing him was precisely what Ted intended to do if Donna refused to comply. There was malice in the grown man's eyes as he held their son aloft. More than that, she thought she could read the notion in his mind like a page from a book. *You'll do what I say, or I'll hurt you by hurting him.*

It was not the first time since they'd been married that she had heard his internal voice so clearly. Ted's rageful thoughts often read like an open book to her when he was sober. Unfortunately, those times were few and far between these days.

She leaped from the chair, arms outstretched for the silent baby. She folded her left arm into a cradle position as she closed in on father and son. Ted seemed to instinctively allow her to take over, dropping the child into her fold much more gently than he had raised him from the crib. Donna was careful to upright Theo's head as he was laid into her breast. She cleared away the saliva from his mouth with a forefinger. Then she placed the palm of that hand on the child's chest and held her breath, waiting for some sign of his own. Only after she confirmed that Theo's tiny diaphragm was still rising and falling did she dare look into his eyes.

They were open, those small dark blue orbs, although unfocused. After a second of confusion, they began to dart about the room, chasing bright spots and shadows created by the sunlight dappling from the window. Theo's arms wriggled against his mother's nightgown. When he kicked her right forearm with his tiny left foot, Donna finally allowed herself to believe that Ted's reckless handling had not permanently injured her baby. She also became aware that Ted was still standing over her, watching as she sat down in the rocker and draped a blanket over Theo's mid-section.

She glared up at him then, feeling the sting of her red rage boiling just inside the rims of her eyelids. Ted looked angry, a sneer on his upper lip. Long creases quivered in the folds along either side of his nose. But his slate-gray eyes, the same color Theo's might eventually become, looked drained and tired. His mouth hung slightly ajar as well, making him look like a brainless fish gazing stupidly at her from the bowl of tap water that served as its universe. Ted would still hate her, but he wouldn't hit her. Not right now, anyway. Not until after he had spent an entire day at work only to return, once again, home to a screaming Theo.

Donna unbuttoned the neck of her nightgown, creating the most prominent V the garment would allow, and squeezed her left breast out the opening. She teased the end of Theo's button nose with the nipple until his mouth popped open, then let him close around it to suckle. It was futile. She knew. She was as dry as the desert sand. The simple act of suckling would pacify Theo for a short time, at least until his father left for work and Donna could get to the kitchen to warm a bottle of formula.

She examined Ted again, not hiding her disgust. He seemed to realize that he had a job to go to suddenly. He rubbed the palm of his right hand under his chin and, with simple amazement, exclaimed, "Goddammit! I forgot to shave." He turned his back to her. Then he strode from the nursery, across the hall, into the main bedroom without another word.

The master bath lay to the back and left of it. Pale, overcast light from the bedroom window fell across his tank-clad shoulders when he turned to enter, highlighting the construction-hardened muscles he had just exercised to not only beat the daylights out of the woman who had given him her hand in marriage but also to brutalize and endanger his newborn son.

Donna felt sick.

Ted had been an angry man before Theo came along. A shouter. But he had never raised a hand to Donna until after the baby was born. With Theo not only a part of their lives but also fussy because his mother couldn't produce milk, Ted's verbal abuse had escalated to physical violence. How long before he killed her? Or worse, killed the baby? Or even worse, killed them both in one of his blind rampages?

Even if he didn't murder them outright in the coming days and weeks, what would stop him from escalating to torture as Theo grew up and started making the mistakes that all little kids make? What would happen when he brought his first F home from school?

Both of Donna's parents were gone to their rewards. A gas leak at home had taken them days after the wedding. Thinking back on it, Donna could believe she saw a premonition in her father's eyes as he gave her away that day; a sadness and helplessness therein that begged her to leave this man at the altar, to not repeat that vow to obey, to come home to Mom and Dad before it was too late. She had nowhere to go, no place to hide if she ran and Ted chased after her.

Gingerly, Donna plucked her nipple from Theo's mouth and tucked her breast inside her nightgown. She expected him to fuss, but he didn't. Not then. Not for the first time, Donna noted that the boy seemed calmer when his father wasn't nearby.

She rose from the rocker with the baby cradled in her arms, then raised him against her left shoulder. She patted him gently on the back with the hand that was not supporting him. He hadn't suckled anything, of course, but he puffed out a satisfyingly large belch anyway. The ritual complete, she laid Theo in his crib and turned to leave.

She was already reaching for the shard of glass just inside their bedroom door when the kid began to wail again. It was a long, distressed caterwauling that pierced the recent silence of the house like the squeal of a teenager's tires on asphalt. Donna snatched the glass from the floor and tucked it close to her right hip, hiding it behind a billowy fold in her nightgown. Not a moment too soon. Ted's bare feet thudded from the main bathroom at a breakneck pace.

"What in the blue fuck is going on out here?" he roared, the lower half of his face and neck covered in thick, foamy shaving cream. In his right hand, he clenched the flair-tip safety razor his mother had bequeathed him as a wedding present (Donna herself had received nothing in the way of congratulations from her mother-in-law). She paused half a breath to thank God that her husband was not a straight razor type of man. He was far too careless and would've most likely slit his throat long ago.

"I told you to feed our fucking kid," he screamed. "If you don't get your ass back in there right now, I'm gonna *make* you!"

He managed three steps toward her, his left hand clenched into a fist and right closed similarly around the handle of his razor. Donna raised the shard of glass that had broken out of the picture frame. She plunged the pointed end into his neck just below his Adam's apple. She held it there, pressing the polished, rounded back of the shard with her thumb. The top side of the fragment cut into the length of her palm below her fingers as the lower half sliced at her radial crease.

Ted flailed. His fists came loose. The safety razor plummeted to the floor. A thick beard of blood ran from the slash across his throat. It mixed and flowed through the snowy shaving cream like fresh lava oozing over the icy peaks of a volcano long thought dormant. A panicked weeping and sucking sound released as air from Ted's trachea seeped in and out around the shard.

He clutched at his throat, trying to shoo the hands of his son's mother from the embedded glass. He struggled to pluck it from his flesh against Donna's surge of empowerment. He scrambled backward at the same time, mashing his back against the main bedroom's exterior wall. Ted's face changed color as he struggled to draw breath. First, it was a winter pale, then a spring pink. Then a summer beet red. And, finally, an autumn eggplant.

As his ability to breathe waned, so did the massive man's strength. His arms, deprived of the blood and oxygen they needed to sustain themselves, fell limp at his sides. An airless matte glaze coated his eyeballs. His tongue protruded from his mouth in a ludicrous, insane parody of a child's playground taunt. His legs gave out as well.

He slid down the main bedroom wall as his stamina waned while Donna pressed on the shard. His head lolled to one side when he landed, palms up at his hips. He looked like a toddler's rag doll tossed carelessly into a corner at bedtime. He looked a lot like Theo had just moments ago when Ted had hoisted him from the crib by the neck of his onesie.

Donna's right bicep and forearm thrummed. She let loose of the shard and backed away from her husband's fresh corpse. Her eyes widened. Her mouth gaped. She had wondered just minutes before whether she could do something like this, could be rid of him. In a heartbeat, she had and was.

A powerful, urgent need to scream bubbled up from deep inside her. She stifled it with both hands, accidentally smearing blood from her injured right palm over her philtrum, lips, and chin. She fought the urge to call out his

name or check for breath or a pulse to verify that he was gone. Instead, she fled to the nursery.
The deed was done.
It could not be undone.
She had to figure out how to deal with it.
First thing's first. She needed to take care of herself before she held the baby again. She and Ted kept some small homemade first aid kits stowed in strategic places around the house: the main bathroom, the hall bathroom, and the garage. The closest—aside from one in the main bathroom that could only be obtained by walking past her recently departed husband—was the hall bathroom between the nursery and the kitchen. She ran there and found the mason jar in the cabinet under the sink. She unscrewed the lid and discovered inside a thin roll of cotton wrap, some bandages, a tiny pair of scissors with single finger-width holes, and some adhesive tape.

She also found a clean washcloth in the drawer just above the cabinet. She laid the rag aside and opened the bathroom sink tap wide. The water was cold, but it felt good. She rinsed away the sticky, foaming mess that coated her right hand. When all the blood and shaving cream had drained away, she examined the cuts the shard had left in her palm. They welled up again and began seeping crimson immediately.

Donna rewashed her hands with soap this time and dried them well. Next, she applied the largest bandages she could find directly to the cuts and wound them with cotton wrap. She had trouble cutting off some of the adhesive tape without the whole thing unraveling. Eventually, she found the correct way to position the fingers of her hurt hand to keep the wrap in place and hold the tape while she cut it with the scissors gripped in her left.

Bandages applied, Donna dampened the washrag with cool water from the tap and dabbed at the cut on her temple. It had stopped bleeding and was already forming a new clot. She scrubbed lightly around the edges of the injury to not disturb her body's efforts to heal. The dried spatters of blood on her skin did not come off quickly, but they did finally clean up. Without the risk of bleeding on her baby, she could now feed him the way the doctors and nurses had asked her to do it.

Donna raised the screaming infant from the crib and carried him to her kitchen. She gently shushed him, trying to soothe him as she warmed his morning bottle. After Theo was fed and changed (and quiet!), she put him back down for a nap. She closed the door to the main bedroom, shutting out the accusatory gaze of her lifeless husband's body. She padded to the garage utility and stripped off her nightgown. There was blood on it, much blood. She was not sure it would come out. She dropped it in the washing machine anyway, grateful that her mother and father could afford to gift her an automatic one.

She found some of her old, pre-matrimony dresses still stowed in moving boxes on a high shelf in the garage. She slid into a spring-appropriate yellow short-sleeved dress from Sears. Gratingly, her only selections of shoes and hair products remained in the main bedroom and bath. She would be forced to confront her husband one more time to make use of them.

The door squealed on its hinges when she pushed it wide. Ted still sat there, gaping at her with his eyes partially lidded, his face and neck splattered with melting shaving cream mixed with rivulets of his drying blood. His tongue—cracked, thick, and gross—lolled from between his lips. She side-stepped him to get to the bedroom closet and the main bathroom. She experienced a second of panicked certainty that he wasn't killed, that he would suddenly stretch out his left arm and wrap his cold fingers around her ankle. She managed the leap despite it, snatched up what she needed, and spent the better part of the next hour making up her face and hair in the hall bath.

Her process complete, Donna packed up Theo's things, including some spare bottles of formula that were already mixed and securely capped. Hours later, when the wash had been completed and she had packed enough baby things for a lengthy trip, she loaded Theo into her left arm and struggled out the door with all she had left in the world. She didn't know where she was going, only that she had to leave. The man who had married her, screamed at her, fathered her son, and then beat the shit out of her would never lay another finger on her or her baby as long as they lived.

The deed was done.

CHAPTER FIVE

L ost Hollow church pianist Peter Mayberry traced a finger down the valley of Sam Brooks's spine. He started at the nape, dragging the pad lazily along the length, and ended at the cleft of Sam's buttocks. The latter's top peeked from its hiding place under the cotton bed linens that draped both men at the hips. Along the way, he allowed himself to linger for a second on one of the randy black, worm-like scars scattered about Sam's back, souvenirs of The Battle of the Bulge embedded in the man's otherwise flawless skin. The texture of the flaw was novel, exciting. For Peter, it conjured images of foxholes and frigid New Year's Day earth, the fog of exploded munitions creeping over it.

He grinned at the goose pimples that prickled Sam's flesh as he drew the remainder of the straight line down his back to its end. Peter liked the contrast of Sam's brown, rose-tinged skin against his near-translucent finger, which was as white as the ivories he tickled on the church piano every Sunday morning. His target acquired, Peter gave Sam's left ass cheek a firm but playful smack, startling him from his slumber. He leaned into Sam's left ear, pressing his lips gently against the lobe, and whispered, "Time to go."

Sam rolled onto his back and craned his neck to see the face of the alarm clock on the nightstand. His soulful brown eyes blinked away the previous night's dreams as they tried to focus on the waking world around him. "It's not even nine yet," he replied. "What's the matter? Mommy calling you names again?" He turned out his lower lip and rubbed a knuckle in the corners of each eye in a mock pout.

"That's not funny."

Peter tossed the bed covers aside. He swung his knees over the edge of the bed and planted his feet hard on the threadbare bedroom carpet. One of them landed with a thud. The left one, attached to the slightly shorter limb that had prevented Peter from serving his country, touched the floor but did not make any noise. Well, the leg was what had been listed on his exemption, anyway. Peter thought his draft officer might have ascertained his homosexuality, although he couldn't say so with any surety.

Throughout his life, Peter had feared that he outwardly presented himself in some telltale unmasculine way that unintentionally revealed what his mother referred to as his *predilection*. He was a slightly shorter than average man with a prominent belly and hips the breadth of his shoulders. He was virtually hairless as well, except for the thin wisps of left-parted chestnut atop his head. Those physical characteristics he could not help, but the way he stood, how he rested his hands, the words he chose, any of those things might give him away in the eyes of his straight peers. Hell, straight guys even accused other straight guys over lesser words or actions.

Peter tried to push himself off the mattress from his seated position. His right fist became entangled in the linens. Sam's prostrate bulk lay partially atop the sheet, opposing Peter's efforts. The result was a whiplash effect that nearly landed him back in the sack. He shook his right hand furiously to loosen himself from the tether. He had been going for an angry and offended exit. Thanks to his gracelessness and Sam's brawny, military-honed frame, it had instead read as cloddish.

Behind him, Sam sighed. "At some point, you're going to have to confront that ghost bitch," he said. He shifted onto his right elbow and stroked Peter's shoulder with the fingers of his left hand. "Hey. Look at me. That's better. I said, at some point, you're going to have to confront that ghost bitch. Especially if you want *this* to work." He wagged a forefinger in the air between them, indicating their invisible connection.

Peter scowled. "Stop calling my mother a bitch," he snarled. He rose from the bed, this time without entanglement. He snatched the pair of wire-rimmed glasses from the nightstand and slid them on. They sharply clarified the vexation on Sam's face. "I have a piano lesson in a few hours. I need you out before that busybody McElroy woman drops her precious little Tony by for his primer."

Sam threw off the covers and bounded from the bed. He stood four inches taller than Peter's five-foot-eight, intimidating with his arms crossed over his broad chest even though he was nude. "You're throwing me out, then?"

Peter wilted. "I—You can't be here while I'm with a student," he said. "What would the stupid kid think? What would his mother tell people?" He turned to face Sam, his arms dangling awkwardly at his sides. "Come on, Sam. I need my income. The church gig only pays a pittance of what I earn from teaching. I'm practically a volunteer there. If the town found out about you and me, I'd lose that *at best*.

At worst, they'd put me in prison. There are sodomy laws in this state. They think what we do is a crime against nature."

Sam's eyebrows shot up. "Is that so?" he asked mockingly. "What do *you* think?"

Peter paused, pondering, then chose to ignore the question. "They'd *murder* you. You can count on it."

Sam scoffed. He snatched his pair of baby blue boxers and his cotton tank from the chair on his side of the bed and quickly pulled them on, covering in seconds what it had taken Peter a half hour to uncover the night before. The older white man felt a discordant pang of loss alongside his sense of relief as he watched Sam's modesty recover itself.

"You think I'm just some toy, don't you?" Sam growled, pulling on his socks. He posed gracefully on one foot as he tugged a sock over the other, a *danseur* without a stage. "You think what we do is unnatural? My whole damn life, you white folks have thought of me as abnormal, or at least lesser than you. Am I just a fetish? Someone you think you can just sneak in the backdoor any time you feel like it and then toss out with last night's meatloaf when you must go back to your *real* life—wallowing in your guilt and wallowing in your self-pity?

"Let me tell you something, Pete," he said as his biceps disappeared into the sleeves of his shirt. He strode to where Peter stood at the side of the bed and leaned into his face. Their noses nearly touched. Peter struggled mightily not to break his gaze. "I'm gonna make this crystal clear right now. I don't care what the white folks around here think of me. I don't care what the white folks around here think of you. There's ways around all of that. You think you're the only man ever been loved by another man? That it? Or are you thinking you're the only white man who's ever been loved by a Black man? Huh?

"I'm telling you, ain't either one of those things true. You ain't special, Peter Mayberry. Hell, you ain't even atypical. Not really. All you are is afraid you're not accepted or not moral. But somehow, you did make me fall in love with you. If you can't accept that, and you can't find it in you to make *this* work, then I don't see any reason for me to come back here anymore."

Sam stomped to the chair where his pants had lain draped for the past ten hours. He slid into them, one leg at a time, and stuffed his shirttail inside before fastening them. Finally, he pulled on his boots. He was nearly out the bedroom door when he suddenly stopped and turned back to face his still-naked boyfriend one more time.

Peter's will to meet Sam's eyes abandoned him. He instead stared at his feet. He caught a glimpse of his naked dick as he did. A fresh wave of shame and vulnerability washed over him.

"You know what your biggest problem is?" Sam said through clenched teeth. He stretched an arm behind Peter and lifted the framed photo lying facedown on the nightstand. He held the image by the top of the frame and forced its subject into Peter's field of vision. Margaret Mayberry's black, narrow slitted eyes glared back at her paunchy, pasty, naked son from within the photo. Her pursed lips twisted sideways and down, allowing him to see her chronic—maybe permanent—disapproval of the man her child had become.

"This," Sam said, stabbing at the woman with the forefinger of his free hand. "*This* is your biggest problem." He tossed the photo facedown on the bed beside them. "Until you get rid of *her*, you're never going to have me." He shook his head. "No. No. It's even worse than that. Until you get rid of her, you're never going to have *anyone*, Black or white or man or woman. Least of all me."

A tense silence enveloped the room while Sam stared at him, waiting. For what response, Peter did not know. He simply stared at Sam's boots, his hands clasped under his belly, attempting to hide whatever amount of his genitals protruded from beneath it. His cheeks were on fire, but the rest of him was cold, as if the temperature inside the room had begun to drop instead of rising with the morning light. He fervently wished he had gotten dressed when Sam had.

"Fine," Sam said. "That's how you want it? Fine. See you around then, Pete. Or not, I guess."

Emptiness, loneliness that started in the pit of his stomach overcame Peter when he heard the back door slam. Seconds later, Sam's Triumph—a gorgeous silver Tiger he said he'd won from a British infantryman near the end of the war—roared to life. Peter listened as the singular joy he'd discovered as a grown man living quietly in Lost Hollow sped out of his life for good.

"Good riddance," the cracked voice of his mother grunted from the photo. The words were muffled because she lay facedown on the bed cover, but Peter could distinctly pick out the sardonic merriment they conveyed.

He sat on the side of the bed and retrieved the portrait, turning it over in his hands to once again face the disapproving woman who had given birth to him in the early days of the roaring decade that had eventually led to the Great Depression.

He had been only ten years old on Black Thursday, that day in 1929 when Wall Street fell down and went boom. Not long after, his father had left him and his mother at home alone in search of employment. He'd never returned. These days, Peter could barely remember what he had looked like.

Meanwhile, Margaret Mayberry had made ends meet by doing odd jobs where she could, such as mending and taking in laundry. The piano lessons she had been teaching to supplement her husband's income dried up almost immediately after the big bust. People were having a hard enough time feeding their kids without having to pay someone to educate them in frivolous pursuits like music, art, or literature.

The hours she did not spend laboring so she and the boy could eat were spent at the altar of the Nazarene church, praying by candlelight that the Lord would find them worthy of respite from this economic plague born of the dalliances, delinquencies, and prideful abominations of the decade prior.

It was on one of those prayerful late afternoons at the church, three years into the tribulation, that Margaret had first come face-to-face with the difference between her then thirteen-year-old son and other boys.

CHAPTER SIX

Peter Mayberry the adolescent sat on a shallow bank of Hollow Creek. The brook babbled along the side of the road directly across from the Nazarene church. While his mother prayed, Peter tossed small stones he dug from the dirt into the crystal running water. He liked to guess whether the rocks were heavy enough to sink immediately or if the current was strong enough to drag them a pace before they settled among the silt and gravel that formed the bed.

Mostly, he was disappointed. The creek had run low and slow for as far back as his young mind could remember. Sometimes he wondered why God had even created it. Hollow Creek at these levels was not capable of providing enough water to quench the thirst of all the wildlife and domestic farm life that occupied the hills and valleys in Lost Hollow. Nor could it provide enough freshwater life to feed the population. Unless you liked frog legs and crawdads, of course. Peter hated frog legs and crawdads. Well, he had never actually tried them. But they looked slimy. He imagined that they would feel the same on his tongue. Also, crawdads could pinch you.

"What you doing?" cried a voice from behind him. Peter snapped his head around to locate its owner. Another boy, one with mischievous blue eyes, peered from under a waterfall of thick black hair. The other boy clenched the narrow handle of a badly rusted tin bucket in his right fist as he approached. In his left, he held a small fishing net. "Quit throwing rocks. You're gonna scare all the crawdads away."

Peter sneered. "So? What are you gonna do? Eat 'em?"

The boy set down his bucket. He plopped himself by Peter's side and grinned, revealing dimples. Peter thought he saw a flash of playfulness dancing in the boy's eyes.

"You kidding? A'course I eat them. Everybody does. They're good, kind of sweet and kind of salty at the same time. There's plenty of them around for when you can't afford to buy no groceries. Momma's been cooking up the crawdads I've been catching for us all week." He cast Peter a sidelong, mischievous glance. "But you *can* eat 'em raw. I like 'em raw."

Peter grinned back, hoping his face showed playfulness in kind. "I don't believe you."

The boy nodded. "I'll show you, then. Name's Joe, by the way."

"Peter."

"Well, Pete, I'm gonna get down in the creek and catch us two crawdads. If I eat the first one, you gotta eat the second one. I'll show you how. If I'm lyin' and I can't do it, I'll give you my bucket of what I catch today so your momma can cook them up. What do you say?"

He started to answer that he didn't like crawdads, raw or cooked. He began to say that his momma wouldn't know how to cook a crawdad if they handed her the instructions themselves. Before he could respond, Joe stood and was rolling up the cuffs of his overalls. He waded into the shallow creek barefoot, bucket in hand and fishnet forgotten on the bank. He began his practiced hand-fishing for crawdads and soon plucked two from the shallows. He captured each of them between a thumb and forefinger that he embedded in their sides just south of their pincers.

Even from this distance, Peter could see the tiny burnt umber creatures brandishing their little natural defenses in the air as Joe raised them from the water and dumped them with a muted *clang* into the bucket. Peter was sorry for them. Pincers or no, they were helpless prey, trapped in a bucket from which they could not climb and deprived of their natural creek water habitat to sustain and comfort them.

When he returned from the water, Joe sat beside Peter and placed the bucket between them. The crawdads were at opposite ends of the disk at the bottom. They rubbed their pincers against the sides of the bucket. One of them attempted to scale it, only to end up on its back with its tiny antenna and walking legs flailing in the space above it.

That was the one Joe selected for consumption. He tumbled it to rights by placing his forefinger under its abdomen, which the crawdad used as leverage. Joe raised it from the bucket, two fingers of one hand behind its pincers and two fingers of the other clasping its tail fin. He dangled the poor thing over his upturned face so that the crawdad stared directly into Joe's maw. Peter winced. Just as he was about to look away, Joe once again shot him that mischievous sidelong glance. He dropped the crawdad back into the bucket and smirked. "Gotcha!"

Peter blinked. "What?"

"I just wanted to see how far you were going to let me go," Joe said, chuckling. "I reckon you were just gonna sit there and let me do it. Boy! You should've seen the look on your face! Your daddy never taught you anything about fishing from the creeks, did he? You don't ever eat bottom feeders raw. At least, that's what my Pa says. If you eat a bottom feeder raw, you're eating everything that bottom feeder has eaten, stuff you wouldn't ever want to put in your mouth. You gotta cook them to get rid of all the junk."

"Oh," Peter said. "So, you were never going to eat that thing?" Joe giggled. "No."

"Then you should put them back in the creek. I don't like seeing them like this." He indicated the second crawdad, which was still attempting to scale the rusty interior of the tin bucket.

Joe turned out his bottom lip in a mock pout. "Oh, what's the matter? Are you afraid the tiny tasties are hurting? They're just crusty fish, Pete. They don't have minds like you and me. I'm gonna kill them, and my Momma's gonna cook them."

"Well, there's no need to make them suffer before that happens," Peter admonished.

Joe snorted. "Fine." He lifted the bucket by its handle and scaled the embankment to the creek bed. There, he flung the bucket without releasing it, propelling the two crawdads from its depths and into the clear running water. He hurled the bucket back toward Peter, although not at an arc that seemed intentionally harmful. He spread his arms wide and glowered. "Happy? There goes my dinner."

Peter, who suddenly found himself feeling guilty about his reaction, folded his hands over his crisscrossed legs and stared at them. "I—I didn't mean you should throw them out," he started. "I just—"

"It's fine," Joe interrupted. "I'll catch more later, and I'll make sure the bucket has some rocks and some creek water in it so the mudbugs don't feel so out of place when I carry them home and cut their heads off. How's that?"

Peter didn't reply. Joe stomped up the embankment as best as he could manage barefoot on a slope covered with sharp blades of grass and not a little shot rock. He strode past Peter and lit near a honeysuckle bush growing along the side of Hollow Creek Road. He plucked a white tubular flower from the bush, examining the complex array of stem-like structures surrounded by its petals, pulled the thickest of the forms from the center, and tossed it aside. Then he placed his lips around the narrow end of the flower and drank from it.

"What are you doing now?" Peter shouted. "What if those things are poisonous? My mom says never to eat wild berries unless you know what they are first."

Joe sneered. "Does this look like a berry to you? It's a honeysuckle bush. It's what you're supposed to do with them. Geez, you may be the dumbest country boy I've ever met. Your folks don't teach you anything, do they?" He plucked two more flowers from the honeysuckle bush and sat beside Peter again.

"Look," he continued, "this is a honeysuckle flower. *Honey. Suckle.* That means you can suck the honey juice out of the middle of it. It tastes good, and it's not poison. I've been doing this since I was small, and it's never hurt me none. I'll show you."

He gripped one of the flowers by its cup and pointed to the small poles in its center. "See the biggest one? The green one? That's the girl part of the flower. All these yellow ones around it are the boy parts. To suck the juice, you have to pull the girl part out of the flower because that's what keeps it all inside. So, you grab the bottom tip of the flower, like this, then you pull on the green plunger at the end of the girl part." He performed the act as he spoke. "There's two ways you can get the juice. You can lick the end of the girl part inside the flower, or you can suck on the bottom tip of the flower. I like to do both."

Joe licked the end of the honeysuckle pistil and then flicked it into the creek. He placed the bottom tip of the flower between his lips and sucked on it. When he was done, he tossed the flower into the stream as well.

"You can eat the whole thing," he added, "but I don't like to do that." He retrieved the second honeysuckle flower from his lap and handed it to Peter. "You try."

Peter accepted the flower. It didn't have a brain like a person or even a fish. It didn't move around or struggle to escape like a crawdad. Joe had swallowed its nectar without any consequences, so why not?

He pinched the flower at its bottom tip and pulled on the pistil. It snapped in half, leaving a small green stigma still lodged in the cup of the flower, blocking access to the nectar.

Joe sighed. "No, you pulled too hard. It doesn't take much. Pinch it between your fingers, just under that plunger on top, and pull *gently*. Not slow, but gentle. It'll pop right out. Toss that one unless you want to eat it. I'll get you another one."

Peter didn't want to eat it, although he thought he might have if Joe had done the same. Instead, he flicked it toward the creek, as Joe had done. It landed about a foot away from his lap, lodging itself in a crevasse between two fist-sized chunks of rock. Fortunately, Joe's back was to Peter at that moment. He was too busy selecting a fresh honeysuckle flower from the bush and did not see the failure.

"Okay, here's a fresh one," Joe announced as he crouched by Peter on the embankment. "Give it another try."

Peter started to take it but changed his mind. He had embarrassed himself enough for one afternoon. "I'll try it sometime," he said.

"Oh, come on, you pussy," Joe replied. "Okay, I'll pull the girl part out for you. Then all you have to do is lick it and suck the flower. How about that?"

Peter shrugged. "Okay."

With the same confidence and practiced hand he had used to retrieve the crawdads, Joe pinched the base of the flower and removed the pistil before Peter could so much as blink. The flower in his left hand, he dangled the pistil by its stamen and presented the trophy to Peter. "Here you go!" Then, with a wry smile, "Come and get it."

Peter stuck out his tongue and leaned in to taste. Before the first drop of nectar touched his tastebuds, he was startled by the loud bang of the Nazarene church door. That sound was closely followed by his mother shrieking his name.

***

"Don't you *ever* let me catch you with the Bayless boy again, do you understand me?"

Peter sat at the kitchen table, his hands folded in his lap, head bowed. Margaret Mayberry stood at the stove, her back to him, stirring a pot of boiling water, her back straight and shoulders squared. If he could see her face just then, Peter knew full well the expression she'd bear: her thin, black eyebrows arched severely over eyes so dark they sometimes appeared black. Her thin lips would be stretched flat in a slant over her narrow chin, pulled so taut that they'd become as white as her scalp. It had taken the water forever to start rolling around in the pot. The room filled with the noise of hot bubbles rising and bursting the surface at a pace faster than Peter could count.

"His family comes from over in Hollow River, boy. Don't you know what they have up there in Hollow River? They have whores there. That's what. They have whores and that Devil music they dance to. And they have man-whores, too. Is that what you want to be, son? Do you want to be a man-whore?"

Peter shook his head.

"Well, you couldn't have proved it today," Margaret snapped. "Outside the church, no less! That Bayless boy has a reputation around here, son. He comes to visit his grandmother so he can put his dirty hands on our local boys. Tries to change them to his type, he does. Did you know his grandmother caught him in her basement with another boy? Huh? Did you know that?"

Peter shook his head again.

"Yeah, you better not have known that. I'll tell you that right now. I can hardly bear to *think* about what they were doing down there. They were kissing like a man and woman. It's unnatural, son. It's the Devil's work, and it's come to infect my baby. I'll be damned—as damned as the fornicator before the throne of God—if I'm going to let the Devil have you."

She opened a drawer and pulled a small pair of pliers from within it. She grasped them in her left hand while her right steadied the pot on the stove. She dipped the jaws of the pliers into the boiling water and fished out a three-and-a-half-inch smooth shank 16-penny nail. She shook it to drip the excess water from the sharp point and back into the pot, then switched off the burner. Peter stared glumly as the last droplet dangled at the nail's end, magnifying its chiseled point. Margaret reached into the same drawer where she had found the pliers and produced a wood-handled claw hammer, a rugged and ancient-looking tool left behind by her husband. She gripped the hammer in her right hand, the pliers with the nail in their jaws in her left, and carried them with her to Peter's side. "Stick out your tongue," she commanded.

"Mom, no!" Peter shouted. The blood drained from his face. "You can't!"

"Put your bottom lip on the edge of the table and stick out your tongue," she said again without hesitation. *"If thine eye offend thee, pluck it out.* That's what the Good Book says. That Bayless boy tempted you, son. I saw it. He wants to lure you into his wicked ways. You will remember this the next time you want to use that organ for evil. You'll remember this, and you'll think better of it. If you don't do this for me and the sake of your soul, I'll have to take your balls instead. I have the snips for it. I can do it while you're asleep."

Peter's hands automatically cupped his crotch. Tearfully, he searched his mother's face for some amount of empathy, any sign of regret or aversion to the task she had set for herself, anything he could exploit to escape. He found only blankness there.

He gripped the table's edge with both hands and lowered his head until his bottom lip was touching the cool laminate. He thrust the trembling organ from his mouth, the bottom of it coming to rest on the tabletop in front of him. He squeezed his eyes shut and tried to stop himself from whimpering. His breath was hot and coppery when he exhaled over his tongue, icy and unfeeling when he swallowed a fresh gulp of air.

Margaret pressed the point of the nail into the median crease of her only son's tongue, pinning it in place on the table without breaking the skin. She held it there with the pliers. Then she raised the hammer, positioning the face of the tool a half inch over the head of the nail.

"And if thy right eye offend thee, pluck it out and cast it from thee!" she shouted. *"For it is profitable for thee that one of thy members should perish, and not that thy whole body should be cast into hell!"*

She raised the hammer higher over her shoulder and swung it hard in a downward arc. It landed with a thud squarely on the head of the nail. Blood squirted from the new hole in his tongue. It dampened his lips and splattered the end of his nose. His body tensed, instinctively trying to pull him back from the threat. But there was strength behind his mother's blow. On its first impact, the nail had penetrated not only Peter's tongue but the tabletop below it.

His mouth wide, straining to prevent his teeth from clamping down on the injured organ, Peter screamed. He beat at the nail with both hands, trying to grab it and pluck it out. When he couldn't, he cried and flailed his palms against the table in frustrated agony. Tears streamed down his face and tickled the unmutilated salty areas of his taste buds. Then the hammer came down again.

And again.

Peter screamed until the hammering stopped. He screamed again a minute later when Margaret used the claw end of the tool to yank the nail free finally, gloriously. When he could move again, he scraped at his bleeding tongue with the fingertips of both hands. He pressed on the puncture wound, trying to shut off the flowing blood and deaden the pain with direct pressure. Still, he screamed. He screamed until he thought his brain was going to explode. He screamed until darkness enveloped him, and he could not cry anymore.

CHAPTER SEVEN

"I should have gone ahead and cut off your balls," Peter's mother taunted from the portrait in his hands. "That nail didn't change anything. You're still sticking things out there for the other boys to play with, aren't you? It's not just your tongue anymore, though, is it? You're sticking your *thing* out there, too. Only they don't want *your* thing. They want to stick *their* things in your mouth. Or in your asshole. Oh, yeah. That's what they want. And you let them."

"Shut up, Momma," Peter mumbled.

"What did you say to me?"

He set the photo back on the nightstand. Then he slid off the bed and leaned against it, sitting cross-legged on the floor. "Nothing. I'm sorry. I didn't mean it."

"Damn right you didn't," Margaret Mayberry chided. "You need to atone for your sins, boy. All that prayer and all that hymn accompaniment down at the church are good for you, but they're not taking away your unnatural carnal desires. *If thine eye offend thee, pluck it out.* Those are the words of the Good Book."

"Yes, Momma. Those are the words."

Peter rolled his tongue over the roof of his mouth. The organ had healed itself over the weeks and months after his mother had punctured it, as tongues do. He'd had to resign himself to bland and soft lukewarm meals for a while. He'd been meticulous about keeping his mouth as clean as possible.

At first he couldn't eat anything at all because Margaret had crammed his mouth with gauze. He supposed he had been lucky that he hadn't bled to death. He neither saw nor felt any evidence that his tongue had ever been injured these days.

"Yes, Momma."

Peter stood up and padded into the kitchen naked, his head buzzing with his mother's words. From a cabinet by the stove, he retrieved a small pot. He filled it with water from the tap and set it on the stove. He ignited the eye, setting the flame to its highest burn. While waiting for the water to boil, he searched the nearby junk drawer. Within it he located his father's claw hammer. After a little more fishing, he came up with a pair of pliers and a shiny one and a half-inch finish nail. It was smaller than the nail his mother had used on his tongue, but it would do. He dropped the nail into the pot of water, which had yet begun to steam.

If thine eye offend thee, pluck it out, he thought.

He decided to practice until the water was ready. He crouched at the knees in front of the kitchen table, settling his penis and scrotum atop it. He adjusted his ballsack so that it dangled below the table's edge but kept his flaccid member lying flat against the laminate surface. It was cool against the sensitive underside, an unusually sensual feeling after having peeled it away from his testicles. He wondered whether it was better to be soft or rigid for an operation of this type. He guessed flaccid would hurt more, but hard might be more dangerous. What if he bled out?

All these things he considered as steam finally began to rise from the pot of water. Stern and silent, his mother peered at him through the bedroom door from her place on the nightstand.

CHAPTER EIGHT

Beard's Grocery sat perched atop a small peninsula, accessible from Hollow Creek Road only by a rickety wood and steel bridge just wide enough for a single car to traverse at any one time. The back of the store opened onto acreage that had, once upon a time, been a dairy farm owned by Jerry Beard's father Jessie. An overturned tractor had taken the elder Beard's life when Jerry was still a tot. Over the years, his mother Kathy had sold off all the cattle and leased the farm's unsaturated acres to local tenant farmers to put food on the table and keep the store Jessie and Kathy had opened as a second business in 1936 operational.

Hollow Creek bordered the three remaining sides of the tiny piece of land on which the store sat. A white-washed board fence ran the length of the creek borders, except for the spot where the bridge connected the store's property to the road. The Beards had considered the geography and its fencing as a beneficial property feature in earlier times. It provided some natural defenses against intruders and a source of distillable fresh water if they needed it. As farm life became too much work for too little profit and the merchant life showed more promise, the creek and the fence with the single-car access bridge seemed more like barriers. For Kathy, anyway.

Jessie had long ago mounted a small five-inch rain gauge on top of the fence post nearest the eastern wall of the store. It was one of several he'd configured around the farm's perimeter to determine which areas were receiving the most benefit from nature's watering can. On the afternoon of March 21, 1955, just as Eli Wynn and Nazarene preacher Mark MacDonald were arriving at Beard's on their errands, the first drops of what the National Weather Service in Hollow River would later call a hundred-year flood collected in the gauge's basin. A bit more than an hour later, that gauge overflowed, and Hollow Creek swelled to dramatic effect, well on its way to flood stage. The bubbling crystal clear creek water over which Eli had trod became a bed of sickly beige, opaque rapids topped with hundreds of tiny cresting waves. The flow bottlenecked under the bridge. The water, too fast and furious to remain contained, began to stretch its fingers in spidery rivulets over its banks. The sun descended rapidly on the horizon as if trying to ignore the impending disaster below.

***

Donna Gilliam's bleeding had not stopped. The bandages in which she had wrapped her hand soaked through in the amount of time it had taken her to clean herself up, feed and gather tiny Theo, secure him in the floorboard of her late husband's Ford F1, and haul ass from the house where his cooling corpse remained propped against the wall in the main bedroom. The two palm gashes she'd sustained while stabbing Ted with her makeshift knife of glass burned when she folded her hand around the steering wheel. Mercifully,

Theo was fast asleep. He remained so when the Ford's engine roared to life.

The nearest hospital stood in Hollow River, a significant trip for her and her infant son on a dark afternoon like this one. It was her only choice for getting herself stitched up. She had also decided to ask a doctor to examine Theo's head and neck. Donna remained unconvinced that Ted hadn't injured the boy when he'd suspended him by the collar in their nursery. He hadn't fussed very much since then. Whether because of injury by his father or the simple death of same remained to be seen. The baby was half-Ted. If Theo's mental connection to his dad was more robust than the one she had unwittingly established, the sudden silencing of rage within his mind must have been welcome.

Large raindrops splattered against the Ford's windshield as mother and son spun out of the driveway. Donna, who drove only occasionally, struggled to find the wiper control. Her fingers stumbled over it and switched it on just as the patter transitioned into a pummel and the gray asphalt of the path in front of her became splotchy and stained black with water. The rain pooled in unmaintained areas of the right-of-way, streaming down man-carved hillsides in long waterfalls and collecting at the shoulders until it formed nearly invisible ponds in places where the asphalt wasn't poured at an angle that allowed runoff.

How long since Ted had bought tires for this bucket? She didn't know. Hopefully enough tread remained to keep the truck from skidding into the verge if she ended up unable to avoid hydroplaning or some road hazard. After passing the Lost Hollow sign, there would be at least another forty-five miles or more of heavy rain and wet road between her and Hollow River. Assuming she made it that far, of course.

The rain flowed in sheets over her windshield as she made the left turn onto Hollow Creek Road, less than a mile from the border of the Blalock farm and Beard's General, but not even close to the center of town. She slowed the F1 to a crawl, searching through the downpour for signs that she was keeping between the lines. She had to fight overcorrecting more than once after bounding over a pothole. With every bump, her fearful brain screamed that she'd accidentally ventured over the centerline, that she was on the precipice of driving off the embankment and into Hollow Creek.

To make matters worse, the windshield's interior kept fogging over because of the sudden difference in temperature and humidity inside versus out. Donna swiped at the moisture with the palm of her bandaged hand. That further hindered her visibility because it left a long wet red streak over the glass in its wake.

She raised her uninjured hand to try again when the taillights of another car swam into view. They were blurry and distorted through the F1's windshield, but the light from them combined with her headlights was strong enough to allow her to see that she was approaching the bridge that marked the entrance to Beard's General. The other car (she couldn't determine the make) was parked on the shoulder of the road just beyond that entrance. Possibly someone had decided that the downpour made driving too risky and had pulled to the side of the road to wait it out.

"Why didn't you just park in Beard's lot?" Donna wondered aloud. Her voice inside her head echoed: *Why don't you just pull into Beard's lot, Donna?*

She glanced at her hand, then at her infant son sleeping soundly in his carrier in the passenger-side floorboard of the

F1. Although her wounds still wept, she was not bleeding out. Theo didn't seem to be in pain. The danger to their lives was greater if she continued the drive to the hospital through flooding roadways than by stopping at Kathy's place to wait out the storm.

There would be questions, of course. *How did you hurt your hand, Donna? How did you get that cut on your head, Donna? Why isn't Ted with you, Donna?* She'd need to answer them, buy herself some time to think through everything that had happened back at the house. It was self-defense. It was *son*-defense, really. But facts never stopped the law from arresting you and labeling your baby a ward of the state while they "investigated."

She'd heard the awful stories about that Georgia Tann woman's orphanage in Memphis. Would Theo end up somewhere like that? There had to be a way out that allowed her to live her life with her son in peace. But until the rain stopped and she could move on to Hollow River, Beard's was as good a place as any to think for a while, to figure out her next move.

Donna turned right onto the bridge, crossing a rapidly rising Hollow Creek already lapping at the top of the barrel. As she rounded the turn, her headlights passed over the car's rear window . Donna caught a glimpse of two figures, silhouettes of a man and a woman, through the stopped care. She wouldn't swear to it, but they appeared to be necking.

***

Peter Mayberry had regrets.

He had intended to use the hammer's claw end to remove the nail from the shaft of his penis after he drove it through. He had wanted the chiseled point of the nail to extrude from the neck of the glans the way his mother's nail had completely penetrated his tongue and embedded itself in the kitchen table. He was circumcised. He didn't know for sure why his parents had made that choice for him, although he thought it was probably his mother hedging her bets Godwise. He'd thought not having a foreskin would make the removal of the nail the easy part. Alas, the pain, blood, and mere sight of the foreign object protruding from the organ overwhelmed Peter just as he'd set about reversing the operation.

Sudden dizziness and nausea caused him to release the hammer. It fell headlong to the kitchen floor, landing with a dull thud. It balanced there, the handle in the air like a diver pointing his toes skyward after a successful jack-knife. Peter registered the novelty of the image—he scored the hammer ten points—before consciousness abandoned him and he collapsed to the floor. The nail remained enrooted in him. As the lights and the room wavered in his vision, he was glad it had not become stuck in the kitchen table as well.

***

Hours later, Peter's eyelids shot wide when he heard a knock at his door. His piano student, no doubt.

He lay quietly, half under his kitchen table, blinking at the hammer beside him, not bothering to call out to his visitor. Shock must not have taken him entirely. Good.

After a minute more of light staccatos on the door, Peter heard the boy's mother tell him that Mr. Mayberry must have gone out. She added that it was just as well because he wasn't any better at tickling the ivories than their pet turtle. The lessons were a waste of good money. She was tired of paying for them. Peter drifted back toward unconsciousness as their footsteps faded from his doorstep.

Much later, he awoke again. The tip of his penis was on fire. With both hands, he pressed on his gut, moving it so he could get a better view of the damage he'd done. The nail was still there. The blood pooled around its head had run down the shaft and congealed in the thatch of pubic hair that surrounded it. Blood clots. He wondered what would happen if blood clotted inside the nail wound. Had he damaged his urethra? What if he had to pee?

These anxieties overwhelmed his shock. Peter scrambled—as well as he could scramble given the circumstances—to his feet and ran for the bathroom. There, he found a small roll of gauze. He wound it around the shaft of his dick, nail and all. He had no medical tape, patience, or steady hand to thread a safety pin through the gauze without pricking himself. Instead, he tucked the loose end of the roll into a previous fold. He hoped it would hold there while he drove himself to the new emergency room at the hospital in Hollow River.

He dressed carefully, sliding first into a pair of loose-fitting boxers. They felt foreign against his skin, as if he'd never dressed before. No surprise, he thought, given he'd spent the previous night and every hour of the day so far wholly naked.

He pulled a pair of beige slacks over the boxers. After a couple of scream-inducing attempts to button them and raise the zipper, he chose to allow the slacks to remain undone in front. The alternative was too painful. Instead, he covered his indecency with a tails-out button-down shirt.

Dressed for his errand, Peter snatched up the keys to his Dodge Custom, a nearly ten-year-old unmaintained rust bucket he'd bought from a junk dealer. He'd only bought it after deciding he might need to venture out of Lost Hollow occasionally to indulge his need for company. Sometimes he wished the thing would break down completely, preventing him from leaving the house.

My luck, he thought, *that'll happen now*. But he was wrong. The Dodge turned over immediately.

By the time he reached the entrance to Beard's General on his way out of town, Peter could barely see the road in front of him. The downpour that the skies threatened when he left his driveway had finally presented itself, and it was a doozy. Unable to clear his windshield faster than the rain could obscure it, Peter edged the Dodge to the shoulder of the road and parked it there. His dick throbbed urgently, frustrated by the foreign object lodged in its neck and requiring attention. Ending up with his car in a flooded ditch or, God forbid, upside down in a rampaging Hollow Creek in no way aided that pursuit. So, he pulled over to wait it out. No blood had seeped from his bandaged member, as far as he could tell. There were no dark stains on his pants or his boxers.

His stomach churned. Despite his best efforts to keep it down, last night's dinner scaled his esophagus and lodged itself at the back of his throat. He gagged and tried to swallow. No use. He threw open the driver's door of The Dodge and lost the previous night's meal onto Hollow Creek Road.

Rain pelted his bare head, gluing what remained of his hair to his scalp. The deluge was cool against his skin, a relief after his convulsions subsided. He cupped his hands and captured some of it in his palms, then pursed his lips and slurped the water from the cup he'd made. The liquid sloshed pleasantly over his teeth and tongue. He spat it out on top of the vomit, most of which the rain had already washed away.

He had grabbed the door to slam it shut again when he caught a glimpse of something, or someone, watching him from the side of the road. He squinted, trying to see through the sheeting rain. Sure enough, there appeared to be a large animal of some kind—a dog perhaps—seated on the opposite shoulder. It had thick, black fur and pointed wolf-like ears, more prominent and longer than any pet he'd ever seen. The creature's jaws hung in a wicked canine grin teeming with jagged yellow shards of teeth. Most prominent of those were its four fangs. The lowers were bent daggers, the uppers extended and poisonous. They dripped with saliva and drops of rain the way a viper leaks venom.

Most hypnotic were its eyes. Peter became aware of them as the thing stalked across Hollow Creek Road, closing the distance between itself and Peter's Dodge. Narrowed above its muzzle, a throbbing red light showed through the slits of its eyelids. The light flowed and pulsed behind the shining lenses, like lava bubbling against panes of glass that were somehow impervious to its tremendous heat.

As the creature drew near, its height inched upward. Its stride evolved from four legs to two. The thick black fur that had dominated the surface of its skin shed in drifts along its path. Long trails of smoke, or perhaps steam, rose from the exposed areas of skin as fat drops of rain landed there. They left behind angry sores in the thing's flesh. Its keen, slitted eyes rounded and became more expressive, sentient, and human.

Lost in those eyes as the creature closed in, Peter next felt warm and loving fingers gently caress his cheeks. He closed his eyes when they slid down his neck. From there, they glided to his shoulders and pressed gently against them, urging him back inside the Dodge. They guided him past the driver's seat to the passenger's, mashing his back against the interior of the opposite door so that his legs and hips—slacks undone at the waist—lay supine on the bench seat. The creature crawled inside the Dodge with him, nuzzling its recently human face into the crook of his neck. Its warm tongue lapped at his jaw chin and lips.

"Sam?" Peter murmured. The pain and discomfort in his pants had been forgotten, replaced with an overpowering sense of relief, nurture, and nourishment. The underlying shame and guilt that had caused him to injure himself was a distant memory. He was in a car with his lover, in public. At that moment, it was only right and good. "Sam? Oh, God, Sam, is that you?"

"No," the creature whispered. Its voice was feminine, tender, and lyrical, a summer breeze blowing softly along the crests of a babbling brook. "My name is Marilyn. I am here to help you, Peter Mayberry. That is, if you are willing to help me."

Her fingers danced down his chest. In an instant, his shirttails had been brushed aside. His bandaged penis protruded from the opening in his boxer shorts. Peter's heart fluttered as the roll of gauze entwined around it came loose and laid in a strip across his thighs. Bursts of electric pinpricks tingled the head of his dick. The sensation ran down the shaft, into his pelvis, and then throughout the rest of his body.

The woman above him pried the finish nail from his flesh and dropped it to the floorboard without resistance. "You will help me?" she prompted. She cradled Peter's exit wound in the palm of her left hand. Bizarrely, he thought he was going to come.

"Yes," he moaned. "Yes. I will do anything."

Marilyn pressed the palm of her right hand over the top of Peter's penis so that her fingertips met the wrist of her left hand, obscuring the injury between her palms. Peter opened his eyes. The headlights of another car briefly filled his rear window. Then they were gone. Soon after that, the interior of the Dodge filled with an unearthly crimson glow. It was accompanied by a fog that obscured everything around him. It billowed gray, tinged with red. The ungodly smell of sulfur found his nostrils.

Peter began to scream.

CHAPTER NINE

Suddenly, she was no longer there. That was Peter's first realization after the hazy glow inside his car dissipated and he swam up from the orgasmic pain and panic to which he had succumbed. The doors of the Dodge were all securely closed. The rain continued to fall hard all around him, pinging the car's metal body like the Lone Ranger's target practice on a tin can.

He grabbed for his penis. It dangled outside his boxers and leaned flaccid against the left side of his pelvis.

He examined it as well as he could in the blackness of the storm. The nail was gone. He had not imagined that. As near as he could tell, the wound it should have left had likewise vanished. He tucked himself back into his boxers and, for the first time since he'd pulled them on, buttoned up his slacks. The act of zipping up brought with it a sense of completion. It made him feel safe again somehow. Only God had to know how he had chosen to atone for his relationship with Sam. Well, God and the whatever-she-was that had found and saved him.

Was she God?

Could God be a woman? He supposed so. He felt an almighty benevolent spirit could take on whatever form it wanted if it chose. Whatever she was, she had in one motion rescued him not only from his injury but from a lifetime of shame.

He straightened his glasses on his nose. The image beyond the lenses looked as clear as ever. He slid them down his bridge for a moment, hopeful, but the world swam instantly out of focus. She hadn't healed his vision, then. Nor his short leg, he'd bet. Yet for the first time since he'd faced the filtered daylight under the covers alongside a naked Sam Brooks, Peter Mayberry's burdens were light. He felt validated. The guilt that had consumed him and compelled him to drive a finish nail through his sex organ had disappeared, along with the injury that it had caused. And, for the first time since he was thirteen years old, he smiled a genuinely happy smile.

If he turned the Dodge around, he should make it home before the storm washed out the road. He might phone Sam to beg forgiveness, to assure his boyfriend he was a changed man. He was ready to accept himself for who he was and for Sam to accept him. Whether God or Devil, the creature that had crawled into his car from the storm and transformed into a woman named Marilyn had freed him. Really and truly released him. Finally.

But she had wanted something in return, hadn't she? his mother's voice nagged him. Marilyn had not been able to eject *her* from his head. *C'est la vie.* It was a distant voice, however. There, but not there. More like a sad memory from a different time, a different life, than the threat to his humanity and salvation he had always thought she'd been. When he returned home, he'd throw away the photo he kept of her on his nightstand. He doubted he could tell Sam about Marilyn. Sam already thought Peter was crazy, but tossing out the portrait of his mother that had haunted them both throughout their relationship would at least prove he had changed.

Peter slid behind the steering wheel of the Dodge and started it up. It was easy to do now that he no longer had to be mindful of his crotch. He shifted into High and made a careful U-turn from the shoulder, not wanting to lose traction to any pools or puddles of rain that lurked in his path. Just as he completed the turn and was about to accelerate, a bright blue bolt of lightning struck near the base of an enormous maple tree that grew along the border of the Blalock farm. The accompanying wind pushed the giant down. It crashed to the pavement in front of him, blocking both lanes.

"Shit!" he bellowed, slamming his fists against the steering wheel. He examined the length of the fallen colossus. There was no way around it, over it, or under it. Not without a chainsaw.

The storm winds whipped at the thin top branches of the tree, waving their long fingers at the rapidly rising waters of Hollow Creek. Peter noted how dangerously close to flood stage the creek had encroached just since he'd pulled over. Small rivulets had already overtopped the bridge that led from Hollow Creek Road to the tiny gravel parking area of Beard's. If the rain kept falling at this rate, both the bridge and the road connected would become submerged, impassable. If the water ran as fast across the street as it was running in that creek bed, it would sweep away both him and the Dodge.

He had two choices. He could make a second U-turn, bolt for Hollow River, and hope there was no submerged roadway in the empty expanse of miles between him and the big city. Or he could cross the bridge and squat in Beard's with people who were at least familiar to him, even if he did not particularly like them. The peninsula on which Beard's sat was on slightly higher ground than the road. There was also all that farm acreage behind it for creek water to flow onto and soak into instead of flood. A safer choice, he thought.

His mind made up, Peter swung the Dodge left and crossed the wet bridge into Beard's. He was out of the car, up the steps, and through the door before the next bolt of lightning and crack of thunder signaled a fresh round of severe downpour.

A HUNDRED-YEAR FLOOD was the 72-point headline the *Hollow River Echo* would assign the story in its March 22, 1955, evening edition. But for Peter Mayberry and the Lost Hollow residents who chose to take shelter in Beard's General on the late afternoon of March 21, it would feel a hell of a lot longer than that.

***

Five minutes after Peter slammed the door of Beard's behind him, the swollen, raging creek waters overcame the bridge that connected the store's parking lot to Hollow Creek Road. Fifteen minutes after that, the bridge itself groaned and cracked from the pressure of the fast-running stream of water channeled through the narrow section of bed it spanned.

Later, large beams of wood and metal struts came loose from the elderly structure and were washed away. Some of the debris tumbled along the top of the rapids for a few seconds before succumbing to the depths. Other pieces skidded across Hollow Creek Road and became lodged in the downed tree that had prevented Peter's return home.

The oval faces of a small and terrified group of Lost Hollow townsfolk peered at the destruction from individual squares of the smudged windowpanes of Beard's General. They bore identical expressions of silent, open-mouthed, awestruck horror.

CHAPTER TEN

She clung to a support beam on the front porch while the rushing waters surrounded the building that The Man, whose name was Peter, had entered. He had not noticed her there, which was good. But she was not invisible. She wondered if their encounter in his car had damaged his mind. That would be bad. He was a fundamentally broken soul, ripe for feeding. She'd sensed that immediately. What she hadn't counted on was using him up so quickly.

She had inhaled his steam for a long time, longer than she'd ever fed on the sins of the souls in her former world. She'd never had much time to hit bottom in that place. She was too busy trying to stay clear of the mountain. The end of Peter Mayberry's steam had hit the back of her throat like the sharp edge of a knife. She'd nearly choked on it.

There had been a moment just after that choking feeling, though, when she thought she could go on. Peter's body had ceased emissions, yet as she continued to drink from him, she thought she could see his skin shimmering. His outer shell had begun to break down. If she'd kept up her feeding, she would have consumed the entire man, body and soul.

The temptation was strong, but she had kept herself in check. She had learned much about this world in her short time here, but she didn't know everything. A native she could no longer feed on would be more valuable alive, especially if he were devoted to her. If she couldn't feed off him, perhaps he could help her find others to satiate the hunger. He thought she was God, something she read in his mind as *The Second Coming*. He thought she was here to save him, to save all of them. She could think of no reason to correct him.

In her old world, guilty souls were provided to feast on. In this world, she had to hunt. That needn't be so much of a chore with a staunch defender like Peter promising salvation as bait.

Marilyn (as she had come to think of herself) first had to survive this storm and figure out a way to follow Peter inside to set her plan in motion. Faces wandered up to the glass in front of the store sometimes. None of their eyes landed on her. They all pointed skyward, the way hers did whenever the eruptions of birthing slime happened in her previous world. Then they shifted toward the rapids overcoming the lot on which they'd parked their dinosaur-fueled carriages. Some of them got angry about that. They pounded their fists against the glass as if venting their frustrations might cause the water to reconsider its course. Others sighed dejectedly and walked away only to return a minute later, unable to tear themselves from the doomsday scene.

A groaning sound followed by a thunderous crash heralded the havoc of the floodwaters that tore up the world below her. It completely obscured the land below. Panic gripped her heart. Raindrops and spray stung her. Beneath the thinning layer of fur on her body, her skin bubbled and boiled as if a million insects were crawling beneath it and desperately seeking a way out. She struggled to hold this bipedal naked ape form. Hair sprouted from follicles in irregular patches all over her body. The humans, as they called themselves, did not look so corporeal when they were only guilty souls. They were more superficial structures of mostly different energy vibrations in her old world. Then again, she was also very different on this side of the tree, seemingly capable of so much more than she had been over there.

The wooden decking beneath her creaked and groaned with the unrelenting force of the water. Here and there, a wave of the stuff lapped onto the porch and bit her. It stung worse than the raindrops. The pain from the biting wounds was deep and throbbing, like a spike driven through her fur, flesh, and muscle and, ultimately, into the bone.

The hunger she had satisfied by feasting on the one called Peter returned. Her body began reverting to its natural state, rebelling against starvation. It was a terrible cycle, she thought. The more she fought against the regression, the more her body waged war against her, and the hungrier she became.

Yellow, thick, pointed claws replaced the delicate, glossy fingernails she had cultivated while feeding on Peter. Her legs drew up beneath her. She could feel her knees slipping out of joint, the tendons cracking apart and reforming, the bones inverting. Her shoulders widened and dove into her biceps. Her laterals broadened and spread down her torso. She opened her lengthening jaws to scream just as the bridge that connected the store's parking lot to the road broke apart and drowned in the overspill.

A succession of thumps followed as the people inside the store slammed themselves against the window to watch the disaster. One of them, a man in a porkpie hat, had a distinctive red haze hovering all around him at that exact moment. His eyes were not as fixed as the others, either. They wandered around their sockets, looking here and there but not at anything in particular, as if he had something much more on his mind than a flood and a washed-out bridge.

Marilyn closed her eyes and inhaled. Yes, she could smell the nutriment even through the wood and glass. It was a minor sin, this one. Half as likely to condemn the fool as most. What he'd done was wrong, but if you were seasoning your immortal soul for the fire, it was no more than a single dash of paprika. He would not make the most filling of meals, but he would do. All she needed was to establish the connection, get him to think about what he'd done, ruminate on it, worry about what might happen if those he knew and loved found out. If she could nurse that smolder of guilt into a flame, she could feed enough to hold onto her human guise for a more extended period. Possibly even long enough to reconnect with the one named Peter.

Thief. It came to her then. The man surrounded by red haze in the window was a thief, but a very recent one. That explained the penetrating guilt. He wasn't comfortable with the crime yet. If he had stolen more than once, it had not yet been enough to embolden him. Marilyn sensed his fears about what others would think of him or say about him if they discovered who he was underneath those—*Bible lessons?*

She grinned, the corners of her canine mouth spreading wide. The red haze man was named Mark MacDonald, and he was a representative of God, what he and those around him called a *pastor*. He might not make such a bad meal after all. Back home, the ones who had in life presented themselves as the most pious were often the most succulent. Well, save for the murderers.

She let go of her hold on her human shape and allowed her reversion to a more primitive form to complete. Sharp, burning pains radiated throughout her body for a time afterward, but they subsided quickly. She felt weak, unsteady on her pins, but otherwise as normal as she'd felt since she'd leaped into this world. Typical for her in the other place was a constant loop of sucking on the souls of the departed and running for her life. Existing here could become a loop of survival as well, but at least it would be a loop of her choosing, not one an eruption of demonic ejaculate forced upon her.

Mark MacDonald, her mind reached out to him. In the window, his eyes drifted her way even though his nose remained pointed toward the spot where the bridge used to be. *You are a thief, Mark MacDonald. You stole from your congregation. Now you want to steal from the person who provides your community with food and clothes. You are an evil man, Mark MacDonald. You don't serve the Lord. You serve only yourself.*

That was all it took. He broke. The preacher's eyes drooped at the outer corners. His eyebrows knitted at a peak above the bridge of his nose. His lower lip trembled pathetically. Beads of sweat began to roll down his face. He removed his porkpie and fanned himself with its brim. The breeze it created wafted the red haze away from his skin. She caught the aroma and began to draw on it. Just an inch closer and she could latch onto its nearest tethers, direct it outside and to her mouth the way a snake charmer hypnotizes a serpent into rising from a basket. But the pathetic preacher stopped fanning himself too soon. He stepped from the window, and the others followed as if understanding without saying that the show outside was at an intermission.

Snarling, Marilyn crept on her belly over the length of the porch from the support beam to the front door. She dared not enter, not yet. If she confronted them in this form, they were more likely to fear her than feed her. Their fear was of no use to her. Pain? Absolutely. Some people use those sensations to relieve themselves of guilt. That was a lesson she had learned only tonight from Peter Mayberry. Alas, if you healed their pain, they mistook the sensation as having washed away their sin.

Fear, on the other hand, was far too primal. It overpowered guilt and tainted the flavor. That was the lesson from the one called Eli Wynn, the younger man on whom she'd first tried to feed in this world. If she hadn't shown him her proper form, he wouldn't have feared her. But she had shown him, and his steam had tasted horrible. It had given her a glimpse into his mind, however. There she discovered the human forms he found appealing as well as the ones that could provoke his sense of shame. They were the same.

Near the door, the scent of Mark MacDonald's steam was much more potent. She pressed the wedge of her nose to the space between the facing and the door and inhaled deeply. Her eyes rolled back in her head. A surge of strength spasmed through her body. The wounds caused by the stinging rain and the splashes of creek water healed themselves instantly. They dried up, scabbed over, and finally crumbled away from the new flesh underneath. The pink of the healed wounds sprouted new fur that filled in almost immediately.

Marilyn lay there for half an hour or more, feeding on the waves of the preacher's steam as they puffed from his pores. When her needs were mainly satisfied, she became vaguely aware of muted shouts coming from behind the door. A loud female voice brimming with a distinctly parental authority was berating someone, shaming someone for something they had done.

A new aroma arrived through the door crack. She recognized it immediately as the sweat-tinged scent of deviance. What in her world was mostly the salty steam of fornicators and adulterers and occasionally perverts was a mixture of salty and sweet in this one, at least as far as the one she sensed was concerned. His name was Jerry Beard, and it was indeed his mother who was giving him the what-for.

The sad preacher's steam had healed her and revived her, but this younger man's was more potent. It was steam that could only be generated in the loving child of a disappointed parent. Forget your gods. Forget your masters. Those were passing things. If your mother was disappointed in you, well, that was the loneliest feeling in the universe.

Marilyn explored his mind and found the source of the strife between them. The boy had hidden a photograph from her that he used to activate his prick, the one like the demon's that towered over the landscape of her original home. Only, this man's was smaller and more desperate for attention. And it was not injured as Peter Mayberry's had been.

She also recognized the image he had been hiding. It was a photograph of the same woman Eli Wynn had been thinking about when she'd encountered him in the woods. She had chosen that form to use on Peter Mayberry because it had, up to this point been, her only reference for what humans found appealing and therefore nonthreatening. This new evidence settled it. She would become the Marilyn figure. When the humans inside the store saw her, they would love her and open their hearts and souls to her.

Then they would feed her.

Because they had no choice.

CHAPTER ELEVEN

"Jerry!" Kathy Beard yowled at her son. "Get your hind-end over here and close the cash drawer. You left it open again. We're not a charity bank." For God's sake. That kid would leave his head at home if it weren't bolted to his neck. Once upon a time, such forgetfulness didn't bother her so much. But as both she and Jerry aged, Kathy found herself more and more wishing that she at least *felt* like she could rely on him some.

Times were pretty good with Eisenhower in the White House making economic recovery from wartime his priority almost a decade after the Japanese surrendered and two years after we left Korea. But that didn't mean they would always be good. If you believed the newspapers, the Federal Reserve was doing everything to hinder the president on that front.

More important, Kathy, Jerry, and a minor assembly of their regular customers were trapped in her store by a frankly terrifying flood. Terrifying at present because they were in the middle of it. The absolute horror would come when she had to assess the cost of the aftermath. Not to mention that the longer they were trapped there. More likely their guests would want to raid their few resources.

The money in the register and the stock on the shelves were as at risk in Kathy's mind as any exterior structures damaged by the weather. She could afford none of it, even in the best of times.

She switched on the Silvertone tube radio that sat on a low shelf behind the cash register. It had been Jessie's when he was alive and had taken on some scarring of its wood grain since. Most of that resulted from her decision to move the device to the store, where she and Jerry were constantly butting against it and knocking it to the floor. It functioned perfectly despite the neglect. It was AM band only and wouldn't tune Nashville's new-fangled FM station even if it *hadn't* been canceled.

W47NV went on air for the first time in '41 but returned its license to the FCC a mere ten years later. However, getting a signal for the defunct channel's AM sister station WSM was no problem. She preferred the sounds of the home of the Grand Ole Opry, anyway. Nashville lay almost as far from Lost Hollow as Hollow River, but—if the previous day's forecast in the *Echo* had any merit—they'd be getting deluged as well.

A *click* reverberated when she turned the knob, followed by a bit of static. Then the front half of Beard's General filled with the voice of a carnival barker shouting the occasional meteorological term from somewhere inside the depths of a tin can:

> *Well, the barometer sure didn't tell us what we were in for today, did it, folks? We're sorry to interrupt the program, but we just received word from Judge Briley that some of our fair city's roads are starting to flood. The Cumber-*

land River is also on the rise, by the looks of things. We're all just sitting here hoping we're not about to see a repeat of '37. We've got our ears pricked up for any word from the Army Corps of Engineers about whether all those flood measures they built up for us a while back look like they're going to hold. For now, you good folks, just stay inside by your radio or your television set if you have one. We'll bring you more information as we get it. Now, back to our program.

Kathy switched the radio off again when the in-studio band strummed out what she recognized as the first few chords of "Cool Water." *Inappropriate choice*, she thought as she about-faced to man the National Cash Register. The cash drawer remained half-open, displaying the entirety of the store's meager intake since they'd unlocked the door that morning. Kathy slammed the drawer shut hard enough to ring the bell, intentionally drawing Jerry's attention. The young man's face had been plastered to one of the panes in the front window, watching the store's closest access to Hollow Creek Road wash clean away in the rapids. Kathy could see the alarm in his eyes as the severity of the mistake dawned on him. He'd ignored her command in favor of the show outside.

"Oh," Jerry called to her. "Sorry, Mom."

Sure he was. That's why, after all this time, he still couldn't remember to shut the drawer thoroughly after a sale. That's why she often found it sitting open when she emerged from the kitchen. She supposed she could count them lucky that they were operating in a small town. Their income was meager, but at least it was less likely to be stolen by hoodlums who could not resist the temptation of an unsecured, unattended cash drawer. For now, anyway.

Times had been tough for the farmers in Lost Hollow not so long ago. Everyone remembered those days. Tough times tended to loosen the moral strands that otherwise bind fingers prone to wander. That twinge of suspicion was enough to prompt her to reopen the drawer for examination. She drew the stack of receipts on the spike next to the register. It was her only reliable record of what came in and what went out over the course of a business day.

"I don't think you'll find anything missing," a booming masculine voice said. The owner's frame created a shadow over the pile of receipts she had been about to slide off the spike. Kathy looked up to see the local Nazarene church pastor, Mark MacDonald, standing over her. He smiled pleasantly when she met his gaze. "I mean, I don't think anyone stole any money from you. I'd just paid my bill when the bridge went out. We all ran to the window at the same time."

Kathy countered with a plastic smile of her own. "Thank you for your concern, Reverend, but I'll verify that for myself all the same."

"Brother."

"What?"

"Brother MacDonald. Or Mark. Or Mister MacDonald, if you really want to address me formally. The Good Book tends to frown on the use of religious titles, you see. Like you, I'm just another child of God. So, Brother."

"Fine, Mark," Kathy grunted. "As I said, I appreciate the concern, but I'll make up my own mind about whether I want these good members of your flock to turn out their pockets for me before I allow them to leave. Okay with you?"

Mark raised his hands to shoulder height, palms turned out in surrender, and retreated. "Indeed, Mrs. Beard. It is your store, after all."

Kathy returned to her work, sliding the day's stack of receipts from the spike and flipping them over to compare the sales figures recorded there with the drawer's contents. "Damn right, it's my store," she mumbled.

She opened a second drawer just beneath the cash register and, without looking, retrieved a flimsy object that had the texture and dimensions of a notepad. She preferred to have her ledger for the task, but that was sitting on her desk back at the farmhouse. It was where she most often did the day's reconciliation after closing the store and filling her belly with a warm supper. She'd long ago discovered that putting time and some distance between herself and the stress of a workday helped prevent her from making too many careless errors in her arithmetic.

From behind her right ear, Kathy plucked a stubby No. 2 pencil. It was dull from the day's use, but another sharpening was likely to render it too short for comfortable writing. Instead, she picked at a couple of taper areas until they flecked off, revealing a rounded but slightly longer core of graphite. Hopefully it would be enough to complete the task.

She flipped the topmost receipt from the stack and was prepared to jot the total sale amount on the first line of her notepad when she suddenly realized that the tablet contained no first line. What she had retrieved from the drawer below the cash register had no lines on it at all, unless you counted the curvy lines of shadows against red velvet created by a photographer's lighting as it fell across the utterly naked body of one Marilyn Monroe.

Kathy gasped. She dropped the pencil, grabbed the girlie calendar by one corner, and flipped it over so that nothing showed except for its blank white reverse. Warmth rose in her cheeks as the blood vessels therein widened, allowing her newly intensified heartbeat to fill them with blush. She straightened her back and closed her eyes, one hand pressing the calendar against the countertop just in case a magical wind from elsewhere in the building tried to flip it girl-side up again.

"Jerry. Matthew. Beard," she said, straining the words through clenched teeth. "Come here. Now."

Jerry craned his neck from the window upon hearing his mother call all three of his names in her irritable staccato rhythm. His Adam's apple bobbed down and then up in a single, fearful gulp.

Kathy noted his wide eyes and the way he stumbled comically around the backs of the tall ice cream parlor chairs that stood in a row in front of that window. His nervous effort to hasten his reply to his mother's call had only sufficed to hamper them. Even so, she controlled her smirk. It wouldn't serve her to let on how amazed she was that she still maintained so much authority over the boy whose father's death had forced him into becoming a man long before he should have.

"What is this?" she demanded when Jerry recovered himself and found his way to the register without falling on his face. She snatched the calendar from the countertop, gripping it between her thumb and forefinger by the hanging hole as if it was a dirty diaper. She dangled the nude Marilyn in front of Jerry's face. Over his shoulder, she saw the Wynn boy from the Blalock farm—Eli—watching them, abject terror etched on his face.

"I—" Jerry began.

"Don't even try," Kathy interrupted. She dropped both hands to her waist. The calendar swayed and rippled against her skirt, causing Marilyn to grind her two-dimensional hips. Jerry's eyes were drawn to it instead of his mother's face. "Look me in the eye, son." He did. "I don't want this filth in my store. Or in my house. I don't know where you got this, and I don't want to know, but it doesn't belong here. Do you understand me?"

He nodded, his enormous ears, courtesy of his father, glowed red at the tips on either side of his head. Kathy had always regretted that he was saddled with that particular characteristic from his late dad Jessie. Minus the ears, both father and son bore a passing resemblance to a certain Mr. Marlon Brando. Except Jerry's hair was jet black like hers and buzzed along the top.

The boy had his father's piercing blue eyes that shone from under a squinting brow. They had the same nose, too. There was a hump off the bridge that caused the front edge to square and drop almost straight down like a cliff. Same square jaw.

Out-of-towners who had never met Jessie sometimes asked how she acquired the framed photo of Brando she kept on the cash register stand. Some of them didn't believe her when she told them it was not the actor in the picture. She hadn't seen *A Streetcar Named Desire*. After all, going to the pictures was a scandalous business, especially for a widow. But she'd read the newspaper interviews with the attractive star. They were accompanied by photos of him, slightly disheveled with a winking countenance and a mischievous grin partially obscured by a cigarette. It was too bad, she thought, that no one printed *him* naked on a calendar.

A twinge of hypocritical guilt gnawed at her for a second following that, but she brushed it aside. She was the mother here, after all. This was her establishment. Jerry, by contrast, remained little more than an impressionable kid in many ways. Who knew what access to this kind of pornographic material might lead him to later? By the looks of it, he might've already passed the corruption on to the Wynn boy as well. Best to nip it in the bud.

She shoved the calendar into Jerry's midsection, causing him to hug it instinctively. He tucked it like a wide receiver completing a pass from the quarterback.

"Take that nasty thing outside and throw it into the creek," she told him. "It was strong enough to wash out the bridge. It may just wash the pervert off you. I'm *very* disappointed in you, Jerry."

Head down and ears still on fire, Jerry retreated with the calendar. He seemed to be trying to keep his back to their audience of regular customers, all of whom were distracted from the deluge and bearing unwanted witness to his chastisement. All except for Eli Wynn, who had managed to find more exciting entertainment in the spaces between the slats on the floor in front of him. His white-knuckled hands were clasped between his knees where he sat in front of the window.

The folks who had packed that row of chairs when the bridge scattered caught themselves staring. They tried to busy themselves with other tasks. Mark MacDonald pretended to browse store shelves but could not stop himself from occasionally peering around them. Donna Gilliam migrated to a small table near the opposite wall. The set had been part of Kathy's trial run of a front-of-store indoor dining experience. It hadn't panned out, but she'd never bothered to move the furniture.

Only Peter Mayberry, the strangely quiet man who played piano for the Nazarene church up the road, met her gaze. He sat at the table nearest the cash register and thus closest to the drama with Jerry. He smiled pleasantly, revealing an odd fresh-looking web of crow's feet at the corners of his glistening eyes. The wrinkles branched out in all directions toward temples that had just begun to exhibit their first tinges of gray.

Had he always looked like that? She didn't think so. Not that she'd paid that much attention to meek Mr. Mayberry before. And not that he appeared unassuming just then, with his kind eyes and smile winking some kind of—what? Flirtation? Approval? If he'd been a character in one of the Edwardian romance novels that occupied her nightstand, he might've stood up and tipped a hat to her.

She put her finger on the difference then. Not only did Peter Mayberry look older tonight than she'd previously noticed, but there was also more confidence about him. More *manliness*. He was attractive when he wasn't avoiding eye contact, uncomfortable as it was becoming for her.

Whatever. She could address that and the fingerprints her new refugees had left all over her front window later if necessary. Kathy wanted only to get back to the till. The calendar drama had drained some of the outrage she'd been nurturing over the drawer having been left open. Even so, not knowing whether cash was missing could become a distraction later. Like when she inevitably tried to cry herself to sleep that night, hugging what used to be Jessie's pillow but hadn't smelled like him in years. She wanted to get it out of the way.

A gust of wind and smattering of heavy raindrops blew in through the front door when Jerry pulled it open to rid himself of the dirty calendar. Marilyn Monroe fluttered madly in his arms, flashing everyone with a glimpse of her hip and legs when she did. Three seconds after he had disappeared over the threshold, Jerry returned from the maelstrom with the drenched and splotchy calendar still plastered against his torso. The door swung to and fro on its hinges, slamming once against the exterior wall as the storm bellowed just beyond.

"Mom!" the young man shouted, startling the customers. Some of them had already lapsed into comfortable interior monologues after Kathy had stopped berating her son. "Mom, help! There's someone out here! A woman! I think she's hurt!"

CHAPTER TWELVE

It finally dawned on Peter Mayberry what the woman in his car had meant when she said she needed his help. While Kathy Beard adjusted the knobs on her lost husband's radio receiver to better hear the news, random scrambled thoughts that were not Peter's surfaced and submerged amid the static in his brain. They startled him at first. The familiar, booming baritone yet peculiarly calm voice of his church pastor Mark MacDonald, who was closest to him among those trapped in the store, piped up there. The voice was so loud and so close that Peter did a double-take to verify that the man hadn't spoken to him out loud.

They're going to catch you. You know that.

Mark strolled to the window and perched in the same place he had been when the bridge washed out. He eyed the ongoing storm damage alongside Kathy's son Jerry and that odd Wynn boy. As Peter watched their backs, Mark's voice broke in again.

So, what of it? This whole town's been scamming you out of your income for years.

A fuzzed but discernable scene appeared in Peter's cortex as if in a dream of the pastor's two hands as they plucked tithe money from the offering plate. Peter then "watched" as the spiritual leader of Lost Hollow's Nazarene community lined his wallet with the pickings. It wasn't much money, probably not enough to be noticed by anyone but the preacher himself because he also happened to handle the accounting. But it *was* theft. Even so, Peter sensed Mark was struggling with feeling guilty about it. As if to underscore this fact, a new thought floated into Peter's mind: *At least I can pay my bills.*

Just as he was becoming accustomed to them, the ebb and flow of Mark's thoughts became intermingled with those of the others around him. It was a jumble of muttering and exclamations not unlike the low rumble of indistinguishable conversation in a crowded auditorium before a show. Except these conversations came with visual aids projected onto his mind. Then a growling, thunderous wail of anguish between his ears interrupted all thought. It barely formed words. It drowned everything else inside his head, including his thoughts.

HUUUUURRRRRRRGGGGAA! the voice screamed. It was a genderless countertenor but bubbly and wet. It lacked clarity, as if its source was gargling mouthwash while it howled.

HLLLLB-P-P! the voice continued. *BURRRRRRNSA!*

Peter started in his seat. He managed to resist clapping his hands to his ears. It would have been a natural reaction to the noise, but only if the others could hear it as well. A brief scan of the room revealed that, indeed, no one else in Beard's General was reacting.

Kathy remained stationed in front of the radio, eyeing it as she listened to a news broadcast about the severe weather out of Nashville. Her rough, workday hands were balled into fists and planted heroically on her hips, showcasing broad shoulders that could be the envy of any 90-pound weakling. When she shook her head over the news, the black bun on the back of her head quivered and loosened a little. A lone strand of silver came free and dangled beside her left ear.

Donna Gilliam, who sat nearby, was using a man's handkerchief to dab a bit of drool from the chin of the infant cradled in her arms. The others—Mark, Jerry, the Wynn boy—all remained plastered to the glass at the front of the store, watching the world break apart and wash away before their eyes.

The next words to gouge holes in his consciousness were recognizable and more obviously directed at him.

PEEEEETEEEERRR, the voice implored him. *DYYYYINGG. MUUUUUST FEEEEEEED ONNNN HIIIIMMM.*

It clicked for him then. Marilyn, the woman beast that had healed him after she crawled into his Dodge at the side of the road, was calling out to him from somewhere in the deluge. She was hurt. She had fed on all the guilt and shame heaped upon Peter his entire life because of his *predilections*, as his wicked mother would say. The beast had taken all that guilt and shame away from him, and it had nourished her for a time. She needed more. He had no more to give her. Not from himself.

Peter closed his eyes and folded his arms across his chest. He concentrated on the warbling, panicked voice in his head that cried out in indistinct howls of pain. It was fading, succumbing to the sea of overlapping thoughts from those in closer proximity to him. He swept aside as much of the clutter as he could and shouted back to her inside his head.

I'VE NO MORE TO GIVE, he said. He attempted to send some empathy with the message, the mentalist equivalent of a facial expression the way one does when one meets with a hurting parishioner in need of counsel. He did not know whether she could receive or even understand such things.

He thought again about what she'd said. She hadn't asked for more guilt and shame from Peter. She'd said she must feed "on him."

The image of Mark MacDonald's thick, blunt fingers paging through the dollar bills in the collection plate surfaced in his mind. Had she sensed that, too?

THE PASTOR FEELS NO GUILT FOR HIS CRIMES, he transmitted. *HE THINKS THE TOWN'S SELFISHNESS ABSOLVES HIM.*

A second passed, no more. Then Marilyn's voice returned: *MAAAAKE HIIIIIIMMMMM.*

Peter's eyes fluttered open. Make him what? Feel guilty about stealing from the church tithes? Impossible. Peter was not even aware he'd taken anything as far as Mark knew. So how was he, the church piano player who knew nothing about the pastor's day-to-day accounting practices, even to broach the subject of missing money? Never mind how he would go about digging out that twinge of doubt in Mark's head so that he might provoke it, cause it to explode in a geyser of remorse.

I wish I could get away with more, he heard the voice of Mark say.

Peter eyed the cash register that Kathy Beard and her husband before her had forever used to tally the cost of weekly groceries for the residents of Lost Hollow. He could not see the cash drawer from his angle but knew that it sat slightly ajar because Kathy herself had just chastised her son in front of God and everyone for leaving it that way. If the right man at the right time was just a wee bit prompted in the wrong way, that man would find himself unable to resist the temptation of repeating a crime he'd recently gotten away with. Success is a powerful drug, after all; an addictive one. When success is born of an act committed against another, it has almost immediate withdrawal symptoms.

Peter directed his gaze toward the back of Mark's head. He imagined the message he'd send as a small rocket fired from the neck of a Coca-Cola bottle tilted at just the right angle.

The cash register drawer is open.

In front of him, the preacher tipped his head slightly to the left as if listening to something. Of course, that could have been because of the news broadcast from Kathy Beard's old radio. Coincidence. Peter pressed on.

She's distracted by the news, you know. Her back is turned. Everyone else is watching the storm or wrapped up in their thoughts.

The fingers of both Mark's hands dangled loosely at his sides. He closed them against his palms. The forefingers of each rubbed lightly at the pads of his thumbs. It was a greedy gesture if Peter had ever seen one.

Do it, he sent to Mark. *You want to. It's money they should have tithed anyway, isn't it? It's money they spent on Hershey bars and cold drinks instead of investing in their everlasting salvation.*

Go on. Do it.

A missing dollar or two won't hurt the Beards at all. You could use that money. An unhappy pastor makes for a misled congregation, don't you think?

After all you've done for them, don't you deserve some happiness?

Mark made his move. Peter was not surprised by it because the preacher had broadcast his surrender to temptation on the same wavelengths Peter had been prodding him. It was almost as if Peter himself had decided to act.

Mark glanced at the folks gathered in front of the shop window, then behind him to where Peter sat. The latter pretended to carefully examine and pick at a hangnail when he did. However, Mark's eyes seemed to pass over the top of him, scanning the store beyond as though Peter was invisible, not even sitting there.

There was an audible *click* from his throat as Mark swallowed the last of his scruples and finally allowed himself to light on the cash register.

Behind it, Kathy remained fixated on the radio broadcast. It sounded to Peter, and probably Mark as well, like the entire Middle Tennessee area was in for a wild night of nasty weather even beyond the deluge that had wrecked the bridge to Hollow Creek Road.

At the window, Jerry Beard and Eli Wynn had begun to pivot away, as if their attention through it had depended on Mark remaining there with them. Peter winced. He could telepathically suggest to the boys that they keep their eyes outside. Or he could push Mark to move faster. He didn't know if he could do both.

They'll stop talking soon and go back to playing music, Peter urged. *Better do it*.

That got Mark moving. A light sweat had broken out on his forehead and glistened in the light from the overheads as he glided into the counter in near silence. He propped his left elbow against it, his back to Peter, and chanced one more look around the place before dipping his left hand into the till. Peter caught a brief flash of faded green when Mark stepped back a second later, shoving his left into the same-side pocket of his jacket as he did.

Peter transferred his energy to the younger men then.

Look outside, he sent. Both boys stopped mid-pivot and returned to the glass. At the same time, the news report about the night's weather ended. Kathy Beard switched off the radio and spun around to face the register, returning quickly to her accounting business. Her eyes landed briefly on Peter as she did. He couldn't help but smile at her.

That's creepy, he heard her think.

He felt a flash of anger but forced himself to ignore it. He'd circle back to Kathy and her son. For now, the pastor with the sticky fingers was the lowest hanging fruit if he was going to feed the (*woman? demon? god?*) who had saved him from self-destruction.

"I don't think you'll find anything missing," he heard Mark say to her. It was out loud this time. Peter took note of the difference. If he were going to use this new power effectively, he'd have to distinguish external voices from internal ones instantly. Mark's comment was followed by some back-and-forth between him and Kathy about how she should address him.

Won't she notice, though? Peter transmitted. *Kathy's been running this business for a long time. She's probably pretty good at balancing the receipts against the cash drawer, don't you think?*

Mark's hands were in the air, a gesture of surrender, as he backed off the angry proprietor. He turned around so that Peter could see his face. A thin, humiliated smile spread over his lips.

She knows, Peter shot at him. *She knows what you did. See those convex mirrors hanging in every corner of the store? She saw you, didn't she? You thought she was just listening to the radio, but she was watching you the whole time from that mirror overhead.*

Bullseye. Mark's smile faded, and his eyes widened in alarm. He strode back to the window and sat, clasping his hands in his lap. His knuckles turned white.

She's just waiting for the right time to confront you about it, Peter continued. *By the way, did you not remember that Kathy and Jerry are trying to run a farm in addition to this store? Did you forget about the Gaskills asking you to pray over Kathy's mortgage a few weeks ago?*

Mark shuddered visibly. He drew a ragged breath and choked on his saliva. Peter thought he looked like a man trying to hold in severe diarrhea when there was no convenient place to let it fly.

Not only have you hurt an innocent family, Peter thought at him, *but you're also going to lose your job or even your ordainment because you let that wily old Devil whisper in your ear. You're the pastor of the Nazarene church, for God's sake. Now you're going to go to jail. What on earth were you thinking?*

Tears welled up in the corners of Mark's eyes. *I— I don't know what I was thinking*, Peter overheard him reason. *I never wanted to hurt anybody. I never wanted to hurt anybody. I never wanted to hurt anybody. I never—*

He kept repeating that last, so Peter tuned him out. He was surprised to find that he suddenly understood how. If necessity was the mother of invention, annoyance was the mother of new telepathic skillsets. More than that, his task with Mark was complete.

Thin crimson tendrils of something that looked like smoke or steam rose from Mark's ears. Also, from his eyes. His nostrils. His mouth. They met over top of his head, winding together into a single cord, the end of which stretched lazily toward the store's ceiling. When it reached the gray painted ceiling boards, the snake bent right and slithered to where the ceiling met the front wall. There it turned again, scaling down the wall to the small gap of space between the door and its trim where it disappeared through a small hole.

After that, Peter heard not a peep from Marilyn wherever she lay beyond those doors. Was she feeding? Or had she died while he dallied with the preacher?

He was just about to transmit a message to her, to inform her that dinner was served. But at that moment, Kathy's rage-tainted voice screeched her son's name in that "boy, you're in trouble, and you'd better be ashamed of what you've done" register that only an astonished and angry mother can achieve. Whatever the problem was, it wasn't the cash register this time. Kathy hadn't had time to count all the receipts or uncover Mark's thievery yet. Mark obviously believed it had something to do with that. His face turned bright red, and the crimson streams from all the orifices of his head pulsed with the renewed flow. Neither he nor the others around him seemed to notice the strange phenomenon.

Kathy was angry about something else, however. It had to do with women and perversion. Peter didn't need his newfound telepathy to know that, either. It was all too evident in her voice, eerily like his mother's at that moment. A familiar sliver of ice glided up his esophagus and into his throat at the recollection. He shut his eyes and swallowed it down again. When he opened them, he thought he saw a tendril of crimson dragon's breath pass in front of his eyes. Then he blinked, and it was gone.

At the front of the store, Jerry retrieved a copy of the famous nude Marilyn Monroe "Golden Dreams" calendar that had publicly outed her pre-fame modeling job a few years ago. Kathy held it out to him pinched between one thumb and forefinger, as if it was a pair of his shit-stained underwear or sweaty gym socks he'd left in a drawer under the counter. She demanded he toss it outside, destroying it in the weather. Her posturing had the effect she intended, Peter thought. Jerry looked suitably ashamed. And Kathy's astonishment *was* an act, partially.

Well, at least I know he's not a queer, Peter overheard her think. His heart dropped in his chest. The thin lips. The narrow eyes. The permanent scowl. Kathy Beard resembled Margaret Mayberry in more than tone.

What was more interesting was the horrified mask on Eli Wynn's face. Peter tried to zero in on the Wynn boy's thoughts. He received no confession there, was barely penetrating the boy's mind. What he did receive was a flash image of Georgia Blalock, her stern face distorted to gigantic proportions, looming large in Eli's vision. She was scolding him, stabbing his forehead with a finger calloused and gnarled from a hard life on a farm.

The vision faded quickly, especially as Eli turned his back on the calendar scene and focused his attention on the storm. The boy placed a hand absently over his left ear. It was meant as a barrier to shut out the drama on that side of him even if it was not physically possible to do so.

What became clear to Peter, as the thoughts of his neighbors and fellow members of his congregation continued to telegraph themselves into his head, was that Marilyn was going to find a nutritious stew of shame and guilt to sustain her within Beard's General. At least until the storm outside finally came to an end and Peter could help her move out into the world at large. After all, there were much more devilish places than Lost Hollow in the world.

New York City? Nothing but gangsters and crime.

Los Angeles? Nothing but glamour and power and the corruption that comes with it, no doubt.

Las Vegas? Well, need he spell it out? There were so many dens of sin. Food would be plentiful, especially if she took Peter along with her.

Could she use his newfound telepathic abilities to coax guilty feelings from those who didn't harbor them on the surface? After all, how many Vegas gamblers experienced profound remorse? Well, at the tops of their minds, anyway.

None of that would come to pass if the woman hadn't fed off Mark. Up front, Jerry Beard threw open the door to toss out the dirty picture of Marilyn Monroe. Peter chuckled. Not only were there two Margaret Mayberrys in Lost Hollow tonight, but there also seemed to be two Marilyns.

He took the opportunity to aim what he was fast becoming to think of as his third eye into the rain beyond the door, searching for some new sign of her. He could see the end trail of Mark's steam dissipating through the opening. Mark himself looked relieved. A good sign. Peter would scan him again later. He was curious. How was Mark rationalizing his deed now that the guilt is gone? Or was he, even? The peace Mark perceived might not come from an acquittal of the theft so much as simple acceptance of it, as had Peter's.

For now, his objective was locating *his* Marilyn and pulling her to safety.

Unable to connect with her telepathically, Peter rose from his spot at the table. He searched for an excuse to follow Jerry Beard outdoors. He wanted to look around to see if he could locate the destination of Mark's red guilt trail. If he could figure out where it was going, he would find her. He could drag her inside from wherever she was, prompt a fresh meal for her from Jerry's guilt over the calendar. Or from the Wynn boy's overpowering feelings of guilt by association.

He needn't have bothered. At that moment, Jerry Beard reappeared in the door frame. His hair was soaked, plastered to his forehead. He was breathless and flush with excitement, although Peter thought he detected the hint of a grin on the boy's face as well.

"Mom!" Jerry shouted. "Mom, help! There's someone out here! A woman! And I think she's hurt!"

Peter leaped from his spot and dashed past Jerry. He stumbled over his uneven legs but quickly recovered himself. Then he and Jerry flew out the door and into the darkness.

CHAPTER THIRTEEN

Donna Gilliam experienced what could only be described as tranquil reflection, a combination of conscious and subconscious thought that bathed her in a simultaneous sense of peace, clarity, and safety.

The storm continued raging outside. She had made it across the parking lot to the building long before the bridge gave way. She had even managed to get food into Theo's tummy before burping and allowing him to drift back into whatever realm it was that enveloped an infant at sleepy time. Wherever he was, he was happy there. Occasional upward twitches at the corners of his tiny mouth gave that much away.

The soreness around the rims of her cried-out eyes hadn't yet gone. She wanted to shut them and rest for a few hours. Or many hours. Her eyeballs itched, sandpapery and burning, as if she'd been swimming in chlorinated water all day long. In any case, there was some comfort for her in the familiarity of Beard's General. Seated in one of Kathy Beard's trial dining areas just north of the mouth of the canned goods aisle seemed somehow safe and comfortable. The snoozing baby only enhanced the effect.

She bore marks from the beating Ted had given her that morning, marks that her makeup had not entirely covered. They included several purpling bruises as well as the scabbed-over cut on her temple. Despite her concerns otherwise, no one in the store had bothered to acknowledge them. Except for Kathy Beard, that is. Kathy shot her a mildly concerned glance when Donna pushed her way through the double-hinged door with baby Theo swinging in his carrier at her hip.

Her physical marks would heal in time. They had before. The ones she'd left on Ted never would. For the moment, she was not ashamed of that. Donna had earlier asked Kathy for fresh bandages to replace the ones she'd wrapped around the palm she had sliced while stabbing Ted to death.

She hadn't said that much, of course. But Kathy didn't ask, either. She had turned over her first aid kit without so much as a cocked eyebrow. Just in case, Donna spilled the story that she'd concocted along her drive. She said that she'd been slicing a substantial Granny Smith apple and had lost her grip in the process. Kathy had simply nodded and gone about the business of wiping away drops of rainwater from the counter on which Donna had set the baby carrier while she'd been talking. Her tacit willingness to accept Donna's story had, perhaps, been the beginning of this beautiful tranquil state. She hoped it would last forever. But then they dragged the naked stranger inside, and the spell was broken.

Donna remained seated at the table with Theo when Kathy, her son Jerry, and that odd Peter fellow dragged the strangely nude woman across the threshold and dropped her in a pink, blistery heap in the middle of the floor. Donna automatically covered Theo's closed eyes as Jerry and Peter hauled the woman inside. Each of the men had her by an armpit, dragging her backward on her heels, allowing the entire store a shameful unobstructed view of her bare ass.

It was an awkward haul for them. Jerry was embarrassed by the real-life nudity and tried to help her *without* touching her. Peter had that limp of his working against them. The woman's head lolled from side to side as they moved with her. She'd be lucky if her rescuers didn't add whiplash to her list of problems because of their jostling. A couple of feet beyond the door, they turned her around and allowed her to collapse.

She lay in a face-down crouch, her forehead propped on the backs of her hands stacked one flat atop the other. She'd bent her knees under her torso so that her bare back curved into a tortoiseshell shape. Her toes pointed outward from beneath the curves of her buttocks. The net effect was that the most sensitive areas of her nudity were hidden from view for the most part. However, Donna surmised that anyone standing in the back of her just then would have been afforded a most unflattering look at her plumbing.

Angry red pimples or boils covered her backside. Some of them had erupted and were oozing a disgustingly thickened yellow pus. Aside from those blemishes, she had the body of an artist's model, from what Donna could see. Her torso and hips had formed a nearly perfect hourglass from the back. She had no visible sags, no apparent cottage cheese or lumps, no signs of the everyday burdens of aging, nor evidence of having endured the travails of bearing a child.

Had he been (*alive*) here and seen her, Ted would have already been flirting in his oafish way, even with his wife and child in the same room. She'd never seen his work toolbox, but she always figured that Ted had the lid papered with pictures cut out from girlie magazines and automotive shop calendars like the one Kathy Beard had just scolded her son about. Respect for his wife and child was not something Ted cared for, nor probably ever thought about at all.

To their credit, most of the living men at the front of the store averted their gazes. The Wynn boy was the one exception. He seemed to be *trying* to avert his gaze, but it proved to be too difficult a task. His wide eyes kept drifting in the direction of the wet and nude woman despite his best efforts to oppose them.

Donna didn't see the lust in those eyes, however. At least not in the greedy, wolf-whistling, tongue-wagging way she'd seen it in her (*late*) husband Ted's. The expression on Eli's face was more like a combination of curiosity, surprise, embarrassment, and recognition.

All the men had moved from the figure as Kathy shut the door against the weather. They positioned themselves so that if they did happen to glance in her direction, they mainly saw the pool of her flopped-over strawberry blonde mane against the floor and not much else.

The preacher, Mark, even had the good grace to button his ratty jacket and clasp his hands loosely together in front of his trousers. Was it an act of prevention or disguise? If he was an honest man of God, why hadn't he simply removed the jacket and covered the newcomer with it?

Peter was the only one who seemed more interested in the young woman's welfare than the novelty of her nudity. He snatched a tarp off a nearby stack of dry goods that had not been shelved. He draped it over her without flourish and pulled it closed around her. With that done, she sat up and began to absorb her new surroundings.

With one petite and pretty hand, the fingers tipped with scandalously red nail polish, the stranger raked long ringlets of hair back from her forehead. It fell into a perfectly parted waterfall, delicately framing her apple pie face and falling softly over the upper lid of one doe eye in a way that presented itself as unintentionally seductive.

Now able to see her face, Donna understood why Eli Wynn had looked so astonished. The woman looked familiar, although she was no one Donna had ever seen in Lost Hollow. After she was covered, both Eli and Jerry stared directly at her, mouths open, like two kids who'd caught Santa Claus in the act of leaving brand new bikes under the tree on Christmas.

The Marilyn Monroe calendar that Jerry had forgotten to toss into the floodwater outside plummeted to the floor at his feet. The rustle caught Donna's attention. It landed face-up and partially propped against the wall. From within the image, a young Marilyn Monroe grinned out at Donna with the sexy knowledge that she was naked and that Donna was observing that nakedness.

Donna looked from the photo to the woman on the floor and back again. She was the spitting image of the nude Marilyn in that "Golden Dreams" photo from 1949. The resemblance was remarkable: from her hair to her eyes to her lines and curves—even her makeup.

Jerry caught Donna's gaze and, blushing, retrieved the calendar. He rolled it up carefully so as not to crease the image and stashed it behind a row of glass jars on a shelf nearby before returning to Eli's side and resuming his agogedness.

Men, Donna thought. She absently stroked the cheek of the infant asleep on her lap. *Predictably intemperate. You won't be like that, though. Will you, Theo? You've got a mommy that's going to teach you better.*

"Can someone get her something to wear?" Peter growled. There was urgency in his voice. He stood protectively over the woman, fixing himself between her and the other men. He set his eyes on Kathy, who was holding the store's telephone handset to one ear and tapping on the plunger. Unable to get a dial tone, she slammed the handset back into its cradle. The telephone responded with a single offended *ting!*

"Can she pay for it?" she snapped back at Peter. When he glared at her, she rolled her eyes and sighed. "I'll see what I can find. I think I have some overalls and a few work shirts in stock. She'll have to do with a pair of rubbers if she wants some shoes, though."

"Just something that will let her cover up will be fine, please," Peter replied.

To everyone's amazement, the young woman opened her mouth and spoke.

"Dry," she said. Her voice was soft and breathy, aspirated, the opposite of the word she'd just uttered. Her eyes were pleading. Something else in them caused Donna to close her arms tighter around her babe. She hugged Theo close to her breasts. He wrinkled his nose and grunted a small protest but otherwise did not stir.

"Yes, you're thirsty," Peter replied. "Can I get you a glass of water?"

Marilyn shook her head. "No," she strained. "Please. I need to be dry. It burns."

Peter barked a follow-up order at Kathy: "We need a towel, too."

"Fine!" came the reply. "I'm working on it!"

A moment later, Kathy returned. In one hand, she held a pair of men's coveralls. In the other was a wadded-up handful of dry dish towels, one of which sported a blotchy purple stain. She dropped the bundle of cloth in front of Marilyn, who flinched. The red blisters, or whatever they were, had spread into the young woman's hairline. One had erupted on her otherwise pristine ivory cheek. For a blink, Donna thought she saw a tendril of red smoke or steam drifting into the air from its core. If it had been there, it dissipated before she could fathom it.

Kathy knelt beside the woman, opposite Peter. "What happened to you, darlin'?" she asked. "Pardon me for saying so, but I know just about everybody in these parts, and I don't think I've ever seen you before. Are you lost?"

"I—I was attacked," the woman replied softly. She sounded uncertain. Her eyes darted left and right under the shadow of her hair as if searching the floor in front of her for what to say.

"Let's get you to the bathroom," Peter interrupted. The anger he had directed at Kathy was gone from his voice. In its place was his typical tremulous tenor. "We can talk about whatever happened to you later." He shot a resentful look at Kathy and added, "When you're feeling better."

"I tried to call the law," Kathy offered. "Phone's out. Because of the storm, I guess."

Neither the woman nor Peter appeared to hear her. Peter clasped the edges of the tarp in one hand and held it together around her. The other arm he wrapped around her shoulders, supporting the woman while she stood upon the shaky legs of a newborn foal. Her small hands broke through Peter's tarp seal long enough to scoop up the coveralls and dish towels (and for Donna to get a glimpse of her knees and thighs). The hands and their contents disappeared back into the folds of her makeshift garment.

Peter and the woman walked in tandem, deliberately making their way past Donna to the tiny restroom in the rear of Beard's General. She caught a whiff of something that smelled like a freshly struck match as they passed. Marilyn did not seem to notice her at all.

The bathroom door slammed shut in the back of the store. Donna craned her neck for a look. Peter stood outside, his back against the door to protect the occupant.

At the front of the store, Mark began to pace the floor like a man awaiting news of his firstborn. Well, an average man, anyway. Donna was pretty sure Ted had spent her time in labor sitting on a stoop outside the maternity with a can of Pabst Blue Ribbon or Busch Bavarian for company. If he couldn't afford his bottle of Jack that week, that is.

Of course, Ted hadn't been a thief masquerading as a man of the cloth, either. Donna wondered if she had been the only one to notice the sleight-of-hand the preacher accomplished while Kathy fidgeted with the radio. He'd pocketed at least two bills, from what Donna could see. She thought Peter had seen it, too, but he hadn't said anything if he did. Of course, there hadn't been much time to sound an alarm between Mark's pilfering and Jerry's discovery outside.

Still, the fact that it was going to be up to Donna to say something irritated her. The more she thought about it, the more her temples throbbed.

It wasn't until Theo stirred and cooed in her arms that she realized she'd been clenching her teeth. This man who was supposed to be a community leader stole from a widow, a woman who worked hard every day to support both herself and her son. What reasonable excuse could he possibly have for that?

At least he's not a murderer, a thin but masculine voice cried from somewhere in her conscience.

Neither am I, she answered it. *What I did to Ted I did in defense of myself and my son. He could have killed one or both of us. No. Not could. He* would *have if given time.*

Oh, yeah? Then why haven't you told anyone about that *yet?*

Fair question, but she was not without an answer. First, they were in the middle of trying to survive a natural disaster. Adding Ted's death on top of that would only compound the stress of an already stressful situation. Second, and unsurprisingly, none of the Lost Hollow townsfolk who had gathered in Beard's General with her that evening had asked after Ted. Not even in passing.

Briefly, the image of her husband's corpse—bloody, bloated, and propped against the wall of their bedroom at home—surfaced in her mind. The memory of his protruding tongue and dead, bulging eyeballs that somehow still managed to convey the shock of his demise made her shudder.

Eventually she would have to explain it all to someone: a friend, a neighbor, a detective, a judge. Eventually she would not be able to justify it out loud as effectively as she had in her head.

The deep cut on the palm of her hand began to sting a little as if she'd touched it with a swab of rubbing alcohol or a dab of Bactine. The sensation killed what remained of the serenity she had achieved before the stranger arrived. A fresh round of tears welled up behind Donna's eyes. She swallowed, choking them back.

The restroom door creaked ajar and slammed shut again, startling her. Donna twisted in her chair to see Marilyn gliding toward her through the middle of the canned goods aisle. She was no longer nude. The men's coveralls were at least two sizes too large for her, giving her the appearance of a little girl playing dress-up with clothes from her parents' wardrobe. Her hair looked completely dry. Her face radiated a healthy pink. Donna could see no sign of the steaming pimple she thought she'd seen on her cheek, not even the beginnings of a scab.

Could it have been just a piece of dirt? she thought.

Kathy had neglected to locate any shoes for Marilyn's bare feet. Donna noted for the first time that her toenails were painted the same sordid red as her fingernails. Were the real Marilyn Monroe's toenails painted that color red in the calendar photo that Jerry Beard had been touching himself over? The question prompted the unbidden image in her mind of the shopkeep's son doing his deed behind the cash register in the store in broad daylight. Donna grimaced and tried to shove it away.

The consequences of the new woman's experiences outdoors hadn't been entirely cleansed from her, however. Bluish purple stains of exhaustion bulged around her lower eyelids. The sparkling, electric blue of her irises shown only partially from behind the droop of her uppers.

Peter strode beside her up the aisle, his hands clasped around her shoulders as if to steady her. She stooped under the weight of them as if he was pressing down on her, trying to prevent her from floating away. Donna thought it was a fear any of the men in Beard's General might have. Slaves to their fantasies, all.

She glanced around at them and noted their identical stares of dreamlike wonder as they watched Marilyn's progress. Of the three men at the front of the store, only Eli seemed to have lost control of the hinge in his jaw. His chin dangled somewhere down around his Adam's apple.

He closed his mouth long enough to swallow the lusty, hot saliva that had pooled inside. Then the slack retook it.

Hot breath wafted across the back of her neck and the left side of her face. She jerked backward in her seat. The sudden movement prompted a single unsettled cry from the sleeping baby in her arms. Donna's eyes darted first to Theo, then to the face of the stranger which loomed inches away from hers as Peter ushered her past. The woman's eyes had gone wide, their irises cracked and pulsating with some kind of fleshy pink substance that undulated wormlike just under the surface. They died in front of her, becoming milky and clouded—a corpse's eyes.

Ted's eyes.

Her mouth, like Eli's, hung open, but not in the same helplessly enchanted way. The stranger's mouth was a rictus. It made her look hungry and snake-like. A tongue that resembled a splintered shard of glass broken out of a picture frame protruded from within. It flicked at her once. Then it flattened and retreated into the thing's mouth. The breath that emanated from within the depths of her blackened, cavernous maw carried a foul and burning shit-tinged odor. Donna grimaced in its wake.

"Murderer," the creature that had a moment ago been a Marilyn Monroe lookalike hissed. Her words fired a fresh volley of the vile stink into Donna's face. "I smell it on you. Scrumptious. Hot. Tasty. Melty. Murder."

Donna freed her right hand from under Theo's sleeping form and pinched her nostrils together, cupping her palm protectively over her mouth as she did. Her squinting eyes watered around the rims, blurring her surroundings. No matter which way she twisted her head, she couldn't seem to find fresh air.

"Well, doll," she managed, "at least I don't smell like shit!" Then the odor was gone, and the world around her fell silent. Donna loosed her nostrils and used the back of her hand to wipe the tears away from her eyes. She blinked twice to clear away the last of the fog and examined the room. Everyone at the front of the store was staring at her. Eli's mouth had closed, at least as far as she could tell. He'd cloaked it with his balled-up left hand as if to stifle a laugh. Mark, Kathy, and Jerry all sported identical expressions of shock mixed with disapproval.

To Donna's side, Peter still had his hands clasped on Marilyn's shoulders, although he was no longer ushering her forward. Instead, he hugged her against him. He had stepped around her, his back primarily to Donna as if to shield the new woman from this foul-mouthed young mother and her infant son.

The Marilyn doppelgänger, all restored to her perfectly seductive and pouty beauty, peered at her from under the shadow of Peter's neck. She pressed her forehead to him like a daughter being comforted by her daddy after having been startled awake from the black hole of a screeching nightmare. Her hands were clasped together under her chin, her doe eyes wide, wet, pained, and sorrowful.

Donna scanned the room once more, seeking an ally but finding none among the host of eyes that met hers.

"What?" she said.

CHAPTER FOURTEEN

Mark MacDonald exhaled an unintentionally thunderous sigh of relief. Eli glanced his way for a second, sizing up what he probably thought was Mark's reaction to the faux pas that had just stunned them all into silence. Then he returned his attention to the etiquette stand-off just outside the canned goods aisle. If Eli thought that Mark's outburst was about the scene, so be it. It wasn't true, but the others could be forgiven for thinking so.

Peter Mayberry had been escorting the distraught and nearly drowned stranger from the bathroom to the front of the store when Donna Gilliam, her baby son Theo clutched to her breast, had pinched her nose and turned her head in disgust.

"At least I don't smell like shit," she'd said out of the blue. Just like that. The stranger shrank back from her as if she'd been struck. She stood quivering in Peter's arms, peeking over his shoulder at Donna and looking like she was afraid the young mother would unhinge her jaw and gobble her up whole.

Peter craned his neck around the woman and stared daggers at Donna as if he expected her to apologize. Donna glared back at them all defiantly. Mark was glad for the distraction. Her hateful outburst had removed all attentions—real or imagined—from Mark's disappearing money trick at the cash register. All eyes were on the woman with the baby and the interloper cowering in Peter's weirdly old-looking arms.

The piano player was in his late thirties, the best Mark could reckon (he'd never outright asked even though the two of them spent hours together at church once a week). It could be a trick of the light, but he looked considerably older than that. The thin lines of crow's feet that mark the eyes of a man nearing his forties were instead deep pockets and oblong folds of flesh indicative of someone much older. The short sleeves of his untucked button-down shirt revealed sagging skin that drooped off Peter's biceps like bedsheets heavy with wash water and hanging from a laundry line.

Sin ages you, they say. Sins like guilt and worry are particularly good at it. If Peter was any indication, the secret life of the church pianist must be even more stressful than what Mark's financial burdens had written across his face.

Of course, Mark hadn't looked in a mirror since he'd stashed his ill-gotten collection plate gains in that Phillies cigar box in his medicine cabinet that afternoon. His new life of rationalized crime might have already taken a toll. He just wasn't aware of it.

Since he'd nicked the two bills from Kathy Beard's cash register, he'd been awash in waves of prickling guilt followed by knee-buckling relief. The waves came in intervals of ten minutes or less, and they were exhausting. Hot gooseflesh drove the hairs on the back of his neck to attention whenever his imagination locked onto premonitions of the town constable, Billy Spears, cinching his wrists in handcuffs and hauling him before the justice of the peace.

"Aren't you supposed to be a man of the Lord?" the judge would ask him.

"Yes, your honor," he'd reply. "But I was weak."

"Well, the Lord will forgive your weakness," the wizened old man would intone as he peered over the top of his glasses mid-review of Billy's police report. "But I'm afraid the State of Tennessee is going to need you to pay your debt."

Mark would flinch when the gavel fell. He knew he would. He'd probably jump when his prison door slammed shut as well. Then where would he be? Alone with his thoughts for a year? Two? More?

The anxiety of possible outcomes scaled the back of his neck, washed down his face, and plummeted straight to his gut. His insides grumbled in protest at the intrusion, sending a horde of barbarians through the tunnels of his intestines in response. They repeatedly banged against the door of his sphincter, threatening him with a foul-smelling liquid exit if he couldn't clench long enough for them to subside.

If he waited them out, all those horrible imaginings and sensations eventually waned. Like magic. Like a miracle. Without rationalization.

Mark did not attempt to lubricate the grinding gears of his squeaky brain with daydreamy scenarios of compassion and understanding on the part of the town or the law. The prickling and washing simply left him, like someone had stabbed an invisible soda straw in his ear canal and vacuumed all the bad stuff from his head. The back of his neck cooled to his touch. He unclenched his asshole without soiling himself.

If he didn't know better, he'd think he was grieving. But for whom? Himself? His *old* self? He'd guided some of Lost Hollow's widows through the process before, not the least of which was one Kathy Beard. She wasn't a regular, but she graced the sanctuary doors from time to time.

When Jessie died, she'd shown up every Sunday in a row for six weeks or more with a toddler version of her son Jerry in tow. On some of those occasions, she'd been accepting of Jessie's fate. At other times, she'd been inconsolable. Often, the two extremes clashed within one twenty-minute conversation, sometimes outside of the church sanctuary.

Mark had been grocery shopping one Monday when she just broke down right there in front of him. He'd lent a pastorally ear even though she wasn't a member of his regular congregation, and her store certainly wasn't a sanctuary. He'd hoped his consolations would help lure her into the flock. She'd never taken the bait, however. But then, he'd never been the most splendid fisher of men.

Were the undulations of uncontrollable emotions he was experiencing like what Kathy had been going through back then? Might he not then play on her sympathy if he had, indeed, been caught pilfering by the townsfolk in the store that night? He thought he might. It was comforting to believe that the woman whose livelihood he'd just violated could be the one person who would understand.

His eyes drifted back to Kathy, who was furiously referencing receipts and writing down numbers beside the cash register. Her mouth was twisted downward at the left corner. Her anxious, bloodshot eyes seemed on the verge of spilling over. The hot pang of guilt again accosted Mark.

Meanwhile, Peter had settled the newcomer into a chair that seemed a bit too close to the Gilliam woman, considering what had just happened between them. Within seconds of her rump hitting the wood, the new woman found herself surrounded by the men. Eli Wynn and Jerry Beard dashed to the young beauty with such hasty abandon that Mark half-expected to see scorch marks on the floor in their wake.

"Hello," Jerry said hesitantly. "So, what do they call you?"

"Marilyn," came the soft reply. After she said it, she smiled at them, grateful for the everyday interaction.

The boys gasped in unison. They locked eyes for an instant, then turned back to her. Eli shoved his hands in his pockets.

Jerry knelt on her right and rested his forearms on one knee, looking like he wanted to propose right then and there. "Where are you from?" he asked. A vibrating twinge of excitement permeated the words as they hit the air.

"Oh, here and there," Marilyn said.

"Are..." Eli began. He swallowed audibly. "Are you *her?*"

She was pretty, Mark thought. That much was a given. Had he not been a couple of decades older than Jerry and the Wynn boy, he might've joined them in what was about to evolve into a friendly contest for her attention. Instead, he allowed himself to admire her with an older man's dissociation: in his head and as if she was not capable of seeing him at all.

He was careful to keep his eyes on her face, however. No gazing downward at the pale smoothness of her neck. And he should certainly not be looking at the hint of bifurcation barely visible at the end of the V created by the collar in the men's coveralls she was wearing when she leaned over in the chair and imitated Jerry, resting her elbows on her knees.

Mark jerked his head upwards and met her eyes. She propped her chin on both her fists and stared back at him, her crystal blue eyes sparkling with bemusement, her abounding lips pulled into the slightest of closed-mouth grins.

Hot blood flooded Mark's cheeks and the tips of his ears. He tried to look away from her, but something out of his control seemed to have locked his head in place. A pair of unseen hands had clasped the sides to prevent him from moving it. Cold, invisible fingers pried his eyelids open with their phantom thumbs and forefingers. He tried to speak, to explain that he was not intentionally staring at her, but his jaw was suddenly locked in place as well.

Long strands of a strange red mist emerged from along the periphery of his vision. They appeared to connect his head to her hands. No, to her mouth just above her hands. She parted her lips to receive the strands, revealing long, pointed canines behind their magazine-perfect lines. From between the teeth, a thick green tongue corkscrewed impossibly out at him. At first, it resembled an enormous painted drill bit. At length, it looked more like a folded-up wad of dollar bills.

Her blue eyes rolled back in her head, revealing blank sockets replete with bright white sclera. They dried up and disintegrated into a wrinkled, yellowy parchment that exploded into an orange-red flame without a blink.

Greed, a voice crooned inside his head. *Avarice!* It sounded like the new woman's voice but with a brutal and sinister growl around the edges. Mark's mouth filled with the taste of warm biscuits: flaky and doughy yet tinged with sulfur and buttered with a mixture of phlegm and snot. His jaw unlocked. He opened his mouth to try to spit, gag, or vomit. Instead, a fresh stream of red mist shot out from him.

Marilyn lunged for it, lapping at it like a dog biting at water sprayed from the end of a garden hose. Now that it was flowing, Mark could not close his mouth again. His hands were frozen in his lap, his feet bolted to the floor in front of him.

Bizarrely, no one else in Beard's General appeared to notice what was happening to him. He rotated his eyes toward Donna Gilliam. She sat with the infant in her lap, gently stroking the thin strands of hair at his forehead and cooing at him. The only evidence that anything bothered her was a gentle furrow in her brow.

Eli and Jerry remained at their same stations on either side of Marilyn. Eli had copied Jerry's kneeling pose. They looked like two country squires bowing before their queen as they awaited knighthood from this angle. They seemed to be carrying on a one-sided conversation with her: goggling at her while they spoke and then waiting patiently for their next turn as if she was replying to whatever they'd just said instead of sucking Mark's life-force from his body. Neither of them paid heed to the tendrils of red mist that floated over their heads and into her maw, nor the giant stream of it that directly connected his mouth to hers.

Peter stood over Marilyn's left shoulder. He was not looking at her, the boys, or anyone else. His eyes were pointed toward the ceiling. They shifted in their sockets uncomfortably, as if he was aware of what was happening but choosing to ignore it.

Mark focused on him, tried to will him to make eye contact. He pleaded with the other man to see what was happening, to intervene. No luck. Without warning and without looking back at him, Peter simply turned and walked away. He dragged over a chair and sidled up behind Donna, out of Mark's line of sight.

Mark rolled his eyes toward Kathy at the front of the store. She remained as she mainly had been since she'd discovered the cash drawer: poring over receipts and math. On the counter in front of her, the last ticket had come off the spike and lay face down on the pile. Kathy scratched absently at her forehead with the eraser end of her pencil. Something did not add up. Why would it?

A fresh wave of hot blood rose in his cheeks. A violent gush of the steam from his mouth and nostrils that sent his head reeling backward. He watched helplessly as Marilyn adjusted her position in the chair to capture the stuff at the end of its powerful new arc.

The last of whatever the horrible stuff was inside him exited his mouth and, apparently, all his head orifices. Marilyn vacuumed up the ends of it from between pursed lips like the slippery last strand on a plate of spaghetti. The invisible hands that had imprisoned him let go.

Mark slumped in his chair, exhausted. His eyes stung. A single hot tear crept from the corner of the left one and rolled down his cheek. His mouth and nostrils felt like they'd been stuffed with sand. The knots that had bound his stomach off and on ever since he'd taken the money from the offering plate loosened. The muscles in his neck and shoulders relaxed, as did those in his thighs and calves.

Relief washed over him. It was the kind of respite that comes from lying back on a cool mattress after ten hours of tossing hay bales under the hot sun and wet air of a Tennessee August. Not that he would know the intensity of tossing hay bales in August. He was a preacher, not a farmer. It was the first metaphor that sprang to mind. He had used it to some degree of success in his sermons to describe how it feels when baptism washes away your sins.

Yes! he thought. *That's it! It feels just like I've been washed in the blood again. I've been made pure.*

He no longer felt guilty about the money he had stolen, neither from the church offering plate nor from Kathy

Beard's cash register. It wasn't the same as the waves of remorse and justification he had been experiencing all day. Even when he'd reconciled and rationalized his deeds before, there had been a twinge of conscience nagging at the back of his mind.

He felt nothing at all. No guilt. No justification. No need to reconcile or rationalize. There was only acceptance that the deed had been done, and it was what it was. He simply did not care.

Behind the register, Kathy's pursed lips curled into a snarl. Mark could hear her exhales, the rage building inside her and getting ready to explode out. She had double-checked her math. She had discovered the missing money.

Not pure, then, Mark thought. *Not freshly washed.*

The Nazarenes taught young pastors that forgiveness and salvation could come only after repentance. Repentance meant admitting your sinfulness, feeling remorse for the evil you have done, and making amends where necessary and possible. That meant acknowledging the wrongs you've done to others and asking for their forgiveness as well as the forgiveness of the Father and the Son.

There was some grace, of course. If the people you've wronged are unwilling to forgive you, even after you've admitted your sins and asked for it, you are still forgiven in the eyes of the Heavenly Father. But not *until* you've first endeavored to make earthly amends.

At this moment, Kathy was only aware that money was missing. Either a mistake had been made during the day's transactions, or a crime had been committed right under her nose. She did not know which of those things had happened. If she alleged a crime, he thought it was unlikely that Nazarene Pastor Mark MacDonald would be her prime suspect. So, until Mark admitted his misdeed and asked for her forgiveness—more than that, until he confessed his sin to the congregation and begged for *their* forgiveness—he could not be truly forgiven.

The freedom he experienced after Marilyn had drained her meal of gunk out of him was false freedom. If scripture was truth (and after a lifetime in service of it, he had no reason to think it was not), this guiltless, sinless state of being he perceived could only be the work of a deceiver.

Mark sat up straight in his chair. Marilyn was not looking at him. Her attention was divided between the two young men at her feet, bouncing back and forth one to the other as they asked her questions and tried to impress her with a few mildly embellished truths about themselves and their daily adventures in the wilds of rural Tennessee. Peter sat still in his hiding place behind Donna, who remained preoccupied with the helpless bundle on her lap.

Mark mashed the palms of his hands into the tops of his knees and stood up. His chair scraped loudly against the floor as he did so, drawing the attention of Marilyn and all those around her. He drew in a deep breath, leveled the forefinger of his right hand at her, and screamed.

"DECEIVER!" he roared. "DEMON! DEVIL! APOSTATE FROM HELL!"

CHAPTER FIFTEEN

Peter launched himself from his hiding spot so fast that he sent the back of his chair hurtling to the floor behind him. Donna flinched when he did. This was the second time she'd been startled in the space of five seconds. The first was Mark MacDonald's uncharacteristic and unprovoked outburst at the odd woman (*is she a woman?*) that Jerry and Peter had rescued from the floodwaters. Both Jerry and Eli had closed ranks around the woman who called herself "Marilyn." Donna suspected that it was not her real name. She bore too striking a resemblance to the famous nude pre-Marilyn woman on Jerry's calendar contraband.

Peter joined the two walking hard-ons at her side. All three of Marilyn's defenders glared at Mark as if daring him to go on.

Kathy reached for something stored beneath the cash register. A baseball bat? A gun? Her back was hunched, with one arm dropped out of Donna's field of view. Whatever it was remained out of sight but within Kathy's reach. She seemed to be waiting to see what would happen next before getting more involved.

Theo squeezed out a single grunt to acknowledge the shouting and crashing furniture, then fell silent again. For as much as now-dead Ted had complained about the constant noise in his life before the storm, Theo had spent hours fatherless without much fuss. He'd done so despite the noise and anxiety of the thundershowers and the unfamiliarity of the surroundings. Since they'd arrived at Beard's, Donna had fed him formula from a bottle that Kathy warmed for her in the store's back kitchen. Feedings were followed by a good burping, a diaper change, and only one tiny spit-up that formed a single cute-as-a-button bubble in the center of the dimple between his lower lip and chin. Donna dabbed it away with a warm washcloth. The baby had fallen fast asleep again right after.

The three fellows who had charged themselves with protecting the pretty lady wore identical expressions of confusion and rage. They were faces that were all too familiar to Donna. They were the faces of the reactive, the "problem solvers." Always they leaped into action, damn the consequences, never aware of the pile of shit they were squishing and spreading under the soles of their superhero boots.

In a way, it was a good thing, or it would have been if Mark's outburst had been wholly without merit. Donna suspected that he had seen something in Marilyn. It could be that it was something not unlike what she had seen a few minutes before. She'd seen something that no one else saw. Hadn't she?

"What's wrong with you, Mark?" Peter asked. Donna could detect no emotional inflections in the question. No clenched teeth. No angry snarl. No empathy. It sounded less like a question and more like an attempt to get at the heart of a simple statement of fact.

Mark blinked at the rest of the men, confused and suddenly alone. "I thought I saw—" he started. "You mean none of you saw—?" He gave up and returned to his seat without looking behind him. He nearly missed the edge of it when he plopped down but managed to scoot backward and situate himself without falling off and landing ass-first on the floor.

"Saw what?" Peter asked after him.

Mark swiped at his face, forehead to chin, with the palm of his left hand and stroked a beard that was not there. "Nothing," he said. "It's just nerves. Got to be just nerves. Because of the storm, you know.

"My apologies, ma'am," he added, tipping his porkpie and nodding in the direction of Marilyn, although he couldn't have seen her from behind her newfound line of guardians.

The trio split up then. Eli and Jerry resumed their chat with the newcomer, albeit at a lower volume. Peter knelt with them at her side. There was something different about the way he treated Marilyn comparatively. It was as though he knew her. He had asked no questions about who she was or why she was here, nor had he demonstrated any interest in the answers she gave the boys. Donna wondered if he somehow already knew those things.

Kathy abandoned whatever weapon she had been prepared to wield and resumed going over her math. Mark folded his hands between his knees and stared at them, searching them as if they were the most exciting hands in the world.

Donna gave the dust a few minutes to settle. When Theo decided to swim to consciousness and fuss, she used it as an excuse to stand up. She placed the baby over her shoulder, cradling his bottom in the crook of one arm and his head and neck in the palm of the other. She strode with a gentle baby bouncy gait over to the preacher. Theo made tiny "uh uh uh" sounds as they walked.

"We've been in one place too long," she said to the preacher. She kept her voice low so as not to exceed the level of the conversation going on at Marilyn's seat. Mark looked up from his hands, eyeing her with a piteously sad, pleading expression. A part of her was disgusted seeing a man of his age and stature sporting the pouty bottom lip of a toddler. She resolved to ignore it.

"Theo needs a walk around the room, I think," she continued. "He misses his father's voice. Ted always spent—spends—an hour or so reading to him around this time of night." This last was a lie, but Mark couldn't possibly know that. "Would you take a walk with me? We can check the weather out there. See if we can find an end to it."

Mark nodded slowly and stood up. Together they walked to the large window at the front of the store and peered into the darkness beyond. There wasn't much to see. Beard's General had no exterior lighting. The sun had already gone down. They could hear the rain still falling. It was their only indication that any world outside of this small-town stockpile of food and assortments still existed.

Donna checked the scene behind them, ensuring that everyone else was too involved in their tasks to care what the young mom and the preacher were doing. Then she leaned in close and whispered in Mark's ear, "I know you saw something." She swallowed thickly, trying to keep the day's odor of snot and tears from wafting into the man's face. "I saw something, too. You're not wrong. She's some kind of monster. I meant what I said before. Her breath does smell like shit."

Mark turned to look at her, astonishment on his face. "You *saw* her, too?" he said, too loud.

Donna glowered at him, motioning with her eyes and head so he would turn his attention back to the window. "Keep your voice down," she replied. "I saw...something when Peter brought her back from the bathroom. But when I told her she smelled like shit, and everybody started staring at me, I thought I must have been seeing things."

Light dawned in Mark's eyes. "Yeah. You told her she smelled like shit," he said, chuckling despite himself.

"Right. When they came out of the bathroom, she leaned down to me and put her face right in my face. She called me...well, she said some things and then her face kind of, I don't know, *transformed*. She didn't look like Marilyn Monroe in that girlie calendar anymore. Her eyes just went blank. Her mouth changed, too. She looked like...a demon, I guess. She looked like a demon with dead eyes and a tongue made of broken glass.

"But there's something else. Now that I'm telling you about it, I have the strangest sense of déjà vu. I feel like I've stood in this exact spot with you and had this exact conversation with you before."

Mark grunted acknowledgment. He kept his face forward and his eyes glued to the windows this time. He shoved both hands into his pants pockets and rocked backward on his heels.

"Well?" Donna said after a moment. "What did you see?"

He answered her question with another question. "Have you ever heard of a sin-eater?"

She shook her head, not looking at him. "Are they demons?"

"Not exactly," he said. "I guess we haven't had *this* part of the conversation before."

Donna sighed. "Please don't be a smart-ass."

He smiled wanly. "Apologies. Religious people in some cultures hire people to attend to their loved ones who have died before they could atone. These people, the sin-eaters, can supposedly consume all the sins of the deceased person, allowing them to pass on to eternity unburdened by any earthly transgressions."

"Oh."

"Nazarenes don't believe in sin-eaters," he added quickly. "That's what we have Jesus for. No human being can atone for the sins of another human being in the eyes of God. Our Lord has already been sacrificed for that. The sins that are after Him? You have to atone for those yourself while you can."

"So, she's not a sin-eater?"

"No, but I think she could be a demon or spiritual parasite pretending to be one. She seems to have the power to draw out guilt from the conscience of the sinner and feed on it like you might imagine a sin-eater does. If you don't feel any guilt, you have no impetus to repent of your sins. If you don't repent of your sins, you can't get into paradise."

"But how do you know she has such a power?" Donna asked.

On her shoulder, Theo had drifted to sleep again. His drool dampened a spot on the back of her dress where his blanket had slipped away. She reinforced her grip on him, suddenly afraid of what the preacher would say next.

Mark looked at her earnestly. "If I tell you what I saw, you have to promise to help me get rid of her. If she's not putting our lives at risk here, she's risking our everlasting souls." He paused, then added, "Do you promise?"

Donna nodded. "I promise."

Mark pulled his hands from his pockets and folded his arms across his chest. "She's been feeding off me ever since she got here," he said gravely. "She might've been feeding off me before then even, hiding outside before they found her and dragged her inside." He tilted his head backward, indicating Jerry Beard and Peter Mayberry. "See, I did something bad today, something I very much want to atone for. The only thing is, thanks to her, I don't have a single regret about it."

"And that's a bad thing," Donna intoned. She stated it, not asking.

"Yes," Mark replied. "That's a bad thing. I could go through the motions anyway, I suppose. I could confess what I've done to the people I've injured and ask them to forgive me. But I don't *want* their forgiveness because I don't feel like I *need* it. Because of," and here he lowered his voice more, "Marilyn, I *can't* repent even if I want to."

"So, what did you see?" Donna repeated.

He sighed and detailed what had happened to him just before he stood up and shouted at the Marilyn woman as best as he could within the limits of his descriptive powers. He also informed her all about the way his guilt and shame had been surging and retreating again for the entire length of time he'd been inside the store. It was like a tide being pushed and pulled along with the waves that were rushing past the store at the level of the rows of wooden slats that formed the front porch treads. When he finished, Donna simply gaped at him.

"What?" he asked.

"I'm wondering what you could have possibly done to create all that fear and self-hatred and doubt," she said. "Oh my God, Mark, did you—did you—" She started to say "kill someone," but stopped herself.

Ted's dead, gray, and bloated face rose unbidden from the depths of her imagination, a wide swath of a manic grin slashed across its face. "Gonna judge him for that, are you?" the corpse croaked. "Gonna judge him for murder if that's what he did? Fine Christian you are, woman. Fiiiine Christian indeed."

"Did you hurt someone that badly?" she finished. She pretended to adjust Theo on her left shoulder. It allowed her to turn her back to Mark for a second and obscure her bandaged palm from his view. Not that he wasn't already aware of it. Mark, Kathy, Jerry, and Eli had all eyed her when she'd burst through the door bleeding, exhausted, and hauling Theo.

"I took some money," Mark said. "I—I've had some trouble paying the bills lately. I took a couple of dollars extra from the church collection plate for myself. Then I, uh, took a couple more from the till while Kathy's back was turned. Everyone else was watching the flood. I couldn't help it." He scoffed. "I thought you saw me do that, though. You were the only one not distracted by something else at the time. I'd hoped that little guy in your arms would've been too much on your mind to pay any attention to me."

"I thought I did see you do it," Donna whispered in reply. "But after the Marilyn thing happened, I was worried this whole night was a weird hallucination or fever dream or something."

Mark nodded. "I've been making excuses for myself all day: I deserved a raise, no one could be expected to live on my take from the collection each week, my car wasn't going to last another year. In the end, the only excuse I have is my pride, I suppose. The church isn't exactly a full-time job these days. Folks worry about the young'uns and the Devil's influence over them, but they don't worry so much that we don't have room in the pews on Sundays." He shrugged. "I could be doing something else during the week to make ends meet."

"Desperation sometimes blinds us," Donna said. She faced him, gently massaging Theo's back with the bandaged hand. "You're not a bad man, Mark. It might feel like it sometimes, but you're not. It's a strange feeling, isn't it? Having a bad time in your life when everyone else seems to be living high on the hog?"

"Yes. Yes, it is. He examined her gauze-wrapped hand, eyes narrow. "Donna? What *really* happened to you?"

"What do you mean?"

He cocked an eyebrow and nodded toward her hand. "Well, there's that, for one thing. My guess is that there are some pretty bad scrapes and bruises underneath all that makeup you're wearing tonight. And if you saw that woman turn into anything like the thing I saw, and I'm right about what she's doing, then you must have a secret of your own."

Donna grimaced. She opened her mouth to reply, unsure about what she would say. Then a new voice answered him instead. It came from somewhere behind them both, lilting and wet. "Why, Pastor Mark MacDonald, hasn't she confessed it to you yet? She sliced the palm of her hand when she slit the throat of her darling husband with a nasty shard of pointy broken glass!"

Donna and Mark wheeled to discover that the mysterious strawberry blonde woman had abandoned her throng of male adorers and joined them at the window. Her words echoed against the sudden silence inside Beard's General. Donna felt the eyes of the entire place trained on them.

"Why don't you tell us all about it, dear?" Marilyn continued. "Sliced him ear-to-ear, didn't you? Left him propped up against your bedroom wall like one of your momma's china dolls. He doesn't blush like they do, though, does he?" She laughed, pressing the delicate fingers of her right hand to her lips in a coquettish, teasing way. "He's quite gray. Why wouldn't he be? All the blood's run from his throat and into his lap!"

Donna's face warmed. Her heartbeat quickened, thumping so hard under her blouse that she was sure Mark and the stranger could hear it. Theo squirmed uncomfortably against the sensation.

"I—" she started, but Mark cut her off.

"Who are you?" he shouted. He took a step toward Marilyn, stretching out his right arm in a sweeping gesture as he did. The back of his hand connected lightly with Donna's elbow. She got the message and took a couple of steps backward so that Mark stood between her and this woman she'd never met who seemed to know an awful lot about how she'd spent her morning.

But not just that. Her mother's china dolls, which had been her grandmother's before her, had been a source of pride for the family. They were original German glazed porcelain dolls from the 1800s, not the reproductions that lady in California had made so famous some years back. Donna could've gotten a pretty penny for them in the antique market if they had not been lost after her parents died. They might've been a hundred years old or more.

Those dolls were popular and widely collected for decades, however. Any good student of Professor Marvel could guess that Donna's mother had owned one. But how did she know about Ted? Or the shard of glass? From deep inside her brain, the realization dawned on Donna that she *had* seen what she thought she'd seen when Peter escorted Marilyn from the bathroom to the front of the store. Marilyn's face *had* transformed before Donna's eyes. She really had spoken those words. In a flash, the idea that Marilyn could be the vengeful spirit of her late husband come to settle a score occurred to her. Only moments ago, she had been celebrating the severing of her strangely psychic connection to the man. The stranger read her mind and had taken on Ted's likeness right before her eyes.

Donna felt faint, as if her blood had suddenly all drained away, leaving her empty, depriving her muscles of the oxygen they needed to remain locked and upright. Her ankles went first, then her knees. As she plummeted backward to the plank floor, someone plucked Theo from her arms. She heard a short grunt of protest escape him. Then a thudding explosion of pain in the back of her head drowned out the sound. She was on the floor. Above her, three faces and the bald back of a baby's head leaned over to peer at her.

"Donna?" Mark mouthed. It was long and drawn out like he was speaking to her from a place of some distance. "Donna? Are you all right?"

Kathy was there, too. She had pried herself away from her math and raced to Donna before the latter had entirely lost her balance. She'd been fast enough to snatch Theo to safety. She held him close to her bosom, supporting his head as she did. Of course she did. It was what mothers did instinctively. No matter how old they got. No matter how grown their children were. A mother remains a mother. Always. Donna smiled sweetly at the notion.

Her eyes next landed on the blonde stranger who stood between Mark and Kathy. She stared down at Donna with the blue doe eyes of Marilyn Monroe. Her pouty lips and perfectly arched eyebrows forecast nothing of her thoughts, no hint of her intentions for using the secrets about Donna she had somehow collected. But there was something else in those eyes. Something dark. Something malicious. Something evil.

Maybe Mark was right. She was the Devil. Or she was some sort of vampire that feeds on the sins of others. Or on the guilt over those sins.

The image of Ted's closed fist barreling down on the bridge of her nose flashed before her. Donna flinched. That image was then replaced with one of his hot blood gushing over her right hand when she cut into him. It mixed with hers as the glass shard from the picture frame cut into her palm. Twin streams of the stuff rolled down her forearm like beads of sweat while she worked.

She searched her heart as the light overhead dimmed around her. She searched her soul as the three faces over her became shadows, then blurs, and then indiscernible from the darkness closing around her. She searched her mind. In none of it did she find a trace of guilt over the untimely demise of Ted Gilliam. She had been a good wife. She was *still* a good mother. She might have been an even better mother for having sliced up the entitled shit who wanted to rule over her and her son.

No, there was no guilt for Donna Gilliam to provide the stranger. What else, then, could Marilyn, the Devil, or Ted want from her?

Before she could ponder it more, darkness enveloped her.

CHAPTER SIXTEEN

Kathy had never wanted to hand a child off to someone else more than that moment. Theo did not fuss. He did not squirm. But because she cradled him while his mother lay crumpled on the floor, Kathy's hands were too preoccupied for her to take a swing at the smug bitch who had verbally assaulted one of her regulars.

Well, *regular* was a loose term. It's not like the residents of Lost Hollow had much choice in the way of local grocery shopping. Kathy was nevertheless relieved that the town hadn't abandoned her and Jerry after Jessie's death. There were plenty of industrious young men in the area, some of them veterans, who could've taken over the place and made a friendlier or more successful run of it. For all her curmudgeonly bottom-line and less-than-personable personality, not a single person in town had suggested to Kathy in the aftermath of those days that she sell the place and start over.

A few of the older kids, a much younger Donna Gilliam née Johnson among them, had helped her ready the site for its grand reopening a couple of weeks after they'd laid Jessie in the ground.

This hussy, on the other hand, Kathy did not know nor had ever seen before. Yes, the woman bore a striking resemblance to the girl in that dirty picture of Jerry's, even as she stood there swimming inside the pair of men's coveralls that Kathy had graciously provided her. What had she been doing hanging around naked outside the store in a storm, anyway? Unlike Donna, who harbored the physical scars of an obvious run-in with someone stronger than herself, Marilyn didn't have a mark on her. Not anymore, anyway.

Instead of searching for a hand-off, Kathy stepped between Mark and the girl. If she wanted to hurt Donna, she'd have to go through both Kathy and Mark to do it. Kathy clutched Theo tight, protecting him with her hands and forearms, then leaned in toward the Marilyn impersonator and glared at her.

"Answer his question," she said through clenched teeth. "Who the hell are you? Come to think of it, how did you get here? Why were you naked when my son and Mayberry over there dragged you inside?"

Behind her, Mark cleared his throat, clearly uncomfortable with the memory.

The woman returned Kathy's gaze and spoke one word, but not to Kathy.

"Peter?" she said.

Aside from the honest Marilyn Monroe, Kathy thought, she must be the only woman in the world who could speak a name that often doubles as a boy's name for his penis in a sexy way. Peter emerged from behind the woman. His face seemed to have withered over the past hour. Crow's feet ran from the corners of his eyes to his temples like gullies in a sandbox after a surprise thunderstorm. He didn't look as tall as he used to, either. He was bent at the middle of his back.

A pained expression passed over his face as he shuffled his way to the standoff. He didn't look *elderly* or infirm to her, but he looked like his middle years had accelerated since he'd walked in her door from the deluge.

Kathy cut her eyes back to Marilyn. "And what have you done to *him*?"

Marilyn smirked. "Tell her, Peter."

He cleared his throat. "She saved me," he said. The words were sandpapery over his lips, and he whistled on each of the ess sounds. He sounded like a man in dire need of a cool drink of water. "She saved me from all my sin and self doubt. She took it all away, and I think she can do it for you, too."

"Sin?" Mark tittered. "Son, there's only one individual ever walked this Earth who can save you from that. And she ain't him. He ascended to Heaven nigh on 2,000 years ago."

"The son of man shall come again," Peter intoned. "Isn't that what the book says?"

"More or less."

"Any reason that son couldn't be a daughter instead?"

Marilyn's smirk became a full-on beam, displaying her top row of gleaming white teeth. Not for the first time, Kathy noted the perfection of her makeup: soft black and brown eye pencil, white eye shadow, and foundation, all topped with comely lips that managed to defy any shade of red lipstick that Kathy had ever encountered. She'd been dragged inside soaked to the bone without so much as a single smudge of her mascara. Combine that with her ability to make every word sound like a sexual proposition, and it was no wonder she had the boys falling all over themselves just to be close to her.

Kathy glanced over her shoulder to make sure Mark hadn't joined Donna Gilliam on the floor. He remained standing behind her, his mouth gaping like a fish while his eyes appeared to search the ceiling for an answer that would limit the Lord's options for arriving in a human body without limiting his divine powers as well.

"W—well," he stammered. "You have to remember, Peter, that Jesus isn't being reborn here on Earth. He'll be descending from the heavens, presumably in the same form with which He ascended from the Earth."

"But that's not what Revelations says, is it?" Peter replied. "Revelations says, 'His head and his hairs were white like wool, as white as snow; and his eyes were as a flame of fire; And his feet like to fine brass, as if they burned in a furnace; and his voice as the sound of many waters.'"

Mark sighed. "Yes, Peter. *His* hairs. *His* feet."

"You know as well as I do that the earliest Christians believed the Holy Spirit to be feminine," Peter continued. "And we—you and I and the rest of your flock—also believe that God himself is The Trinity: the Father, the Son, and the Holy Ghost. It is reasonable to think that the Son of God could choose to come back as the Daughter of God if he really and truly wanted to. He could come back as a dog, even. Or a wolf." Peter's eyes drifted to the back of Marilyn's head. "Or even looking like someone famous."

Mark clapped a hand to his forehead. He slid his palm upwards, pushing the brim of his hat up. It made him look like he was wearing a baby's bonnet. "You can't believe that a naked woman you and Jerry rescued from the rain is the Lord," he said. "I'm sorry, but that's fucking stupid."

The novelty of hearing the local pastor swear was too much for Jerry and Eli. The younger men turned their backs to the group and tittered into their fists, their shoulders quaking. Peter rolled his eyes.

"Well," Mark continued, "it *is* stupid. Look, Peter, we Nazarenes are a modern lot. We've been ordaining women since we were founded fifty years ago. Many churches won't do that. We have women elders and deacons, too. We don't have any of them here in Lost Hollow, but churches in some cities do. Hollow River's church has two women in leadership. Nobody is saying a woman can't save souls. But Jesus was not a woman, and I doubt He'd want to come back in a form that's hard for people to recognize. Kind of defeats the purpose of coming back to lead."

Peter sneered. He side-stepped Marilyn, who was eyeing the argument between the two men with all the relish of Darla in *The Little Rascals* when both Spanky and Alfalfa were trying to woo her. He made two long strides to where Mark stood. His weirdly old eyes glared at him. There was insanity in them, rage. It sent a shiver up Kathy's spine, palpable enough to cause Theo to grunt against her shoulder. He could sense what she was thinking and feeling through their contact. It was a unique sensation for Kathy. All Jerry ever did as an infant was snore.

Theo's tiny body tensed in her arms. There was a series of vibrations against her left forearm where his bottom was propped. Okay, fine. He just had gas. All this religious talk was spooking her.

"You want me to prove it?" Peter asked. "You Doubting Thomas. You want me to show you the wounds in her hands and her sides? Well, I can't do that. But I can tell you this: *we know what you did*. Just like she knows what Donna did. She *knows*. And because she knows, I know." He broke his staring contest with the preacher and threw up his hands, looking around at the others as if testifying at a revival meeting.

"She saved me from my sin, and she healed my wounds!" Peter boomed, pointing at Marilyn. "I was a broken man! I confess it. She came to me in my darkest hour when I lay broken and bleeding and in danger of being washed away by the flood of my wickedness. She healed me! She healed my flesh and at the same time chained the demon of shame that had hold of my heart!"

He lowered his voice to a stage whisper and leaned toward Mark MacDonald. The preacher's hands trembled at his sides. "Ever since she saved me, I've been able to sense the thoughts of some of my friends and neighbors here in the store," he hissed. "You've been wondering why you kept feeling those twinges of guilt and then not feeling them, haven't you, Mark? I watched you. More than once, you've been full-up of the crimson smoke of guilt, so much of it that I thought you were just going to melt away. But then it rose from your body, letting you have some relief.

"Do you know why, Mark? It's because of this woman, your savior. She was right outside pulling it all out of you. She *wants* you to be saved, Mark. But she can't take it all away until you repent."

Peter glanced at Kathy, who blinked back at him. She was suddenly very much afraid. Peter pointed at her. "You need to tell *her*, Mark. Confess what you did. Ask for her forgiveness, then ask for forgiveness from the savior." He indicated Marilyn. "Only then can your soul be saved."

Mark's face changed. His mouth dropped at the corners. His eyes softened. He faced Kathy, shoving his hands in his pockets as he did. He seemed to be rooting around in there for something. That, or he was adjusting himself in front of her, which was the only thing that could've made the moment even more uncomfortable.

From his pocket, he produced two one-dollar bills. He stretched them out to her, palm open, pressing them loosely there with his thumb. He cast his eyes at the floor, offering her the money but unable to look at her as he did.

Kathy cleared her throat. "What's this for?" She thought she already knew.

"Take it first," he replied.

Kathy did as he asked with her free arm. She dexterously folded the bills with one hand like a woman who had been handling money all her life. Then she slid them into the front pocket of her store apron. "Okay. So, tell me. What's it for?"

Mark settled the brim of his hat to its proper place on his head. He straightened his back and shoulders and stood at full height, meeting her eyes.

"Redemption," he replied. "It's for my redemption." Then he balled his hands into fists and launched himself at Marilyn.

CHAPTER SEVENTEEN

For Mark, the final minute of his life as the pastor of Lost Hollow's Nazarene church seemed significantly longer than sixty seconds. In the first second of that minute, he shoved Peter out of the way. The man was less fragile than his aged appearance suggested. It took one flying elbow to the ribs, followed by Mark planting both palms in the middle of Peter's chest, to send him to the floor.

In the next second, Mark pinwheeled his arms to keep from losing his balance and toppling onto Peter. Then he pivoted to run at Marilyn. Bizarrely, her face bore no expression of alarm as he closed in on her. There was, in fact, a surreal expression of serenity around the edges of her eyes. No sign of strain in her arms nor crouch of her legs betrayed her preparation for his oncoming bulk. Her arms hung at her sides, her body contrapposto, unshielded.

Granted, Mark was no fighter. But compared to her five foot, five inch frame and 120 pounds soaking wet, the preacher was a steaming rodeo bull charging a toddler who'd fallen into the arena from the stands. He was five feet, 10-inches tall, and just a hair over 210 pounds at last check.

Peter would scramble to his feet soon. In his heightened state of awareness, Mark thought he could already hear the man clawing at the floor, trying to recover himself. From his periphery, he could see the two younger men, Jerry and Eli, rushing toward him, their eyes wide in alarm. All they could intuit about what was happening was an angry older man hurling himself at a defenseless and pretty young woman. They didn't know, couldn't say, what she was.

Kathy knelt beside the unconscious supine body of Donna. With Theo still resting on her left hip, she pressed two fingers against Donna's windpipe, just below her jawbone, checking for a pulse. Mark felt a pang of guilt over that. The fainted mother hadn't been his priority. Instead, he'd wasted time arguing theology with Peter.

A plume of red steam arose from Mark's shirt collar. It wafted in front of his eyes, then changed direction in midair, racing ahead of him toward the Marilyn woman. He watched her inhale the steam. It went up her nostrils and down her throat as she rapidly grew more significant in his field of vision. For a fraction of a second, Marilyn's face elongated. Her cheeks and nose tightened and stretched into something canid. Her tongue protruded from between her lips and split in the middle at the seam. Thick blood drooled down her chin from the wound. Then the split healed just like that and sculpted what had previously been the singular tip of a human tongue into a serpent's fork.

Mark squeezed his eyes shut and flung them open again, trying to force his brain to focus the image and make some sense of what he was seeing.

He was disappointed. The thing that had been a woman named Marilyn stood before him as a hairy wolfen giant. Its mouth gaped in a salivating, ravenous lupine grin, the greedy smile of hunger about to be satiated. He was the willing morsel.

More than that, that guilty twinge he'd felt over Donna Gilliam was gone. It had dissipated as soon as the beast had guzzled the last of the red steam down its gullet. His suspicions had been correct after all. That meant that Peter was wrong. Marilyn was no savior. Not even close. She *was* a demon, here to feed on the quickly replenished remorse of a small town jam-packed with people keeping secrets, generations of them.

Just before Mark landed in the middle of the thing's chiseled chest, Marilyn inhaled again. Her eyes were closed, her mouth still wide. Claw-tipped hands the size of catcher's mitts pawed at the air in front of her, like a cat making biscuits. Her muzzle rooted the air like a blind puppy searching for its mother's tit. But Mark's milk had run dry. With no guilt left inside him to feed on, he thought, he had a shot at taking her down.

The collision landed more like a lover's embrace than a takedown. Bristly, feverishly hot arms closed around him, wrapping him in a thick down of black fur. Marilyn's biceps and forearms squeezed his ribs. He heard them groan and crack in her grip. It was like someone had snapped a thick cord of uncooked spaghetti right beside his ear. They collapsed against the pressure on the walls of his torso.

He couldn't breathe. He expanded his diaphragm against the creature's belly and inhaled what he could. Then he lifted his head from Marilyn's chest and stared up at her. Her eyes were too wide, red-rimmed with tiny black pupils and sickly yellow corneas streaming thick mucus from their corners. Rage overflowed them.

Her breath stank of sulfur and rotting flesh. It gusted hot against his skin, welling up tears in his eyes. The muscles under her thick pelt trembled, using up all their oxygen as she strained to squeeze one more gleaming drop of steam from his poor and battered soul.

He could not allow it.

It was not to be.

"I," he grunted, "Am. A. Thief." The four words exhausted his air supply. He rested a beat and then tried again. "The. Lord. Forgives. Me." Another breath. He closed his eyes and wrenched his last words from somewhere deep inside him.

"*I* forgive me," he shouted. His eyelids fluttered wide then, making him look surprised at the strength of his affirmation. His body fell slack in Marilyn's arms. His chest heaved one final time.

In the distance, he saw a pinprick of bright white light. He was dying. At least, he thought he was at first. After some indeterminable amount of time passed without the ability to draw a breath, Mark wasn't at all sure what was happening to him. His body compacted. His skin pulled taut around his muscles, bones, and organs, wrapping him like a sausage casing. The pressure from his shrinking shell imploded his lungs, heart, kidneys, liver, and stomach. Anything that took up space inside him collapsed in on itself, folding over and over until it was no longer recognizable as human anatomy.

His brain hurt. A pair of enormous, invisible hands gripped the sides of his head, pressing at his temples with the balls of their palms until the fissures in his skull cracked and began to separate. It was becoming difficult to process what he was seeing and feeling, as though someone had yanked all the wires from his brain and replaced them with cotton batting.

Suddenly the world around him looked much more significant than it had before. He recognized that he lay on the floor, although he couldn't remember how he came to be there. His eyes bulged from their sockets. He felt it happen. A sense of satisfaction came with it, like squeezing the head out of a particularly painful zit.

He could move his eyes independently of one another. Had he still relied on inner ear fluid for balance, the effect would have been dizzying. Everything around him had taken on a shade of red or blue. There were no different colors except for those. He could no longer recall having ever discerned colors except red and blue.

The last thing Mark recognized before the world around him became nothing but a strange duotone landscape of odd structures and alien creatures was Peter Mayberry's gigantic ancient fingers descending over top of him. The pianist towered over him, the pads of his fingers practically the size of Mark's face. Peter, the giant, used those pads to pinch Mark under the armpits and raise him into the air. He hovered there for a minute before Peter's thunderous footsteps stomped across the floor of Beard's general with him in tow.

The forward motion created a wind that stung his new eyes. He wanted to blink against it, but he no longer had eyelids. Every signal he sent to the muscles that should move them went unheeded.

Then he was falling. The rough and dry pads of Peter's thumb and forefinger fell away from him. The electric shock of impact in his limbs followed a sensation of tumbling through the air.

He hit metal. Or something that sounded like it, anyway. Mark sensed it in more than just his arms and legs. There were extra sensations of impact along his belly and down around his jaw. It was like he'd grown a series of new limbs on every side of his body. His entire field of vision was suddenly surrounded by metal as well. He pondered it for a moment, but a moment was all he had left.

Cognition faded. He had no more brainpower for thinking and reasoning.

He was hungry.

Nothing more.

CHAPTER EIGHTEEN

Donna stirred to the screeches of Theo howling as though he'd just lost a limb. She rolled her head to the right and located the infant, who was cradled in Kathy Beard's lap. Kathy herself sat crisscrossed on the floor less than a foot away. She attempted to soothe Theo by cooing at him and making funny faces, but to no avail. The infant's face was a crimson mask of upset. His tiny balled-up fists trembled over his belly.

"That's his hungry cry," Donna managed groggily when Theo paused for breath. Her voice was weak, low, and raspy. Her tongue was thick in her mouth, making it difficult to form words.

Kathy examined her with relief in her eyes. "Well, look who's up!" she said in the same baby voice she'd been using to entertain Theo. "It's your momma! Yessiree, your momma's awake!" Then, in her normal voice, "How are you feeling, Donna? Do you think you can sit up?"

Donna pulled her legs into arches at the knees and propped herself on her elbows. A wave of dizziness turned the wall of Beard's General into a Vaseline smear for a second, but it dissipated quickly. She sat up and propped her forehead on the fingertips of her left hand. Her bandaged right one rested in her lap.

"I think I'll be okay," she replied. It was a struggle to talk over Theo's police siren-like wails. "I don't know what happened. The last thing I remember was Peter and Mark—"

She glanced around the room. Peter Mayberry and the stranger they all thought of as Marilyn stood together beside a mop bucket. Jerry and Eli leaned against the wall of shelves opposite them, staring. Just staring at Marilyn, mouths hanging stupidly half-open. "Wait, where's Mark?"

Kathy smiled at her piteously. "There's no Mark here," she said. "You went down hard. It's got you confused. You're in my store. It's been raining for hours, and the bridge is washed out. We're kind of sitting ducks until the weather passes and the water recedes. Or until some kind soul brings a boat for us. We need to get this baby fed." She passed Theo to Donna and then waited expectantly. After an awkward few seconds of silence, "Do you need me to get you something to cover up with? A blanket?"

"I don't, uh, breastfeed," Donna answered, tucking her chin.

"Oh. Right."

"There's another bottle of formula in my bag," she added quickly. "It's the last one. It should hold him for a while if you could get that for me. I need you to help me mix up some fresh for him later. I can pay for it. It's just about 15 ounces of water, boiled, mixed with a tablespoon of Karo, and about 9 ounces of unsweetened evaporated milk. Oh, and we'll need to pour that off into bottles to cool it."

Kathy nodded and stood up. "I remember. I'll see what I can do. Meantime, let's get you back over to that table so you can feed this boy."

She stretched out her arms and retrieved Theo from Donna so she could stand. Donna planted her bandaged right hand palm-down on the floor for leverage. It landed in something wet. Surprised, fearing she had reopened the cut, she jerked her left hand away from Kathy and raised her right palm to her face. It wasn't blood, whatever it was. The liquid she'd slapped on the floor was translucent, if a tad ruddy after soaking her bandage. It wasn't viscous like blood or mucus. It was just plain brown creek water.

"Oh!" Kathy exclaimed. "I forgot about your hand. Did you hurt it?"

"No, not at all," Donna replied, still mesmerized by her palm. She looked at the floor where she'd braced herself. A small puddle of dirty brown liquid oozed through the crack in the floorboard near where she sat. Some of it overflowed the bevel and stained the gray planks on each side of it a darker color. "Oh. Oh, God."

"What is it?"

Donna helped herself to her feet and took Theo. The boy had stopped fussing about his hunger pangs and drifted into an unsatisfied slumber again.

"Uh, does this place have a second floor? Or an attic?"

"No," Kathy replied, glancing up at her store's ceiling as if she'd never seen it before. "Nothing but ceiling and rafters up there. Why?"

With the baby in her left arm, Donna dabbed her right palm on her dress. She hoped the water hadn't soaked through her bandage enough to expose her wound to infection.

"Because the creek's decided to come inside."

She pointed to where she'd been sitting. Kathy followed her finger. She gasped as together the women watched a fast-running trickle of rain-swollen creek water roll out of the space between two floorboards nearer to the door. Suddenly the stuff was everywhere. Donna could hear the floorboards groaning, see them bulging against the pressure of the flood's assault.

"Well, shit," Kathy said matter-of-factly. "Jerry! Get the push brooms!"

Behind them, Jerry grabbed Eli by the overalls strap and dragged him into the employees-only room behind the cash register. Seconds later, the boys emerged from the depths of that space, each with a sizeable wood-handled push-broom in hand.

"What do we do with them?" Jerry called.

"Sweep the water out the door!" Kathy snapped back. "What do you think?" She looked at Donna and rolled her eyes. *Kids*, that look said. *They're a handful.*

Kathy put a hand on Donna's shoulder, urging her farther into the store. A few paces backward, and the women were standing on the linoleum that covered the aisles of stock. The floorboards only accounted for a fifth or less of the room's square footage by Donna's estimate. They spanned the width of the building from the cashier's stand to the far wall, laid parallel to the door and window in the front.

"That area used to be part of the front stoop," Kathy explained as if reading her mind. "We closed it in because we didn't need that much porch. We didn't want to take up potential aisle space when we added the cashier's stand."

"What's under us?"

"A crawl space walled in with cinder blocks, I think," Kathy answered. She looked at the floor, shaking her head. "In all my years, I've never seen that creek come out of its banks like this. I mean, how high can it go? It's got to be over five feet from the bottom of the bed."

"It covered the world after God commanded Noah to build the ark," a male voice from behind them said.

Donna pivoted to discover Peter strolling up to them. She had half expected Mark MacDonald, the Nazarene preacher, for reasons she couldn't quite pinpoint. The Marilyn woman stayed several paces behind, seemingly transfixed by the intruding water. She looked confused, even fearful.

Jerry and Eli continued striving in vain to direct the liquid toward the door. The speed of their broom pushing was no match for the expediency of the flood. Their brooms made *swish* sounds with each forward stroke. After each swish, the gaps in the floor cleared but immediately filled and overflowed again.

Jerry was better at the job than Eli, who kept forgetting to lift the bristles off the surface before he pulled the broom back to himself for another push. He was making ripples and waves more than guiding the flow of water.

Kathy was on Peter before Donna could fully process what he'd been saying.

"You," she strained, "go back over there with your friend. I still haven't figured out what happened to Mark MacDonald, but it's not happening to anyone else here if I have anything to say about it. And soon as I can, I'm getting the law out here on both of you."

A lump rose in Donna's throat. "Kathy? Where *is* Mark?"

She opened her mouth to answer, but Peter interrupted her.

"The false prophet is gone," he croaked. "He doubted. He denied. He shall be cast into the lake of fire along with all of those who deny her."

"Peter!" Kathy growled. "Shut the hell up and go stand over there." Then, to Donna, "Mark might be dead. I'm not sure. He attacked that woman over there, and she did... something...to him. I don't think I can describe it." She craned her neck toward Peter and Marilyn. "She's *not God!* She's a *goddamn witch!*

"Come on, Donna. Let's get your baby fed."

Kathy snatched Donna's bag from the floor beside the chair in which she'd spent much of that late afternoon. She bade Donna sit while she rooted for the bottle of formula. She found it quickly and handed it to Donna, who capped it with its nipple. Donna cradled Theo in a gentle slope conducive to feeding and teased the baby's lips with the formula. He took the bottle without question, sucking it down greedily. He chugged a third of the milky stuff in what seemed like seconds.

Donna beamed at her infant son while he supped. Such peace! He did not worry about where his food came from. He was not concerned about when or where his next meal would be provided. He knew only that he had been hungry, and he was being fed.

Donna closed her eyes and listened to the sounds of Theo gulping, sucking, gulping some more. He paused for a breath now and then, but mostly he fed. For a few minutes, everything seemed normal. The downpours and thunder and lightning outside faded into the background. The sickly bright lights inside Beard's General dimmed into the warmth of flame. The *swish, swish, swish* of the push brooms all but disappeared. But most of all, she and Theo were safe and warm, away from bad weather as well as bad husbands and fathers.

Kathy's voice in her left ear startled her out of her reverie.

"He gave me back the money he took," she said softly. "Mark. He gave it back. Even though I didn't say as much,

I'd already forgiven him for taking it. But that doesn't explain how Peter knew, how *she* knew he'd taken it."

"He told me he did it," Donna replied. She'd located the memory of it, although it was distant in her mind, like something that had happened decades ago. "He did feel guilty about it, I think. But he told me something else, too. Something...crazy."

Kathy met her eyes. "Yes?"

Donna swallowed and followed that with a long sigh. "Well, you heard him call her an apostate from Hell. What he told me is that she'd been *feeding* on him all night long, ever since Jerry and Peter dragged her in here. It was some kind of mental connection, I guess. He said she was eating his guilt, like a...well, something he called a sin-eater."

Kathy nodded. "Go on."

"Here's another crazy thing. The whole time he was telling me about it all, I had the weirdest sensation of déjà vu. It seemed like he and I had had that exact conversation before. But we hadn't. Well, there wouldn't have been any reason for us to have, would there?"

"No," Kathy said. "Did you kill Ted?"

The abrupt change of subject startled Donna so severely that she gasped aloud. It dawned on her then that the entire store had heard everything Marilyn had said to her: about her mother, about her china dolls, about Ted and, most significantly, about her having sliced him up with a shard of broken glass that had subsequently dug itself into her palm.

She considered lying to Kathy, but an entire day and evening of unreality had cured her of any notion that she wouldn't be caught. Someone would eventually find his body, no matter what happened tonight. No matter how far she and Theo had run by that time. A woman and an infant on their own amid the economic boom of the past few years would not precisely be inconspicuous.

Instead of manufacturing a cover story, Donna nodded, adding a meek "Yes" just in case Kathy hadn't seen the gesture. A beat of silence passed between them. Donna squirmed in her seat. Theo's feeding position in a short wooden chair intended for use at a kitchen dinette was putting a strain on her back. She opened her mouth to add to her affirmation when Kathy finally spoke up.

"You're about to say he was hitting you and that you were afraid for the baby."

Those were the precise words Donna had been about to utter. She gaped at the woman. "Is it that obvious?"

"I've been getting that same feeling of déjà vu all afternoon, too," Kathy continued. "I can't say for sure that's how I knew what you were going to tell me. I mean, everyone in town knew Teddy had a temper. With that bandage on your hand and those bruises on your face—the makeup doesn't cover the swelling that well—it's an easy guess. You said yourself that any conniving old fortune-teller could hit this stuff on the nose."

"Yeah," she said. "Wait. I said that out loud? I don't remember that."

Kathy smiled. "Well, maybe I just saw it in your face. But I can't shake this feeling, either. I have memories of the boys trying to sweep the water out, even though water has never come into the store before, as far as I know."

Together they eyed the work still going on at the front of the store. Eli had slowed, obviously tired. Jerry swept furiously still, although there didn't seem to be much water to push around anymore. The torrent that had pounded the roof overhead had slackened, and they could no longer hear it over their voices. Donna allowed herself to feel a twinge of hope. This could be the end of it. That was fine with her. Whatever came next, at least she wouldn't be stuck in a general store with a zealot and his weirdly sexy God anymore.

Kathy piped up again. "Have you looked at Peter lately?"

"He looks older somehow."

"Like, older just since he walked in the store today?"

"Yeah," Donna said.

"Yeah."

CHAPTER NINETEEN

Eli's shoulders, biceps, and triceps screamed at him to stop swinging that broom. His gluteus maxima and biceps femora weren't happy, either. Smarty Marty Blalock would have bopped him on the back of the head if he heard him say things like gluteus maxima and biceps femora out loud. He only knew the names of those muscle groups by listening to some of the doctor shows Mrs. Blalock enjoyed on the radio. Besides getting peeks at Jerry Beard's stashes of contraband, listening in on the radio programs was Eli's only real entertainment.

Several of those shows had ended their radio runs and been adapted to television over the past year. Mrs. Blalock said television was of The Devil, however. It was meant to turn Loyal Patriotic Americans into Pinko Commies—mainly that *I Love Lucy* show. To top it off, television allowed young men like himself a window into the glamorous and hedonistic world of Hollywood. It was an invitation to think naughty thoughts that could lead to doing naughty things.

Mrs. Blalock didn't know about Jerry's dirty pictures. She would positively shit her britches if she knew he'd seen a real-life naked woman just an hour or so ago. And she'd double-shit if she could hear him thinking about the word *shit*.

Eli wasn't even sure Marilyn *was* a woman. When he turned his head to catch a glimpse of her as he pushed the creek water around, he felt torn. His emotional reaction to what had happened to Mark MacDonald was shock, revulsion, moral outrage. There was also an intellectual reaction: curiosity and awe at the strange transformations he thought he had seen come over Marilyn and the preacher.

In tandem, those reactions were enough for him to decide that he wanted nothing more to do with the woman who looked like the sexy famous girl from the calendar but was some kind of monstrous (and hungry!) shapeshifter. Then again, she looked like the sexy famous lady from the calendar. *And* he had seen her naked.

The image of that earlier moment in the evening rose to the front of his mind, quickening his heart. He stooped deeper over his work, embarrassed by the physiological consequences of thinking such thoughts. The beads of sweat that had broken out on his forehead from pushing the broom rolled down his cheeks like the heavy rains that had created this chore in the first place.

Suddenly, she was behind him. Watching him. He sensed her there. A shiver of excitement traveled up his spine. He stopped sweeping, propped both hands atop the broom handle, and turned around.

"Hello, Eli," she purred. "I love watching a man work. I'll bet your muscles are just aching, aren't they?" She emphasized the word *aching* in a way that Eli surmised was a double entendre, although that term was not in his vocabulary. They'd never used it in church, on the Blalock farm, or any of Mrs. Blalock's favorite radio shows.

Beside him, Jerry had also stopped working. He eyed them both, lips parted and uncertainty etched across his brow. Jerry's mother and Mrs. Gilliam were occupied with the baby and his bottle. Peter Mayberry crouched by the mop bucket into which he had dropped that thing he'd found on the floor after—

After what? Something had happened a few minutes ago that had involved Peter and Marilyn and someone else whose name was at the edge of his mind but wouldn't tip over. Whoever it was, it was something Marilyn had done to them that had caused Eli to grow suspicious of her. But it must not have been significant after all. If it had been important, like getting Mrs. Blalock's flour, he would remember it.

Peter's right hand rested on the rim of the bucket. He seemed to be teasing its tiny occupant with his fingers from here. Eli took all of this in while trying to avoid Marilyn's gaze without looking like he was trying to avoid Marilyn's gaze. With no help available from the others, he finally allowed his eyes to meet hers.

"Uh. Me?"

Marilyn smiled at him. When her lips pulled back from them, the teeth revealed were pointed and yellow. Eli blinked and looked again. No, they were regular teeth. Well, they were normal Marilyn's teeth, brilliantly white and squarely human behind her enticing, voluptuous lips.

"Of course, you," she replied. "I've seen the way you keep looking at me. You like me. Don't you?"

Eli's chin dropped toward his knees. Blood rushed to his cheeks.

"Come on," Marilyn said. "You don't have to be embarrassed."

She leaned forward as she said it, offering Eli a glimpse down the neck of the coveralls the reluctant Kathy Beard had gifted her. Sometime between when she had walked up to him and her last words, the zipper had magically lowered itself, creating an unobstructed view of her cleavage. His head and neck locked in that space, unwilling to pry himself from the vision.

As if sensing his distress, Marilyn stretched out her right hand. She placed her forefinger on his chin and delicately nudged his head upward. Eli's eyes tracked the motion up her neck to her angelic face.

"Look at me, Eli, you naughty, naughty—"

Something happened to her then. The smooth neck of the girl in the calendar photograph wrinkled and sagged under her chin. It jiggled like a rooster's wattle when she moved. Her cheeks filled out in a way that approached jowly. Her nose became bulbous and speckled with dirty pores. Enormous purple bags bulged under her eyes.

Those eyes! They were no longer the dreamy blue-green he'd been entranced by a moment ago. They were hard and brown, the eyes of someone who had deprived herself of living life and believed everyone else should be just like her. The woman standing before him was not Marilyn Monroe or anyone who looked like her. It was Georgia Blalock.

"—naughty, dirty, evil, sinful BOY!" she screeched at him.

Her lower limbs grew upward like double tree trunks, raising her to ludicrous height. She towered over him the way she had in his head ever since he was orphaned. She trained the finger she was pointing at him between his eyes. Instead of the smooth, young, and pink fingers of Marilyn

Monroe with their sexy nails, the fingers on the hands of *his* Marilyn had grown coarse patches of white hair along their backsides. They ended in yellow nails caked with visible layers of keratin that split in multiple places along the tips.

"Why didn't you come home, boy?" this lunatic incarnation of Mrs. Blalock demanded. Her jaw unhinged and reconnected with each word she spoke, making her look like a sinister ventriloquist's dummy come to life. "You were supposed to buy some flour. Then you were supposed to come home."

The thing rolled her head to the left and glared at Jerry, who gaped wide-eyed at them over the handle of his broom. "You!" she shrieked. "It was your dirty pictures that kept him so long. You are the corrupter. Devil boy!" From thin air, she produced the Marilyn Monroe calendar, pinching it between her knotted fingers in a fashion that resembled the way Kathy had toted it across the room to Jerry when she'd discovered it in the drawer. The smiling strawberry blonde in the glossy photo belly rolled for him as the thing that was and was not Georgia Blalock shook the calendar in his face.

"What were you planning to do with it, Eli? Did you study her long enough to commit her to memory? Her naughty points, too? Were you going to touch yourself in the bathroom tonight while you thought about her? Were you going to stroke your prick *in my house*? Under *my* roof? Where *my God watches over me and YOU*?"

Laughter erupted from elsewhere in the room. Eli scanned the area to see Peter sitting by the mop bucket, an enormous shit-eating grin on his face. One hand rested on his belly. It rode the waves of his abdomen up and down as he chortled.

Across the aisle, Donna and Kathy stared at him. Their faces bore twin shocked expressions, mirth gleaming in their eyes. He didn't even need to look at Jerry. Eli could hear him laughing from somewhere behind him. It was a braying laugh, the kind that made you tilt your face at the sky when it overcame you.

Hot shame burned his skin. His eyes felt funny, like his eyeballs were melting in their sockets and running down his cheeks. The world went red before him. It wavered in his vision like steam rising from hot asphalt on the first cool rain following a late July drought.

"Aren't you ashamed?" Mrs. Blalock asked him, her voice hoarse with rage.

Eli met her black onyx eyes with his tearful pleading ones. "I *am* ashamed!" he replied. "I am ashamed!"

"You should be, boy. You're damned to Hell on account of your lust. There's no forgiveness. No redemption. You're guilty. You're a bad, bad boy. Shame!"

Eli searched his mind for something to counter her judgment. He went to church sometimes with Mrs. Blalock. But did he *really* pay attention when he did? Like a good boy would?

He did his chores every day. That was good. But was his heart *really* in them? Didn't his mind too often wander back to Beard's General and, more specifically, Jerry's frequent new additions of lovelies that were not hidden well enough from his mother's discovery? In the end, he could not conjure up any good thing he had done that outweighed the bad.

Red steam exploded from him and streamed from his eyes, nose, ears, and mouth. It escaped from the cuffs of his shirt, his collar, the flares around his work boots. It oozed from his pores like the creamy contents of erupting cysts.

Mrs. Blalock lapped at the rising stuff like a thirsty stray dog laps at a puddle in a pothole. Her ample, middle-aged bosom expanded toward him as she sucked the stuff down her throat and up her nostrils.

And then he was spent. Eli collapsed to the damp planks of Beard's General, his forehead making a bone-chilling *smack* sound. He did not fall unconscious, but his head did feel lighter somehow.

All the burden of his lust had been drawn out of him. He might not be forgiven, but he suddenly no longer experienced guilt over the sensations that arose in his pants when he gazed at the naked woman in the calendar photo. Nor was he ashamed that everyone knew the pictures made him want to touch himself at night when everyone except him was asleep, when the memory surfaced unbidden of a nude Marilyn Monroe smiling at him from beyond the frame of some bizarre distant dimension.

The patter of approaching feet came from every direction. Shadows surrounded him the way they must have covered Donna when she went down earlier in almost this exact spot. There was something familiar to him about having fallen on his face here, more so than watching Mrs. Gilliam's fainting spell. He couldn't quite put his finger on it. It was like he'd done this before in a different age, a different life. Yet in this same place.

Hands gripped his shoulders and raised him. He opened his eyes to see Marilyn sitting on the floor by the mop bucket beside Peter. Her coveralls were zipped up to her neck. Her face and hands bore no signs of stretch or strain, no indication that she had ever transformed into anything resembling Mrs. Blalock. She was the picture of disinterest in whatever was happening with him and the folks at the front of the store.

"Are you all right, hon?" he heard Kathy say in his ear as she and Jerry raised him to a sitting position. "That was quite a fall."

He didn't answer at first.

Was he all right?

He wasn't sure.

CHAPTER TWENTY

Jerry joined his mother at his goofy friend Eli's side and helped him up from the floor. Together, they walked him to Kathy's stool behind the cash register. The drawer was sensibly closed, although Kathy's stack of receipts, pencil, and arithmetic remained scattered and forgotten on top of the stand. She scooped up the pile of papers and shoved them in a lower drawer, one slot above the one where Jerry had hidden his girlie contraband. Out of sight, out of mind. At least until this hell night ended and she returned to her entrepreneurial senses.

Kathy fetched Eli a glass of water from the back, placed it in his hands, told him to sip it, and left the boys to rejoin the only other mother in the place that evening.

Eli looked white as a sheet. In his mind, Jerry had already diagnosed the problem as overwork. God knows what heinous physical activity Eli had been forced to perform over at the Blalock farm before they sent him on his flour errand that afternoon. He'd jumped up to help Jerry sweep away the flood water on top of all that. Poor guy must be exhausted.

"Did you see that?" Eli asked him, looking sidelong at Jerry. His eyes were wide in their sockets. Haunted. He gripped his unsipped glass of water loosely in his right hand. It tilted precariously, the contents lapping at its lip.

Jerry gently pried the vessel loose from Eli's grip and placed it on the cashier's stand in front of them. "I *heard* it, man," he replied. "You went down hard. Those boots of yours must've got some creek slime on the soles or something."

Eli shook his head vigorously. "No, man," he said. "That wasn't it. Come on, don't fuck with me. I saw you watching us. Everybody in the store saw it. That woman, she changed. She turned into Mrs. Blalock, started getting on me about that calendar. She had it in her hand. She shoved it in my face and told me I do sissy stuff like touch myself at night. She said I was hopeless. Ruined because of my l—lust."

A gigantic tear crept from the corner of his left eye. Jerry watched it roll down his cheek, drop off his jaw, and splatter on the floor. It blended easily with the dark stains from the creek water.

"Hey, man—"

"Then something else happened. My head got, I don't know, *hot* is the best way I can describe it. This stuff, this weird red smoke, started coming out of me. She was eating it. Snorting it, more like. Or inhaling it. Looked like she was having a ball."

"Eli," Jerry said, lowering his voice. He leaned in so that his friend could hear him, hoping that the others in the store could not. "I think getting stuck here is doing something to your mind, man. The chick who looks like Marilyn Monroe has been sitting over there by the mop bucket with Peter Mayberry ever since we grabbed the brooms. Before that, even. I wasn't paying a whole lot of attention to what was going on behind us, but I never saw her get up and walk over to you. Not one time. One minute we were sweeping water, the next, you were on the floor. That's all I know."

He scanned the shelf on the opposite wall where he had stowed the calendar after he and Peter had dragged the naked woman in from the rain. There it remained, rolled up in a paper telescope from all the handling of it after his mother had discovered it in the cash register drawer. Jerry elbowed Eli in the ribs and indicated the spot with his finger.

"There," he said. "That's where I put the calendar after I found her outside. It's still there, exactly where I left it. Nobody's touched it, buddy. You just hit your head. Had a bad dream or a hallucination or something."

Eli looked him in the eye. "What about the other guy? The one she ate, or crushed, or whatever it was she did to him?"

Jerry frowned. "What other guy?"

"What do you mean 'what other guy?'" Eli snapped. "The other guy. The church guy. M—uh. Well, his name started with an M and—"

"And what?"

"And something happened…" he trailed off. His face screwed up in befuddlement as if the name and event he thought he was remembering sat just on the tip of his tongue but was stuck there.

"There's nobody else here, man," Jerry said after a beat. "It's you, me, my mom, Donna Gilliam, Peter Mayberry, and the pretty lady we saved from the storm." An idea occurred to him then. "Hey! What if you're dehydrated? Your mind can play tricks on you when you haven't had enough water. Mom's always on my case about drinking enough water." He grabbed the glass from the cashier's stand and offered it to Eli again. The boy accepted it and began to sip.

"That's it," Jerry said. "Sip it. Don't gulp. If you're dehydrated, gulping it will make you barf. Ironic, huh? We're surrounded by it, but all you can do is take little sips out of this glass. 'Water, water everywhere but not a drop to drink,' huh?"

"You make that up?" Eli said, grinning. A wave of relief washed over Jerry when he saw his friend's face alight.

"Nah. Some dead guy did, I guess. Ancient mariner or some damn thing. I don't know. They talk about it in school sometimes."

"I don't go to school anymore," Eli reminded him.

"Oh, right." Jerry punched his friend playfully on the shoulder, nearly spilling his water. "You're too smart for us educated folks."

That made Eli snort laughter out loud, music to Jerry's ears. He plopped down on the floor beside Eli's stool and surreptitiously examined the state of the store. Peter and Marilyn remained by the mop bucket. The former occasionally played with whatever that thing was he'd trapped in it. Probably something washed in from the creek when the water lapped up through the floor planks.

The Marilyn lookalike had a strangely serene expression on her face as she sat with a straight back and her palms on her knees. It was a look of satisfaction, as if she'd just cut a long and particularly odiferous fart.

Jerry's mom and the Gilliam woman fussed over the baby. Mom's back was turned to them, which was great. She had ears like radar dishes, but they didn't seem to work as well when they weren't pointed in his direction. She always told him that he got the big flaps on the sides of his head from his father. He thought it more likely that they'd come from her side.

"Psst. Eli," he said, tugging on the boy's pants leg. "Hop down here. There's something else I want to bash ears about."

Eli did as he asked. The legs of the stool scooted a volley of staccato *clack* sounds over the floor as he slid out of it. They reverberated throughout the front of the store. Jerry winced and glanced around again. None of the others paid the disturbance any mind.

"What's up, doc?"

"You know what you were saying before?" Jerry whispered. "About 'sissy stuff?'"

Eli grimaced but nodded slowly.

"Listen, man, I know it hasn't been easy growing up around old lady Blalock. She's square, always gets hacked when she thinks somebody enjoys something she can't have for herself. I hope I haven't been getting you into any trouble with the girlie pictures."

Crimson blossomed in the boy's cheeks. "She hasn't—" He paused as if struggling to remember. "I don't *think* she knows anything about it. But that doesn't stop her from accusing me of stuff."

Jerry nodded. "I get it. So, I'm gonna let you in on a secret that's gonna make you feel better. Everybody—and I mean *everybody*—flogs their log."

Eli snorted, his lips spread wide across his face. He shaded his eyes with one hand and then ran the palm down to cover his mouth. Jerry smiled along with him.

"Cross my heart," he said and then did so with the forefinger of his right hand. "If I'm lyin', I'm dyin'. Every man you can think of and every boy over the age of thirteen beats their meat from time to time."

"Even President Eisenhower?" Eli asked, chuckling.

"Especially President Eisenhower," Jerry answered. "How else do you think he keeps his cool when he negotiates all those peace treaties with the Ruskies? He blows off the steam the night before. To pictures of Marilyn Monroe, I'd guess."

"What about Mamie?"

"I doubt Marilyn's her type."

Eli howled. He couldn't help it. He laughed so hard that his belly ached. He gripped it with both hands, trying to hold it steady as tears streamed from the corners of both eyes. Donna and Jerry's mother looked at them from another part of the store, trying to see what was so funny. Although they were not in on the joke, they open-mouth smiled at the two young men as if about to break into laughter themselves.

"All right, all right, simmer down. Do you get it? Cool?"

Eli's grin faded, the calculations going on inside his head etched across his brow. A second later, his smile resurfaced. "Yeah, man," he said. "I get it."

"Good." Jerry leaned back against the wall, narrowly avoiding a bump on the head from a low shelf. He sighed, satisfied that he might've solved a problem he hadn't even known he'd caused. He'd need to be more careful about how he shared his treasures in the future. He could ask Eli about his day at the Blalock farm before he offered to let him see any new pictures. If the square was having a really quadrangular day, he'd skip it and wait for a better time. No sense in causing Eli any more trouble than he already had at the place.

"Hey, Jer?" Eli's voice called.

Jerry sensed exhaustion in it. "Yeah, man?"

"Do you think Joseph McCarthy flogs his log?"

Jerry smirked. "Yeah, probably over Lucille Ball. Or maybe Desi Arnaz does it more for him. I told you. Everybody does it."

"Even girls?"

"Girls don't have logs to flog, Eli. How sheltered *are* you?"

"Then how do they feel...you know?"

Jerry thought for a moment. "That's a good question," he said. "They have to have something in there that gets rubbed the right way, don't they?"

"Yeah, I guess so." He shifted uncomfortably, not happy with the answer.

Jerry nudged him. "Hey, I've got an idea how we can find out." He cocked a thumb at the woman in the coveralls.

Eli's eyes narrowed. "What are you talking about?"

"Why don't we ask our friend Marilyn over there?"

"We can't do that!"

"Well, you want to know, don't you? Would you want to ask somebody from around here? Want to ask my mom or Mrs. Gilliam? I reckon they'd both know, but I don't think I want them gossiping about how much we *don't* know at the next church social, do you?"

"Your mom doesn't go to church socials."

"You know what I mean, goof," Jerry chided.

"Yeah, I know what you mean."

"Come on. I double-dog dare ya. We'll go over there together, see if we can pry her away from Peter Mayberry and his pet long enough for a chit-chat."

"I don't know, Jer."

"Nope. We're doing it." He stood up, pulling Eli by the back of his collar as he did. The two young men glanced first at each other, then at Marilyn. Jerry noted that she was looking back at them, a pleasingly sensual curl of a smile played across her lips. She raised her right hand and beckoned to them with her forefinger.

Jerry's heart beat fast in his chest, pounding against the wall so loud that he thought he could hear it in his ears. A startling clap of thunder caused the floor beneath them to tremble. Then the lights went out in Beard's General.

CHAPTER TWENTY-ONE

"Well, shit!" an angry feminine voice shouted through the darkness. "Jerry! Find the emergency candles. I forgot to grab them before it got dark outside."

Eli heard, or rather intuited, Jerry's departure from his side as the young man divined his way through the blackened void that enveloped everything. He reckoned that a bolt of lightning must've hit a pole somewhere and exploded a transformer. That, or it struck a tree that fell onto a line.

Mr. Blalock often complained about Lost Hollow's lackluster maintenance of the overhanging tree branches that lined the roads throughout this area of Hollow County.

"We'd spend a lot less time in the got-damned dark if they'd just cut the got-damned trees back every got-damned August like they're supposed to," he'd moan whenever the farmhouse lost power. Meanwhile, Mrs. Blalock would chide him for taking the Lord's name while she gathered up any nearby emergency candles and ignited their wicks with a match from the box she kept in her apron pocket at all times. Ever-prepared, that woman was.

Eli occasionally wondered if the old lady had a secret smoking habit. It would've been her *only* vice if she had, at least as far as she was concerned. Well, unless she had a log she could flog.

But that wasn't a vice anymore, was it? The more Eli considered what Jerry had explained to him about jacking off, the more enraged he became over how the woman of the farmhouse had shamed him. He'd been lied to. There were layers of injury because of it. First was her assumption that he was doing it at all, let alone in inappropriate places. He *was* doing it but, as it turns out, that's none of her business. Did she want to know when and where he was taking a shit, too? How much different was shooting a load than squeezing a turd, anyway? At least in terms of privacy. Shitting was a release, too, although it didn't cause quite the same tingle of electricity in his nerve endings that flogging did.

"Shitting is something everyone has to do," the quavering, sharp-edged voice of Georgia Blalock cut through the darkness. It sounded like she was standing right in front of him, close enough for him to feel her breath on his skin. Eli let out a loud yelp and took a single step backward, thrusting his fists out in a defensive stance as he did.

"Everybody shits," the voice continued. "Because everybody eats. It's what God intended. But God did not intend for you to go around always playing the fiddle on your diddle, especially not in *my* house!"

Eli squinted. Jerry had yet to return with the candles. Even so, Eli's eyes were beginning to adjust to the darkness. He could discern the outline of Georgia Blalock standing a few inches in front of him. She wasn't a giant this time. Not yet. She was shorter than the Marilyn woman, stooped with age and the wear and tear of life as the farmer's wife.

"Nuh-uh," Eli retorted. "You've been lying to me. Jerry says everybody does it. Probably even President Eisenhower."

He paused, then added, "I'll bet Mr. Blalock does it, too! I'll bet he does it all the time when you're not around!"

A snarl vibrated the dark around him. It was not like any animal he'd ever heard on the farm. It was terrifying yet familiar. Then it clicked with Eli that he was remembering what had happened to him once before in this same space. Marilyn had transformed before his eyes. She had grown into a gigantic vulpine caricature of Mrs. Blalock. She had chided him for his wandering hands then, too. When she had succeeded in forcing the shame from him, he had started to, to *steam*. She had absorbed it, inhaled it. Although crystal clear in his mind, the memory seemed as though it was from an event that had happened to him long before. Decades, possibly. How could that be?

Something else had happened before, too. She had eaten up the preacher, Mark MacDonald. She had fed on him until there was nothing left of him to feed on. Instead of inhaling red steam from him when he ran at her, Marilyn had sucked on him until every bit of his humanity had simply dried up. Had he known what she was? What she was doing? Why hadn't he spewed red steam like Eli had that time?

"You're a bad, bad boy, Eli Wynn," the thing growled at him from the darkness. "You should beg for forgiveness. Plead your case before your God. Let it be known before him and me that what you do is sinful. You condemn yourself every time you think about the sexy ladies and every time you touch yourself to them. Every. Time."

Eli's clenched fists trembled. Nothing had changed except that the Marilyn-Georgia Blalock thing had laid it all out loud in the middle of the store. Talking with yourself and your best friend about jacking off was one thing. Coming from her, it sounded like he was doing something sinister, shameful, something he should feel wrong about. Then he did. Red steam wafted from his nostrils, his mouth, his collar, his ears. It was hot where it caressed his skin as it rose into the night.

"No!" Eli shouted. He shut his eyes and conjured Jerry in his mind. Jerry, who always seemed to have it all together. Jerry, who never lost his cool, even when rising creek water threatened to overtake his momma's store. Jerry, who perceived no shame when looking at pretty gals. The Jerry in his mind reminded him that everyone does it. Even President Eisenhower. Even Joe McCarthy. "Everybody touches it sometimes! I'm not doing anything wrong!"

"Your friend hides his girlie pictures from his mother," came the hoary old woman's response. "He knows it is shameful. He knows he is depriving your soul of eternal life in paradise. Shame!"

"No!" Eli shouted again, opening his eyes. Although wrapped in total darkness, he could clearly see the angry bitch Mrs. Blalock. She stood nose-to-nose with him, her hateful eyes narrowed to angular slits. Yellow pointed teeth lined her cracked and blackened gums. She inhaled while he stared at her, seeking more of the red stuff. There was no more to be had. The corneas of her wolfen eyes splintered bloodshot.

Eli's confidence soared. He leaned closer to her. "Just because another person thinks something is shameful doesn't make it so. Sometimes you just want to do things without worrying about people's opinions. *That's* why Jerry hides it. Not because he's doing something wrong."

Rage made itself known in the Georgia Blalock creature's face. Her hairy, clawed hands stretched out for him. Before he could reverse course, she had pressed a palm into each side of his head. Eli grabbed her by the wrists, hating the way the coarse furriness prickled his fingers and palms. He tried to yank her hands away from him. Her vise-like grip would not be loosed. She only squeezed harder.

Eli wanted to scream. The pressure inside his skull was too intense. His eyes felt like they were bulging so far out from his eyelids he could no longer blink. They burned when the hot breath of the beast breezed against them. Fluid drained from them, something thicker and slower running than tears. His tongue protruded involuntarily from between his lips. A drop of the stuff from his eyes ran over its tip. It was salty but had a chunky consistency to it as if he'd just eaten a booger.

The sensation made him want to gag, but that reflex seemed to be out to lunch for the moment. Before him, the Mrs. Blalock thing transformed into something unrecognizable. She was no longer the stern farmer's wife, nor Marilyn Monroe lookalike. She was only a wide mouth with a cavernous, red-ribboned throat undulating behind it. The floor of the mouth was carpeted with a mucous-glazed tongue that forked at the end. It wagged separately from the undulating throat, greedily seeking that first succulent taste of him.

Eli's entire face pulled away from his skull and into a jet engine as the maw closed in, obscuring his entire field of vision. His mind fogged over, too. Words became more challenging to find. More than that, his ability to remember how to remember words had diminished. Except for occasional flashes of cognition, he was forgetting how to think.

Something new was happening to his body, too. It wasn't like changes he'd experienced before, not like the ones from his early stages of puberty. It was painful, but not like the growing pains in his legs that had sometimes awakened him from sleep screaming back in those days. They were also not slow changes, like the peach fuzz he used to have to shave before his jawline finally became peppered every morning with the sandpaper stubble of a man. His body collapsed in on itself, imploding.

The final coherent thought to cross Eli Wynn's mind wasn't a thought at all. It was a snatch of a song he'd heard not too long ago. Or was it a long, long time ago? It might have been from a Western movie. He couldn't remember. The lyrics were there one instant and gone the next, drifting in and out of memory like the detritus of sea life in the tide. The words had something to do with a river. Something about returning to the river. Or not returning to it. And Marilyn Monroe was there.

Then the song, along with the rest of his humanity, was gone from his memory. Eli Wynn was out of his mind.

CHAPTER TWENTY-TWO

The passing aroma of sulfur fast followed the sound of a struck match. A radius of orange light floated a few inches across the room in front of Donna Gilliam. It flared bright on the wick of the first of four emergency candles that Jerry had placed on the table near the front center of the store.

Three more candles ignited in quick succession. Their combined flickering created dancing shadows that elongated and contracted all along the walls of Beard's General. Donna's eyes adjusted to the new environment in time to see Peter Mayberry pluck a small dark object from the floor nearby. He strode purposefully with it back to where he had been sitting when the lights went out. There, he dropped the thing into the mop bucket alongside the first critter he'd been babysitting.

Where were those things coming from anyway? They were small, but Donna thought it odd that a second one had been capable of squeezing through the cracks in the floorboards. Especially now that the water running fast and high beneath the front of the store had receded some. It had seeped into the building like a roach or a spider. Or a field mouse. Both things in the bucket were closer to the size of a field mouse.

Something else was wrong. It could be an illusion of her new perspective by candlelight, but the group of neighbors gathered in the store seemed smaller suddenly, like one of them had sneaked out the front door and swam away in the flood under cover of darkness.

"Something's different," Kathy Beard intoned from beside her.

Donna inhaled profoundly and sighed it out, relieved that it wasn't just her. "You feel it, too, huh?"

"Yeah."

"I can't place it. It's like someone's missing. I keep looking around for another person, but my head is telling me everyone is accounted for."

Kathy raised her accounting finger and enumerated heads out loud. "There's you, me, Jerry, Peter, and the weird chick."

Donna dropped her eyes to the infant in her arms. Theo had taken the power outage as a cue and drifted into whatever magical land it was that babies dream about. *If* babies dreamed. Kathy caught her gaze.

"And Theo there makes six," she added. "Sorry. I don't think of young'uns that small as being separate from their mommies yet."

Donna smiled. "Well, he is pretty much a wiggly accessory."

"Enjoy it if you can," Kathy replied, a wan smile surfacing on her lips. "I was grateful when Jerry over there got old enough to wipe his butt instead of shitting a diaper and squalling about it."

She paused, then added, "Honestly, Donna? Sometimes I feel guilty about thinking it, but his daddy's passing opened my eyes to a few things about myself. I wasn't that great a mother. Well, I wasn't a *bad* mother, but my heart wasn't really in it, either.

"Jerry's a good kid, and I think I did a decent job of raising him. If this was a different world or even just a different time, I'm not sure I would've gotten married in the first place. I love Jerry, and I wouldn't take anything for him, but I *know* that if I had it all to do over my way, I wouldn't have had a kid."

Donna shifted uncomfortably in her seat, drawing Theo closer to her bosom. Kathy patted her on the knee.

"Oh, I'm not saying what's right for me is right for every woman," she said. "I like running a business. More than that, I like *owning* a business. Sure, it's a struggle sometimes, more stress than I'd like to have on my mind while I'm tossing and turning in the bed at night. But I can tell you that I know a hell of a lot of women who are housewives and addicted to Valium. Me? I don't even smoke cigarettes."

She scoffed. "I guess what I'm trying to say is that not having a man around isn't the end of the world. In the end, you and Theo are going to be better off than if you had kept living under Ted Gilliam."

A tear streamed from Donna's right eye. She dabbed at it with her bandaged hand. "Even if I'm in prison and he's a ward of the state?"

Kathy pursed her lips together, glowering. Her hand left Donna's knee and landed on her own. She stroked the tops of her thighs with her palms and opened her mouth as if to speak, but no answer came.

"That's what I thought," Donna replied. "Listen, I appreciate what you're trying to do. But you didn't kill your man. You didn't suffer through all the hitting and screaming. You weren't constantly afraid he would kill your son just for doing what babies do. I admire what you've done here,

Kat. I do. But you've achieved what you have under very, very different circumstances from mine."

"You could run," Kathy said. It came out in a quiet monotone, betraying neither opinion nor judgment. "Like you talked about before. You could leave Theo here and run. I promise you he wouldn't live out his youth in an orphanage. I'd make sure of that. I may just be another woman, but as a business owner and the only source of trade for miles, I do have some political muscle I can flex around town."

Donna hadn't considered that prospect. She'd thought about running with Theo but nixed the idea because a single woman with a baby stood out like a sore thumb in a world where everything you did or said or thought had to be approved by a man first. She would have to allow people to assume her husband had died naturally or run off. Or that she'd had the kiddo out of wedlock. None of those options sounded as freeing as adopting a new name and going out on her own. She could find a job waitressing or as a secretary. Without Theo to burden her—

But no. She couldn't.

"I love him," she said matter-of-factly. "I can't leave him."

Kathy stared straight ahead. Still speaking in that monotone voice, she said, "If you love him, then at this point, the best thing you can do for him is leave him."

Fury boiled in the center of Donna's chest. Her lips drew up in a tight sneer over her chin. Her nostrils flared in a distinctively masculine way. If she could have seen herself in a mirror, she would've recognized the face she was making as the same one her dear departed hubby Ted used to make whenever dinner was late to the table.

Kathy had stepped over a line. No, not stepped over it. She had trod directly *on* the line. Then she'd ground it into the dust with the heel of her boot.

Donna wanted to lash out at her, give her the what-for about lecturing another parent on what she should do with her child. She didn't, however. Because she recognized that much of what Kathy had said wasn't infuriating because of the line-crossing. It was infuriating because she was right.

A loud grumbling sound from across the room caught her ear, shoving her anger to the back of her mind. She followed the sound and noticed Marilyn, legs splayed unsexily in front of her. She sat on the floor beside Peter and the mop bucket. The candlelight created shadows that licked greedily at the hollows of her cheeks. The woman's right hand was on her belly. Her nose was screwed up in a sneer. Her eyes were squinted in a way that made it look like someone had glued her asshole shut and she needed to squeeze out a turd.

She noticed Donna's gaze and met it unflinchingly, adjusting nothing in her expression or posture. There was unashamed evil in that look that shocked Donna down in the depths of her flailing humanity. Ordinary people instinctively changed their behavior when being watched, even if they weren't doing anything embarrassing or wrong. This woman, this sensually beautiful woman who looked like a movie star, had no such instincts. Or she had trained herself not to obey them.

A cold chill ran up Donna's spine. She tried to tear her eyes away from Marilyn. Instead, her head only trembled on its stalk and refused to comply. Donna's mind raced, searching for something to say or do that could break the tension between them.

Marilyn's stomach panged again. She winced as her body made involuntary efforts to process food that was not there.

"H—Hey!" Donna managed finally. Her voice quaked shrilly in her ears, and it felt humiliating. "Are you hungry?"

Peter looked up from his mop bucket long enough to grace her with a smirk. "What do *you* think, Einstein? We can all hear it."

A sly grin curled Marilyn's lips.

"Well," Donna said, casting her eyes to the floor, "I just thought Kathy might have something she could eat. You know, if it's bothering her."

"*For I was hungry, and you gave me food,*" Peter intoned. "*I was thirsty, and you gave me drink. I was a stranger, and you took me in. I was naked and you clothed me.* Matthew 25, verses 35 and 36. That what you're getting at, Donna Gilliam?"

Donna cast a glance at Kathy and rolled her eyes. "I guess," she said. "Just seemed like the decent thing to do."

"The *godly* thing," Peter admonished. "For our Savior was naked, and we clothed her. She is hungry. We should feed her." He glared at Kathy. "*You* should feed her."

"Fine," Kathy replied. "Did she happen to have some cash stashed somewhere we couldn't see when you dragged her in from the rain?"

Peter huffed. "You would deny her when she is obviously in need?"

Kathy stood up and dusted imaginary dirt from her hips. "I'm not your church, Peter Mayberry. I don't have anything against charity, but you two have acted weird ever since she got here. It's like she's got a hold on you. She's pretty, Peter. We can all see that. But that's all she is. She ain't Jesus. If you just get your hands out of my dirty mop bucket for a minute, you can dig in your pockets and buy her some food if you're so worried about her.

"You'll have to wait for the electricity to come back if you want something hot, though. The range is electric. I modernized some of the appliances in the back a couple of years ago, including the range and the freezer. I still need somebody to haul away the old one that's sitting against the wall over there. I bought the new ones in the days when people paid their bills and before they started begging me for free stuff, though."

As if they'd heard her, the overhead lights in Beard's General suddenly buzzed back to life. The *click* sound and flare of sudden brightness startled a short gasp out of Donna. Her heart skipped two beats. It had just settled back into its normal rhythm when Theo started screaming.

"Oh! I guess someone else is hungry, too," Donna said to the baby. She bent to find the bottle he'd been working on when he'd drifted off. It was nearly empty, which wasn't good because neither she nor Kathy had yet found occasion in this mess of a night to mix any fresh. She raised the nipple to Theo's lips and allowed him to take the bottle. He began to suck immediately.

"Well, look at that," Marilyn's voice echoed in her ears from inches away. "He and I have something in common!"

Donna looked up from Theo to find Marilyn standing directly over her, a malicious rictus spread over the lower half of her face.

CHAPTER TWENTY-THREE

Buster McNath was already pissed off when he sank ankle-deep in the mud outside Ted Gilliam's home that night. It hadn't been pouring when he'd left the job site to pay the lazy bum a visit he really couldn't afford. He could barely see through the sheets of water falling from the skies. The trip down the backwoods lane to Ted's house had been easy enough for his pickup. He hadn't expected the ground to be so soft and deep. Water brimming with clumps of saturated earth poured into a hole in the sole of his boots. He aimed the beam of his Rayovac at his feet and groaned.

"Goddammit!" Buster gruffed. Those Montgomery Wards Powr House boots were practically brand new. He'd already cussed that dumb son of a bitch Roy Robinson for dropping planks nails-up where people have to walk. While eyeing the oncoming weather, Buster had stepped on a protruding nail and driven it entirely through the sole. He'd been lucky, however. The tip of it had only penetrated the space right between his first and second digits. Should've fired Roy's ass for that, but Buster already had too much on his mind.

The wet sock inside his boot was the final straw. If he'd had any inklings about a change of heart when he'd arrived outside Ted's house, they were gone. He was going to get fired tonight.

The mud yanked at his boot as he wrenched it free. He shook that foot wildly in front of him, trying to rid himself of the annoying slosh in the moc toe. The ooky stuff had found its way inside easily enough, but it wasn't keen to leave.

"Shit," Buster mumbled. "Forget it." He glared at the front door of Ted's house which, bizarrely, was standing partially open despite the nasty wind and rain. It creaked on its hinges with each powerful gust and then slowly returned to its original angle, not quite closed but not entirely open.

"Damn thing's not plumb," he said. "Just like Gilliam. Should've fired him a long time ago."

He stormed to the door and pounded three times on the facing with the ball of his right fist.

"Gilliam! Where you at, boy? It's Buster!" He waited. The only response was the driving rain pouring from the gutters on each side of the front porch.

"Mrs. Donna?" he called, softening his tone a bit. "It's Buster McNath. Ted didn't show up at the job site today. Any idea where he is?"

No reply.

Buster sighed. *Well, now you gonna go and make me feel bad about firing ya if something's happened to ya.*

"Ted?" he tried once more. When that produced no response, Buster placed a palm on the front door and pushed it inward. He stepped across the threshold into total darkness. He fumbled for a light switch on the interior wall with his left out. He found one and flipped it up. Nothing.

"Power must be out. This just gets better and better, don't it?"

Suddenly glad he hadn't left the flashlight in the truck, Buster aimed it into the rooms beyond him and scanned from right to left. No sign of life. He had walked into what looked like a living area. A kitchen opened to the right. A hallway in the back of the room led into darker depths than the beam of his Rayovac wouldn't reach.

"Ted? Mrs. Donna?"

He treaded cautiously through the living area. The bedrooms were probably in the back of that hall. Buster had never made a habit of walking into folks' houses without an invitation, much less their bedrooms. But something about the quiet here wasn't sitting right with him. He wondered whether Ted missed work for some reason besides being a lazy, good-for-nothin' drunk who probably belonged in a prison pulling levers on a license plate press more than he belonged on a construction site with a saw in his hand.

The first door he arrived at was on the right side of the hallway. Buster peered in without stepping through, shining his flashlight in every corner. *This must be the nursery.* Baby Gilliam's crib stood against the far wall. Beside it sat a rocking chair with a small blue blanket draped over one arm as if waiting for mother and child to return. The room was stacked with stuff mothers require for baby care, at least as Buster understood it. There was no indication that the family had packed up and left town.

He backed out of the room and turned to examine the door on the left side of the hallway. This one was closed. "Ted?" He knocked and waited. Silence. The doorknob felt weird in his grip. A shiver of either fear or excitement crept from his balls and into his belly when he turned it and pushed the door.

Buster trailed the beam of his flashlight over what looked like drops of black and dried-up liquid on the floor. He followed their trail to the rear wall of the room where sat a bloated and milky-eyed Ted. Rain poured through a busted window above him where a tree had uprooted and crashed into the house, thanks to the saturated ground surrounding it, no doubt. The rain had soaked Ted's hair and ran down the sides of his face like water from a showerhead.

The corpse's head was cocked to one side. The puffy purple bags under his eyelids drooped over ashen cheekbones. His jaw was slack. He had a questioning look as if he'd awakened from a nice, normal nap seated against the bedroom wall in a pool of his coagulated blood only to find himself drenched in rainwater while his boss stood over him. He looked like he was about to ask Buster what had happened and what the hell he was doing there. He wore a surreal man-in-the-moon expression on his face. It would've been funny if it wasn't so abjectly terrifying.

The soft flesh of Ted's second chin sported a jagged line carved across it, made more prominent thanks to the way his slump against the wall bent his neck forward. To Buster, it looked like the blood of four or five men Ted's size had poured out of that wound, painting the man and everything under him in the viscous oil of life.

Buster's heart throbbed in his temples. The pain broke his paralysis, enabling him to think again. It must've been a break-in, possibly even a robbery and kidnapping. Whoever had killed Ted had taken his wife and brat along with them to—well, to God knew where. Or Donna and the kid were still hiding somewhere in the house.

Oh, shit, he thought. *The* robbers *could still be here, too!*

He was suddenly aware that he was utterly alone on a stormy night in an unlit, unfamiliar house turned crime scene. Buster decided to scan the room as quickly as possible, then retreat to his pickup. He could drive down to Beard's and call the constable from there. If the power was out here, it was a safe bet that the telco's party line was down as well. If Ted even *had* a telephone hookup. Buster had never needed to call him before.

Except for the corpse, the main bedroom was empty. Buster tried to leave the room without turning his back on the corpse. He was a grown man. He'd seen dead people before. He knew better than to think one could sneak up behind him when he wasn't looking. All the same, the prospect didn't feel quite so far-fetched as it would if he'd been standing there on a balmy day in the middle of the morning.

A lamp that sat beside an alarm clock on the couple's nightstand flared to life. Buster yelped in surprise. The surge of fresh electrical current through the bulb created a bright burst of light like a newspaper photographer's camera flash. The glow settled into a steady burn that shone in beams from the top and bottom of the shade, creating an hourglass shape. It steadied bright enough to illuminate all but the farthest corners of the bedroom.

Buster cut his eyes to the dead man, who had risen from his slump against the wall. Ted stood on his knees, gaping at his living boss with the same milky, listless eyes and slack jaw that he'd been wearing when Buster first walked in. In the thickness of the solidifying blood pooled beneath him were distinct handprints and smears where the dead man had propped himself up and shuffled his calves under his butt so he could sit on them.

The nearest Catholic church was hell and gone over in Hollow River. For that reason, Buster McNath hadn't attended a single day of Mass since moving to Tennessee in the '40s. He crossed himself anyway.

Better safe than sorry.

"Holy Mary, Mother of God, pray for us sinners, now and at the hour of our death," he whispered. Not once did he take his eyes off the thing staring back at him. Then it spoke. The voice it exhaled was flat, unreverberant. It contained neither emotion nor inflection.

"There is no God in heaven," it said. "There is only empathy. And the ones who feed on it. Ravenous. Relentless. Must be relentless."

Ted straightened its head briefly and then allowed it to loll over his left shoulder. Its eyes grew wide, bulging outward, imitating the horror of the dawning of knowledge of impending doom. "The soul bugs. Skittering."

It stretched its arms toward Buster like a toddler gesturing for his mommy to pluck him from the ground. It shuffled forward on its knees, creating thin wakes of blood as its calves surfed through the stuff.

"Starving," it shouted hoarsely. "Skittering. And she's starving."

Buster matched each of Ted's shuffles forward with a panicked step backward. His heart performed a somersault and lodged firmly in his throat. The clarity of thought restored to him only a moment before it was entirely gone from him again. His mind raced, furiously seeking a rationalization for what he saw and heard. At the same time, another part of him tried to form a plan to save his skin and not make him feel like a coward when he told this story to the guys at the job site. Assuming he survived it.

In the end, all Buster could think to do, if he wanted to live long enough to tell anyone what he'd seen, was turn tail and run. He'd worry about appearances later.

He fled just as the Ted thing came within striking distance. Its crimson-stained fingertips brushed against the cuff of Buster's sleeve, leaving a dark red skid mark as the burly construction site foreman dashed from the room, his Rayovac still burning. Its beam bobbed up and down over the floors, walls, and ceiling as Buster pumped his arms and made tracks down the hall, through the living room, and out the front door. He only chanced one look behind him after he leaped over the threshold toward the driving rain. No Ted. No human-sized thing shambling after him on wobbly legs. No formerly living person crawling along the floor of the hallway that he'd just left in the dust.

The ground, engorged with rainwater, tried to stop him. He stomped his way through it without bothering to shake the water from his boots but without falling. He yanked open the pickup door and threw the flashlight inside, not bothering to switch it off. Then he slammed the door closed, slapped the lock down, and started the engine. He yanked on the shifter and felt the transmission settle into Reverse. He eased off the clutch, stopping himself from smashing the throttle to the floor lest the engine stall. The rear tires of his pickup spun in the muck, splattering clods of wet dirt against the windows as they did. Buster was stuck.

"GODDAMMIT!"

CHAPTER TWENTY-FOUR

That fearsome grin spoiled the soft, wet features the real Marilyn was so known for. Donna cradled Theo closer to her bosom as the baby downed the last of the formula. Marilyn paid it no mind, maintaining her unblinking glare straight into Donna's soul. She could feel the strange woman inside her head sifting her memories, settling on Ted just like she had when Peter had escorted her from the bathroom before. It was a familiar feeling for Donna, not unlike how she'd believed Ted could read her thoughts. She had come to think that one of these two things was true: either her head was simply an open book, or evil incarnate had an uncanny ability to see into places where no one should.

"You know, he's lucky," Marilyn said. She cast her eyes on Theo. "He's far too young to remember his daddy, isn't he? He could go his entire life and never know anything about what his mommy did. Is that what you want for him? To go through his whole life not knowing his *real* mommy? The murderer?"

All around Beard's General, time slowed to a crawl. Everyone except Donna, Theo, and Marilyn frozen in place moved in slow motion. Donna could see Peter from where she sat. He was in the process of turning his head toward their conversation but at a pace that rivaled the sun's dawn to dusk journey across the sky on any given summer day. She couldn't see Jerry or Kathy because they were somewhere outside her periphery. She didn't dare turn her face away from the Marilyn manifestation before her to look for them. She couldn't hear them, however. They must be affected by the slowdown, too.

"I'm not a murderer," Donna replied. Her voice was firm. She surprised herself by stating it with conviction and believing it. "Ted was a violent man. He was going to kill us." Her mouth tasted like a boy's gym sock. She licked her lips. They were cracked and flaky on the tip of her tongue. Marilyn's, to the contrary, were as ripe and beautiful as ever.

"It was self-defense," Donna continued. The firmness became distant in her ears, more robotic, was like she was reciting the ingredients on the back of a tin of Van Camp's Pork and Beans. Something was wrong inside her head, more than it had been when she'd first sensed Marilyn inside it. Her thoughts became muddled, less coherent. They drifted, unable to focus on a single idea for any length of time. Her attention bobbed from notion to notion, color to color, memory to memory in a rapid succession of mental photographic stills. On some different plane, she heard Marilyn speaking to her again.

"You *are* a murderer, Donna Gilliam," she lilted. "Where is your steam? The guilt of the murderer tastes *so* sweet. Come on. You cut your husband's throat with a shard of glass from a picture frame. You took him by surprise, didn't you? Do you not remember the innocent look of betrayal in his eyes when you cut into him? Do you not remember how he slumped against the wall, bleeding all over himself?

How the blood and white shaving foam mixed and drooled down his chest?

"You took his life from him. He was a son. A father. A provider. *You* took all that away. Why? Because he was scary? Did that give you the right to become his executioner?

"Give me your steam."

Yes. She had killed Ted. She remembered it vividly. She could see him in her mind. Marilyn's presence within had brought it all back as if she was still standing in the dark of her bedroom, staring down at the corpse with its sad, shocked man-in-the-moon face staring back at her in a permanent expression of disbelief.

It wasn't right, though. It had been morning when Ted died. There was darkness from the window over Ted's head in her memory, no sunlight. She could hear the storm outside beating through the glass. Some of it poured in on top of Ted through a broken segment where a branch of their maple tree was lodged. The lamp beside the bed was dark, yet she could see dead Ted splayed in a bright beam of yellow light in front of her. It was as if her memory had trained a spotlight, or a flashlight, on his corpse. The shaving foam was all gone from his face and clothes, melted and disintegrated the way snow does on an asphalt roof on the first sunny day after an accumulation.

Then the lamp was on again. She glanced at it when it came to life, startled. When she looked back at Ted, he was upon his knees: staring, stretching his arms out toward her. It was without menace, however. She could sense it.

Donna tried to speak to him. She wanted to tell him that she was sorry. She was sorry he had to die, but not that he was dead. She was sad that Theo wouldn't grow up with a daddy, but not that he wouldn't grow up with *Ted* for a daddy. She was sorry that things would be harder financially for her and the baby. But she was not ashamed that she would no longer have to worry about him drinking the grocery money.

She meant to say all this, but Ted opened his mouth first. She couldn't hear what he was saying, not exactly, but she could read his lips. It was a skill she hadn't even known she had. Or it was that psychic connection between them again. With Marilyn staring her down as she sat in her chair at Beard's General and Theo in her lap, Donna Gilliam repeated her late husband's words aloud as she recognized them.

"There is no God in heaven," she said. "There is only empathy. And the ones who feed on it. Ravenous. Relentless. Must be relentless.

"The soul bugs. Skittering.

"Starving! Skittering. And she's starving."

The vision cleared as if someone had pulled the plug on a television set mid-broadcast. Marilyn's face came into focus inches from Donna Gilliam's. Her eyes were wide and furious, her nostrils flared, her lips twisted into a snarl. At some point, while she was reading dead Ted's words, the woman had clamped hold of Donna's head with both hands. She was leaning in, tongue moistening her lips as if to plant a kiss directly on Donna's mouth. Except her tongue wasn't a regular tongue, her lips and teeth no longer human. Flames erupted from somewhere behind her eyes, making her pupils glow fiery red.

"If you don't feed me your shame, murderer, then I will eat *all* that remains of your soul," she growled.

Donna's lungs began to ache inside her chest. Marilyn's mouth had nearly closed around hers, drawing the breath of life away from her the way a vacuum cleaner sucks at the nap of a carpet. Donna tried to halt her exhalation—to close off her airway and trap what oxygen remained in her lungs—but the searing pain in her chest prevented it. Trying to inhale hurt as well. Every attempt began and ended in short gulps that used more oxygen than they could provide. Her nostrils were on fire.

The edges of her vision blurred and began to blacken. The world around her was growing larger, or she was shrinking. Her head was lighter. It felt like it was about to pop off her neck and float into the air. It was like the feeling she'd had when she'd fainted before, but not exactly. There was a finality to it. If she went through the tunnel that closed in on her, she could never return. Theo really would be alone then. Would he be Marilyn's next meal?

Donna's adrenaline surged. The thought of this creature forcing her to abandon Theo kicked her fight in hard. She flailed against the attacker, or thought she did. She might have been only flailing in her mind. Whatever in the world Marilyn was, she was far too powerful for the young mother. Exhaustion inhibited the beating she meant to administer. The urge to surrender overcame her. She could just let go, let her consciousness drift away, fall asleep and never wake again. She could. She *should*.

And then it happened. Her muscles relaxed. Her lungs were empty. As fast as it had surged, her fight was gone.

A crashing sound followed by a loud thud somewhere nearby snapped her back from the brink. Air filled her lungs again. Consciousness fluttered in like a momma bird bringing the worm home to her nest. Her vision returned. The first thing she became aware of was Theo's face staring up at her from behind his bottle. She was still holding him *and* still tilting the pretty much empty formula bottle up for him to suck on. She plucked the nipple out from between his lips and set the bottle down on the floor. Her head spun with effort, but she managed to steady herself in her chair.

Marilyn lay on her back on the floor several feet away, Kathy straddling her. Away from them rolled the remains of a baseball bat, broken in the middle. It must have been the weapon Kathy had been reaching for behind the cash register earlier that night. The store owner landed punches left and right on Marilyn's pretty mug. The little bob tied on the back of Kathy's head trembled with each blow. Her closed fists made thick slapping sounds as they found their targets.

Donna smiled wanly despite herself. However many years had passed since Kathy abandoned physical farm labor for selling goods to shoppers, she still fought like a country girl.

Peter clambered from his spot by the mop bucket and tried to pull Kathy off Marilyn, who was not fighting back. The stranger absorbed each blow to her jaw and chin without so much as a wince. And was she laughing? Donna thought she was.

There was the staccato of boots against wood and linoleum, and then Jerry joined the fray. He pried Peter off his mother and flung the weirdly ancient-looking fellow across the room. He skidded into the mop bucket he'd been pondering all night. It rolled a few inches and stopped next to the wall. Peter hit the floor hard. Donna grimaced, confident he'd broken a hip or collar bone, but Peter was on his feet again within a moment, evidently unhurt despite his deteriorating condition.

Jerry hugged his mother around her waist, tugging her far enough away from Marilyn to prevent her from landing more punches. Then he lost his grip and fell backward on his ass. Kathy sensed her freedom and dove for another round of battle, but she would never land another punch.

Marilyn's face elongated and transformed into something in between human and canine. She sucked at the air in the room the way the Big Bad Wolf did in those "Three Little Pigs" cartoons they used to show before the movies over in Hollow River, back when Ted used to take Donna to movies. The thing craned its neck from the floor, its jaws kissing distance from Kathy.

Jerry scrambled to gain his feet, but not soon enough. Kathy's body dried up like a mummy. Her eyes rolled back in her head. Her cheeks sunk into her skull. Her limbs all withered at once, darkening to a ruddy brown and crinkling like a paper sack. The bob on the back of her head came loose and fell off, vaporizing on its way to the floor along with the rest of her hair.

In an instant, Kathy Beard no longer resembled Kathy Beard in any way. Her entire body deflated like an unknotted balloon and crashed to the floor with a thin *clack* sound.

From Donna's vantage point, Marilyn appeared to have turned the woman into some sort of weird bug. She gaped at the small shining creature that had moments before been her confidant.

Jerry fell back to a seated position on the floor, his face gray, his chin practically in his lap. He gripped his stomach with both hands as if trying to prevent himself from throwing up.

The tiny black Kathy thing began to skitter toward the front door. It looked like it was trying to run from the fate Marilyn had already dealt it.

They're skittering.

Kathy had crawled half a foot when Peter approached behind, on his hands and knees, and snatched her up from the floor. He groaned as he raised himself to full height. He was bowed at his knees. One hand gripped his lower back. Nevertheless, he held his grip on her the entire way to the mop bucket. He dropped Kathy inside.

Donna thought she heard a tiny distant scream as the small black thing plummeted into the bucket with the others.

On the floor and cradling his knees to his chest, Jerry rocked back and forth on his butt, wailing.

CHAPTER TWENTY-FIVE

Doubts crept into the back of Peter's mind. They were subtle at first, like when you watch a stage magician slice a woman in half. You want to believe what your eyes are seeing. You will allow yourself to believe it. Still, you know that it was only an illusion. How many times over the course of this longest of stormy nights had he watched Marilyn try and fail to "save" the others gathered here as she had saved him?

First had been Mark MacDonald, the preacher who had proclaimed his forgiveness and salvation without her help with his last breaths. He was the first that she had reduced to—well, whatever these things were he had collected in a mop bucket. Peter was not clear on *why* he was collecting them, either. She hadn't told him to do it, not even through their telepathic communications. With Mark, there hadn't even been any thought about it. Peter had simply snapped the thing up from the floor and placed it in the first container he'd seen.

As for the Wynn boy, the desire to collect his remains (if that's what these things were) psychologically overpowered Peter. He'd tried to resist it just to see what the creature would do and where it might go. Mainly, he'd wanted to find out whether there were any remnants of the kid still in there somewhere. Instead, he'd compulsively leaped from his spot by the mop bucket and scooped it up for safekeeping.

Kathy joined them. Already her son Jerry was beginning to look confused about how and why he came to be rocking to and fro in tears on the floor of his mother's store. Those sadly masculine blubbering gulps of snot and sobbing had waned to a single final tear. Then it was all over. Jerry stood up and glanced around the room, blinking.

"Where's Mom?"

That was another problem, wasn't it? Throughout the night, Marilyn had knocked multiple times on the doors of those whose souls were lost before condemning them. Peter had seen the sin boil and rise as red steam from Mark even before she had made her appearance inside the store. At the time, it had seemed like a test, like she meant to verify the charity of the group of survivors before she saved them. *I was naked and you clothed me* and all that. But Mark had proven to be a thief. He had asked for forgiveness but then attacked the one who could provide it and dared to proclaim he had it anyway.

Poor Eli was simply too consumed by his lust. Multiple times, Peter watched Marilyn confront him and try to rescue him. She had finally decided he could not be saved the last time. That's what she had transmitted to Peter, anyway. The boy could not be saved. So, Peter had watched with morose understanding as she committed his soul to eternal damnation.

But Kathy? Not once during the years of hours in the evening had the store owner displayed any kind of guilt or shame or suffering from sin. As near as Peter Mayberry could tell from the limited access to her mind that he had, Kathy was as close to sinless as you could come without being an infant like Theo Gilliam, nestled soundly in his mother's arms on the side of the aisle end caps.

Donna had just surrendered her last chance for salvation when Kathy interfered. Peter had seen it enough times to recognize the moment by then. The steam stopped flowing, the sucking sounds began, and everything became a blur of rapidly changing shapes and colors until the little bug-like remains of the sinner and Marilyn were all that remained.

Now, *where's Mom?*

Forgotten, that's where. That bothered Peter most of all. No matter how many times Marilyn tried to save them, the remainders always forgot the lost. They don't remember their local Nazarene pastor being trapped among them. They don't remember young Eli falling all over himself along with Jerry to impress the pretty new arrival. They don't remember what happened to Kathy. Peter tried to take some small amount of comfort because Jerry seemed to recall *having* a mother, but that was all.

Marilyn's voice spoke in his head. He turned to face her when it did. She was looking at him, sensing his thoughts and confusion.

Have some faith, she said. *The Beard woman tried to intervene in my work. That cannot go unpunished.*

So, you damned her for all eternity? Peter shot back.

She only smiled at him in response.

Jesus asked forgiveness for those who tormented him on the cross, Peter continued. *Kathy was protecting her friend. Isn't that right?*

He considered Donna. She was focused on the baby. She bowed her lips in a gentle, loving smile that betrayed no knowledge of the events that had just occurred in front of her.

In front of her? Sakes, they had directly involved her! How was Marilyn to save anyone if they could not remember the consequences of remaining lost?

Trust in the Lord, came the reply.

Trust in the Lord. Easier said than done. He would have to force himself to comply, however. Thinking such faithless thoughts while she was in earshot of his psychic waves was dangerous. He was allowing his Earthly contemplations of God's mysterious ways to override the primary tenet of his faith, which was, of course, faith itself. Who was he to question the decisions of The Almighty? She would know better than he the nature of Kathy's soul, the truth about her intentions.

Peter plopped down beside the mop bucket again, grunting as his joints groaned with the effort. He eyed Marilyn, who sat a short pace away from him. She twiddled her thumbs in her lap, watching Donna. Her mouth was turned down on one side, her eyes narrowed. A casual looker would think she was simply contemplating their predicament. Peter could sense the rage boiling and burping like a cauldron overflowing with hot lava in her skull. Waves of steaming molten stuff pounded between his ears with each transmission from her to him. Some of them were sent to him deliberately. Others felt like an accident, as if her thoughts were a radio broadcast that leaked into an adjacent frequency.

He rested his elbow on the mop bucket and propped his forehead in the palm of his hand. He rubbed his temples, trying in vain to massage the fury away.

Distantly, he could hear Jerry padding about the place, checking every nook and cranny of the store for some sign of his mother. The boy wasn't panicked. Not yet. But Peter had no doubt that he probably would before too much time passed.

He tried to shift his mental energy, focus on Jerry's thoughts instead of allowing himself to be bombarded by Marilyn's. What he discovered therein was a whirlwind of compulsion and confusion. No sooner had Jerry explored a corner of the building, all the while calling out for his mother, than he forgot that he'd already checked there. He ran circuits through the aisles, around the exterior walls, into the employee area, and out again.

Peter sympathized with the kid. As cruel as Peter's mother had been to him, he could remember times as a youngster when he'd lost sight of her and fallen into a panic, thinking she had somehow forgotten he existed and gone home without him. That terrifying feeling of being alone in the world—really and truly alone—for the first time was like swallowing a cannonball. It was a fear that sat on your stomach, pressing on your bowels to the point that you feared you might have an accident even though you are a big boy and know how to use the commode. Then comes the relief when your dear ol' Ma suddenly appears from around a corner or through a door and smiles down at you with that loving look of compassion and understanding. Sometimes she would pluck you up from the floor and hug you and remind you that she would never, ever leave you. In your exhaustion and your consolation, you might shed a tear on her shoulder or drift off into a comfortable nap, secure in the knowledge that Momma was here, and you were safe. At least until next time.

But for Jerry, that moment would never arrive. In the back of his mind, Peter sensed that it was dawning on Jerry himself. His circles around the store shortened in their diameter. Once, he'd even stepped through the front door and outside. A Niagara Falls-style wall of water poured off the metal awning over the porch. Peter sensed Jerry contemplate leaping through that downpour into the overflow for an instant. Instead, he cried out for his mother again, screaming against the noise of the rushing water.

Unable to locate her there, he returned to the store's interior, awash and dripping trails of long rivulets behind him. He collapsed to his knees and hung his head. His thick black hair flopped down over his forehead, obscuring any tears he shed behind the water that dripped from his wet strands.

The show had been enough to turn Marilyn's attention away from Donna. Both she and the young mother stared wide-eyed at the man-boy who crouched before them with his heart breaking, his whole world newly in doubt. A fresh message, bright and hopeful, arrived clearly in Peter's mind. Marilyn would focus on saving Jerry, allow Donna to stew in her juices some more before circling back to her. There was some sin in the boy, some life regret and shame causing him to act out so. She could find it, rescue him from it...*feed on it.*

Feed on it?

That's what he'd heard. He was sure of it.

He rose from the floor with her, albeit slower and with more effort. He meant to reach out to her, touch her on the shoulder, force her to pause a beat. He meant to confer with her about the best course for dealing with the hysterical boy who had just lost his mother, then forgotten he'd lost his mother, and thereby lost her again. He was too slow.

Marilyn crossed the room and knelt beside Jerry, cradling his damp shoulders with one gray coverall sleeve that was entirely too long for a woman of her size.

She allowed her hair to tumble over her face as she crouched beside him, held him close to her the way a pastor offers graveside comfort to a new widow. Peter could not decipher what she was saying to him, but whatever it was didn't seem to be doing him any good. The psychic connection between them dimmed. He received only brief sensations of emotion as she chatted with the young man: a flicker of hope, a beam of excitement, a flash of hunger. It hadn't been so intermittent with the others. Was she shutting him out intentionally?

Jerry's back and ribs heaved with every sob of pain and loss while Marilyn patted him on the shoulder and whispered in his ear. It was a delicate touch, a sensitivity Peter hadn't seen in her since she had come to him for the first time in his car out on Hollow Creek Road.

He began to hobble his way over to them. To help Jerry? Yes, but more to get within earshot of their conversation. Why shut him out?

A surge of jealousy swelled within him. Was she replacing him already? Had he been too weak, too unable to keep up with her? Grown too old, too fast? Had he lost her trust?

He halved the distance toward the duo when time stopped around him. Again. It had happened with Mark MacDonald. It had happened with Eli Wynn. It had recently happened with Donna Gilliam and then, unexpectedly, with Kathy Beard.

The entire world came to a stop. He could still move, still think. It was like he was trudging through a mud bog, however. His feet were too heavy to lift. One step toward Marilyn and Jerry lasted eons. He wanted to turn his head to see if Donna and Theo were stuck in molasses as well.

Doing so meant extra effort that detracted from his forward momentum, if you wanted to call it momentum.

Meanwhile, the image of Marilyn and Jerry before him blurred. It jerked and fritzed, cutting in and out of his ability to comprehend it like a shitty television signal scattered by interference from an electrical storm.

He had seen that before, too—more than once.

He knew what it meant.

She had given up on saving him. Kathy Beard's boy would become the next creature Peter escorted to the mop bucket.

CHAPTER TWENTY-SIX

The right rear tire of Buster McNath's pickup truck could've dug a hole to China by way of the slick mud in Ted Gilliam's driveway if he kept on the gas much longer. That didn't stop him from laying the throttle to the floor one more time in his increasingly futile effort to flee the scene. Motor oil-scented exhaust belched from the tailpipe each time he hit the gas after shifting from First to Reverse and back again. Each time he changed gears, he clung to the desperate hope that the solution he had just tried seconds before would magically work this time.

"Goddammit!" he roared, slamming his shifting fist against the AM radio's volume knob when he transitioned to First again. "Goddammit! Goddammit! Goddammit!"

The rain that had soaked his hair on his way from Ted's front door to the pickup ran down his forehead and into his eyes. Buster liked to think of himself as a man who did not cry. He couldn't remember having shed a single tear since toddlerdom, not even when his saintly mother went to be with the Lord. Tonight, part of him wanted to burst into tears out of frustration alone.

He took some comfort in those raindrops running down his face. They could fool his eyes into thinking he was already crying, so they wouldn't do it for him. He wiped at his face with the palm of his left hand, unwilling to remove his right from the shifter knob. He flicked the rain droplets off the tips of his fingers, splattering the windshield with them when he did.

"Shit!"

He snatched a handkerchief from his back pocket and wiped down the glass. It was hard enough to see through without adding water spots inside.

Buster was in the process of stuffing the handkerchief back into his pocket when he noticed movement in the beams of his headlights. Specifically, he saw it in the opening of the front door. In his mad dash to his truck, he had neglected to close it behind him. He let off the gas, watching, and kept the clutch fully engaged as a precaution.

There it was again. Something vaguely human walked past the door, just inside it. If he'd only bought that new truck he'd been wanting, the one that had those fancy new European sealed headlamps with high beams, he could switch those suckers on and get a better view of whomever it was.

His head insisted that it couldn't be Ted. Ted was dead. Killed. Despite what he'd seen in the house, he wasn't ready to believe the man's corpse was capable of pacing about the place like it was Sunday morning, and he was waiting for the missus to finish getting ready to go to church.

His balls, contrariwise, were believers. They prickled with gooseflesh and squeezed themselves against the wall of his body for warmth and comfort.

"Somebody else is in there," he said. The certainty in his voice cemented the idea. "It was a trick of some kind.

There's somebody in there messing with me trying to get rid of Buster. Ain't gonna be that easy. No, sir."

Steeling himself, Buster killed the pickup's engine. He allowed the headlights to continue shining. Without the motor to charge the battery, the beams dimmed. Their brightness petered out just before the front door's threshold. If anyone walked by, he might not see them.

He bent forward and ran his hands underneath his seat, seeking the .357 Magnum he kept loaded there. Mostly, it was there just in case there was ever a dispute about his bar tab on a Saturday night or a paycheck he handed out at the end of the month. Finest revolver Smith & Wesson ever forged, in any case. At least, that's what he'd been told. He'd had the gun for five years but had only fired it twice, both times in his backyard after a few too many High Lifes.

He gripped the revolver in his left hand. With this right, he snatched up the flashlight he'd thrown across the cab when he'd leaped inside. It was still burning because he hadn't bothered to take the time to switch it off.

He shoved the pickup's door open, careful about where his trigger finger rested while he did. He'd almost shot off his big toe the first time he'd fired the thing because he couldn't keep his thumb from fidgeting with the hammer and his forefinger from the trigger. His granddaddy would've smacked him on the back of the head for that if he'd been alive to see it. "Who taught you how to hold a gun, boy?" He couldn't afford to be that careless tonight.

The rain hurt when it hit his face as if someone sitting in a tree above him pelted him with small stones. He shielded himself with his left forearm. Aiming the light toward the front door wasn't as easy this way, but it did help clear his vision. The palm and fingers of his left hand remained firmly wrapped around the revolver's grip.

Halfway to the door, his boots filling with slimy wet muck again, it occurred to Buster that this configuration would not work if he needed to fire the gun at something (or *someone!*). He was right-handed and couldn't aim for shit with his left.

"Goddammit!"

He tucked the flashlight under his right armpit and transferred the revolver. When it was secured in his right hand, he grabbed the flashlight out from his armpit with his left. There. Better.

He shined the beam in the space beyond the doorway and nearly fell backward when he did. A startled gasp escaped his lips. There in the door frame, slack-jawed and staring at him, stood the milky-eyed corpse of Ted, just as he had looked when Buster had discovered him leaning against the wall in the main bedroom.

Buster's knees tried to buckle under him. He locked them in place and spread his feet apart in the shooter's stance his granddaddy had taught him. A surge of power thrummed through him when he pulled back the hammer and raised the .357 with one extended arm. He leveled it at the thing standing in the doorway, not exactly sure of where he was aiming but figuring he was well within the ballpark of Ted's heart.

"I don't know what kind of game this is, mister," he shouted over the rain. He imagined himself looking and sounding a lot like Jock Mahoney in *The Range Rider*. "I don't know how you're doing this, whoever you are, but I knew Ted. He was a drunk. He was lazy. But he could swing a hammer, and this is the only time in the five years he's been working for me that he ever failed to show up for work. You put him back how I found him, then come out here and face me."

In the doorway, the corpse cocked his head to the left as if trying to process what Buster had just said. Part of him wanted to shout at the thing. Something like *I'm not talking to you! I'm talking to the man behind you!* But that would've made him look crazy. Instead, he forced himself to take two steps closer to the front porch. He wanted to show whoever was using his dead friend's body for a marionette that he meant business.

The corpse did not budge from its spot at the threshold. It began to work its jaw, struggling to regain control of the atrophied and decaying muscles within. "There is...no God," it said through strained breath. "There is...only empathy... and those who...feed—"

Buster's hand tightened around the revolver. It trembled in the air before him, muddling his aim. "What do you want from me?" he cried.

Ted cocked his head the opposite way. He tilted it back some as well, pointing his dead man's gaze toward the sky as if searching for the answer in the driving rain. After a moment, he straightened up again and fixed on Buster.

"The water cleans," Ted said. He seemed to have found his voice. "The water purifies. Tell Donna. There is no God in heaven. But the water. The water. The water—"

Then, the thing trailed off and gazed back at the sky, taking a step over the threshold as it did. Seconds later, it had shuffled onto the porch. His arms dangled at his sides as he moved, made unnaturally long by his derelict shoulders and sloping back. His feet shuffled forward rather than walked, like a kid's doll with its feet glued to a pair of Popsicle sticks.

Buster's eyes stung. He'd forgotten how to blink. He squeezed them shut and popped them back open to clear them. Ted moved closer, sliding forward, his face upturned to the water falling from the sky. Ted was not blinking, either. If he genuinely was still alive, or somewhere between dead and alive, the heavy rain was pelting his eyeballs with the same force that made the drops feel stone-like on impact with Buster's skin. The corpse's mouth remained open, too, so a not-insignificant amount of the rain had to have been running down his lifeless throat. Yet he did not blink. Nor did he drown or even gag.

An abomination. That's what Ted had become. Buster's granddaddy taught him about shooting, but his gramma filled his head with stories about ghosts, goblins, and ghouls. She'd tell him all the old stories before she shut out the lights and bade him drift off to sleep. Then she'd shut the door to his room, sealing his fate.

As a kid, he'd loved the creepy thrill those stories ginned up in him. Thinking about them kept him awake far longer into the night than was healthy for a growing boy. But he didn't mind. He both loved them and was terrified of them, and it was good.

The thrill was gone. There was only terror.

The closer the Ted thing shuffled toward him, the more he wanted to drop everything, turn tail, and run. He doubted he would get as far as the end of the driveway without tripping over his feet thanks to the mud and his water-logged boots. The pickup was no good, either. Stuck. Just like him.

Out of options, Buster McNath did the only thing remaining he could think to do. He squeezed the trigger and fired a round from the .357 Magnum at the thing that meandered toward him. It took the bullet in the throat, rocking its upturned head backward. The gaping slash there grinned back at Buster during the recoil, but Ted himself did not react, did not even flinch. He did not pinwheel his arms to try to maintain his balance. He did not stumble over his feet. There was barely a slowing of his forward momentum.

Buster screamed. He pulled back the hammer twice more and fired as many shots. One struck Ted in the top of the right shoulder, exploding bits of flesh, bone, and red gore out the back of him. Another hit him squarely in the chest, again to no effect but the sudden appearance of a blackened, smoking hole in the middle of the bloodstains that ran from his slashed throat.

Two more shots rang out in the night, both aimed at Ted's kneecaps. If he couldn't stop the thing by shooting it in the head and chest, he could at least destroy the bone and muscle it needed to walk. One shot went wide. Buster heard it ricochet off some piece of metal junk somewhere. Probably an old hubcap carelessly discarded near the porch. The second bullet hit its target just above the right knee. Buster saw the leg threaten to give way. A spark of hope kindled in him when it seemed like the Ted thing might tumble face-down in the mud. It stopped, seemed to test the injured leg for stability, and then resumed its forward trek. Ted's arms had left his sides and stretched outward into space. Reaching. For him.

"Tell Donna," it croaked. "The water."

But Buster wouldn't tell anyone anything ever again. After two more rounds went wild, he had precisely one left in the revolver. He pulled the hammer back one more time. Then he pressed the barrel firmly to his temple and squeezed the trigger.

CHAPTER TWENTY-SEVEN

Time was no longer out of joint, at least as far as Beard's General was concerned. The rate of movement of everyone who remained there had been restored to normal. Peter sighed as he stooped to pluck the tiny black creature that was all that remained of Jerry Beard from the floor. He examined his gnarled fingers, which were tipped with the thick and sickly yellowed nails of an older man. The skin on the back of his hands was a faded farmer brown, speckled here and there with irregular gray dots. The hand he used to capture Jerry trembled with the effort. That was new.

Whatever kind of *Alice in Wonderland* fantasy garden Marilyn had created when he and Jerry had dragged her in from the storm, Peter seemed to be exclusively immune to its time-preservative effects. He alone could avoid the odd loops and holes in time and memory it had created. He alone suffered the natural consequences. While everyone around him remained the same age, including the infant Theo, Peter's body moved on. For most of the hours (*years?*) they'd been trapped there by the storm, Peter had convinced himself that it was Marilyn's generosity and desire to save souls that prevented them from seeing the sunrise of March

22, 1955. Hell, Marilyn herself had transmitted as much to him through the psychic tunnel erected between them when she freed him from his guilt and restored his penis to its unmutilated state in his car.

Marilyn. The One. His Savior. More and more, Peter was beginning to doubt that these titles were an accurate label for the stranger's role in his life. It was time, then, to stop referring to her that way. If she lacked an actual name, then Marilyn it would have to be, but no longer could he think of her as God or daughter of God.

The decision diminished her hold on his mind. It *felt* like it had subsided, anyway. Maybe he only perceived it that way because she was busy digesting the life and soul she'd just drained from Jerry. Or Peter had simply awakened from the delusions she had encouraged in him.

He dropped Jerry into the mop bucket and watched as the creature squirmed its way around the sides of the container after it hit bottom. It first searched for a means of escape, then settled among the three previous critters. It seemed to latch onto one, following it wherever it moved and ignoring the rest. Was that one Kathy? Was there even enough of Jerry left in the tiny beast to recognize his mother in this form? Thinking about it hurt Peter's head. He crouched down to his former place beside the bucket and exhaled a breath of simple exhaustion.

"What's happening to you, Peter Mayberry?" said a female voice from somewhere on his periphery. It sounded remarkably like the voice of his dead mother when he'd been ill as a child. But that was only an illusion, an auditory hallucination. When he twisted his head in the direction of the voice, only Donna Gilliam sat there, her baby in her lap. Her brow was furrowed and her eyes scanned his features for an explanation.

"What do you mean?"

Donna grimaced, clearly uncomfortable. "I don't mean to offend you," she said. "But you look really—well, *old* suddenly. Are you sick?"

Peter smiled at her. "I know." He licked his lips, noting the dry, salty taste. "I have been under much strain lately."

She nodded. "Me too. But I wonder why yours has had such a, uh, dramatic effect on you." Her gaze drifted somewhere above him. "I can't imagine your soul more burdened than mine."

Donna's thoughts, or a representation of them that appeared to him like a series of pulsating still images, flashed across Peter's mind. Marilyn, who grinned stupidly from the spot on the floor where she'd consumed Jerry, must have finished digesting her latest meal. The mind tunnels were opening again. Before him floated the image of a pregnant young woman dressed in a Puritanical white apron and cap. An accusatory sans-serif scarlet letter A was embroidered in the middle of the breast. Peter recognized her as a somewhat childlike impression of how Hester Prynne, the protagonist of Nathaniel Hawthorne's *The Scarlet Letter*, would have looked had she been more than a figment of that author's imagination. Except that this Hester Prynne bore a striking resemblance to Donna Gilliam.

Before the picture vanished, the middle of the A on Hester's chest slid loose from its anchors and began to change. The right side of the open end of the letter reconnected, approximating an isosceles shape with a slight gap between the leftmost angle and the bottom line. The right descending side then broke in half and bent upwards at the break, transforming the scarlet letter A into a scarlet letter M.

M for Murder, Peter thought. It was not a perfect M. Some part of Donna knew that, and that was what had been frustrating Marilyn's attempts to feed on the young mother all night long.

"I know the truth," he said to her, not realizing he was going to say the words out loud until he opened his mouth and did so. "You did what you had to do. For you. For Theo." He cocked his head at Marilyn. "I think that's why she can't save you. There's nothing in you that needs to be saved."

Donna only looked at him, uncertainty evident in her eyes.

"I know," he said again. "It doesn't always feel like killing Ted was the right thing to do. But that's not God talking to you. It's not your conscience, either, if that's what you're thinking. That's your fear. You're worried about what will happen to Theo because you can be damn sure the State of Tennessee won't see it your way. You're concerned about what others will think, what they'll say.

"It doesn't matter." He swallowed audibly. "It's a lesson I've only just learned myself. Most people are afraid of others hearing their thoughts, knowing their minds. But I saw it all in yours. I saw Ted slam you against the door this morning. I saw him blame you and threaten you because the kid there is colicky, because you can't breastfeed him."

A tear crept from the corner of Donna's left eye. She did not wipe it away. Peter's eyes welled up at the sight of it. A new connection formed between them, one that bypassed Marilyn and didn't offer him insight into her thoughts. For the first time since he'd climbed into bed beside Sam the night before, Peter sensed the warmth of an unspoken human connection kindle in the middle of his chest. It expanded throughout him, raising gooseflesh on the back of his neck as it chipped and melted away the frost of antipathy for the flaws in humanity that had enveloped him after Marilyn healed his wounds.

"I see the truth," he continued. "Everything that I've ever been taught was true about sin and redemption and forgiveness is all steeped in power. It's all about controlling others, not saving anyone from eternal damnation. It's all about forcing them to submit to a way of life. It happened to you when Ted tried to force you into his mold of the perfect wife and mother."

"And Theo into the perfect baby," Donna added.

"Yes. And it happened to me—"

Donna's mouth dropped open. Her eyes widened. She had received his transmission loud and clear. "Peter!" she said. "I had no idea."

He smiled at her. "Because of my vigilance and the everyday assumptions people make about their neighbors," he said. "If you're careful about giving people reasons to think things about you, they're more likely to ignore you. They're more likely to think nothing as they go about their mundane lives. But I think I've always been more attracted to men."

"But the church," Donna started. "Sodomy—"

Peter shook his head. "It's not all about the sexual stuff. That's how they confuse you. They *make* it about sex because that's the only way they can frame it in their heads. As natural as sexuality is for humanity, our collective discomfort with it is the easiest tool for dehumanizing those on the margins of what society wants to believe is *normal*."

"You've thought about this a lot?"

He laughed. "Not at all. I'm just now thinking about it. Out loud." *Although in some ways I've been thinking about it for decades*, his brain added, but he did not say. *All of that thinking over all those years happened all at once in this very same spot.*

"It's not easy," he said. "There's a nervous part of me that's screaming at me to shut the hell up. Telling you this stuff—trusting you with it—could get me arrested or even killed if you ever felt the slightest twinge of vindictiveness toward me for any reason."

"Well," Donna replied, holding up her bandaged hand. "I mean, we're in the same boat as far as secrets go, aren't we?" She laughed. It was an easy laugh, the ironic last laugh of the man standing on the trap door with a noose around his neck just before the hangman pulls the lever. Laughter bubbled up from Peter, too. It felt good.

"I won't tell your secret if you won't tell mine," he said.

Donna grinned with mock excitement in her eyes. "We should run away together!"

Peter raised a finger as if the idea had just clicked for him, too. "Yes! We could get married! You force me to keep my dick in my pants and keep the house. I'll drink too much and smack you around a bit when you get out of line! We'll be the picture of the nuclear family!"

That set them both off in a fresh round of guffaws.

Mirthful tears streamed from both of Donna's eyes. She wiped at them absently. "I'd—" she started but had to stop and catch her breath. Through huffs and puffs of giggles, she finished: "I'd make a great Audrey Meadows with a black eye!"

Peter howled. "I don't know who that is!" he shouted. He was equally lightheaded and out of air. The words exited his mouth much louder than he had intended.

"Bang! Zoom!" Donna shouted back, imitating the Ralph Kramden character from *The Jackie Gleason Show*.

"Oh! Yeah!"

"Yeah!"

Peter clasped his belly with both hands. His abdomen ached from exertion and a lack of air. He rocked back and forth as he did, trying to settle down before he accidentally soiled himself. A loud, long, and wet fart momentarily dried up their laughter.

At first, Peter thought he *had* soiled himself. He looked at Donna, who looked back at him. They then looked down at Theo, whose eyes were closed but whose nose was wriggling in an expression that resembled disgust.

"Oh, my!" Donna said. "Well, we know who smelt it, so I guess we also know who dealt it!" She waved a hand in front of her nose, grimacing as she did. "Whew! And *I* can smell it, too! Peter, would you mind grabbing a fresh diaper and a blanket out of my bag there? Hopefully Kathy won't mind if I change him on the table. That bathroom in the back is too tiny. There's no place to put him down."

Just like that, he was sober again. All the humor drained from his face. Whatever breakthroughs he and Donna had made here tonight—even in the past few minutes—there were still things she didn't know, things she *couldn't* know because she hadn't been "saved" by Marilyn. For her, all the events that led up to this conversation were brand new. They had all occurred over the same evening on March 21, 1955. For him, it had been—well, he didn't know how long it had been. In most ways, it felt like hours, just like it did for the others. But hours don't age a man physically like this, no matter what traumas he's faced. In those ways, it seemed like he'd been riding out this storm for forty years or more. Then Donna twisted the knife.

"Where is Kathy, anyway?" she asked innocently. "I'm almost positive she was here when the buckets started pouring from the sky. It feels like I haven't seen her all night."

"Yes, Peter," said Marilyn from somewhere off to his right, "where *is* Kathy?"

He turned to look. She stood at his side, having managed to creep up close without making a sound. He hadn't sensed so much as a warning tingle through the mind tunnel—more evidence she had changed her mind about his role in her play.

"She must be in the back," he said to Donna, gritting his teeth. "I haven't seen her in a while either."

"Well," Marilyn replied, "why don't you go look for her, then? Donna and I can use the time to get acquainted. If we're going to be stuck here for a while, we might as well get to know each other, hmm?"

Donna smiled sweetly at her, but Peter detected some trepidation behind it. Something around her eyes made it look forced. She might not remember the surface of everything that had happened to her and the others as the storm ran its course overhead and the flood washed the world away below, but something about Marilyn wasn't ringing true to her. Her guard was up. That meant Marilyn would be unlikely to succeed in getting her to steam.

Peter was beginning to think that the best way, the *only* way, to be rid of the false prophet among them was to starve her to death.

You're an idiot, his mother piped up. Her voice in his head startled him. She'd been gone since his first encounter with Marilyn in the car. Now that he recognized the creature for what it was, she had returned. His heart sank inside his chest. Suddenly he was hopeless to uncover a way to escape both Marilyn and his mother forever. *If she doesn't feed the demon her guilt and shame, the demon will feed on her body and soul instead. Have you been asleep all night? Dreaming of sticking your dirty thing where you oughtn't to stick it?*

"No, Momma," he mumbled. Then he realized he'd said it out loud. He looked from Donna to Marilyn, who were both staring at him. Confusion was etched on Donna's face, exasperation on Marilyn's.

After a beat, Marilyn laughed. "I'm not your mother, silly boy," she cooed, but not without some condescension. "Be good and go find the nice store lady while Donna and I bash ears."

But before he could rise from his spot on the floor, Donna Gilliam surprised them all.

"There is no God in heaven," she said suddenly. Her eyes had rolled back in her head, showing only bloodshot whites. Her voice was deeper, too, not her own. "There is…only empathy…and those who…feed—" She trailed off. Her arms slid off her lap. Peter was up in a flash, scooping the infant from her arms before he crashed to the linoleum. There was a twinge in his knees and hips as he whisked Theo to safety. He was sure he would pay for the burst of adrenaline later.

At present, Theo was secure from whatever weird thing was happening to his mother. For the second time tonight, the baby had been rescued from Donna, although Peter was sure neither mother nor child would remember the first one.

The words she spoke were familiar, he thought. They were like what she'd said when Marilyn was trying to save her (*feed on her*) before, when Kathy had understood what was happening and fatally intervened. They weren't exact, but close.

Donna slumped in her chair. Almost immediately after, she sat bolt upright again, eye sockets wide and arms outstretched into the space in front of her as if reaching for someone. For Theo?

"Water!" she shouted, again in that flat, gravelly voice. "The water cleans! The water purifies! There is no God but the water."

CHAPTER TWENTY-EIGHT

By all rights, Sam Brooks should not have survived the night of March 21, 1955. On his side were his war-honed reflexes, an adrenaline-fueled ride from regret, and a handful of luck. The raindrops that pelted his bare face beneath his motorcycle helmet arrived like thousands of tiny needles pricking him in rapid succession.

Rain rides on the Triumph were not unusual for him, but this was an unusually hard downpour. It was also a high-speed ride. What he wouldn't give for a face shield or a fairing with an attached windscreen. A pair of leather riding gloves and an out-of-season jacket that zipped to the top of his neck protected the rest of him from the tiny onslaughts. His eyes were most important to him, and they were under attack. Sam squinted hard against the wind and rain, relying on his memory as much as his eyesight to guide him through the storm and back to Pete's.

He hadn't left on good terms. He had left on no terms at all. Since late morning, he'd cruised the scenic route between Lost Hollow and Hollow River, hoping nature would help him clear his head. When the clouds turned sinister that afternoon, he'd stopped to fill the Triumph's tank and then set out for home.

But his mind wandered to the argument he'd had with Pete. Over two or three miles, the urge to turn around strengthened in his heart. A twinge of guilt warmed the back of his neck, pinching at it. When the pinches escalated into full-blown twists of daggers that caused his head to buzz and throb with thoughts like *what have I done*, Sam spun the bike a hundred and eighty degrees in the middle of the two-lane and hauled ass back the way he'd come.

"I must be crazy," he said aloud, the wind from the ride blowing out his cheeks slightly as he did. "I'm riding back into a storm to try to save a relationship with a nutcase white man who thinks his dead bitch of a mother talks to him from a picture on the nightstand.

"I *must* be crazy." He chuckled. "Well, I'm talking to myself, ain't I?"

Now, Sam was caught in the storms he'd intended to outrun. By the time he reached the outskirts of Lost Hollow, near that general store name of Beard's that he'd never dared pop into before, Hollow Creek Road had become completely engulfed in the overflow of the creek that ran alongside it. The bridge that connected the road to the store's parking lot was gone, as was most of the parking lot itself.

Sam thought he could see a few lumps of solid matter standing like flat stones among the rapids in the darkness. He recognized them as the tops of submerged cars. That meant there were people trapped inside. He could see several figures standing in silhouette in front of the light that spilled through the large window on the front of the building. The water rushing beside it hadn't torn away any of its supports yet, but if this rain kept up and the flooding fattened on it, Sam could foresee a time when it might.

The rapids shimmered in the crests and valleys as they passed through the light from the store's interior. The effect was like the sheens oil created when it seeped from destroyed military hardware, except it was red instead of black rainbow. Tendrils of the stuff snaked toward him across the top of the flood, seemingly independent from the motions of the water beneath them.

Must be a trick of the light, Sam thought. *Nothing I need to focus on right now, anyway.*

The Lost Hollow Constable's Office, the Hollow County Sheriff's Department, and Peter Mayberry's house lay on beyond the wash that had flooded the road in front of Beard's. Sam halted the bike parallel to the water's edge and strained to determine its depth. Tiny waves of cruddy creek water lapped at his boot. If the pool was just the tiniest fraction of an inch of depth across the surface of the road, he could probably pass through it, make his way to Pete's house, and call for help. If it was an inch or more, he was apt to lose control of the bike, plunge into the creek rapids, and end up a casualty of the storm himself.

Sam was tempted. In the end, his better judgment won the day. He aimed the bike toward Hollow River and set off away from Lost Hollow. Hollow Creek was the main road into the town, but it wasn't the only one. There had to be a byroad, a cow path, a foot trail, or some space nearby where he could circumvent the flood. Even if it meant getting slapped in the face by a few wet branches of cedar or pine along the way, Sam was confident he and the Triumph would be more likely to navigate some soggy, clumpy Tennessee earth than survive a flailing trip down an engorged Hollow Creek into God knows where that shit dumped out. Deep, chunky clay mud was no friend of a street bike, but it was better than dying.

He trundled away from Beard's, but not at great speed, keeping an eye out for a trail, path, or side road he failed to notice on the way in. Thin trails of the red mist that had meandered their way across the gulf of the creek bed and onto the road closely followed. They nipped at the knobs of his back tire, his taillight, and the heels of his boots as he rode. Eventually, they became too thinly stretched to maintain cohesion and dissipated, absorbed by the dampness. Sam rode on, his pursuer unnoticed.

Less than a quarter mile later, he caught sight of a promising break in the tree line. He stopped and pivoted the bike so its headlight shone down what appeared to be a narrow but well-worn cow path off the highway and through the woods beyond. Pete had once told him most of the farmland and wooded areas on this side of Lost Hollow belonged to the Blalock family. This trail could dump into a clearing somewhere on their farm. Since no driveways seemed to connect the Blalock lands directly to Hollow Creek Road anywhere nearby, there must be another road on the far side of their farm that runs parallel to Hollow Creek. If he could get to that road, he could use it to get back to Pete.

Sam downshifted into First and opened the throttle enough to easily walk the bike across the road toward the mouth of the path. The beam of his headlight didn't reveal as much as he'd like, but he could see it widened a bit just a few feet ahead of him. It seemed to make a straight course. If he kept his feet off the pegs (but ready to ground them, should he start to spin) and maintained a good forward momentum, he could navigate it.

Fifteen minutes later, with the soles of his boots covered in muck and his arms and legs dotted with triangular clumps of stick-tights, Sam barely managed to dodge a headlong plunge into a burned-out tree that had crept up on the periphery of his headlight's beam. A mouth-like hole gaped at the bottom of it. Dirty smoke, some of it pulsing red in his light, belched out of that hole. The branches of the tree were charred and black. Embers of flame clung to some of them. Despite the dampness, they brightened in the wind, then dimmed again when the breath died down.

Must've been struck by lightning, Sam thought. The layer of electrical aroma combined with the odor of burning wood was evidence enough of that. He noted the gaping maw still belching its gusts of fumes and blackish gray fog. *Jesus. Looks like a portal to Hell.*

Glad that he hadn't collided with it, Sam chose to forget the tree and press forward. He opened the Triumph's throttle, allowing the heels of his boots to skim the top of the earth along the way. His thighs screamed at him, unaccustomed to the strain of riding in such an awkward position. It would be easier to use the foot pegs, but if the bike slipped in the muck and went down, he risked breaking an ankle or worse. Better to walk away from a stuck bike than to become stuck beneath one.

Sam caught the occasional flicker of lights through the darkness ahead of him. They were not reflections of his headlights off exposed granite and flint, nor glints off the ashen bark of barren trees. They were electric lights, the lights of the Blalock's farmhouse. The urgency was getting the better of him. He had to force himself to stay in a low gear and burn minimal gas. His mind kept insisting he was lost, that the lights he was seeing ahead of him weren't anything but his illusions. Yet they were getting closer.

When the Triumph finally escaped the woods, Sam was dumped onto a gravel path that stretched parallel to the tree line on both his left and right. It wasn't a road. Not exactly. It looked like a driving path the Blalocks had cut for themselves to travel some of the longer distances over their farm. On Sam's right, it bent a curve and climbed a slight rise. At the top of that rise was the back of the Blalock farmhouse and, God willing, his way back to an actual county road of some kind.

Sam paused long enough on the gravel to scrape the muck from the soles of his boots. Then he shifted the bike into gear and sped toward the house.

Irritatingly, the front facade of the Blalock farmhouse was Antebellum, also known as plantation style. It was two stories tall, blindingly white, with a front door on the opposite side of a deep front porch. The porch itself featured three square columns on either side of a set of three steps that led to the arc of a keyhole-shaped, gravel driveway. It was made to resemble the home of a high-ranking government official. Or a pre-emancipation slave owner.

What's the difference? Sam thought.

That impression was most likely the Blalocks's intent, even though the sides and the back of the place more resembled a plain old Tennessee farmhouse. On any typical day—because he certainly would not be out here most nights—Sam might have shot the place a sly middle finger. It would not have been observable from a distance as he dashed past on the Triumph, but it would have been satisfying.

Tonight, however, was not the night for such luxuries. Sam shifted the bike into Neutral at the spot where the driveway met the steps that led up to the front door. He propped the kickstand in the gravel and dismounted, leaving the engine idling. The foot of the kickstand sank into the soft belly of the gray mud created by the deluge, even on the Blalocks's tightly packed gravel driveway. The Triumph remained upright, so that was something. He did not bother to remove his helmet.

Although Pete had mentioned them off-hand a few times, Sam Brooks had never come face-to-face with the Blalocks in Lost Hollow. Sam doubted Pete had ever mentioned his Black lover to the lily-white farm family. Tennessee farmers were not exactly known to be friendly to a stranger's nighttime knocks at the door, either, so he needed to be prepared for anything. He inhaled a single deep breath, exhaled long, and mounted the steps.

He'd barely rapped his knuckles on the facing for the third time when the heavy wooden door swung to reveal a darkened tunnel of hallway. The beam of a flashlight hit him square in the eyes. He winced and raised a hand against it. Before his vision cleared, the cold steel of a wide-mouthed gun barrel kissed him firmly under his chin. It forced his gaze skyward. His hands automatically followed suit. He raised both, open-palmed and thumbs outward, just above shoulder height.

"What the hell do you want?" the gruff voice of James Blalock growled from somewhere in the darkness. "What you got pressed against your scruff is a .410. It's loaded, and the safety's off." The not-so-subtle *click* sound of the shotgun's hammer locked it into the cocked position. "You better have a got-damn good reason for setting foot at my door, or I swear to God I'll scatter your skull six ways from Sunday."

"We don't keep money around here, if that's what you're after," a shrill, tremulous voice called from inside the house. Georgia Blalock's words came from slightly farther away than her husband's. The beam of the flashlight trembled in his face as she spoke, which meant she was the one holding it. Sam's heart sank. If James Blalock had been managing both a flashlight and a shotgun, Sam would have had an opportunity to take advantage of the awkwardness to disarm him. He swallowed thickly.

"I don't want any trouble," he said. The end of the gun barrel pressed harder into the bone of his chin with each word. "I just came from Beard's General. The bridge is out, and the road is flooded. There are people trapped inside. I just need someone to call for help. If you've got a phone, you could call the constable. Or the sheriff."

There was silence from behind the barrel of the shotgun.

"I swear," Sam tried again. "I just need you to report the trapped folks. Then I'll be on my way. I was just coming in from Hollow River to see a friend of mine who lives a ways down past the store."

"Jimmy?" he heard the woman stage-whisper. "Eli's been over at Beard's for a long time today, even for Eli. I thought he'd be back before supper, but he wasn't. I figured he and that Beard boy must've just lost track of time. I was going to send him to bed without supper when he got home tonight."

James Blalock seemed to ignore this tidbit from his wife. "If the bridge is out and the road is flooded, how do you know there's people in there?" he demanded. "More'n that, how the hell did you get to my place from over there if you're coming in from Hollow River and the road's out? Knob's Mill don't connect to Hollow Creek for another five miles in that direction." He shoved the end of the barrel to

Sam's left to indicate a direction, then settled it back where it had been.

Shit.

Well, at least he knew which road and which way he had to go to get back to Pete's place. Knob Mill to Hollow Creek would have him on his way after riding here. *If* he rode from here.

Trespassing was a capital offense out in the boonies, especially if you were Black. It was a crime for which many white folks believed themselves judge, jury, and executioner. Blalock hadn't yet hurled the T-word at him, but Sam hadn't told him that he'd found his way to the house by traipsing over his border and through his lands. If he did, the man might decide that—trapped people or no trapped people—killing Sam was his civic duty. Or moral obligation. Or some other legal rationalization bullshit dreamed up by white men who chose to feel threatened by Sam's mere existence.

His chest tightened. The muscles in his calves, thighs, forearms, biceps, shoulders, and neck all pulled taut at once. His breath came in short, hot bursts through his nostrils, creating a dragon's breath effect when it hit the cold air the thunderstorms forced to the ground. He remembered these sensations well from his soldier days, but mostly the nights. Whether he willed it or not, his body was gearing up for a fight. He fought against his instincts to keep from balling his raised hands into fists.

"Answer me, boy!" echoed the voice of the man he could only vaguely see through the gloom from inside the house. "How'd you get here? You been trespassing on my property?"

James Blalock lunged forward with that last sentence, pressing the barrel of the shotgun so far into Sam's jaw that it caused him to bite down hard on his tongue. Self preservation took over. Sam grabbed the barrel with his right hand and snatched it out from under his chin, shoving it broadside into the exterior trim of the door. A loud *crack* and a hot yellow flash deafened and briefly blinded him when it went off.

Flecks of white-painted pine blew apart from a nearby porch column and scattered in all directions. The sting of heat and black powder singed his cheek. His ears filled with a cotton-muffled ringing sound. The Blalocks screamed in unison. Or they were shouting something at him that he couldn't understand. In the confusion, Sam wrapped a hand around the shotgun's barrel and pried the entire thing out of a stupefied James Blalock's grip.

He tossed the weapon off the porch, flinging it as far as he could into the storm. It spun longways in an arc that carried it somewhere beyond the range of his vision. Sam bolted, leaping over all three porch steps and landing gracefully on the gravel below them. Once in the saddle of his Triumph, he had it in First with the throttle wide before he'd even raised the kickstand. He turned to look at the startled white couple who had moved outside to their front porch. They gawked at him.

"Call the goddamn sheriff!" he screamed, not knowing whether they could hear him over the roar of the bike, not to mention their tinnitus from the gunshot. "Get help!"

The bike's rear tire spun gravel when he let out the clutch. Part of him hoped he'd sprayed James and Georgia Blalock with some of it as he rode into the darkness, into the rain, onto Knob's Mill Road.

Hopefully to Pete.

CHAPTER TWENTY-NINE

Marilyn shrieked. The sound shook the walls around them, rattling cans on shelves and vibrating a framed photo of Kathy Beard's late husband Jessie off its spot near the cash register. It clattered to the floor without breaking its glass. For Peter, that was both a blessing and a disappointment. It was a blessing because he'd had his fill of sharp things slicing and impaling his skin over his time in this world. It was a disappointment because he remembered how Donna Gilliam had made a simple tool of the broken glass from a picture frame. With it, she had wrestled ownership of the rest of her life from Ted.

Ted. Ted was dead, but Peter thought he recognized the tremulous, haunting voice that had echoed from the well inside Donna's throat a moment ago. Something besides Marilyn had used Donna's inner turmoil over killing Ted to speak through her. Peter wondered whether Marilyn's inability to feed on Donna was because someone else—*Ted?*—had gotten there first. But how?

Throughout the long night, Peter had watched the red steam rising from Mark and Eli and even from himself. For Mark, it wafted to the ceiling and out the door before they'd discovered Marilyn. Could the psychic abilities Marilyn had bequeathed him when she healed him have also infected the others from whom she'd drawn the stuff? Donna had some of it, too. Maybe even enough of it to connect with her late husband somehow.

It was useless to ponder that much more. The mysteries of Marilyn were too vast, even with his deep connection to her. Best to concentrate on what Donna had said, not how she had come to say it.

"There is no God in heaven," she had said. "The water cleans. The water purifies. There is no God but the water."

What did it mean? Beard's General was surrounded by filthy creek water. The people of Lost Hollow had become careless over the decades since a much younger Peter and his brief acquaintance Joe Bayless had plucked honeysuckles beside it. Drivers threw garbage out of car windows as they sped past. Once during a late summer drought, when the creek ran exceptionally low around the segment that flowed past the church, Peter had even seen a complete set of car tires laying in it. Easy times brought with them wastefulness.

The congregation used that part of the creek bed for baptisms whenever someone decided to become a member or if they just wanted a second chance at redemption. Most times, they just went home stinking of frog piss and cow shit after Mark raised them from the depths, no different than who they were before. Not really. But they felt better about themselves for having taken the plunge for the Lord, cleansing the slate of the markings of sin with a dab of babbling country runoff.

There is no God but the water.

There was God *in* the water.

That was another curious thing. When they'd brought her inside, Marilyn's naked body had been covered in pinpricks of red that had healed instantly after she had dried off. Well, as far as he could see. The coveralls Kathy had provided hid most of her, but Peter distinctly remembered a few of the boils on the parts of her neck that protruded from the coveralls. Her face was clear, too. Perfectly.

Then, when the creek water had threatened to flood the store itself and rose through the cracks in the floor planks at the front, he had sensed uneasiness in her. As they watched Jerry and Eli try to fight back the tides, that uneasiness had transitioned into fear. It had evolved into near terror before Marilyn sensed Peter's connection to her and shut him out. He had yet to master that skill, and he envied her for it. If more people understood what it truly meant for others to know their thoughts, they would not be so eager to share them.

It hadn't been until the rain slacked off and the waters receded some that Marilyn dared to approach the front of the store. The water had injured her. She was afraid of it. The panic episode had sapped her strength. That's why she had fed on poor Eli immediately after the water had subsided: to regain the energy the stress of the situation had cost her.

Peter had an idea.

Earlier that night (or possibly years ago), someone had set a glass of water on the cashier's stand. He couldn't recall whose glass it had been, only that his eyes had passed over it multiple times over the evening. He'd noted it most recently when the picture of Jessie fell over. He enjoyed the simple beauty in how the ceiling lights played on the glass and in the liquid itself. He eyed the stand and was relieved to find that the glass remained there, still half full.

"Hey," Marilyn demanded, startling him. "You just going to sit there looking stupid, or are you going to do what I asked?"

Peter smiled. She had, without realizing it, provided him with some cover. He bowed his head smartly toward her, careful not to allow Theo's head to roll around in his arms as he did. "Whatever you say," he said. "I'll go check on the porch first. Could be she stepped out to check the damage."

Donna snapped to her senses then, looking alarmed. "Oh! Give me my baby!"

Peter returned the infant, who slit open his eyes just enough to make sure everyone knew that he knew something was happening. When he was secure in his mother's arms again, he allowed them to close.

Donna looked at Peter urgently. "Kathy can't be out there by herself! Peter, please do go find her."

Whatever had happened to Donna a moment ago seemed to be lost on her, as if it had never occurred.

Peter nodded at her. "I'm going to look."

Theo pursed his lips, poked the tip of his tongue through them, and made a raspberry sound. Peter smiled sadly. *My sentiments exactly, kiddo*, he thought. *My sentiments exactly.*

He hobbled to the front of the store and grabbed the glass of water from the cashier's stand, chancing a look behind him to make sure Marilyn was not watching when he did. She wasn't in his head. Had Donna's outburst rattled her enough to forget about their connection? That, or she indeed had given up on him. Or he had successfully shut her out by himself. He doubted that last, however.

Wary that thinking about his connection to her might somehow reestablish it, Peter instead decided to concentrate on the shape and feel of the glass in his hand. He walked with it clasped in his left, holding it in front of his belt so that Marilyn couldn't see it even if she happened to look at him. With his right hand, he opened the front door. The air outside had cooled significantly compared to how it had been when he'd arrived at Beard's. A mist of rain and creek water sprayed him in the face when he stepped over the threshold. Frog piss and cow shit? Probably. But at that moment, it felt nice.

Propping his right hand against a support beam, Peter lowered himself into a kneeling position. He winced at the grating sound in his knees as they fought his attempts to bend them. The pain was excruciating, like someone had filled his joints with hot, pulverized glass. When he was finally down, he had the requisite old man moment of terrible fear that he might not stand up again. Funny. He'd always thought the old-timers meant that as a joke.

He shoved the fear aside, then transferred the glass of water from his left hand to his newly freed right. He dumped its clear contents into the rapids. Next, he dipped the glass into the running water, allowing it to fill until the flood tugged on it nearly hard enough to tear it away.

He turned the glass toward the light pouring from the front door and held it up close to his nose, peering at its new contents. It was nasty stuff, all right. It bore a striking resemblance to the contents of his commode after a bad church chili dinner fundraiser. It didn't smell as rank as that. Not quite. It was not something he'd want to drink, much less have splashed on him by someone who thought he was an apostate from Hell.

"We baptize people in this shit," Peter mused. "Might as well piss on them and tell them it's raining."

He shook his head sadly and began the long chore of regaining his feet. His shorter leg made that difficult even without the joint and tendon problems his rapid aging had thrust upon him. He wobbled when he gained his height and came close to tipping off the porch into the rush. His heart leaped into his throat over the falling sensation. But, he thought after he recovered his balance, there was also a part of him that had wanted it to happen. Drowning in a flood would be easier than what he had to do next if Mark had been right about Marilyn. If *he* was right about her.

Peter poured a tiny amount of the creek water back into the rapids, just enough to prevent him from sloshing it all over the floor while he limped inside with it. Marilyn watched him when he pulled the door and stepped over the threshold. Donna peered around from behind her.

"Well?" Marilyn said, cocking an eyebrow. She might have wanted to pretend to wonder aloud if he had found Kathy out there, the same Kathy that she had eaten alive and transformed into...something else. But before the words were out of her mouth, her eyes lit on the glass of creek water he carried. They widened in alarm. "What do you have there, Peter?"

He grinned sheepishly, not bothering to act as if he didn't know what she was talking about, and continued his stride toward her. He paused once mid-stride to wince when he felt her searching around in his mind. He imagined a brick wall, trying to shut her out. "Oh, just a glass of Hollow Creek water," he said. "Dipped the glass off the side of the porch, and this is what came up." He held it up so she could get a better look. "Nasty, ain't it? All brown and sick-looking. If you look close in the light, you can see weird things floating in it."

Marilyn's wide eyes narrowed to slits. "And what do you intend to do with it? I am sure Kathy will give you some clean tap water if you want something to drink."

"Oh, no," he replied. "It's not for me. I wouldn't drink this stuff if you promised me a million dollars and the keys to my very own palace. As I was outside looking for Kathy, it occurred to me that this water, this…stuff is the same stuff we dunk our congregation in to purify them, to cleanse them of sin and iniquities. Ironic, isn't it? Something with so much of our pollution and shit in it, something so powerfully destructive that it trapped seven of us in this store with a demon from Hell, is the same stuff we use to perform one of the most sacred acts of our faith."

"Seven?" Donna called. "Who else is here?"

Peter ignored her but noted that she didn't ask about his demon from Hell remark. Dimly, he hoped it meant that somewhere inside her were still memories of all the previous events inside the store, from all the time and memory resets that had led them all to this point and him to his enfeebled age.

"You look scared," he said to Marilyn. "Did I strike a nerve? Hit the mark? Nail the bullseye? Dunk the clown? No? Then I need more *practice!*"

On the last word, Peter flung the glass of creek water directly into Marilyn's face. The airborne wave of brown muck struck the center of its target, dampening her nose, eyes, forehead, lips, cheeks, and chin. The pores under her apparently waterproof makeup enlarged and began to gasp clouds of crimson smoke. Many of them bubbled and became engorged with something. They inflated smooth and blackened, bulging outward like spider eyes. Then they burst and drooped down her cheeks and forehead like melting pocket watches in a Salvador Dalí painting.

Peter backpedaled as fast as he could without falling on his ass. He had expected—well, he hadn't known *what* to expect. Whatever it was, it hadn't been this. Marilyn lurched toward him, her arms outstretched. Her nails were ragged. The tops of her fingers and the backs of her hands had grown thick patches of long brown hair.

"You!" she gargled. A viscous black liquid poured out of her mouth when she opened it. Peter could see the points of fangs descending from her gums through the stuff. "You were supposed to help me! You were supposed to feed me! I saved you. I *healed* you." She sounded genuinely hurt. "Why have you forsaken me?"

Peter snarled back at her. "I didn't forsake you," he shouted, hot tears welling in his eyes. "You lied to me. I thought you were here to help *all of us*. You let me think there was something *wrong* with all of us. You didn't save me. You didn't absolve me. You just preyed on the guilt and shame my mother instilled in me about who I am. *YOU LET ME KEEP THINKING I WAS A BAD MAN!*"

He kicked at the floor with his shorter leg and flung the glass against the wall in frustration. It shattered and collapsed to the floor in a heap of fragments, none of them conveniently shaped like the blade of a knife.

"I *was* saving you!" Marilyn screeched. "All I needed was your help feeding and then I could keep you. I could protect you. We could have protected each other."

Peter clapped his hands over his ears. He could feel her trying to burrow inside his head. It was like sticking a finger into the middle of a wet sponge. He shut his eyes, held his breath, and imagined himself squeezing the sponge dry so that it was no longer so pliable. That shoved her out. For the time being, anyway.

"You're trying to manipulate me again," he said. "Poor, broken Peter Mayberry, is that it? Not enough confidence in who he is to bother standing up for himself? There's a saying around here. 'Fool me once, shame on you. Fool me twice, shame on me.' You've shown me who you are. You're no friend. You're no protector. And you're no savior. Not for me. Not for anybody."

The pupils of Marilyn's eyes filled their entire sockets, blazing a bright red. She stooped over, ape-like, and Peter watched in astonishment as her shoulders broadened and her biceps and forearms thickened underneath her coveralls.

"I. AM. HUUUNGRRYYYYY!" She leaped at him. The claws on her right hand passed in front of his nose as he struggled to back away. Miraculously, she missed and tumbled to the floor. She landed on her face and the palms of her strange simultaneously human and canine hands. A satisfying *crunch* thundered through the air when her face hit the floor. It sounded like a thick branch collapsing to the ground from the top of a dried-up black walnut tree.

Peter blinked, unable to comprehend at first what had happened. Then Donna Gilliam was standing over Marilyn's sprawled body. She had quietly placed Theo in his carrier during the drama and set him on the floor. When Marilyn lunged at Peter, Donna had simply stuck out her foot and tripped her.

Peter and Donna shared a sigh of relief over the demon's body. There was something different about the young mother. Crow's feet had spread from the corners of her eyes, forming fault lines that fanned out toward her temples. Her soft, young woman's hair had become coarse and gray in spots. She seemed smaller somehow, too.

"Donna," Peter started, but she cut him off.

"I remember everything," she said, a bittersweet smile on her lips. "Kathy. Jerry. Eli. Mark. I remember them all.

I don't know how." She glanced around them at the store, which had not aged at all. "How long have we been trapped here? How many times has that *thing* fed on us and forced us to forget so she could do it again?"

Peter shrugged helplessly. "I don't know," he said. "She only fed on me the one time. I suppose that's why I look so much older. Time has kept its hold on me. She told me she wanted my help, but I still don't understand what she meant by that. Unless it was just to help her find fresh, uh, food."

"Well," Donna replied, "what are we going to do?"

Before they could decide, Marilyn heaved a ragged breath and was on her feet again. She leaped up facing Peter but spun on her toes and ran at Donna instead. She wrapped her hairy, elongated fingers around the woman's shoulders and drew her close as if in a lover's embrace. She tilted her head to one side, canine jaws parted. Then she sank her fangs into the soft flesh of Donna's cheeks, piercing the skin through and into the void of her mouth as she screamed.

"*NO!*" Peter shouted. He launched himself at the two of them, wrapping his sagging arms around Marilyn's newly narrow and muscular abdomen. He braced himself and yanked backward, hoping gravity would aid what remained of his strength in toppling her to the floor. He had no plan for what he would do once they impacted. But that didn't matter. Right now, he wanted only to pull her off Donna.

She was too strong.

Peter slid his arms up her torso and crawled onto her back as best he could. He wrapped his legs around hers, pulling his feet together into a V-shape between what would have been her thighs if she had been a human woman. With his elbows as taut as he could stretch them in her armpits, Peter yanked backward with all his might.

When Marilyn did not budge, he balled his right hand into a fist, raised it into the air over his head, and brought it down hard on the back of her skull. It was like hitting a wall of solid granite. His pulse throbbed in the meat of his palm as each punch landed.

"Please," he cried. "Please, don't take her. She has a baby, for God's sake. She has a baby!" He gulped down a sizable wad of mucus. "Listen. Listen to me. If you let her live, I really can help you. I'm the church pianist. I worked closely with Mark. I know things about the people who worship there. I know which ones hide guilt and shame. You'd have enough steam to feed you for the entire rest of their lives."

"And then?" the creature snarled at him. She allowed Donna's body, shriveled and charred but somehow still alive, to fall to the floor in front of them. Peter slid off Marilyn and moved backward a few steps. Marilyn turned to face him. She had regained much of her human shape, although her shoulders remained broad. Her arms were enormous as well. They thrummed with the bulging muscles of a Greek statue, muscles the real Marilyn Monroe would never possess.

Peter's mind raced. "Well," he said, "then I don't know for sure. But we'll find someone, something. The world is bounteous with people who have said and done horrible things that they'll regret all their lives. It doesn't matter how often they are told they are forgiven for most of them. For a lot of us, forgiving ourselves might as well be traveling to the moon. It's something that's beyond what we'd achieve in two lifetimes, let alone one."

Was she grinning at him? "You did it," she said. "I took your steam and healed you, and you were done. You have no more steam to feed me."

Peter sighed. "No," he replied. "I didn't forgive myself. I just realized that I felt guilty and shameful about something I should not have been. I was ashamed of who I am. Not because I did something wrong or because I was a bad person, but because I grew up with people *telling* me I was a bad person."

"And all these others?" Marilyn countered, sweeping a hand at the room as if Mark, Kathy, Jerry, and Eli were all still standing there with them. "They all ran out of steam, too, didn't they? I fed on them for years and years. But they all eventually forgave themselves, didn't they? And we are down to this."

She looked tired suddenly, dropping her gaze. Her eyes drifted to the door, beyond which a fresh volley of pounding rain, lightning, and thunder was firing up. "I cannot hold this all together for much longer," she said. "This pocket of time and space. This body. I thought I had created a new eternity in this place. I wanted it to be a place to survive, rich in food and flavor. I thought it was safer here. But it's not. It's not safe at all. It's just a different kind of Hell."

Peter nodded. "Fine," he said. "You didn't get your Eden. Then why not give up? Stop what you're doing here and let us go? Go back where you came from or just wink out of existence. It doesn't matter to me either way."

She cut her eyes back to him, anger boiling behind them. "You don't understand the hunger," she said. "There's a need inside me that I can't control. It is overpowering, and it is urgent. I will do anything to satiate it." A long line of saliva drooled from her lower lip and dangled there, the weight of its wobble stretching it toward the floor as she spoke. "Anything. Even if it means draining you all down to your insignificant, primordial cores."

"Then you're going to force me to fight you," he replied.

She tossed back her head and laughed at him, her Marilyn hair tousled. It would have been pretty on a movie screen, except it was speckled here and there with blood and long black, brown, and strawberry blonde strands of animal fur. "You can't fight me, Peter Mayberry. Not if you had size and strength and youth enough even to come close to matching me. Whether you understand it or not, you are an old man. Feeble. In pain. Your *fight* is as useless against me as your words. When I'm done with all of you, I will leave this place and hunt again, no matter what futile end it may lead to."

Peter's blood burned. He knew that many in Lost Hollow had thought him weak, a momma's boy. They had whispered as much behind his back. He was only the church pianist and a piano teacher, after all. He had the long and slender fingers to prove it. His digits must look quite the mismatch against his unequal frame.

But hearing Marilyn, a stranger, pick up on that and state it out loud enraged him. He looked down at his hands and imagined himself sinking those thin fingers into the flesh around her temples while he plunged his thumbs into her eyes. The thought of it filled him with strangely manic glee.

"Well," he replied. "We'll just see about that." He skirted Marilyn and knelt beside Donna, intending to lift the gasping living mummy to her feet. He meant to stand in the way of Marilyn making the rest of a meal out of her. "I'm not going to let you take her away from her baby."

The next thing he knew, Peter was skidding on his ass across the linoleum tiled floor section of Beard's General. The back of his head and his shoulders slammed into the far wall, sending a shock wave down his spine and into his legs and toes. He thought he heard something snap when he hit and momentarily feared for his neck. A quick rotation of his head in either direction and a test wiggle of his toes convinced him that the sound must have been his imagination.

When the world stopped spinning, and he located Marilyn, she was already on Donna again. A disgusting wet squelching sound ripped the air as the woman's muscles and tendons imploded and her skin drew up tight around her bones. Then came the crunch of the bones themselves. They snapped like dry twigs. Peter recognized it as the sound he'd heard when he'd hit the wall. He had just been wrong about its source.

The snapped bones grated against each other as they collapsed and were ground to powder inside Donna's body. Peter grimaced and plugged his ears. He'd seen a lot tonight, but somehow watching (and *hearing*!) Donna Gilliam being consumed while her infant looked on serenely from his carrier on the floor was more than he could bear. He laid on the floor and curled up in a fetal position there, screaming, hoping he could somehow drown out that god-awful chewing sound.

His scream trailed off into a hoarse whimper, and, after he had no more air to give voice to it, he realized that the eating noises had stopped. Peter opened his eyes and blinked away the glaze of moisture that his cries had left behind. He pulled his hands away from his ears and sat up. In the spot where Donna Gilliam had lain rested a shiny, bony black creature. Stalks or feelers waved independently of each other on what Peter had to assume was its head. He stared at it, and it seemed to notice him. It crawled toward him, moving slowly but deliberately over the linoleum.

Marilyn sat on the floor beside it, paying it no mind. Her face was a mask of serenity. Her eyes were upturned so that the irises were mere crescents under her eyelids as if she was in intense orgasm or ecstasy. Even from this distance, Peter thought he could see the throbbing pulse of her heart in the cords of her neck.

"Monster," he whispered.

He stood and met the tiny creature halfway. As he'd done with the remains of all the others that evening, he pinched its mid-section between his thumb and forefinger and hoisted it into the air. He took a short trip to the mop bucket and dropped it gently inside along with Mark, Kathy, Jerry, and Eli. There were five of them crawling around the bottom of the bucket. Five *things* that used to be human beings, his friends and neighbors.

Behind him, he heard a soft grunt followed by a whine. Theo began to fuss. Peter turned toward the sound and saw the boy's tiny fists loosely balled over his head, trembling there with that classic baby reaction to being too hot or too cold or too hungry or too bored. How did you know which one was the problem? It was just him and Theo against Marilyn: a senior citizen and an infant.

Attempts to plan his next steps faltered in his head. He wanted to fight, but he also wanted to flee. He thought of leaping into the Hollow Creek overflow while Marilyn busied herself with her food-induced orgasm.

He could try swimming against the current for the road, but that would leave Theo here all alone. He didn't want to do that. He couldn't make the swim with the kid in tow, either. He and Theo both would surely drown.

Unable to think, Peter collapsed beside the carrier that held Theo and soothingly stroked the thin lock of hair closest to his wrinkly forehead. When the baby settled again, Peter rested his elbows on his knees and cradled his head in the palms of his hands.

He wept.

CHAPTER THIRTY

Why was he holding onto them all? Aside from distant hope that there was some way to restore his fellow castaways to their human forms, he didn't know. He only knew that through all these hours (*years*, he reminded himself) he had experienced an irresistible compulsion to gather them up and place them somewhere that seemed safe after Marilyn had sucked out their souls. That was more than he could say for himself and Theo. They were alone in the wolf's den and, as Marilyn had pointed out, he was just an old man. Against her, he was as helpless as Theo, only an infant.

She sat across from them still, reveling in whatever sweet sensation her consumption of Donna Gilliam's soul had instilled in her. She would snap out of it soon. Her irises had already returned to their rightful forward positions in her eye sockets. Her lips, by contrast, remained frozen in that psychopathic grin of post-feeding revelry. Peter wanted to punch her right in the gleaming white teeth that sparkled within it. Her stare prevented him from acting on the impulse. Her eyes seemed to follow him when he leaned left or right in their path, daring him to act while she was digesting her latest feast.

Beside him, Theo cooed. He broke the staring contest with Marilyn to check on the boy. Bright blue eyes radiating the pure light of innocence and trust beamed from them. Theo smiled. Peter hadn't seen him do that before. Was it the kid's first smile? The thought prompted a sympathetic pang of loss in Peter, a loss that Theo wouldn't feel or understand until much later in his life. If he *had* a much later. Peter smiled back at the baby automatically, although no part of him felt like smiling at that moment.

I must get him out of here.

Beyond Marilyn lay the broken remnants of the glass he'd thrown against the wall in anger. He regretted that deeply. A simple glass of creek water had temporarily disabled her. If he could do that again, he could find some way to keep her out of commission until it was safe for him to carry the baby outside and away. He'd need more than a tiny glass of creek water for that, but even a glass seemed like too much to ask now that he'd shattered the only one sitting out anywhere.

There's the mop bucket, his mother's voice buzzed inside his head. *Holding water is what it's for, dummy. Dump the stupid critters out and fill the mop bucket. Drench her while she's still sitting there catatonic. She'll melt like the Wicked Witch of the West, and you can focus on finding a way through that flood out there.*

Right. The mop bucket. Why hadn't he thought of it before? What to do with its residents in the meantime?

Forget them, his mother snapped.

"I can't do that, Momma," he said aloud. *If I turn them loose, they'll run away. How will I explain that to Theo when he grows up? How will I explain it to the church when Mark doesn't come to preach on Easter? How will I explain it to the* town when Kathy and Jerry Beard suddenly aren't here to run the store?*

A pause, and then his mother's voice returned: *How are you going to explain it anyway? They're not people anymore.*

Good point.

You're running out of time, boy. It's now or never.

Peter scanned the store, searching for any container he could use to hold the remains of the residents of Lost Hollow or as a substitute for the creek water reservoir he needed. The shelves in Beard's General were stocked with all kinds of can-shaped things. Coffee tins, jars, sacks, and boxes all caught his eye. He considered dumping out a large can of Brim coffee. It was less than half the volume of the mop bucket. It didn't have a handle, so it wouldn't be as easy to carry back and forth from the risen creek. But he could easily keep the critters together by transferring them to it.

The problem solved, Peter climbed to his feet. He walked three steps toward the shelves that held the ground coffee when Marilyn's left arm shot out from her side. She clamped her hand around his ankle, holding fast. Peter gasped and tried to jerk his leg away. He succeeded only in throwing himself off balance. He pinwheeled his arms and miraculously righted himself, but not before he caught sight of her seething mouth filling up with fangs again.

"What are you doing, Peter?" she asked. The menacing rictus she'd borne since devouring Donna did not fade with the effort.

"I—" he stammered, then decided it wasn't worth trying to fabricate excuses. She could read his mind if she wanted to. "I don't have to tell you that. You already know what I'm doing, don't you?"

She tilted her head, batting her eyes at him coquettishly. The flirtatious gesture added a cartoonishly surreal quality to her face that would have been funny if he'd seen it in a Looney Tune from the safety of a cushioned seat in a movie theater. Animated, she would have looked like the Big Bad Wolf in an adaptation of "The Three Little Pigs" or "Red Riding Hood." In real life, she was utterly terrifying. Peter's heart raced. She seemed to sense that, too, because her grip tightened on his ankle. Blood pulsated maddeningly in his temples.

"I *want* you to tell me," she said. "You offered to travel the world with me, remember? If you want that, shouldn't we begin by being honest?" Her face softened. "It's lonely being me, you know. I've been thinking about everything you said. I don't want to have to kill you, Peter. Not if we can help each other."

He nodded, sighing. "I know. I know."

"Then tell me what you were going to do."

Peter drew wind through his teeth and then spilled it. "I was going to fill that mop bucket over there with creek water and dump it on you. I hoped it would stop you. Or kill you." He looked at her. Her gaze was expressionless. He tried to probe her mind but was met with a blank wall.

"You don't understand," he continued. "I've seen what happens when we run out of guilt for you to feed on. There are only two of us left here. The water outside is showing no signs of receding. Hell, it's still raining! If I don't stop you, and you stay here, you're going to feed on either me or on the baby. Or both of us if it lasts long enough."

She grinned at him again. "And?"

"And then we'd be dead!" he shouted back at her. "If you're not lonely enough to stop yourself from eating me, can't you at least stop yourself from killing an innocent?

Theo's a baby. He doesn't even have the capacity for sin or guilt yet."

Marilyn pursed her lips. At least, it *looked* like she was pursing her lips. It was difficult to read her expressions through all the canine features that had overwhelmed it. Was she hungry again already? Less than five minutes after she'd come out of what he was beginning to think of as her digestion coma? If so, he thought, the odds of him and Theo escaping her alive dropped dramatically. The longer she stayed satiated, the less likely she was to attack. But if her hunger was returning more frequently, like an opium addict needing bigger and more frequent doses to get any joy—well, then, he didn't have time to plan anymore. He needed to act.

From somewhere around Marilyn came a low, long growl. Peter thought she was grumbling at him. Then she pressed the distinctly paw-like free hand to her stomach. He recognized the sound for what it was: a hunger pang.

"Oh, dear," Marilyn said, not taking her eyes off him. "I do love the steamy flavors of sin. But, as you just heard, in the end, it comes down to what's available. I like you, Peter. You believed in me, and you wanted to help me. You can *still* help me. I'll tell you what I'm going to do. I'm going to give *you* a choice. I can either eat you next or eat the baby over there.

"If you choose the baby, I won't be hungry for a while. You'll have a chance to decide whether you want to kill me or join me when the rain lets up, and the waters recede enough for us to get out of here." She chuckled. "Of course, if that doesn't happen, I'll just end up having to eat you anyway, I suppose. But at least you'll have a fighting chance.

"If you choose for me to eat you next out of some sense of heroic selflessness, all is lost for both of you. But you know that already, don't you? You said that the baby is too young to sin or feel guilt. Therefore, it's also too young to reason. *Therefore*, it cannot help me, and it is helpless against me."

Marilyn let go of his ankle and stood up, folding her arms in that smugly patient way women like his mother did when she knew she'd won no matter what Peter said or did.

"So," she said, "what do you choose?"

Peter glanced at the ceiling and then down at his feet, avoiding her eyes, trying to keep the surface of his mind blank so she wouldn't sense what he was thinking. The coffee can idea was a no-go. He'd tipped his hand there. He doubted he'd have time to rip open a container, dump out the coffee, and fill it with creek water before she chomped down on him. The mop bucket had no lid, but it held the somewhat living remains of his friends and neighbors. It was also farther away than the coffee.

"You have five seconds," Marilyn intoned.

"What? You didn't say there was a time limit for this."

She shrugged. "I don't like waiting for food."

Peter sighed. "All right, then. I've made my decision."

"Which is?"

"Neither!" He dashed for the mop bucket, fully expecting Marilyn to fling an arm over his chest or throw a foot under his legs as he ran. When those things didn't happen, a spark of hope kindled inside his heart. She hadn't been fast enough to stop him. If he grabbed the bucket and let the critters inside it be damned, he might reach the creek water before she could stop him. He wanted to look behind him, to check whether she was in pursuit. But he dared not. He'd falter if he saw her on his tail, and his balance wasn't all that good anyway.

His right hand closed around the metal handle fastened to the lip of the mop bucket. He hoisted it, contents and all, into the air. He pivoted to make a dash for the door but stopped dead in his tracks when he caught sight of Marilyn in his periphery. She hadn't budged from the spot where she'd stood with her arms folded. Not at all. The spark of hope ignited only a second before was just as suddenly extinguished. Ice gripped his heart when its warmth winked out.

"You're not going to try to stop me?"

She laughed. "I already have."

Peter's mind whirled with possible interpretations of what she'd just said. He looked down at his feet to make sure she hadn't magically nailed them to the floor. He looked at the door and listened to make sure the storm was still raging. He looked in the mop bucket to verify that there was no giant hole in the bottom of it. There wasn't. It was still crawling with the soul remainders of his friends and neighbors. Then he looked back at Marilyn.

"It doesn't seem to me like you've stopped anything."

He was about to break for the door again, but she broke first. In a flash, Marilyn was at Theo's baby carrier. She reached into it and plucked him out by his onesie, holding him aloft by the back of the neck in a fashion that Donna would have immediately recognized as a drunken Ted Gilliam special.

"No!" Peter screamed. He dropped the mop bucket, not caring how it jostled the tiny creatures trapped inside, and raced toward the monster. He was running on rubber legs, his arms outstretched at their full length but somehow never long enough to reach the dangling infant.

Theo kicked at the air, fussing. His tiny face was screwed up in a purplish twist of uncomprehending pain and rage.

His arms flailed wildly up and down. The boy was a tufted titmouse lying injured on the ground, desperately trying to take flight while a predatory house cat bore down on him.

"I take it back!" Peter shouted. "I take it back! Just give me a minute to think!"

Marilyn came unhinged at the mouth. She tilted back her head. Her lower jaw dropped away at an obtuse angle that would have been impossible for any native creature of this world. She raised Theo high above her head and dangled him over the gorge. His eyes bulged angrily from their sockets. Tiny spit bubbles foamed on the edges of his lips. One expanded from his right nostril and burst in a wet spray that dotted his cheek and upper lip.

Peter closed in on the two of them, his hands nearly under Theo's armpits. Then Marilyn let go. Theo plummeted. And fell.

And fell.

Peter's arms closed around nothing. Marilyn's mouth snapped shut. She swallowed audibly. Then they looked one to another in silence. Peter's eyes were wide and alarmed, tearing up. Marilyn's cheeks bulged and relaxed as if she were swishing mouthwash. She belched then, spewing out a tiny black object that landed on the floor of Beard's General at Peter's feet.

At first, it appeared to be a shiny black ball of metal or plastic. Then it unfolded itself. It was another one of those creatures he'd been dumping in the mop bucket all night long.

It was all that was left of baby Theo Gilliam.

Peter was alone.

CHAPTER THIRTY-ONE

The five miles from the Blalock farm by way of Knob's Mill to its mouth at Hollow Creek Road might as well have been fifty. The needle pricks of the pouring rain against his gunpowder-scorched face forced Sam to slow the Triumph to thirty miles per hour and soon to a measly twenty-five. Occasionally, he glanced at the road behind him to make sure he wasn't being followed by the Blalocks or, God forbid, a sheriff's deputy after having left things the way he had at the farm. It was something he could have to answer for later, but it would have to *be* later. With each mile he put between himself and the Blalock farm, his need to locate Pete grew more urgent. He couldn't shake the feeling that something was wrong.

By the time he reached the T at the end of Knob's Mill and turned right onto Hollow Creek Road, the rain had slackened again. On more familiar ground, he opened the throttle and made the trip to Pete's house in less than five minutes. The bike skidded some at the end of the driveway when he leaned into the turn. Otherwise, the last leg of the trip was uneventful.

Sam rode the bike to the back of the house out of habit and parked it under the awning over the back porch. There it was out of sight of any curious passersby. It would be out of reach of the weather there because Pete, at some point after his mother died, had had the foresight to have the hillside behind his place graded so that any water that happened to overflow his gutters would drain away from the house and not into it. It was beautiful work, too, lined with riprap rock like the walls of the creek bed along the side of the highway. Sam's tires left a thin, muddy trail against the smooth, sterling white concrete back there. He would clean it up for Pete later. If he remembered.

Without knocking, he shoved the back door and stepped over the threshold onto a bristly welcome mat. Dripping and covered in stick tights and chunks of mud and gravel, Sam called out.

"Pete?" he shouted. "It's Sam! You here?"

He waited, but no answer came.

Shit.

Sam dropped to his left knee, unlaced his boot, pulled it off his pruned foot—his sock came off with it—and laid it considerately on the welcome mat. He shifted to the right knee and repeated the process. Barefoot, he trod cautiously through the house room-by-room, glancing in every corner before again calling out to the strangely neurotic white man he'd come to love.

He entered the main bedroom from the back hallway and stood in nearly the exact spot where he'd stood naked earlier that day. The memory of the anger, his argument with Pete, seethed there. Light from the room's far door, which led to the kitchen, fell across the floor and onto the nightstand like the blade of a knife. It half-illuminated the severe black-and-white portrait of the Mayberry matriarch. Sam could see only her unsmiling mouth and the tip of her nose in that light. That was all right with him because her eyes were the most severe of her features. He'd never liked the way she looked at him from whatever slice of time that photograph held within its frame.

"Pete?" he called again. "It's Sam. Listen, I'm sorry about this morning. I just want to talk to you. I need to know that you're okay. We can talk about the rest of the stuff after that. If you want to."

No answer.

"Pete?"

Sam walked the length of the bedroom, carefully avoiding line of sight with the image of Mother Mayberry, and entered the kitchen. He was not a screaming kind of man. The war had stomped most of the screaming out of him while he was overseas. But what he saw on the kitchen floor of his boyfriend's house that night was enough to startle a yelp from the former soldier. He stood frozen, unblinking and unbelieving, over the purplish crimson wash that had dripped from the kitchen table and pooled into a congealing mass on the floor.

"Pete?" he shouted it this time at volume, only because he couldn't scream it. His eyes registered the hammer lying on the floor beside the red goop. Had someone broken in? Had they bludgeoned Pete to death at his kitchen table? Sam's heart beat fast and hard inside his chest. It filled his head with repeating surges of pressure, roaring in his ears and pounding against the walls of his forehead and temples like furious ocean waves crashing cliffside during a hurricane.

"Pete! Where in God's name are you?"

He stepped farther into the kitchen to see across to where the floor met the house's exterior wall. No sign of Pete, nor any indication that someone had dragged his, *uhm*, remains over the colorful splatter-patterned kitchen linoleum. Sam rushed to the bathroom. There were no bloody fingerprints or smeared handprints on the mirror. No signs of a struggle. No body in the bathtub.

"Pete!" His voice reverberated against the tile. The echo made the place feel emptier, crypt-like.

Panicked, Sam ran through the rest of the house: the utility, the living room where Peter taught his piano lessons. He threw open every closet door he could find. He even yanked on the pull string that opened the mouth of the attic. Finding no evidence that it had been recently used, he released his grip and let the springs that connected the hatch's arms to its frame pull it closed again.

Dammit.

Out of ideas, Sam returned to the kitchen. He reached for the telephone handset, which sat cradled on an older-looking wood-paneled device mounted to the kitchen wall. He was prepared to tell the operator anything, everything if it meant getting someone out here to figure out where Pete was, what had happened to him. The risk to him was enormous. Here he was, a Black man from out of town standing on the bloodied floor of a white churchgoing pianist's kitchen. There was every chance any responding officers would arrest him, if not outright murder him, just for being here. Add to that the missing homeowner and the gruesome scene and, well, it could only end with him either murdered or in prison, especially if Pete himself never turned up again.

Sam supposed he could report the problem without identifying himself. He could flee the scene before the cops arrived and cross his fingers that no one noticed him. The memory of the Blalock man shoving a shotgun in his jaw less than an hour prior surfaced.

With his free hand, Sam absently stroked the spot where the jackass had embedded the barrel under his chin. How much had he told the Blalocks about where he was going and what he was doing? It had all happened so fast. Would they remember him if they heard Pete had gone missing and blood was found at his home? Would they make the connection and report what had happened? Hell, he'd asked them to call the police in the first place. If they'd heeded his call for help, they might have *already* reported him as well.

"Suspicious character," the police report would say. "A suspicious character showed up at the Blalock farm that night. He rode a motorcycle in the direction of Hollow Creek Road. He was being suspicious. An hour later, a mystery telephone caller reported Peter Mayberry missing or dead."

Not reporting what he'd found would look even more suspicious if the authorities did manage to connect him to it through the Blalocks. Still undecided, Sam plucked the handset from its cradle, placed it to his ear, and was met with deafening silence. There was no dial tone nor operator asking for a "number, please." No snippet of conversation transmitted to him from someone else's call on the party line. Much to Sam's annoyance, Pete had yet to pony up the dough for a private line. Over the years, he had found that communication—whether with a friend or a lover—was crucial for establishing trust and love. A private line would have facilitated that effort for them both. With the party line in place, neither man dared to call the other over the wires.

Sam tapped and released the switch hook in a rapid one-two-three pattern and listened again. Nothing. The storm must have knocked down a line somewhere. Now what?

He slammed the handset into its cradle and leaned against the wall, propping his heavy, pounding forehead against the palm of his right hand. Through the door that led to the bedroom he could see the cold eyes of Peter's dead mother glaring at him from the black-and-white photo on the nightstand, accusing him. Even sans color, she seemed alive inside the world behind that frame and glass. Hateful. Smug. She was daring him to keep on trying to insert himself into her son's life.

Snarling, Sam stalked into the bedroom and snatched the photo from the nightstand. He tucked it inside his motorcycle jacket, carrying it with him to the back door of Pete's house. He knelt there, pulling on first his left boot, then switching knees and pulling on his right. When he opened the door, the cold and wet storm wind tried to shove him back inside. Sam pushed past it. He fastened his helmet, climbed onto the Triumph, started it, and rode around to the front of the house.

He hadn't noticed when he'd arrived, but it occurred to him that he'd seen no sign of Pete's car. It was neither in the driveway nor around back where he'd parked his bike. There were also no signs of other automobiles. Either Pete had hurt himself and tried to drive himself to the hospital, or someone else had hurt him and had help getting rid of the evidence.

Then why not clean up the blood? he wondered. Lost Hollow had no hospital, at least as far as Sam knew. The nearest one would've been in Hollow River. If Pete had gone there, Sam was sure they would've met somewhere along his ride to the small town after his change of heart and before he'd encountered the flooded road with the bridge out at Beard's.

The corner of the picture frame poked him in the ribs as he leaned the Triumph into the turn onto Hollow Creek Road, rain pelting his face again like arrows launched from hundreds of tiny bows. A memory bubbled to the surface of his mind. On one of the few occasions Pete had allowed alcohol to loosen his tongue and cast off his armor, he'd told Sam all about the horrid Mother Mayberry and the hot nail she had once driven through her own child's tongue. He'd also told Sam about how his mother still spoke to him sometimes from inside his head; how she urged him to repent for what she called his *predilection*. The only way to repent? To bleed.

"If thy hand or thy foot offend thee, cut them off, and cast them from thee," Pete had said. He was quoting the book of Matthew from the King James Bible but imitating the shrill and scratchy voice of Margaret Hamilton as the Wicked Witch of the West from "The Wizard of Oz." He'd never met the woman, but Sam reckoned it was probable that Mother Mayberry sounded very much like that old green lady. "It is better for thee to enter into life halt or maimed, rather than having two hands or two feet to be cast into everlasting fire."

Before he could continue with the next verse, the one about plucking out your eye, Sam placed a finger against his lips, shushing him. He hadn't intended to get Pete drunk that night. He wanted and appreciated the honesty and the insight, but it would be better coming from a sober Pete, not a drunk one who might wake up the next day with a hangover and regrets. Anyway, he'd heard enough. This man who sat drinking with him was still a boy in a hell of a lot of ways. He hated his mother but also loved her and obeyed her because that's what a good boy is supposed to do, even after Momma has long decayed in the earth.

Maybe their fight that morning had triggered another round of penitent pain. If Pete had tried to drive himself to the hospital but had only made it as far as Beard's, he could be trapped inside by the flooded creek and the washed-out bridge. Now that he'd made it to Pete's, Sam could come at the store from the opposite direction on Hollow Creek Road. Hopefully he could find a way across. It would need to be a secondary road that could get him somewhere around the back of the peninsula on which the store sat. At this point, even a downed tree stretched across the creek bed would do.

Less than one mile after he'd turned onto Hollow Creek Road, Sam slowed the bike at a part in the trees and scrub along the shoulder. Beyond it, he could see risen creek water rushing along the top edge of its bed. Soon, this branch of the flow would hit flood stage. It would cover this section of road just like the section around Beard's. If he continued beyond this point, there was no turning back. He would either find a way into the store or spend what was left of the storm out in the rain and lightning, trying to avoid being washed away.

He unzipped his motorcycle jacket enough to get an arm inside it and retrieved the picture of Pete's mother from its depths. He turned it face up and examined it. In the darkness, he couldn't make out much of the monster's image. Yet he could still *feel* her staring at him from within, hating him.

"He's not yours anymore," Sam said. He flung the photograph, frame and all, through the part in the shoulder growth and toward the creek rapids. He lost sight of it in mid-arc thanks to the darkness of the night. He thought he heard a slight splashing sound a second or so later. He might have imagined it. It was possible that the photo was lying somewhere near the creek bed instead of drowning in the rushing onslaught. Either way, she was gone from him. With any luck, she was gone from Pete as well.

Sam shifted the Triumph into First and opened the throttle, feeling somehow lighter than he had a moment before. Wherever Pete was, Sam was suddenly sure that he was still alive and safe from the storm. Together they would be safe from the ghost of his mother here on out and forever if Sam had anything to say about it. He would make sure of that. Somehow.

Minutes later, he arrived at the mouth of an unmarked secondary road that led away from Hollow Creek and possibly to a way around the flooded areas. Sam was a half-mile down that road when he came upon what was once another tiny bridge. It had collapsed into a ragged, gaping chasm of asphalt with black-as-night creek water ripping along the other side of it. He was lucky he'd seen it or he could've plunged headlong, bike and all, into the rush.

He pounded a closed fist against the Triumph's gas tank, swore, and turned the bike around again. Back to Hollow Creek Road it was, then.

Hang on, Pete.

CHAPTER THIRTY-TWO

The Marilyn thing lay propped against a shelf of dry goods, awake but not exactly alert. Her hands, with fingers interlaced, rested against her tummy. Though ragged at the tips, the nails had mostly returned to their red-polished human form. Her eyes were half-lidded. Only a glimmer of red crescent peered through the fences of the luxuriant eyelashes growing out of her upper lid. An alarmingly wide, shark-toothed grin spread over her lips, stretching them the width of her head. It was a grin of satisfaction, of satiation, of a woman content in the smell of her own farts.

"Th-That was just a baby," Peter said. He waited, but she made no indication that she had heard. Her voice inside his head remained quiet as well, leaving his mind feeling like an auditorium after the crowds had left and the janitor had shut off the lights. "I said Theo was just a baby," he said louder. "He's innocent. He had his whole life ahead of him to make secrets and do things he'd regret. Why did you do that?"

Marilyn remained still as if she hadn't heard. As if he didn't exist.

Peter crossed the store to where she sat, legs splayed like some creepy Raggedy Ann doll that a child had tossed in the corner after having had their fill. He dropped to his haunches (as far as his arthritic hips would allow, anyway) and looked her in the eyes. God, her breath was rank.

"Marilyn?" he whispered. Then, straining his vocal cords: "WHY DID YOU DO THAT?!"

He resisted the urge to grab her by the collar of her coveralls. A mixture of viscous pink and white drool had collected there. Some of it clung to her lower lip. It slid down her chin in one elongated, bulbous drop, buttered molasses off the edge of a biscuit. Her eyes flickered, the lids rising to half-staff. She turned her head slightly toward him, the grin on her face never faltering. She raised both hands to his face, lightly caressing his jaw with her gangrenous fingers.

"Because," she said, "I was hungry." She pinched both his cheeks and bit the air playfully in front of him, a dog snapping at the water from a hose.

Peter stood up and backed away from her. He ran one papery hand through what remained of the hair on his head. The image of baby Theo imploding played over in his mind, his cheeks and skull caving in on themselves as Marilyn drank his life away. He was helpless. He hadn't protested, not a single cry of discomfort. He had even cooed once when Marilyn scooped him up from the spot where Donna had been sitting with him all night long. All of it together was too much for Peter. He pressed the palms of his hands against his temples and wailed at the ceiling as fresh rain pummeled the roof beyond it.

"I THOUGHT YOU WERE HERE TO SAVE US!" he screamed. "I thought you were God or at least sent by Him to absolve us." He grabbed fistfuls of his hair and tore at it. "How? How am I still here if you're not what I thought you were? Why am I not like them?" He swept a hand toward the Schlueter De Luxe mop bucket containing the oddly living remains of the Lost Hollow townsfolk who had sheltered with him in the store that day. "Why am I still me?"

Marilyn erupted into laughter. It was an evil, demonic sound. It made him shiver despite the humid night.

"You thought what you thought," she said, her wet, lilting voice turned dry and gravelly, a talking corpse with a plenteous mouth of earth and decay. "I'm not your fucking God, you stupid, naive little man. I am no one's god. I am hungry, and you are my food. You poor human souls. You have no idea. You're constantly wringing your hands with your shame, guilt, and self-inflicted sinfulness. Constantly worrying about what comes next, trying to figure out how to get yourselves out of the cages you yourselves built.

"The thing is, there *is no way out*. There is no absolution. There isn't a soul that's passed from your world that hasn't landed in the simmering pots of mine. Beings from your world or beings from worlds beyond, they all become my food. Even before you come squalling into the world, your journey's end is in the depths of my belly. You've always been my food. You always will be my food."

She eyed his fallen face, chuckling. "There it is. You know it's true, don't you?"

Marilyn stood up, graceful even in a half-human form, and danced toward him. She wrapped her arms around him, dragging one long fingernail up the middle of his back when she did. Peter was suddenly locked in place with his arms at his sides, unable to move all but his head. He twisted his face away from her as she stood on tiptoes to meet him. Her long, pointed tongue flicked out of her mouth and dealt his silver stubbly chin a glancing blow.

"Look at me, Peter Mayberry," Marilyn said. "Look me in the eye, and I'll tell you *my* secret, *my* sin. Don't you want to know?"

"Let go of me," Peter replied, looking not at her but at some point over the top of her head.

"Do you remember when I found you, all alone in your car? All hurt and alone with your impaled dick out?"

"Of course I do."

"Yes," Marilyn said. "When I was watching you sitting in your car in all that rain, I recognized something in you. You're alone in this world, Peter. One of a kind. So am I. I didn't come here because I *wanted* to, just like you didn't choose to be born who you are. But here I am, and so are you.

"We don't have to be lonely, Peter Mayberry," she added. "We don't have to be lonely ever again. *That's* why I've spared you." She paused, then added, "Well, so far."

Peter's eyes met hers. "I can't love you, Marilyn," he said. "My heart belongs to someone else."

She smiled at him. At some point, her lips and mouth had regained their pouty innocence, transforming from the gaping, razor-lined maw that had devoured his friends and neighbors into the Marilyn Monroe calendar girl. It was a mouth that Jerry Beard and Eli Wynn had probably imagined pressed against theirs on countless hot summer nights past.

"Sam Brooks," she replied. "I know."

"Sam Brooks," Peter echoed.

"But you don't understand. I'm not asking you to fall in love with me or even with Marilyn Monroe. I'm asking you to *be with me* like you said before. I am powerful in your world, but I'm still a stranger here. You've seen what your world's *wetness* can do to me when I am weak. You saw the blisters on my back when you pulled me from the storm. That's why I need you, Peter. You can go places I can't. You can protect me from the things in this world that can hurt me when I'm hungry.

"And you can feed me. As you said before, you know these creatures. You know their secrets, what makes them feel the things I need them to feel to feed on them.

"You've lived your entire life in this world among people just like you, yet you're completely alone. We can help one another. I'll show you. If it's Sam Brooks you want," she said, her voice deepening as she talked, changing timbre, becoming more masculine, "I can be him for you."

Peter hadn't even blinked but was suddenly staring straight into the collar bone of the muscular, brown-skinned man who had ridden away on a Triumph motorcycle that morning. Marilyn's metamorphosis had been instantaneous and, as near as Peter could tell, perfect. It was unlike any of the transformations he'd seen in her earlier that night. She had Sam's short and crisp hair, a holdover from his tour of duty. His face, the imperfections here and there, was mirror accurate.

Most striking was the way she had reproduced his eyes. It wasn't just that she had managed to capture the exact shape and set of them in his face, not to mention the right shade of brown swirled with black in his irises. She had also somehow, impossibly, captured the *soul* of them. In faux Sam's gaze, Peter could see the actual man's confidence, warmth, and humor. He could see the same passion and strength that had sent him tumbling ass over end in love.

Tears welled up in Peter's eyes. His chest tightened. An uncomfortable bubble of hot air from somewhere in the pit of his stomach found its way up to his trachea and into his mouth. Mixed with these sickly sensations was a lit fuse inside his brain. It was rapidly burning down, inching closer to exploding all the pieces of Marilyn's usury that had been allowed to coalesce in his mind over the past few minutes.

"You're not Sam," he said to her. It came out as a whisper, so he cleared his throat and repeated it at a normal volume. "You are *not* Sam."

The doppelgänger's grip around his torso tightened. It only made him angrier. He struggled against it, writhing his shoulders, shimmying to loosen himself.

"You are not Sam," he said again.

"You are not Sam.

"You are *not* Sam.

"You are *NOT Sam*.

"YOU ARE NOT SAM!"

Peter pressed both of his palms against the pectorals of the audacious thing that completely resembled his beloved companion and shoved with everything he had. The Marilyn/Sam thing reeled backward, opening enough space between them for Peter to follow through with a swift kick in the balls. Marilyn/Sam screamed and went down on its knees then, hands cupped over its groin, head upturned, howling at the ceiling.

It had been a gamble. Peter had hoped that a thing that would take enough care to replicate the expression of his boyfriend's warmth and compassion in the eyes would also have duplicated his testicles, not to mention the sensitivity that is native to the appendage. He experienced a moment of marvel at the ability of the creature to recreate a person so accurately it had never met based exclusively on his memories of that person. Peter let it pass. This was not the time to dwell on such things.

Sam boiled away before Peter's eyes in a bulbous, melting haze of hair, skin, sinew, and bone on the floor. The nasty soup writhed and flowed and caved in on itself like molten metal being poured into a vat from a flask. Whatever the thing was changing into, it was happening at a much slower rate than the transition from Marilyn to Sam. He had hurt it. Surprised it. Made it angry. It could be transforming into something even more complex and dangerous than either of its human forms. Peter sensed an opportunity.

His eyes passed over the mop bucket in which he'd dropped the creatures, considering it again. He could dump them out, race that bucket to the floodwaters that had at this point encroached nearly to the door of Beard's General. If there was a chance he could find a way to restore them, it would be a bad idea to allow them to run free.

He next landed on the dry goods shelves that lay just beyond the writhing creature. On it sat a row of one-pound coffee tins: a small section of Folger's that stood alongside a slightly larger selection of Maxwell House as well as the Brim tins he had previously noticed. That would have to do.

Peter leaped past the beast and grabbed a Brim tin from a shelf. He accidentally knocked two others onto the floor in the process, neither of which spilled. He tucked the coffee tin into the crook of his left arm and pried off the lid. The homey aroma of the ground tickled his nostrils immediately. He had a moment to wish he was at home, enjoying a fresh cup of the stuff instead of fighting for his life against this, this whatever-it-was. He dumped the contents of the one-pounder onto the floor. A small pile of the grounds landed on the waxy edges of the Marilyn thing. They were quickly absorbed by it and, Peter would swear it, accelerated its throbbing.

He dashed to the front door and threw it open. The fresh cycle of the unrelenting downpour was falling still, some of it with enough force to bounce off the front porch and splash him in the face. With a firm grip on the edge of the coffee tin, he dipped the container into the floodwaters just as he had done with the drinking glass. It filled immediately. He retrieved the can of dirty liquid and ran back inside. Some of it sloshed from the container and onto his pants as he did, but not enough to matter.

Without ceremony, Peter dumped the creek water directly on top of the thing on the floor. In return, it emitted a sizzling, whistling shriek that fired invisible arrows with razor-sharp points directly into his eardrums. Thick gray billows of steam drifted up from the red and yellow sick that had formed on the beast where the water landed. The blob folded over on itself and plunged its injured top mound directly onto the floor of Beard's General like a toddler doing a headstand.

Peter raced to the floodwaters and refilled the coffee tin. On his way back, he caught the toe of the shoe he wore on his shorter leg on the threshold and went sprawling. His knees and the palms of his hands absorbed the shock when he landed. The thrum ran up his forearms, through his elbows, and into his shoulders like bolts of electricity. The Brim tin had flown from his hands as he braced for impact. It landed on its side, rolling in a semicircle from the cashier's station to the giant front window that looked out at Hollow Creek Road. Fortunately for him, the water had all spilled out before the can rolled away.

The momentum of his fall had sent the creek water creeping across the linoleum side of the shop floor, where it pooled around the not entirely formed "feet" of Marilyn. The thing responded with a fresh round of shrieking and began to slink away from both Peter and the puddle of water. It moved like a discolored segment of inchworm, undulating its way toward a large commercial freezer that had leaned against the wall of Kathy's store since forever.

It wasn't a working freezer. Peter had once inquired whether Kathy was willing to sell it or donate it to the church for charitable functions. Kathy, with the help of Jerry and a couple of burly guys who had delivered her latest selection of cold beverages, had lugged the thing out here from the back of the store. She'd intended to have someone haul it away for her after she bought a replacement. But like a lot of small-town business proprietors, more immediate concerns piled up and took precedence over maintenance. So there the freezer had remained.

Peter distinctly remembered a toddler who'd played an involuntary game of hide-and-seek from his mother inside it. When she finally found him, she'd one-arm dragged him out of the store, screaming and rubbing one sore butt cheek. You couldn't open that freezer door from the inside. If you got yourself closed in it, you were trapped. That prompted a new idea.

He gave the thing crawling on the floor as wide a berth as he could. At one point, a weird octopus-like tentacle stretched out of it and tried to wrap itself around his ankle. He avoided it. Narrowly. He pulled on the freezer door handle, then rushed back around the thing and snatched the coffee tin from where it had come to rest.

Seconds later, he tossed another round of dirty creek water onto the thing. It had begun to mold itself again, this form more dog or wolf-like. Peter wondered whether Marilyn was trying to again form the creature that had come to him in his car. The water was causing her pain, but not enough to prevent her from reforming herself. The downpours hadn't killed it, either. Marilyn had been hurt but very much alive when he and Jerry had dragged her inside naked. A large enough volume of water—a flooded creek, say—might completely dissolve her, kill her dead.

He could grab the thing while it was still smaller than him, wrap his arms around it and throw it as far as his floppy old man arms would allow off the front porch into the storm-forged drink just outside. But there was something more than mildly unpleasant about that idea. He'd seen it absorb the pile of coffee grounds he'd spilled nearby. He'd also seen it try to grab him. What if it could absorb him, too?

The thing had been reading minds and copying what it found inside them. She had become Marilyn because of the Marilyn Monroe calendar that Eli and Jerry had been gawking over before she arrived. Who was to say that she couldn't simply absorb another person and take them over?

It was kind of funny. All night long, Peter had thought Marilyn was someone he knew and understood. His mental connection to her had exacerbated that feeling. He realized he didn't know her at all. He felt silly and stupid for having ever believed he had.

He didn't want to sink his arms into the blob. He couldn't trust that he wouldn't be killing himself in the process. But if he could herd it into the freezer, secure it there for a while, he'd buy himself some time to figure out how to get it outside.

Peter refilled the coffee tin and slung another wave of creek water at the thing. This time, he intentionally tossed it in the hand-to-hand firefighting style rather than dumping it on top of the blob. The water flew sideways from the bucket and landed in the floor space between him and Marilyn, next to her. It rolled over the floor and pooled against her edges, causing her to leap forward as if Peter had set off a firecracker by a frog's butt.

There were no signs that she could sense what he was doing. He wondered whether she possessed any kind of *sense* at all in her state. Mid-change, she resembled an overgrown amoeba more than a being of sentience. He ran outside and refilled the coffee tin. If he could keep her on the same path, one or two more splashes should send her leaping right into the back of the empty freezer. He threw the water at her again. The resulting leap caused the thing to smash headlong (if she had a head) into the grill at the bottom of the freezer. She rebounded an inch from it and sat there, trembling and wobbling like the disgusting gelatin dishes his mother used to take to the July church picnics when he was small.

"Shit!" Peter cried. He bolted for the front door, tin in hand. The Marilyn thing had already slithered its way another foot from the freezer by the time he returned with a fresh load of water. He tossed it the way he had before.

Marilyn sprang back toward the freezer again. This time, she came down half inside it and half out. Flagellum-like appendages oozed from her edges, inching toward the floor. She seemed to be trying to wrench herself from the box before he could slam the door and cut her in half.

"Goddammit!" Peter shouted. Fuck the water, then. By the time he could run back for more, she'd be completely free of the freezer again, and he'd be right back where he started.

He knelt in front of the throbbing blob, both knees firing painful shots when he went down, and grabbed the part of the thing still attached to the floor. It was the same tactic he used to playfully grab at Sam's ass: palms up, fingers curled. His fingertips sank into the pliable goo past the distal joints.

The stuff sucked at his fingers, sticking to the pads and then pulling free again. It was like pieces of Scotch tape were attacking him. But it burned, too, like Scotch tape on the eye of a hot stove.

One quick upward shove and the mass of Marilyn landed inside the freezer. Finally.

Peter pulled his hands free, but not without some effort. He checked his fingertips, verifying that they were all still attached. They were there, all right, but they glowed a bright red. The top layer of skin was cracked and flaky. The middle finger of his left hand sported an angry, festering blister. He started to shove that finger into his mouth but then thought better of it. Instead, he cursed himself for not taking off his shirt or grabbing the towels that Kathy Beard had given Marilyn to dry herself. He could've used either of them as a buffer between himself and the goo.

Furious with himself and the thing that called herself Marilyn, Peter slammed the freezer door shut.

CHAPTER THIRTY-THREE

Somewhere in the drowning darkness beyond the walls of Beard's General, a feeder line poorly maintained by Hollow County Power Utility swung violently in the thunderstorm's gales. The line bowed with each fresh gust of hot breath from the atmosphere. Repeated strains against the cable's splice separated it enough to create an arc of brilliant orange-yellow light. The current that flowed through it made valiant efforts to continue its journey through Lost Hollow, only to find itself channeled into the wind, rain, and thunder. The winds were not enough to sever the line entirely from its mooring. When they finally bellowed themselves out, the line settled back into its groove, as did the current.

Inside Beard's General, the event created a frustrating and terrifying strobe effect. The store's overhead lights flickered on and off as the cable outside strained and relaxed. With every dive into darkness, Peter worried that the beast would waken and burst from the depths of the freezer before he could secure the door. With each flooding of brilliant interior light that followed, he waited for his eyes to adjust before he resumed the work he'd been only feeling his way around seconds before.

Peter stood with his left foot planted firmly in front of the freezer box. The right was pressed hard against the door, leaving a smudgy sole print on the Arctic White enamel that he doubted would be noticed among the debris from the damage the creature had caused. He'd found a tow chain looped around a hook nearby. It was just the right length and link width to thread around the complete circumference of the appliance once, with enough left over at each end to wind multiple passes in a square knot at the door handle. Hell, it may have been the very chain used to move the thing out here in the first place.

Peter threaded the two ends of it through the handle and used the force of his legs and back against the weight of the box itself to pull it taut. He had just enough time to fix the knot before the next round of darkness enveloped him.

He relaxed his hold on the chain ends and stepped back from the freezer, not taking his eyes off where it should have been sitting even though he couldn't see anything now. His shoulders, biceps, thighs, and calves sobbed with relief. He could feel the pattern of the steel chain links sunk into the palms of his hands. He must've been gripping them hard, indeed. Would the makeshift prison box hold her? For how long? With the others reduced to—well, whatever they had been reduced to—he'd just have to pray that it would, at least until the thunderstorm and its downpours passed. Or sunup. Whichever came first.

The lights flickered on again. In front of him, the freezer door held fast. Peter sighed, relieved. A skittering sound from somewhere behind him made short work of his comfort. He wheeled to find five of the six tiny, shining black creatures had escaped. They gathered in a loose semicircle on the floor before him. They had somehow scaled the smooth interior of the Schlueter De Luxe mop bucket he'd dropped them into one by one over the course of the night. They stood still as if they'd been watching with interest his progress on Marilyn's new holding cell. The smallest of them (what remained of Theo, he presumed) held a scrap of the bucket's peeling manufacturer's label in one minuscule claw.

Peter crouched on his haunches in front of the group and pried the scrap of paper loose from the critter's grip. Pinched between his thumb and forefinger, he turned the paper over and held it close to his eyes for examination. White block letters E and A floated before him on a black background. They'd been ripped from the word HEAVY in the company's logo. QUALITY HEAVY METALWARE, it had originally read. Meaningless. He released the piece of label. As it fluttered to the floor, he regarded his new friends through narrowed eyes.

"What are you?" he asked them. "What do you think I should do?"

There was, of course, no answer. Every pulse of telepathic connectivity he had established with the others while they were human was gone. That might have been because Marilyn was no longer conscious, assuming his powers depended on his connection to her. He suspected that they did. Then again, he wasn't sure the beings on the floor in front of him could communicate on the level of a human brain, even if they wanted to.

Peter shut his eyes and tried to reach out to them anyway, any of them. Well, he reached out to all except Theo, who even when he was human had been nonverbal, his mind bursting with flashes of light, color, random noises that could have been words if he'd heard them with an ear that understood them, and the face of his mother. He signaled the others by calling out the names of the five adults who had taken refuge in the storm: Kathy, Jerry, Eli, Mark, Donna.... He imagined his psychic sweep operating like sonar on a submarine, scouring the area around him, waiting for that one *ping* that would echo the presence of another vessel. Alas, none arrived.

Peter looked behind him. The door of the freezer remained shut. No banging. No rocking. No rattling. No signs of life from within. His sonar picked up no signals from Marilyn herself, either.

Satisfied that he was alone with the skitterers, at least for a while, he seated himself on the floor in front of them and leaned forward. He rested his elbows on his knees and propped his chin atop steepled fingers. He stared at the tiny creatures for a few seconds. They were all a gleaming, squid ink black. There were no other markings, nothing that would enable him to determine which had been whom, save for the smallness of the smallest one.

Each of the skitterers had a long, segmented abdomen that tapered off into a wedge-shaped tail. The tail thinned and fanned at the end to become almost transparent at the tip. Each abdomen was connected to a generously broad thorax. The underside edges of the thorax sprouted spindly legs, four to a side. Those legs consisted of two long, muscular segments separated by some backward-looking knee or elbow joint. Attached to the front of each critter, just under its beady black eyes and long, quivering antennae, was another pair of legs. These were thicker than those of the thorax. On each end of those front legs sat two lobster-like pincers.

Crawdads, Peter thought, shocked that he hadn't noticed the resemblance before. He gently retrieved a larger one from the floor and held it belly up so he could examine the underside. It did not protest. *They look almost exactly like the crawdads Joe Bayless and I fished out of the creek that day.* Well, the crawdads *Joe* had fished out of the creek, anyway. He hadn't wanted to touch them back then, wouldn't have even considered it except for an adolescent desire to impress the boy.

These were not crawdads. They resembled them, but they weren't fish, and he hadn't caught them in the creek. They were people. They were what remained of people after Marilyn had fed on everything they had. They were living souls, reduced to nothing but somehow still alive and trapped with a monster in a small-town general store in the middle of a thunderstorm so severe that it had wiped out the only means of escape. They were soul-dads.

A thin, crunching sound woke him from his reverie. The sixth soul-dad, the last of them, had clawed its way to the top of the mop bucket, vaulted the rim, and landed upright on the floor. On its way down, it tore off another piece of the bucket's label. It held the scrap of decal aloft in its right pincer as it skittered its way across the floor to join the others. It took its place in the semicircle and faced Peter, holding the scrap high as if urging him to accept it.

Gingerly, Peter extracted the decal from the soul-dad's pincer and held it up for a look. It was one character: a T, probably the T from METALWARE. He strained to read the decal that remained on the bucket across the way. Sure enough, the motto over the stylized De Luxe logo now read QUALITY H VY ME ALWARE.

Peter grinned. He sought and located the first scrap he'd dropped and sat it on the floor in front of the soul-dads. He placed the new scrap to the left of the original. T and EA. TEA. That made no sense. He transposed the pieces so that the T piece sat on the right of the EA piece. EA and T. EAT.

Something about that struck him funny. Peter chuckled. His sagging old man belly jiggled visibly under his shirt, slapping against his lap.

"Are y'all trying to invite me to tea or tell me I need to eat something?" he asked the soul-dads. "You're probably right. It feels like I haven't eaten anything in a week."

He was about to stand up when the lights in Beard's General cut out again, leaving him, the six soul-dads, and the monster chained inside the freezer in total darkness. Peter made an effort anyway, wobbling on legs of pins and needles that refused to allow him to remain upright. They crumpled beneath him. He landed flat on his back. He had one second to hope he hadn't landed on any of the soul-dads, and then the first atomic blast of Marilyn's fists against the inside of the freezer door pounded in his ears.

She was awake and probably congealed into something much more substantial than blob form.

She wanted out.

A new sensation crawled up the flesh of Peter's left arm. It felt like an insect, an oversized cockroach creeping over his knuckles, past his wrist, along his forearm. At one point, somewhere below the crook of his elbow, the thing slipped and nearly tumbled off him. He sensed it right itself by clamping a pincer onto a crop of his silver arm hairs. It was one of the soul-dads. It had to be.

He wanted to shoo it away, swipe at it with his right hand, swat it like a fly. He fought the urge, reminding himself that the soul-dads were not insects. They were human and, if he dared to allow himself to believe it, trying to communicate with him.

It waited a beat after it righted itself. Then the creature resumed its trek up his arm. For a second, he feared it would crawl under his shirt sleeve, a sensation that could override his willpower to not swat at it. Instead, it surmounted the hem, crawled over his shoulder, climbed his jaw, and perched on his chin.

"What?" he started.

The soul-dad leaped into Peter's mouth. It performed something like a handstand on his lower lip. Then it bounded off him like a diver, plummeted into the cavity, and slid eye stalks-first with legs flailing over his tongue and down his throat. From there, it crawled down his esophagus. It forced its way past the involuntary spasms of his gag reflex, his body's attempt to reject the object. Its spindly walking legs felt like fork tines poking and prodding their way toward his gut.

When it landed there, Peter sensed absolutely nothing. No fullness in his abdomen. No movement or digestive noises. Then, suddenly, there was warmth. It began in the pit of his stomach, a glowing ember that pulsed slowly, trying to feed itself, trying to light. A hot gasp of warm, foul air escaped his mouth. His eyes rolled back in his head. His entire body locked up and spasmed, alternatively arching his back and caving his abdomen like a fish flopping around on the floor after having leaped from an aquarium.

The lights inside Beard's General flickered on again. A surge of electricity ran through Peter at the same moment. The spasms stopped. His eyeballs righted themselves. The world he saw through their lenses was more apparent, as if someone had adjusted the rabbit ears or the sharpness dial on a television set. If that television set showed colors.

A burst of strength followed. The loose old man's skin on his arms tightened. His biceps filled out again, more like they had been when he was years younger, long before he had walked through the door of Beard's General that evening. His calf muscles expanded, tightening the skin around them as well. He sat up. None of his joints screamed at him for trying it.

"What the hell did you do to me?" he asked out loud.

Added my strength to what's left of yours, came the reply from somewhere within but also outside of his head. The voice was distinctive and familiar, full of masculine youthfulness and the blissfully ignorant confidence that is often its hallmark.

"Jerry Beard?" Peter said.

That's me, was the answer. *Well, that was me, anyway. I'm you, and you are me. Sort of. Soul-dads, huh? That's a funny word for us. I guess we do kind of look like crawdads. Well, I don't anymore, but all the rest still do.*

"What have you done to me?"

A short burst of sardonic laughter ensued. *You weren't getting the message. I had to take matters into my own, uh, claws, I guess would be the right word.*

"Pincers."

All right, pincers then. The only way we will beat the demon lady is if we band together. We all see that. We could have done it when we were still human, before she sucked all our lives away, but we didn't see it then. All we saw was a pretty woman and our secret shame. We let the stranger take advantage of our humanity, Mr. Mayberry. We let her take advantage of all our fears, secrets, and judgments.

"Our sins."

Yes! Jerry exclaimed. *Our sins. But it wasn't our sins that did us in. At least, that's what Pastor Mark thinks. It was our willingness to judge, to raise ourselves as judge and jury above one another for sins that aren't even really sins. Or at least they shouldn't be. Not where there's love. I don't think they should be, anyway.*

Peter smiled. He knew what Jerry meant, even if the young man remained too judgmental to state it directly.

The thing is, Jerry continued, *the only way we can bond together is if we combine. We can give what's left of ourselves over to you so you can use our strength along with yours. We're not crawdads, you know. That's just how you see us. I'm not sure what we are, but we're powerful now that we don't have shame holding us down.*

Peter nodded. It made sense, he supposed. The dots that marked the most significant events of his life had connected in a way that seemed suddenly obvious. Joe Bayless had tried to feed him crawdads on the bank of Hollow Creek in front of the very Nazarene church where he'd played piano for years as an adult. His mother had instilled the shame in him that day, puncturing his tongue with a nail. She forged the shame and guilt over who he was, and it had pursued him for his entire life. On top of that, she had nurtured his anxiety about others uncovering his secret. Similar fear earlier that day had cost him the great love of his life. The shame, which always followed closely on anxiety's heels, had caused him to mutilate himself.

Marilyn had offered him false absolution, forgiveness for a sin that wasn't a sin, and healing for an injury that should never have been there in the first place. The thing about shame and anxiety is that they're cyclical. You climb their mountain, fighting the abuse they heap upon you. Then, just when you think you've overcome them by reaching the summit, you discover that you weren't climbing a mountain at all. You were just walking along the rim of a wheel the whole time.

He was at the start of that wheel again. He had returned to the creek banks in a way, once again confronted with performing an act of faith, of confidence in who he was. It would be an act of absolution not for the shame his mother had instilled in him, but for the sin of having spent his entire life denying who he was, allowing others to deny him who he was.

You're going to have to absorb us all to win this battle, Jerry said, unbidden. *Use us. All of us. It's the only way.*

Peter placed a hand palm-up on the floor in front of another soul-dad. It climbed onto his fingers and came to rest in the valley of his relaxed grip. Its eyes seemed to be focused on his, even without irises. Its face, without countenance, encouraged him, prodded him to eat. It let him know that everything was going to be okay.

He raised the soul-dad in front of his face. He pinched it at the tail with his free hand and dangled it upside-down over his mouth.

"It's the only way," he echoed. Then he dropped the soul-dad into his mouth. It did not struggle.

His body was less reactive to this new surge of soul energy, although Peter did feel a burst of physical strength. A new serenity swam about his head, as if the addition of—*Eli*, the soul-dad whispered. As if the addition of Eli's soul-dad to the stew in his belly had triggered sprays of happy juice into his brain's chemical receptors.

Without hesitation, Peter grabbed the third-largest soul-dad from the floor in front of him and turned it up. Like Eli before it, this one went down without a fight. When it hit bottom, Peter was flooded with purpose. His imagination swam with variations on possible scenarios for dealing with the thing in the freezer. He considered ways to engineer the release of the freezer door without getting stomped by Marilyn in the process. He pondered ways to rid Lost Hollow of the creature forever. Elements of logic and calculation he had never understood suddenly swirled in his mind like the water around Beard's General.

That one must have been Kathy Beard, she of the cash register, pencils, and ledgers. Somewhere within him, he sensed her acknowledge that she was, indeed, a part of him.

Peter took up the next soul-dad in line. A quaking *thoom* from behind him shook the room. He twisted around and saw an indented relief of enormous knuckles in the surface of the freezer door. A second set of the same appeared instantly below the first as he watched. It was accompanied by another *thoom* that vibrated the floor beneath him.

"Oh, God," he said, swallowing hard. A wad of saliva started down the wrong pipe, tickling his throat and forcing him into the convulsions of a coughing fit. Fortunately, there was no regurgitation of soul-dad pieces in the fluid he coughed from his windpipe. *Oh, God. I'm running out of time.*

When the coughing fit subsided enough for him to breathe, Peter plucked the fourth and fifth soul-dads from the semicircle, one in each hand. He considered sending them down the gullet together but didn't think he could prevent himself from choking on them that way, even if they aided their descent. One of these soul-dads would be Mark MacDonald. The other was Donna Gilliam, mother of the infant Theo. Peter supposed it didn't matter which of them he consumed first, although part of him hated to think of Donna leaving Theo behind for any amount of time. He turned up the soul-dad in his left hand, thinking it was probably Mark since the one in his right had been standing closer to the Theo soul-dad.

Just as Mark slid past Peter's epiglottis, the store was rocked by another thunderous explosion of fists against the inside of the freezer door. She wasn't strong enough to break the chain yet but, by the sound of it, Peter didn't think it would be long before she sent it hurtling off its hinges and across the room, tow chain and all.

More than startling, Marilyn's efforts were distracting. Had Mark's soul-dad been any higher in his mouth when that last blow landed, Peter's gasp might have lodged it in his windpipe. A stuck soul-dad, he thought, seemed a hell of a lot more hazardous than aspirating his spit. He needed a getaway, somewhere he could hole up and finish this— ritual? job? meal?—before Marilyn could get free and sink her claws into him.

Scanning the area, his gaze landed on the bathroom at the back of the store. He'd ushered Marilyn there to dry off and put on her men's coveralls when she'd first arrived. It wasn't a great *hiding* place. She'd sniff him out there even if she didn't connect with him telepathically. But with its door closed, the bathroom would dampen the grating noise of Marilyn's work and allow him to finish consuming the last of the soul-dads without killing himself in the process.

The Donna soul-dad gently cradled in his right hand, he scooped up the smaller Theo soul-dad in his left. Then he stood and strode for the bathroom, the door of which stood partially open already. The baby soul-dad felt different in his hand than the others had. It squirmed a bit, as if not entirely comfortable with the plan after all. Or it wanted its mother.

He transitioned the Donna soul-dad from his right hand to his left, allowing the mother a moment with her infant son. He used his left to shut the bathroom door. Safely enclosed (more or less) in the Beard's General bathroom, Peter Mayberry propped himself against the wall and slid down it, landing on his butt. He was careful not to crush his two-remaining soul-dads. He examined them, sitting side-by-side in the palm of his left hand, watching him watch them.

"I guess it's time," he said. He retrieved the larger soul-dad, Donna, by her tail and tossed her into his mouth. Like the soul-dads before her, she put up no fight at all. When what remained of Donna evaporated inside him, Peter became flush with urgency, a literal craven need to consume the soul-dad of her offspring as well.

He's an innocent. The voice of Donna floated in his mind like leaves on top of Hollow Creek at its most serene. *Theo is the purest of us all. Take him, too. We won't have enough light to fight back against that monster if you don't.*

I sense hesitation in you, she added. *You can't save him, but he can save us.*

Do it.

Please, just do it.

CHAPTER THIRTY-FOUR

Peter crouched between the sink and the restroom toilet in the back of Beard's General. Over his head, he dangled the last of the soul-dads, this one only a baby. The tiny black thing grunted and mewled as it squirmed between the thumb and forefinger of his right hand. It was all that remained of Theo Gilliam and, unlike its predecessors, it seemed to be fighting him.

Theo's mother had given Peter her permission to consume the little one. Theo's innocence was paramount to their plan for confronting Marilyn. A newborn had neither time nor enough life experience to sin or develop shame. Could that be why Marilyn had left him alone for so very long?

There were Christians who believed that a stillborn is destined for a "cooler place in hell," regardless of their innocence. Logically, if the babe is too young to sin, it is also too young to accept Jesus. Therefore, it cannot enter Heaven.

Peter had never believed that. A God that refused to accept the innocence of a newborn into paradise was cruel, even if the souls of those newborns were provided with a less-fiery separation from Him in the afterlife.

Peter's reluctance to drop the remains into his mouth came not from fear for Theo's everlasting soul, then. He'd had no trouble swallowing the prior soul-dads who could consent. Theo couldn't agree. He thought it possible that the simple concept of eating a baby could have created a barrier in his mind.

From somewhere beyond the bathroom door, he heard a loud *rrrrrip*, followed by a crash. The cacophony startled him. He dropped the baby Theo soul-dad into his lap. It scurried away and headed toward the light that shone under the bathroom door.

Peter scrambled to his knees and cupped both hands over it before it could. He collected it between the fingers of his right hand and again settled himself between the sink and toilet. It occurred to him that if he hadn't consumed the five soul-dads, the joints in his hips, knees, and hands would have been screaming in burning pain thanks to arthritis that had hatched in his bones over the course of the night. Not all the pain was gone, but it had diminished. It could return.

Just in case, Peter raised his left hand, curled it into a loose fist, and lightly bit down on it to stifle any pained outbursts that could reveal his hiding spot. His skin was salty and thin as tissue paper against his teeth and the tip of his tongue. Too much pressure and he would break the surface. Best not to draw his blood in case the thing thrashing in the other room could smell it.

Outside, he heard another crash, metal groaning against metal, followed by a thud that shook the floor beneath him. Marilyn must have torn free from the restraint he had fashioned. It would not be long before she discovered him.

Come on, you pussy! the voice of Joe Bayless taunted him.
There's no need to make them suffer, he heard himself retort.

Another voice, this one female, chimed in. This one sounded closer, as if Donna sat right beside him, whispering in his ear instead of boiling alive in his stomach acid with the rest of the Hollow Creek flood survivors.

"He's suffering," she said. "We need him. Eat."

With a trembling hand, Peter raised Theo's soul-dad over his head the way Joe had done with one of the two crawdads he had captured in his bucket from Hollow Creek decades before. He opened his mouth and tilted it toward the flailing creature so that gravity could take over and guide it home when he let go. He closed his eyes and released Theo, reopening them just as the small one curled shrimp-like in the air and disappeared behind the horizon of his cheeks and nose.

The thing struck and then bounced off the front of his bottom row of teeth. It arced upward, then landed on his tongue, lukewarm and not a little slimy. The critter's dual antennae stalks grazed the roof of his mouth just before his swallow reflex took over. The sensation left a burning itch in its wake. He had an overpowering urge to rub at the area with the tip of his tongue. For one horrifying moment, it felt like the thing was going to lodge in the back of his throat, that spot in the back near the tonsils that's impossible to clear even after gargling with a glass of water. He imagined choking, his uvula clasped in a death grip by Theo's pincers. Then a second swallow forced the tiny beast into his esophagus, where nature took over.

A wave of regret washed over him when the lump of the soul-dad finally went down. For the greater good or not, swallowing a squirming baby was a clear violation of human empathy, selfish and animalistic. He didn't need decades of shaming by his mother or Nazarene church doctrine to understand that.

Peter pressed the palms of his hands into his eyes and dropped his head. He sobbed, resting his chin against the top of his chest. He knew that the others were with him, could feel them convalescing within him as they dissolved into pure energy in the pit of his stomach, but he had never felt more alone than he did at that moment.

Swallowing the baby dragged some fresh self doubt alongside it. What if they weren't enough? What if Marilyn remained stronger than all of them put together? What if they were simply wrong? She had no reason not to feed on him now that he had turned on her.

Theo is with us, the voice of Donna assured him. It sounded weaker than it had before, emerging from somewhere inside his head, not whispering in his ear. As if aware of this, its next words were accompanied by a chorus of familiar voices. At the bottom somewhere was Mark MacDonald. At the top was Donna Gilliam. Between them were Kathy Beard, Jerry Beard, and Eli Wynn.

You have Theo's purity, they said together. *You have all our remaining strength. Shut down your rational mind. You have no reason to feel guilt or shame. You have no reason to doubt yourself. Help us. Help yourself. Let go.*

"And let God," an earlier version of Peter Mayberry would have automatically finished. This Peter, the man sitting between a dirty sink and a dirtier commode in the bathroom of a small-town general store, instead said nothing. It wasn't up to God. Not this time. This time it was up to him and a smattering of Lost Hollow residents who had sacrificed their humanity to shut the mouth of the thing that, left alone, might consume the whole town—possibly the entire world beyond it.

Marilyn could be a world-eater, but Peter was a soul-dad-eater. He might even be a sin-eater and had been all along.

It would sure as hell explain a lot. Lost Hollow was only a tiny part of the world. If he could keep her from taking it, he could stop her from spreading out, save the souls of millions without having to consume them himself.

Three loud thuds reverberated through the bathroom, their vibrations scattering his thoughts, followed by a single, more deafening thud against the bathroom door. The force was significant enough to bow the face of it. A thin crack appeared at the top of the distortion. It spread out across the wood in a web of smaller splinters. They enlarged, becoming parted lips that opened onto cavities of solid white pine, disappearing when everything settled back into place.

She had discovered him. Marilyn was throwing herself at the bathroom door, trying to bust it in. Peter wondered what form she'd taken: woman? Wolf? Dog? Gigantic crawdad? Whatever it was, it was strong enough to need only two or three seconds to recoup its strength for another launch. The second thud split the entire thing straight down the middle. To Peter, it sounded like the crack of a wooden bat against the hide of a baseball, only amplified by a few hundred decibels.

One more solid hit with a modicum of force behind it, and she'd have him cornered. Time to act.

Peter stretched his right hand over his head and grabbed the side of the sink. With his left, he gripped the toilet seat. He pushed himself up from the floor, half expecting to plummet right to the ground if the arthritis in his hands, hips, and knees protested at all. Thankfully, they didn't. All his joints worked together in a well-oiled motion to help him gain his feet. It was effortless, a range of movement he didn't even recall having since childhood.

A brutish snort echoed from behind the door, then it was torn in half. Both pieces crashed inward. The side jamb came loose from its hinges and fell forward, its head hitting the rear wall of the bathroom. The doorknob side was flung in Peter's direction. He watched it fly at him as if in slow motion. He shoved both hands forward in a warding off gesture. When the head of the door piece connected with his palms, he closed his fingers around it, halting its forward momentum in mid-air. He thrust the plank downward. It slammed harmlessly against the floor, bounding on the bathroom tile a single time before falling still and silent.

The next thing Peter noticed was the snout. It appeared, sniffling and snarling, from behind the door frame. Soon it was accompanied by the attached mouthful of dagger-like canines, fiery-red eyes, and matted, oily fur. Marilyn's shoulders and dog-like torso were too broad to fit through the door. For a second, it seemed as if she'd become wedged in the frame. She snarled in protest. A horrific stench of rotten eggs permeated the air between her mouth and Peter's nostrils. He gagged on the stink, fighting to keep his hands free and avoid pinching his nose or covering his mouth. He could taste the odor. It was like swallowing flaming balls of pig shit. It singed the hair in his nostrils and the lining in the back of his throat. His eyes welled up, too, blurring his vision, obscuring the heaving beast before him.

No longer able to help himself, Peter raised both hands to his face, wiping hot tears away from his eyes. He followed that by swiping a forearm along his nose, which came away coated in a thin layer of mucus. He reached for the bathroom faucet and twisted the cold tap wide open. He cupped a handful of chilled water and splashed it in his eyes, grateful that the deluge had not corrupted the store's well water system. Blessed relief.

He turned from the sink to find Marilyn forcing herself through the bathroom door. She lunged at him, snarling with her dirty yellow fangs bared.

CHAPTER THIRTY-FIVE

Without thought, Peter thrust his right-hand palm up under the faucet. The cup of his hand filled to overflowing almost immediately with cold tap water. He threw it at the beast, who had closed enough of the distance between them that he could feel her broiling sulfur breath huffing into his face, singeing his eyelashes.

The water arced over Marilyn's snout and splashed her directly between the eyes, scattering drops over her muzzle and forehead. They sizzled when they landed, burning away the thick fur and opening fresh, blood-red sores on her demon skin as they settled. One drop ran from the top of her forehead and down to her right eye, carving a repulsive bubblegum pink gulley through the upper eyelid before plunging into the depths of her impossibly crimson iris. Tendrils of black and gray smoke billowed from her eye socket as the water scorched away her cornea and began to soak into the lens beyond.

Marilyn howled, a twisted mask of agony and rage stretched over her features. Peter hurled a second stinging fistful of water directly into her eyes. That one sent her scrambling in reverse through the bathroom door. He could hear the wretched, ragged claws of her hind paws floundering for purchase. A huff and a snort, and she was through. She left behind a significantly wider passage in the doorframe than the one she'd created.

Peter considered trying to angle and jam the door itself into the hole, but what good would that do except to slow Marilyn down long enough for him to toss a fresh handful of water her way? It injured her. Mildly. In the end, she would exhaust him.

A younger Peter with no will to live would have accepted that fate, even embraced it. The older and newly emboldened Peter who crouched in the bathroom of Beard's General was not so willing to surrender without a fight.

Soon, Marilyn would recover enough of her sight and strength to come at him again. Peter scanned the bathroom around him for anything he could use as a container. His eye fell on an empty Coca-Cola bottle that stood on the sill of the small square window in the rear wall. The window itself had been painted over, presumably to prevent perverts and the cows that grazed in the field beyond from looking in on unsuspecting ladies doing their business.

He grabbed the bottle, dumped the decorative silk daisy out of it, and shoved it under the tap. It was one of the soda pop company's new ten-ounce King Size bottles. The mouth wouldn't fit directly under the flow without a tilt. The tap was immobile, and the sink basin was not deep enough. He wouldn't be able to fill the bottle to the top, but so be it. Any more water than the two handfuls he'd already thrown at her would be better than nothing.

Peter did manage to fill the bottle to overflowing, even at its tilt. However, a third of it spilled back into the sink basin because of the way he had to twist the bottle to get it out from under the tap. He pulled it free, then he heard Marilyn winding up for another charge. The bottle in his right hand, Peter covered the top with his left, spun from the sink, and raced from the bathroom into the open arena that showcased the shopping aisles of Beard's General. The front door of the building lay ahead of him but might as well have been miles away. Between him and it stood the massive canine form of Marilyn.

She looked larger, standing primarily on her hind legs in the half-light of the derelict store and with none of the citizens of Lost Hollow around for perspective. Anthropomorphic paws swiped the last of the pain and sightlessness from her fiery eyes. The digits on each of them were tipped with cruddy yellow spikes for claws. She sprouted impossibly long thumbs where there were dewclaws on an ordinary wolf or dog. Peter wondered if all of Marilyn's feasting during the night had led to an evolution for her, transforming her into a much more demonic, werewolf-looking creature than the canine that had climbed into his car. Was she changing still?

Smashed against the right side of the store lay the door of the freezer into which he had shoved Marilyn while she'd lain mostly incapacitated in her blob form. Debris containing burst bags of sugar and flour, among other baking staples, surrounded the door. The thin red fingers of breaking dawn flexed through the remaining windowpanes on the opposite side of Beard's General and glinted off the savagely twisted steel frame and hinges that had once secured the door to the freezer itself. The latter component miraculously remained upright on the left side of the store.

He couldn't shove Marilyn back in the box. The door was damaged beyond repair, and Marilyn stood at least a foot higher than the freezer. She was at least two feet broader than it at her widest point.

As if sensing his thoughts, the beast threw back her head and howled at the ceiling. Then she grinned at him. A long line of what looked like blood mixed with thick saliva ran from the right side of her mouth and dangled off her mandible. She licked at it with a long bluish tongue, flicking it onto the floor beside her. An excruciating assault of radio static shrieked in Peter's cortex. Securing the Coca-Cola bottle in his armpit, he clapped a hand to each ear, trying to shut it out, struggling to remain upright. His knees betrayed him, however. He collapsed in a partial squat. A few seconds later, the static resolved into the familiar voice of Marilyn inside his head.

Look at how strong I have become, she said. It was a statement of fact, without arrogance. *Look at how strong you could be if you joined me, Peter. Feel what the souls of those people did for you. Think of what more could do. I can make you just like me. Together we can feed on this world of yours forever.*

Her voice filled his head just like the storm had drowned the parking lot of Beard's General. The pressure of her words against the sides of his cranium made it feel as if it were bulging outward. She had nearly shut out his thoughts in the process.

Peter grabbed the Coca-Cola bottle from its place in his armpit. He gripped it by the lower half of its contour and aimed the neck of the container toward Marilyn as if it was a gun, a sword, or a magical talisman.

If you're still with me, he signaled to the soul-dads, *this would be a great time to come forward.*

And then they were there, the combined community of Lost Hollow's lost souls. They poured strength into the muscles of his inner thighs, his quads, hamstrings, and glutes. He rose on what had not long ago been shaky elderly legs. They were stronger, thrumming with fresh currents of electric power. They toned up and tightened, becoming more robust than at any previous time in his life. The energy flowed up his spine next, flexing and sizzling the strands of muscle in his arms, chest, and back. The not inconsiderable paunch he'd sported for most of his adult life, which had drooped and sagged ever more over the course of the night, tensed and shrank into his abdominal cavity, stretching taut over muscles he never even knew he had. The skin around his biceps and forearms stretched and pulled tight against mountains that erupted beneath them like the steroidal effects of spinach on Popeye the Sailor. Peter then became aware that his hips, forced into an awkward angle from years of his slight limp on one leg that was slightly shorter than the other, no longer hurt even though his legs remained of disproportionate length.

Distantly, there were sounds of ripping fabric as his old-age growth spurt stretched the seams of his pants around his thighs and the armholes of the slightly oversized shirt. The collar shrank to choking. Peter snapped it loose from his throat with one finger and watched as the button hurtled through the space between him and Marilyn. It struck the floor a few feet away from her, bounced once, and then came to rest at her side.

The current zapped his head then. His blurry old-man vision cleared, providing him with crystal clarity of his surroundings as well as the beast in front of him. Her thoughts were gone from his head, shoved out of it by the burst of community power. She had given up trying to convince him to join her and instead collapsed into a runner's crouch.

Explosions of soul-dad synaptic activity fired in his brain, slowing down the world around him. The earth spun at three-quarters of its regular rate, slowing Marilyn's crouch enough for Peter to admire the way her thick demon fur rippled as the muscles under it expanded and contracted with her movements. He saw a kind of terrible beauty in it that he might've wanted to preserve on a canvas had he been an artist instead of a musician.

Marilyn's mouth opened wide. Her lips peeled back, revealing the inside of her dripping shark mouth of sword-like fangs. Blood caked the narrow gaps between her teeth and speckled her elongated wolf tongue. She slammed both of her front hand-paws onto the floor in front of her and launched her back end into the air.

She's attacking. Now.

The slow-motion perception turned out to be no advantage at all. Before he could block her—or even sidestep her—Marilyn crashed head-first into him. The blow struck him square in the middle of his newly drum-like abdomen. It knocked the breath from his lungs and thrust him backward. His arms and legs splayed before him, and Peter slammed back-first into the rear wall of Beard's General.

A selection of nostalgic folk art that had been tacked there fell around him as he slid to the floor. A bizarre watercolor imitation of a famous Hilda Clark Coca-Cola advertisement landed face-up in his lap. Hilda stared dead-eyed and unsmiling at him from under a white hat with some flourish. She held a mug of the cold nickel beverage in her right hand aloft. It made him realize that he had lost his grip on his soda pop bottle when he was hit. He glanced around the room, seeking it, and hoping that it had not spilled. Then a grave-cold hand clasped him around the throat. A second one wrapped itself around his balls. The next thing he knew, Peter had been hoisted high over Marilyn's head. His back very nearly touched the ceiling.

A half-second later, he was plummeting through the air again. He thudded to the floor chin-first. His jaw crunched against the wood. He heard it inside his skull. There was no time to acknowledge the pain. Instead, he used the momentum to roll toward the opposite side of the store, coming to rest in the space of wall that stood between the front door and the giant window through which they'd all watched the flood take out the bridge.

The door bounded slightly ajar from the force of his impact. A gust of wind from outside carried the odor of natural disaster to his nostrils as he clawed his way back to his feet. The breeze held aloft the ozone smell of heavy rain and the pungent aroma of rotting animal flesh mingled with fish. There might have been some sewage in it, too. Not surprising if the rush of the floodwaters had broken any of the clay pipes under the building tasked with sluicing years of shit and piss to the septic tank.

Peter peeked through the gap in the door before it could slam shut again. The creek bed remained indistinguishable beneath the sludgy brown water that completely covered Beard's parking lot from what he could see. The rain had stopped or had at least slackened from this spot. A glint of new morning sunshine sparkled along the crests of the waves that lapped at the sides of the porch outside.

He staggered upright again, his back to the wall by the door, just as Marilyn charged at him. She kicked his discarded Coca-Cola bottle away. No matter. Peter could see that it had spilled to empty.

She ran at him full tilt, her sinewy arms outstretched, hairy palms out and fingers bent. He bent at the knees and raised his palms to shoulder height, a high crouch that he hoped would stabilize him and enable him to absorb her impact as well as wrestle her hands away from vulnerable areas of his body. It was a move he'd only seen a few times on the television wrestling matches he used to watch with Sam at a club in Hollow River. Peter was never interested in the wrestling itself. Not really. That was more Sam's thing. But he was suddenly glad he'd paid attention.

His fingers interlocked with hers. The bulk of her supernatural frame pressed against him as they grappled like the ram of one of those new-fangled hydraulic trash compactors they used to crush metal for recycling. Peter leaned into his right shoulder and straightened his elbow. That forced Marilyn's left arm into a crooked position, which had the unintended consequence of Peter getting a whiff of the matted, sulfur-tinged fur that coated her shoulder. He gagged, wrinkling his nose in disgust. Marilyn shoved his left arm back so far that it closed the distance between them. Her hot breath tainted his naked neck, raising gooseflesh on the nape. Before he could shove her away again, she sank her fangs deep into his left shoulder.

Hot blood ran down his back beneath his shirt, although he barely felt it thanks to the searing pain from the fresh puncture wounds in his deltoid muscle. Peter relaxed his grip on Marilyn's hands. Instead of pulling away, she leaned into him and ripped upward, trying to dislodge her teeth from his rage-tensed shoulder. He took advantage of the position and wrapped his arms around her waist, locking his hands together behind her. He squeezed, forcing her diaphragm to contract, depriving her of air. Miraculously, her grip on his shoulder relaxed. Her teeth were loosed from inside him.

Trapped, Marilyn reared back her head. Her saw-toothed maw gaped wide and careened toward him. The fine points of her nasty fangs could've struck him between the eyes had he perceived them in real-time. The slow-motion effect that had addled his brain at the beginning of their conflict seemed more like a blessing now.

Peter hefted Marilyn off her feet, causing her to overshoot her mark. Her chin bounced off the top of his head. He rocked backward on his heels, using Marilyn's weight against him along with gravity for momentum. He rolled onto his butt, the creature still in his arms, and slammed her forehead against the floor. He tumbled with her, crashing against the front door. It gave way to them, allowing the combatants to slip over the threshold and onto the porch beyond. They were wrenched loose in the process. Peter impacted the planks on his hands and knees, precisely between the front door and the expanse of water that used to be Hollow Creek but was now more of a pond. Marilyn was not so lucky.

He had only seconds to act. She had rolled to the porch boundary, inches from the murky risen floodwater. She lay on her side, facing the muck. She had already begun to stir when Peter got his feet under him. He ran and, like the high school football punter he never was, thrust the toes of the foot on his shorter leg under her ribs with all his might. There wasn't much room for follow-through, but the impact was enough to both startle Marilyn and shove her overboard. She rolled off the porch and tumbled into the depths without much in the way of splash or fanfare at first.

A great sizzling sound arose from the water. Billows of crimson steam followed it. The vapor fluttered back and forth in the winds of Marilyn's flailing. She thrashed hard in the surf, at one point gaining a tenuous one-pawed grip on the porch. She was trying to pull herself back onto it when Peter lunged forward and stomped on her fingers.

Marilyn howled in pain and frustration. She glared at Peter through the smoke of her disintegration. Marking him, he thought. Cursing him.

All around her, the filthy water bubbled and boiled, rising and bursting along the sides of her arms, neck, and torso as she fought to stay afloat. Her fur was falling out, exposing the pink flesh beneath. Where it was missing, gaping, blistering sores had burst, their rims rising and turning outward on themselves. To Peter, they looked hilariously like rolled-up rubbers. They oozed a bloody, gelatinous material into the soup. Turd-shaped seepages plunked into the water on every side of the floundering beast. Therein, they seethed and cooked themselves into a bright red foam that radiated outward from Marilyn in concentric ripples.

The stench was unlike anything Peter had ever experienced. It smelled like someone had set fire to a field of diarrhea-drenched wheat by bombing it with shells of rotting eggs filled with lit sulfur matches. He covered his mouth and nose with his right hand and gagged.

He turned his head to try to avoid the stink, but not so far from the scene that he couldn't see her. Had he not been alone, he could have gone back inside the store and insisted someone else ensure that Marilyn's death was final. But he *was* the last of the Beard's General flood refugees, the only survivor of that hellish first day of spring. It was, therefore, up to him.

But I'm not alone, he thought. *Not entirely. Not really.*

Marilyn stopped thrashing. Her head, nose pointed toward the sky, disappeared into the foaming mud water. Satisfied,

Peter stepped inside Beard's General. His skin tingled and burned. He was changing again, aging rapidly. He held his hands up to his eyes and watched them deflate. His knuckles became more prominent under the back of his hand as the skin there wrinkled and shrank against them. Age spots that had vanished when he'd called upon the soul-dads had not only returned but multiplied. His fingernails grew longer, yellow, and thick, cracking his cuticles. The hair on his forearms grew longer, coarser, and turned silver.

His legs gave way beneath him. He collapsed to the floor in a seated position, his head spinning, and glanced at the structure around him. Not only was he changing, but so was everything else.

The interior of Beard's General grew more prominent and more derelict as if time had sped up for everything but his perception of it. Papers and pictures came loose from the walls and tumbled to the floor. Paint flecked off surfaces here and there. They fluttered into disintegration like the pappi of a red-seeded dandelion swept aloft by the wind. At one point, a jagged, palm-sized rock crashed through a rear windowpane in the wall on his left. It rolled across the floor and came to rest at the lip of the freezer, the interior of which appeared to be covered in some form of green and black mold. Other windowpanes cracked and fell inward here and there, although Peter saw no evidence of more rocks. Cobwebs formed in corners and vanished almost immediately, only to be replaced with new ones.

Along with the structural changes, Peter saw the faint shapes of figures around him. Alternating phases of darkness and light created a strobe effect on the building's decay. All the while, the forms moved about the store, essentially blurs of motion. They cleared the place of appliances and furniture. They carried with them shelves and stock. He could not see their faces. Nor could they observe him, disguised as he was by the rapid passage of time.

"What's happening?" he cried aloud. His voice was raspy and hoarse. Elderly. Frail. He waited, but no one answered him. The rotation of the Earth made him dizzy.

He laid on the floor, face-up, and closed his eyes, shutting out the bizarre scene, allowing himself to recover some sense of stability.

Are you there? he called, sending psychic feelers from his cortex throughout his body, trying to reach every nerve ending. *Mark?* he cried. *Kathy? Jerry? Eli?* Then finally, with slightly more guilt: *Donna?*

Anyone? How long have we been stuck in here?

There was no reply.

When Peter opened his eyes, they focused on a rotten, peeled ceiling. Against his back was a floor that felt soft, pliable, in danger of collapsing under his weight. Bright sunlight streamed through the remaining panes in the front window of Beard's General, peaceful and warm.

He sat up. Outside were the sounds of birds and what might have been a passing car.

The storm was over. It had ended years ago.

He had caught up to the world.

APRIL 17
1975

CHAPTER THIRTY-SIX

Sam Brooks knocked the Triumph's kickstand down on the shoulder of Hollow Creek Road. He'd killed the motor at the mouth of the bridge that connected the road to the grassy peninsula on which the dilapidated structure that used to be Beard's General sat. He dismounted and strode cautiously over the bridge and into the dandelions that painted a picturesque, folksy landscape around the building. The morning sunlight danced blindingly over the dew and in what remained of the dusty windowpanes that lined the front of the place. For just one second, he thought he saw dark shapes of people inside; ghosts pressing themselves against the glass, eyeing the trespasser who stood at its boundaries. Then the vision was gone, if it had ever really been there.

One terrible night more than twenty years before, Sam had sat astride the same Triumph in the middle of the road, watching the cops from a safe (and, he hoped, anonymous) distance. The Hollow County Sheriff's deputies who had blocked the road on both sides of the ponding hemmed and hawed about whether anyone was trapped inside the store and how they would reach them if they were. They'd arrived before he had. So it seemed that the Blalocks, who had shoved a gun in his face when he rode upon their plantation-style farmhouse and asked them for help, had taken his report seriously after all. But any hope Sam had held for getting across the creek himself had vanished as soon as he'd rounded the curve and seen the first signs of flashing lights.

Defeated, the Sam from that night had turned his bike around and ridden back the way he'd come, back to Pete's place. There he'd waited helplessly for a sign that Pete had been trapped in the store by the flood and, more than that, had survived. No sign ever came.

The sounds of rain and thunder waxed and waned throughout the rest of that night. By daybreak, it was all over. The storm dumped buckets of rain over Lost Hollow and the rest of Middle Tennessee for more than twelve hours. Finally, it crawled off toward the northeast. Along the way, it lost its rage, dissipating first into a moderate rain, then a gentle mist, then clouds and cold wind gusts, and finally nothing. It left behind a swath of destruction that some folks would still be repairing or cleaning up a year later. Roads, bridges, fences, roofs, driveways, power lines, and telephone wires lay in pieces throughout Hollow County. Only a few residents of the town of Lost Hollow seemed to have suffered the brunt of the storm's fury.

The official theory put forth by the Hollow County Sheriff's Department was that Kathy Beard and her son Jerry had become trapped in their store along with some of their customers. Given the lack of bodies inside the place after the floodwaters receded, they'd probably all been washed away by the rushing tide while trying to escape. Door-to-door welfare checks as the days and weeks passed revealed that Nazarene pastor Mark MacDonald, pianist Peter Mayberry, farmhand Eli Wynn, and mother Donna Gilliam, along with her infant son Theo, all went missing sometime during or after the storm. No remains were ever discovered. Unless, of course, you counted the body of Ted Gilliam.

Deputies discovered Ted's cut-up and rotting body propped against the Gilliam's main bedroom wall a day after the flood. Beside it, a bullet in his head, lay the body of Buster McNath. The saturated ground of the Gilliam property had loosened the roots of a large walnut tree overnight. It collapsed onto his home and broke the bedroom window. Crows had been at their lips and eyeballs by the time the bodies were located. The County Coroner found glass embedded in Ted's throat despite the decay. Along with signs of a struggle in the home, authorities labeled the deaths homicides. Buster McNath's revolver was in the front yard. The killer must have turned it on him and then dropped it when he fled the scene.

Their murders remained an open case twenty years on. The Tennessee Bureau of Criminal Identification arm of the state's Department of Safety maintained a lookout for his wife, their prime suspect, and son as the years rolled. Whether Donna had escaped and was living elsewhere in the United States with her child, or whether they were among the casualties of what came to be known as Hell Spring, remained a mystery.

Privately, most folks thought she had probably been washed away with the people who had been trapped in Beard's General that night. They found her car (along with Mark MacDonald's and Pete's) still standing in the parking lot as the creek water drained from it, after all.

Sam Brooks had learned all this information over years of repeated visits to the small town. Each time a new story remembering Hell Spring appeared in the local paper or on the evening news, Sam absorbed it like a thirsty sponge. Even after all this time, he remained hopeful that some new information or break in the case might reveal what happened to the folks who mysteriously disappeared that night in 1955. Most importantly, he prayed that someone would discover what had happened to Pete. To date, nothing new had emerged.

To the left of the storefront, the carcass of one rusted-out automobile stood among the tall grass. Long ago, Sam had recognized it as Pete's Dodge Custom. The other two vehicles had been towed away at some point, claimed by junkyards, or hauled off by Kathy Beard's youngest male cousin. That man had bought the property from the county government and took over its operation after having Kathy and Jerry officially declared dead. He'd constructed a new bridge between the lot and Hollow Creek Road but had never bothered to repair and reopen the store. He was afraid another storm would destroy it all again. Or maybe he just didn't want to be bothered with it. Either way, Sam had considered asking the new owner about the Dodge, thinking he could offer to haul it away. Until last week, though, he'd had no place to move it *to*.

In January of 1975, the Hollow County Commission voted to place some abandoned houses and acreage in Lost Hollow up for sale for a song. One of those places was Pete's. It had stood for twenty years as it had on that first night of spring in 1955. Well, minus the pool of congealed blood, which Sam had been thoughtful enough to clean up before he left the place for good on March 22, 1955. Decades of hard work, plus some modest savings and a discrete sympathetic banker, had enabled him to buy the home for himself, contents and all. It would need much work. *A lot* of work. But at this point in his life, Sam was beginning to look ahead toward something resembling a retirement. Any work and money he invested in the place would be to the good.

He trudged through the high grass, stomping it down in places and shoving it aside in others to get a closer look at the Dodge. It sat on four empty rims, the tires that once shoed them either removed at some point or rotted away after years of exposure and neglect. The car's formerly polished black exterior was dull and lifeless, pocked with a few rust-ringed holes. A long, spidery crack stretched diagonally from the lower corner of the driver's side to the upper corner of the passenger's. Both headlights had been broken as well. Bits of glass lay scattered about inside their housings.

The driver's door hung slightly ajar on its hinges. Sam pulled it slowly, fearing that it might fall off the frame. He winced at the rusty *creeeaaaaak* it made, his arms and chest reacting with chills. He shuddered despite the warmth of the sun beating on his shoulders.

He stooped and crawled behind the wheel of the beast, spooking a tiny flower crab spider that had mistaken the car's interior as part of the wild hunting ground that surrounded it. The tiny white creature scurried over his hand, down the seat, through a crack in the floorboard, and disappeared. Sam watched it go, admiring the effortless way it maneuvered the path. How long had the spider been living here? Long enough to plan an escape route. That was more than the casualties of Hell Spring in Beard's General could say.

Half an inch from the gap into which the spider had fled lay a thin, cylindrical metal object. It caught Sam's eye just as he was about to exit the car. He reached for it, pinched it between the thumb and forefinger of his right hand, and held it up to the sunlight for examination. It was a nail, the kind carpenters and cabinet makers use to fasten baseboards and trim to furniture or rooms.

    Sam suddenly remembered the drunk story Pete had once told him about how his mother had driven a similar nail through his tongue when she caught him playing by the creek with another boy whom Pete thought she suspected of being gay. This couldn't be the same nail (unless Pete had carried that nail with him as a reminder for the rest of his life, which Sam would not have put beyond him). It looked weirdly disjointed, though, even in a car as bizarrely out of place as this Dodge Custom.

    Sam dropped the nail into the breast pocket of his work shirt. He snapped the pearl fastener into place to keep it from tumbling out and patted it twice. He didn't know why he wanted to keep the thing. The memory of Pete's tongue story was one reason. Or it was just the nearest piece of history in reach. Either way, it was going home with him.

    He ran his fingers along the top of the Dodge's cracked steering wheel, most likely one of the very last objects Pete had touched way back in 1955. Then he climbed out of the car. He pushed the door as closed as gravity and the ravages of time would allow and turned his sights toward the store.

    The temptation to explore it was intense. Technically, he was already trespassing. He had asked no one's permission to cross the bridge onto the Beard property, nor had he yet approached the Beard cousin about taking ownership of the Dodge. He didn't think anyone would prosecute him for it, even if he were caught. He'd been seen around town often enough in the years since 1955 to have become a familiar face to some residents. Even so, Sam closely examined his surroundings and listened carefully for anything that sounded like oncoming traffic. When he was sure he was alone, he walked up the crumbling steps to the porch, pried open the door, and stepped inside.

It wasn't much to look at. The floorboards groaned with exhaustion when he crossed the threshold. He stopped just inside. He remained there for a moment, absently holding the door to the relic. A tiny part of him feared the place would trap him inside along with all its ghosts if he allowed the door to shut. Instead, he scanned the interior from the safety of the space near the threshold.

There were all the things you would expect to find in a weathered building that lacked use: insects, cobwebs, dust, pieces of debris that had either accumulated here over time or had fallen off larger objects as they were toted out. Briefly, his gaze fell on the shell of a freezer leaned up against a far wall. As he looked at it, he thought he saw, in his periphery, figures moving about between the light and shadow cast by the sun through the broken and time-tinted windows. When he turned his face to them, they were no longer there, like an afterimage caused by staring at something for too long in bright light. Not ghosts, but apparitions of light created by the science of the human eye's reactions to it.

The effect was spooky enough to drive Sam back outside, into the welcoming sunlight of a fair-weather day. Having made his mind up about the Dodge (he would telephone the Beard cousin about buying it when he arrived home that evening), Sam strode across the narrow bridge and back onto the shoulder. The reliable Triumph roared to life beneath him just like it had every day since he'd brought it home from the war. No traffic approached, so Sam shifted the bike into gear and rolled into the lane that led farther into Lost Hollow.

To Pete's house.

To *his* house.

To home.

CHAPTER THIRTY-SEVEN

The warmth of the morning sun embraced him when Peter Mayberry emerged from the shadows cast by the porch canopy hanging over the dry-rotted door of Beard's General. He blinked against it and shaded his eyes with one withered and spotted hand. The thick silver hairs on the back of that hand caught his eye as he raised it to his forehead. He was reminded that not long ago—just about twelve hours—he was barely a middle-aged man. He'd been soft around the middle but unwrinkled and fragile only of mind. Even a shorter time ago than that, he'd been superhuman. Thanks to the soul-dads.

He was still standing on the front porch of Beard's General, on a peninsula surrounded on three sides by the babbling water of Hollow Creek. That much he knew. Everything else—the woods that bordered the Blalock farm across the street, the street itself, the bridge that once spanned the gap between Hollow Creek Road and the store's parking lot—looked different. There should not have been a bridge there at all, not after he and the others who had encamped in Beard's during the deluge had watched it break apart as the rising waters whisked it away.

The flutist's song of a nearby wood thrush broke his reverie. He followed the sound and soon found himself at the top of the stairs that led from the store's front porch to what had once been its parking lot. The white gravel lot had been entirely replaced with long stalks of Kentucky fescue, clover, crabgrass, dandelions, and weed grasses he could not identify. There were no cars in sight, not even his Dodge Custom.

A glint of sunlight bounced off something lying in the grass a few feet away from him. Cautiously, Peter gripped the splintered wooden railings on either side of the stairs and scaled them to the ground. The journey was made treacherous because of his one short leg. Not to mention the onset of age and the arthritis that came with it. Each of the three downward steps jabbed flaming swords into his worn-out hips and knees. He wobbled on them until he found himself standing over the shining object.

With the toe of his short leg, he brushed away as much of the clover as he could and peered at a metallic shape. It looked like a Dodge medallion, probably even the one from his car. Peter tried to bend and pluck it from the ground, but his screaming hips would not allow it. Instead, he toed it loose from the soil in which it had been partially buried, dusting it off as best he could with the sole of his shoe.

It was a Dodge medallion, all right, rusted around the edges but otherwise in excellent condition. If it was his, how long had it been out here?

"Hey!" shouted a masculine voice from somewhere on his right. The sound startled him. He teetered as he turned to face it. "Hey! This is private property. Fuck are you doing here, old-timer?"

A man Peter had never seen before climbed off a sizable green tractor, on the front of which was a dirty but equally green bucket that had been lowered to the ground. Had he heard a tractor running when he walked outside? Peter didn't think so.

The man approaching him wore blue denim overalls over a beige work shirt. Atop his head was a green ball cap embroidered with the silhouette of a leaping six-point buck and the words John Deere. Peter recognized the brand, but the tractor didn't look like any he'd seen before. It had a broad front, and its lines were sleek and curved, like a sedan.

"Answer me, dude," the man said, closing the distance between them. "You gonna make me call the cops?" He snatched a palm-sized rectangular thing from the right pocket of his overalls and brandished it at Peter, who flinched, fearing that the man was about to throw it at him.

"I, uh," Peter stammered, his voice tremulous and weak. "I got lost, I guess. Where, uh, where am I?"

Understanding dawned on the man's face. He lowered the brick-shaped object to his side and chuckled. "Oh," he said. "Wandered away, did ya? My granddaddy had the Alzheimer's, too. Only he used to call it 'the Sometimers' because it was only sometimes that he lost his head. 'Course, by the time the good Lord took him, he couldn't even remember his name. Do you remember your name, old-timer?"

"Peter."

The farmer nodded. "Well, Peter, my name is Tim Beard. Right now, you're on the backside of my family farm. The building you're standing in front of used to be the family store. It was my great aunt's side business until a hundred-year flood wiped it out back in 1955. Besides her farmhouse on the opposite side of that hill, the closest house along this stretch is miles away. You must have been toddling around all night."

Peter nodded, unsure how to answer. "Must have."

"You remember where you live?"

He nodded again. "I think so."

Tim raised the rectangle from his hip again and examined it. "Well, give me the number, and I'll call somebody to come get you. I got to wait on the developer. He was supposed to be here fifteen minutes ago and—*goddammit*!"

Peter stumbled backward in alarm. "What?" he cried.

"No bars," Tim said. He sighed and shoved the rectangle into the front right pocket of his overalls. "Damn phone companies give all the rich folks in the cities the cell service and leave us out here with rotten cables they won't maintain." He scoffed. "Truck's back at the farmhouse. I won't drive it across that bridge there. Don't trust it to hold up. Just wait for me here. I'll go get it and drive you home. If that damn developer shows up while I'm gone, just tell him I've gone to get my truck and I'll be along shortly. Can you remember that?"

"Yes, sir," said Peter, who had no idea what cell service was and probably wouldn't know the developer if he bopped him on the back of the head. "I'm sure I can remember that."

"Awesome," Tim replied. "Just have a seat on the porch steps over there if you get tired. I won't be too long."

He strode to the tractor and climbed aboard. After a loud choking sound, it belched to life. Tim raised the bucket enough to clear the terrain before turning his back to Peter and motoring away through the tall grass behind the store.

Peter watched him go. After the tractor disappeared over the crest of the hill, he permitted himself to examine the front of Beard's General. It was a nightmare version of the building he'd walked into the night before. The front windowpanes were all cracked or broken. A few were missing entirely. The brilliant white paint that had covered the entirety of the structure's facade had long flaked away, leaving behind only gray wooden beams and planks bleached by years of unrelentingly hot Southern sun. The Beard's General sign that once hung above the canopy was gone, replaced by bare gray wood. There was no evidence that it had ever been there.

Peter turned his back on the store and wandered over to the bridge, the structure that shouldn't have been there at all after the previous night's flooding but had miraculously been replaced before sunup. It wasn't the bridge he remembered, not the one he had driven over to escape the storm. This bridge looked more expansive than the previous one. Its width was bigger than one car but not quite big enough to allow two to cross in opposite directions simultaneously. Like its predecessor, this bridge was constructed almost entirely from wood. Like the building behind him, said wood was sun-bleached, worn, and weak. It could splinter and crumble to dust beneath any brave soul who dared tread it.

Peter stepped from the bridge and peered into the creek bed. Hollow Creek ran low and clear. Along with the smooth shapes and rainbow colors of creek rock and, no doubt, crawdads that resided in the flow were clumps of what looked like newspaper. He spotted several empty beer cans, some broken glass bottles, rusty oil cans, and a wealth of types of packaging that were simultaneously shiny and trashy looking. Either the flood had washed away someone's garbage, or the constable's apathy about litterbugs had gotten worse.

The crests of the rippling water sparkled in the sunlight, just like it had on the day Joe Bayless had fished two mudbugs from it and dared him to eat one raw.

A familiar-looking bush thrived between the creek bed and the bridge railing on the opposite bank. Tiny white and yellow flowers, each with a green stamen poking out of its center, dotted the ends of the bush. Honeysuckle. How long had it been since he'd dripped the nectar on his tongue?

He dragged his taste buds along the roof of his mouth. Dry. Like a cat's tongue. He doubted that the drop of nectar from a honeysuckle flower could quench him. It was safer than scaling the creek bank and drinking from the filth that ran through it, though. Assuming the bridge didn't collapse out from under him, of course.

Peter treaded a few careful steps onto the bridge. When he was satisfied that it was unlikely to crumble, he strode across. He managed the entire trek without tripping over his feet and without much sound of protest from the boards beneath them. A wave of relief washed over him when he reached the end that connected to the road not only from crossing the bridge without plummeting through it, but also from adding distance between himself and the store. Being on the other side of the creek made the night before's events feel less tangible somehow.

Peter plucked two flowers from their stems on the honeysuckle bush. The first one was for himself. He pinched the valley of the flower between the thumb and forefinger of his left hand and deftly pried out the stamen with the thumb and forefinger of his right. Pursing his lips around the narrow end of the flower, he suckled it. Sweet liquid washed over his tongue for an instant.

Peter tossed the used-up flower into the creek. He watched the tiny rapids carry it aloft for a few feet and then smash it against the remains of a tire that lay half-buried in the mud. Buried alongside it was something rectangular and metal with what looked like a sheet of paper inside. It looked like a picture frame. The image within was too faded and washed from days of creek and sun to be recognizable. He let it be.

The second flower was for Joe, the boy he'd met along the banks in the minutes before Peter's mother had whisked him home and driven a nail through the middle of his tongue. Joe, he understood, had been the first spark of what would later become his full-blown attraction to members of his same sex. Perhaps in another world or another time, he could have referred to Joe as his first crush. He didn't know if Joe had felt the same about him. He would never know. But his mother had intuited it, which was why she had punished him.

Peter pulled the stamen from the second flower and drank its nectar. He tossed the remainder into the creek and watched as it missed the tire. It rode the creek's current until it was out of sight.

Peter plucked a third flower from the honeysuckle bush. That one was a struggle. The age in his hands made them tremble and ache. It was hard to close his fingers around the correct part of the flower to snap it from the bush without destroying it. He broke it off clean, though, and removed the stamen. He tilted back his head and tipped the narrow end of the flower toward his lips, squeezing his eyes shut against the brightness of the morning sun. A single tear crept from the corner of his left eye, rolling and bobbing its way down the craggy fault lines in his ancient cheek.

This one was for Sam.

CHAPTER THIRTY-EIGHT

The ride home was terrifying. After he'd tossed his third honeysuckle flower into the shallows, he heard a series of repeating thuds approaching. At first, he thought it was a stray rumble of thunder from somewhere in the distance. That startled him, and suddenly he understood why Sam had never liked sudden loud noises when he'd returned from the war.

More thudding sounds followed fast upon it. They reverberated in regular beats, a giant's footsteps growing louder as they approached. The muscles in Peter's legs begged him to flee back across the bridge. Then a beast of a vehicle rounded a bend in Hollow Creek Road and slowed to a stop in front of him.

The thing was black and shiny. Its color was like how his Dodge Custom had looked in its heyday, but significantly larger. It sat upon tires nearly as large as the ones on the back of the John Deere tractor Tim Beard had driven away a few minutes before. The front grill sported a metallic-looking ram's head. If it had windows or a driver behind a steering wheel, Peter couldn't tell. The glass on the beast was as black as its body.

The thudding sounds he was hearing came from inside the vehicle. Each new pulse rattled Peter's teeth and vibrated the ground beneath his feet.

It drew up in front of him, after which the thudding ceased, and the engine—or whatever marvel of engineering propelled the thing—stopped roaring. A door opened on the left side and out dropped Tim Beard. He ran to the passenger's side and pulled on the lever to a door there, motioning for Peter to climb aboard.

The truck's interior (well, *Tim* called it a truck; it was unlike any truck Peter had ever seen) was overrun with lights, bells, and buzzing sounds. Thankfully, Tim had either fixed or disabled whatever was causing the repetitive bass drumming. He watched the man pull a strap around his waist and shoulder and clamp it into a slot. Peter located a matching strap on his side and, not without some effort, performed the same task, hoping he looked like he knew what he was doing.

When his seatbelt clicked home, the beast silenced one of its annoying chimes. A display in the center of the truck's dash appeared to indicate the time of day. If accurate, it was three o'clock in the afternoon. Just above and to the left was another display that showed the date: *APR 30 2010*.

Peter thought he was going to faint. Tim shifted his beast into Drive and mashed the throttle. Fear for his life subsequently replaced any inclinations Peter had had toward unconsciousness. He clung white-knuckled to the front seam of his seat as Tim rocketed the truck over several miles of a very different-looking Hollow Creek Road. The lines on the pavement had changed. They were brighter than they had been before. There were no longer any potholes to be seen, no trees down anywhere. With Peter's direction, they finally came to a stop in front of what had only last night been his house.

"Here y'are," Tim said. He stretched an arm over the older man's lap and pulled on the truck's passenger door latch when Peter couldn't figure out how to pop it for himself. "Welcome home, Mr. Brooks."

Peter paused mid-step down from the truck and searched his rescuer's eyes. "Brooks?" he said.

"Yeah," Tim replied, a piteous smile curled his lips. "That's your name, right? It's right there on the mailbox." He tilted his head to the left.

Peter glanced in the direction he'd indicated. Sure enough, a large gray mailbox with its flag up had replaced the small silver one that had stood at the end of his driveway for the entire time he'd lived in Lost Hollow. A small plaque engraved with the single word *BROOKS* sat atop it. A series of numbers ran down the length of the post on which the mailbox was perched: *1101*.

"Yeah," he said quietly. "Peter Brooks. That's me."

Tim cleared his throat. "Well, anyway, I got to be goin', Mr. Brooks. I got a text from that developer saying he was running late, but he oughta be there by the time I get back. I think he's gonna buy it from me. Turn it into a subdivision or something. About time someone did. I can't keep up with the taxes no more.

"You take care. Do what them doctors tell ya."

Peter nodded, not paying attention. When he was safely on the ground, he gave the truck door a hard shove and heard it close behind him. A moment later, Tim Beard and his truck that sounded like a giant's footfalls had vanished from his sight and out of earshot.

Brooks. The name on the mailbox was Brooks.

He followed the short path of the driveway to a small garage that sat detached from the house. It had not been there the night before when he had still been a relatively young man. The structure stood open. Its single wide mouth revealed a collection of tools hanging on a pegboard, a shiny white automobile with the word TOYOTA emblazoned along its back end, and a smaller structure with two tires that poked out from beneath the hem of an Army green tarp. A tingle of recognition tickled the skin on the underside of Peter's scrotum. The sensation ran up the length of his spine and culminated as frost on the back of his neck.

After checking to ensure that he was not being watched, Peter padded into the garage and bent to get a closer look at the shape under the sheet. It was a motorcycle. The horizontal shape of the handlebars and the horse-like quality gave that away immediately. But was it *his* motorcycle?

Unable to contain himself, Peter clenched a tent of tarp fabric in his left hand and pulled. The covering slid up and off the front of the bike easily. He pushed it back far enough to examine the logo on the gas tank. The single word TRIUMPH in serif letters and with a smile-shaped trail connecting the tail of the letter R to the right side of the bar in the letter H greeted him. It lay against the backdrop of a gas tank painted in precisely the right shade of silver.

Hope welled up in him for the first time in—well, ever. The night that Sam had left him (only last night, in fact) had been one of his lowest. Peter thought he'd gone for good. Aged though he was and as different as the world seemed to be now that Marilyn had gotten her comeuppance, the only person he had ever truly loved might have returned after all.

Peter covered the bike again, making his best effort to leave the tarp in the same position and condition that he'd found it. Just as he bent to adjust the hem over the front tire, he heard what sounded like the springs of a screen door being stretched to their limits, followed by wood slamming against wood. Then the approach of footsteps. Methodical. Slow.

"Who's out here?" a voice called from somewhere outside the garage. "Better show yourself, or you're gonna get my boot in your ass when I catch you."

Panic replaced Peter's euphoria. What if it wasn't Sam? What if he had somehow traveled through five-and-a-half decades only to find his home, everything in it, and everyone he knew replaced by strangers? The panic seized up his body. Try as he might, Peter was unable to move his legs. Not that he could have outrun the man, Sam or not. The overnight onset of arthritis and his mismatched leg lengths would see to that.

Terrified, Peter latched onto the one hope he'd discovered after Tim Beard called him by the wrong last name. He closed his eyes, inhaled deeply, and shouted, "Sam? Sam Brooks! It's me, Peter! Peter Mayberry from 1955! Please! Please don't hit me!"

He grimaced, awaiting the blow to the head that would follow. Instead, he heard a *thunk* as something ahead of him hit the ground outside the garage. He peeked from his left eye. Lying on the ground just outside was an aluminum baseball bat. A pair of well-worn leather work boots stood beside it. The legs that extended from inside those boots were clad in a pair of gray sweats. Brown hands with a red tinge to them lay at the hips.

"Oh my God," the baritone voice rang in astonishment.

Peter thrust open both eyes and gazed on the face of the man who lived in the house he had accidentally abandoned on the first day of spring fifty-five years ago. The man's face showed a definitive sadness, the weariness of lifelong patience with the world and its ills. It was embedded in the crow's feet surrounding those deep-set eyes. Yet life danced in them still. Shoulders, once broad and having borne the weight of wounded and dead compatriots in the Battle of the Bulge, hung low at their ends. The years had eroded the muscles there until skin draped over bone the way so many flags had draped man-sized boxes after the war. Yet there was still some strength in them.

The man stepped over the garage threshold and strode toward Peter with effort, awe in his eyes. He raised an open hand to Peter's face and brushed a stray strand of wispy white hair off his forehead.

"Pete?" he said, unbelieving.

"Sam," Peter replied.

MAY 1
2010

CHAPTER THIRTY-NINE

No one, not even the most astute meteorologists on the Hollow River news stations, expected the training line of heavy rain that began on that Saturday morning to result in the devastation it ultimately wrought. Over two days starting on May 1, 2010, and ending sometime Sunday, May 2, slow-rolling thunderclouds drenched parts of Mississippi, Tennessee, and Kentucky with nearly 20 inches of precipitation. It saturated and drowned floodplains, overflowed creeks and rivers, and took more than a few lives in the process.

Famously, a metal temporary school building was at one point spotted floating along a bed of rapids that had previously been part of the local stretch of the Eisenhower Interstate system. By Monday, May 3, newspapers and weather experts were calling the deluge a one-thousand-year flood, upgraded from a one-hundred-year event in the early hours of May 1 and a five-hundred-year event the next day. Recovery efforts for Tennessee cities and small towns alike would take years and millions of dollars.

But in the earliest hours of Saturday morning, a completely unaware Peter Mayberry and Sam Brooks lay together on Sam's bed. The former was snuggled in the fetal position with his back pressed firmly into the latter's chest, protected by his arms.

Peter snapped awake briefly when he heard thunder rumbling in the distance. Or was it? It could be Tim Beard, the fellow of the John Deere hat and matching tractor, driving his truck home after a long meeting about selling the farm to that real estate developer. Sam had told him that younger folks, those from something called Generation X and Millennials, sometimes installed radio systems in their cars that were very heavy on bass. That must have been the "giant's footsteps" Peter had heard.

A second rumble echoed over the hill somewhere south of them, but Peter did not hear that one. He had already drifted back to sleep in the warmth of the arms of his best friend and the love of his life. He had thought that worrying about the next day and the day after would prevent him from getting to sleep that night. After all, how was he to explain where he'd been for the past five decades? What would become of him when people suddenly found out that one of a group of people thought washed away by the angry waters fifty-five years ago had suddenly resurfaced alive and well in 2010? Or would anyone except the government even care? Sam had assured him that they would think of something together. And that was good enough. For tonight.

Miles from them, along the stretch of Hollow Creek Road that extended between what had once been the Blalock farm and what had once been Beard's General, a bright blue bolt of lightning descended from an angry thatch of black clouds. Its spindly fingers crackled in the pockets of air it displaced as it drove itself into the soft earth. The arc struck the base of a thick and ancient black oak tree just a few rows inside the woods lining the Blalock side of the road. It lit up the surrounding forest as if it were suddenly high noon on a cloudless day and then vanished, returning the land to its rainy-day gloom.

As the black smoke of singed and burning debris along the forest floor wafted from the ground toward the sky, a sinister red glow began to pulse from within a rotted and hollowed-out section of the black oak's trunk. Enshrouded in a cloud-like mist not formed of water, the light burned brighter with each pulse, as if something from somewhere inside was rapidly approaching the portal.

After another loud *crack*, both the mist inside the tree and the red glow from within the fog vanished. In their place, a dog-like creature lay just on the verge between the shadow world inside the oak and what folks in Lost Hollow who were not Peter Mayberry called reality. It was a furry creature, large with a long snout and pointed ears. When it turned its head to the sky, its eyes scanned the alien landscape with a combination of fear, disgust, and ravenous hunger.

Thick drops of rain began to fall from the darkened clouds overhead. One of them landed directly in the center of the beast's long, lolling tongue. It sizzled there, like acid stinging her, burning off her taste buds. Then it melted away.

If more of these stingers landed on her while she was weak and hungry, they could hurt her more seriously. But she couldn't go back to the arena. Not now. The mountain would kill her for escaping. She would have to find shelter here. And food.

A loud clap of thunder boomed overhead. More drops of pain-makers pelted the ground around her.

Soon, she thought.

AFTERWORD

The weather event that is described in the preceding pages is fictional. However, some of it was inspired by flooding accounts reported in the pages of The Tennessean newspaper's March 22, 1955 edition as well as a 1961 report on floods and flood control by the Tennessee Valley Authority (TVA). A heavy storm coalesced west of the state on March 20, 1955. It ended sometime in the early morning hours of March 22. While over the mid-state, the storm dumped rain from three to eleven inches over a 650-mile length and 170-mile width of Tennessee. Flooding records were broken in several areas and nearly broken in others. In southern Middle Tennessee, only the floods of 1902 and 1948 at that point rivaled the severity of the one in the spring of 1955.

If you fast-forward fifty-five years and six weeks like Peter Mayberry did, you arrive at the date of the devastating flood that drowned Middle Tennessee on May 1, 2010. The May 2010 deluge was first labeled a 100-year flood by local weather nerds. Later it was upgraded to a 500-year flood and then a 1,000-year flood by folks in the local news media and on social media. Nationally, media attention was primarily focused on the BP Deepwater Horizon oil spill that had begun less than two weeks earlier. Until they were presented with local complaints about lack of coverage, a video of a portable school building floating down Interstate 24, and stories about people being washed away, CNN and others failed to take notice. Then they did.

At least twenty-one people lost their lives because of the 2010 flooding. Around 30 percent of Tennessee was declared a major disaster area. Damage to Nashville alone was estimated by its then-mayor to be $1.5 billion. Recovery for iconic Nashville landmarks like the Grand Ole Opry House took weeks to months. Recovery for people and property of less renown took years. Some never recovered.

Since May of 2010, Middle Tennesseans tend to compare every new significant flooding event with the one that occurred that year. They do so with good reason. Whether you do or do not buy the science of climate change, anecdotal evidence that extreme weather is more common now than it used to be is hard to dismiss. After all, we live in an era where the weather reports on the nightly news regularly contain wildfire reporting. At least one report cited by The Weather Channel in April of 2022 indicated that the world could see up to 500 catastrophic disasters a year by 2030.

When it rains, it pours the old idiom states. A sprinkle becomes a patter. A patter becomes rain. Rain becomes a downpour. The downpour becomes a flood. And the flood? That becomes power outages, health emergencies, economic disasters, and—for some—an opportunity. Like the folks on the nightly news always say, have your safe space ready. Get to know your neighbors and have a plan. You can predict a storm's timing, but you can't predict its wrath.

Or the wrath of the thing that comes in from it.

ACKNOWLEDGMENTS

It can never be stated enough that no author produces a novel-length work of fiction without a tremendous amount of support from others. I owe the following unique and talented individuals a debt of gratitude for their hard work on *Hell Spring*:

- The poet Richard Bell for taking the time to read an early beta draft and for offering his valuable feedback to make it a better book.
- Starr Waddell and Fiona from Quiethouse Editing for their beta reading services. *Hell Spring* and my previous novel *The Gordon Place* are both better off for having passed through their hands.
- Megan Harris for being a true professional who edited the work you just read. Any mistake or awkwardness you find herein is my fault for overriding her suggestions.
- Sean Duregger, audiobook narrator and more, for his award-winning work on my previous novel *The Gordon Place* as well as his willingness to work together again on the forthcoming audiobook edition of *Hell Spring*.

- Paula Rozelle Hanback for the beyond-my-wildest-expectations cover design that evokes small-town 1950s America, Hollywood, and oncoming disaster all at once.
- And, finally, you readers. Thank you to everyone who read my previous work and asked me for another. Thank you to everyone who reviewed *The Gordon Place* and wanted more from the little town of Lost Hollow. Thank you to anyone at all who buys and reads my work, regardless of how you ultimately feel about it.

ABOUT THE AUTHOR

Isaac Thorne is a Tennessee man who has, over the course of his life, developed a modest ability to spin a good yarn. Really. He promises. The screenplay adaptation of his short story "Diggum" from the collection *Road Kills* is the winner of several horror film festival awards. His previous novel, *The Gordon Place*, was a finalist in the 2020 Readers' Favorite Book Awards. The audiobook edition narrated by Sean Duregger won the 2020 Independent Audiobook Awards horror category.

You can find Isaac on Twitter, Facebook, Instagram, Pinterest, and TikTok at @isaacrthorne or on his site at isaacthorne.com.

Just don't corner him during a flood.

ALSO BY ISAAC THORNE

THE GORDON PLACE is Isaac Thorne's 2019 debut novel. In addition to placing as a finalist in the Readers' Favorite Book Awards, *The Gordon Place* won the Horror category in the 2020 Independent Audiobook Awards.

Lost Hollow constable Graham Gordon just walked into his abandoned childhood home for the first time in twenty years. Local teenagers have been spreading rumors about disembodied screams coming from inside. Now, thanks to a rickety set of cellar stairs and the hateful spirit of his dead father, he might never escape.

It's a fight for the future and the past when spirit and flesh wage war at the Gordon place.

PRAISE FOR THE GORDON PLACE

"With the right amount of gore and a permeating sense of dread, this work proves Thorne to be a gifted storyteller."
—*Publishers Weekly*

"...a thrilling throwback horror tale that tears through the pages like a hound from hell." —David Simms, *Scream Magazine*

"...every time I jumped back into *The Gordon Place*, I was easily whisked away to Lost Hollow." —Steve Stred, Splatterpunk-nominated author of *Sacrament* and *Mastodon*

"As comforting as sliding into a warm bloodbath. And just as soothing and nerve-jangling." —Drew Rowsome, *My Gay Toronto Magazine*

"Even the most strange and otherworldly scenes in the book are so well described that you feel like you're there in the midst of the action." —Yeti, *TN Horror News*

MORE BY ISAAC THORNE

ROAD KILLS is a 2017 collection of short tales of dark horror from the mind of Isaac Thorne. These stories are all connected to travel, to the road. It is always lurking there, just waiting for you to come out for a drive or a walk or a jog.

However you next confront it, the road is already there, plotting.

And waiting.

For you.

Available as an audiobook, in paperback, and as an ebook at retailers everywhere.

PRAISE FOR ROAD KILLS

"Different types of horror are explored fully, with a killer style." —Jim Uhls, screenwriter of *Fight Club*

"You'd be hard-pressed to find that much entertainment for a dollar anywhere else." —Danger Slater, author of *Impossible James*, review of "Diggum"

"I'm convinced Isaac could be the next great horror writer." —Dave Karner, filmmaker, review of "Diggum"

"…you'll feel and see every bump under granny's wheels…" —Joanie Chevalier, author of *Deadly Dating Games*, review of "Decision Paralysis"

THANK YOU

Isaac Thorne and Lost Hollow Books appreciate the time you have devoted to this novel. If you like what you've read, please consider rating and reviewing this book on your platform of purchase or any other platform of your choosing. Ratings and reviews help books like these get discovered by readers like you.

You can find links to popular review sources and more at Isaac Thorne's landing page:

isaacthorne.contactin.bio